VIGILANTES

SUPERPOWER CHRONICLES BOOK 3

ARTHUR MAYOR

ONE

My previous principal's office was not like this. I guess this guy was my principal now. According to the huge grandfather clock in the corner, as of ten minutes ago he'd become my principal. No, sorry, I'm on the Island now. He's my Headmaster, not principal.

The chair I was in was built to impress donors. The fact that it also intimidated punk kids from the Kages was pure gratis.

The desk was bigger than my room. Well, not my room now. Bigger than my room at my mom's place.

Oh, boy I was having a tough adjustment. Even the stupid navy blue blazer I was in made me feel ridiculous.

The headmaster entered the office, not from the same door I'd come in. No, he entered from his office in his office. You would hate to only have one office. "Ryan, can I get you some water?"

A quick look at the gold-embossed nameplate reminded me what to call him. "No, thank you, Mr. Paris." Crap, I bet it was Dr. Paris.

He took his seat.

This guy didn't look anything like my principal, either. I mean my old principal. No well-worn tweed blazers and frumpy khakis. This guy could be an investment banker. Not that I've had a lot of contact with investment bankers.

He didn't have a manila folder in his hand. It was a deep blue folder with the same lion and horse crest I had on my stiff blazer.

He took his chair. If I was a Bond villain, I still wouldn't have a chair that nice.

"Well, I've looked over your records." He opened the file and flipped through the sheets of paper. I couldn't tell if those were actually my records or if they were just random news articles. "A lot of truancy. You're behind in credits."

Nope, that was my file. "Lovely family." Behind him, among the leather-bound books and award plaque things, was a silver-framed picture. A younger Dr. Paris, still with some brown in his hair, but just as whip slender as now. The pretty blond woman next to him had a dated hairstyle and blouse, so an old picture. Between them both sat an East-Asian girl of about eight or ten, smiling ear to ear.

He followed my finger, then looked at me over his glasses. "Thank you. That's an old picture. My daughter is your age now." He looked back at the file.

It was at that time that I noticed the good doctor didn't have a ring on. So there was trouble in paradise and I'd just pointed it out. Good call, Ryan.

"Listen, Ryan." He flicked the file shut and leaned back, letting the chair rebound a little before he said whatever he wanted me to listen to. "I have my concerns about how well you're going to do here at Hellington."

You and me both. "You do?" It must be because you can read.

"I look at your file and I see someone not making

school a priority." To his credit he wasn't being judgmental, he was just calling it like he saw it. And he saw it dead right.

"Well, I'm making some changes." For a comfortable chair, I was really uncomfortable.

"Hellington is not going to be an easy transition from Jefferson. The academic standards you find here are going to be higher."

I nodded.

"And you'll have to make school a priority," he continued. "For example, what did you do last night?"

"What?" That's the word I used, but my tone said "GUILTY!"

"Last night?" Dr. Paris asked again. "How did you spend your time?"

"Ah... I just hung out with some people."

Let's talk about last night.

I was hanging over a five-story drop. The only thing stopping me from plummeting to my death was a hand around my neck.

Did you see what I did there? "Hanging out with people"? I'm a funny, funny man.

It was hot. August is always hot in Darhaven, but this was roasting hot. Even on top of a crappy apartment building it was still hot. Didn't make it any better that I was tripped out in my Guard uniform. Absolutely no skin exposed, black and grey with a raven on my chest. I was sweating like a beast. Sweating and gasping for air.

The hand that I both depended on to keep me suspended and was choking me was attached to six-foot-five-inches of loony psycho killer. I had last seen him when he'd planted a bomb and blown Red Knight to wherever evil people go when their van explodes.

"How did you find me?" Osprey yelled in my face.

I tried to answer him, but he had his iron hand around my neck.

"How did you find me?" He yelled louder because, you know, the reason I wasn't responding was I didn't know he was asking a question. "Why are you here?"

Now *that* was a good question.

Let's talk about why I was there.

I'd left the Book Room. I know I left the Book Room because I wasn't there now. But I didn't remember doing it. I was in a daze.

I was given this note by Raptor. Yes, that Raptor. The legendary superhero, leader and founder of the Guard. He'd sent me a note. It was more complicated than that, but that was my mentor -- it was always more complicated than that. One of the last things he'd done before he died was fire me from the team. I don't know when before that he'd put in the failsafe to get me this note, but I got it. I finally found out how to decode the note -- like I said, complicated. I thought maybe the note would be some last words, like: I know I was hard on you, but you got what it takes. Or: I fired you, why are you reading this? But no, it was only my last mission.

I'd taken out my translation and read it again. I was three blocks away now.

Is it called a translation or is it just a decoding? Well, whatever it was it was darn perplexing.

I'd read it again. And by again I mean again again. I had gone over the decoding three different times when I did it, six more just to be sure. So what I had was the same sentence written out nine times. Warn Caesar, the Legacy is coming.

Couple problems with that, Raptor. One, Caesar is the biggest, baddest super villain in Darhaven so he's probably the biggest baddest super villain in all the world. So why would I be running a message to him, anyway? Two, and this is a fun fact, he's dead. There's no one to tell. I guess I could go tell Caesar's second in command and heir apparent -- oh wait, he's dead, too. And the next guy and the next guy. In fact there was nothing left of Caesar's criminal empire. It was being gobbled up by whoever could swing their elbows hard enough at the trough.

So not only did I not know who to warn that the Legacy was coming, I had no idea what the Legacy was.

I'd looked at the clock readout on my display. I had to catch a bus to the subway and take the subway to the Island to make it home. That added an hour to my day now that I was living with my dad.

That's complicated, too.

Fine, I only had one person that would know anything about this. I could ask him and make choices from there.

I'd been sitting on an air conditioning unit, and it was difficult to get up. I'd thought I was done. I'd thought I'd fought the good fight, and now I was done. But here was Raptor telling me no. Not done. There was a time when all I'd wanted was to be a Guard, but that was when Raptor, Landslide, Orion, and Cat were alive and there to tell me what to do. Clockwork was there too, but it turns out he was a force of Evil manipulating the rest of the Guard to their dooms. I'm less nostalgic about Clockwork. Now it was just me and four other apprentices as lost as I was.

Four apprentices as lost as I was and one career criminal

with a psychic link to a six-inch statue of Anubis. Yeah, that was complicated, too.

It was the statue guy that might have some information.

Oh, side note, there's also a spooky smart cat named Feral who had some connection to Cat, but I hadn't seen him for a while. I hoped he was okay. The last time I saw him was in a fight with Osprey. He saved my ass by causing a distraction.

I'm worried about me, the city, and whatever the Legacy is, but I'm also worried about Feral.

In a fit of youthful rebellion, I'd thrown the statue off a building. But I'd found it again. Yes, it was more complicated than that, but let's just say I found it again and re-hid it in a plastic bag duct taped to the inside of a vent stack of the tenth floor of an abandoned building.

I fetched it and the small wooden sculpture fell into my hand. In the last few weeks this thing has been my most constant companion. Without it I would be dead a couple times over. Downside is the guy who makes this magic happen is Jackal. Yes, that Jackal. The super villain that five years ago plunged this city into chaos as he fought a war with Caesar, then was caught by Raptor, handed over to the Darhaven police department, and convicted of multiple counts of murder for about a dozen life sentences. His superpower, the ability to copy superpowers, was cool, but not a problem in the general population of Irondale prison.

We hang now.

It's complicated.

I'd given the statue a rub. Rubbing didn't do anything, I was just being a jerk. "Jackal."

Nothing.

I shook it. "Jackal."

He might have been asleep, sometimes it took a little to wake him. "Jackal."

The eyes glowed, then the entire statue. "What's going on? Problem with the delivery?" I'd made a deal to get his help. I got access to his years of criminal experience and I dug up a stash of cash and gave it to a single mother living in the Kages. Her husband was killed in the war I mentioned earlier and this was his way of covering that debt.

"No, the delivery went fine." After I'd made darn sure she was just a single mother trying to make a living in the crappy of crappy holes in the crappy section of town.

"Good. Then what's the problem?" He always talked like he didn't have time for the conversation and had to move on to the next thing. He was in prison, he had time.

"What do you know about the Legacy?" Might as well cut to the chase.

"Wow, just calm down. If you want something from me, what do I get?"

"What do you want?" I'm not a good negotiator and he knows it.

"There's a man I need some information from. If I tell you what I know about the Legacy, then you go find this guy and get the information I need."

"And how will I get information from him?" I couldn't buy it and I wasn't going to beat it out of him.

"I'm sure you could be persuasive. Be intimidating." That seemed to solve the equation for him.

"I am not your strong arm." No way was I going to do that.

"Cards on the table, I was going to string you along and see either how outraged I could make you or what I could get you to agree to. But I'm already onboard. I got nothing, kid. Until you said the word Legacy, I'd never heard it used except for sports teams and rich people."

I'd thought maybe he wouldn't help, or make me do something stupid and or illegal, but it had never occurred to me that he couldn't help.

I was a little stunned. I didn't really have a next move.

"Give me some coordinates here. What is this Legacy thing, what context?" he asked.

And now the dance. Everything I said to Jackal could and would be used against me. He had plenty of information that was dangerous. He knew for sure that Caesar was dead, commonly suspected but not known. He knew that the Guard were all dead. Their deaths were not public record and there were always enough bogus sightings reported in fan sites that only a few people were starting to realize the Guard hadn't been around lately. But Jackal knew the truth, and I doubt he was sharing that info with the guys on the inside. The cherry on top, he also had my first name.

"I translated the letter," I said.

"That code thing Raptor's widow gave you?" The statue flared a little more yellow.

"Yeah, it said that I had to warn Caesar that the Legacy was coming." Might as well tell him everything.

"Okay, going to jump to conclusions here, but then this dates back before my time in Darhaven," Jackal said.

"So you can't help?" What now?

He must have heard the despair in my voice. "Wow, when have I not delivered? I've never heard of them, so you need to talk to someone who predates me in Caesar's organization." For about five years, Jackal worked for Caesar until he wanted to go out on his own.

"Well, who?"

"The Worm would know." Jackal said it like he was thinking out loud. For all I know he was just thinking out loud. I don't know how his power works. He copied it from one of his employees, Angel. And I don't know how her power worked either, except that she used carved little cherubs to get blackmail information.

When he didn't say anything else I said, "the Worm lured me into a trap and almost got me caught by the federal government. I don't think he likes me."

"I'm sure he just hasn't gotten to know you." The statue's glow dimmed then flared. "Alright, you'll need to talk with Zed."

I didn't know who that was, but Zed hadn't tried to kill or capture me, all plusses. "Who is Zed?"

"He was an enforcer for Caesar, in the inner circle until he was replaced with more powerful supers."

Caesar's inner circle had at least two of the most deadly supers in the city, Mindraker and Toxin. Both of them were dead. I know they're dead, I saw the bodies.

"What's his power?" If Zed had worked for Caesar, he must be a badass.

"He's a P1, Maybe a 1.2." Jackal was not impressed. "I met him a few times, and didn't feel much to copy."

I was a Paralevel 1.3. Level 1's don't have any actual super powers, we're just better at doing what normal people can do. For me, I have photographic muscle memory. "But what is his power?" A level 1 could be great at chess or be able to punch through 40 planks of wood.

"He's a paragon." Again, Jackal was unimpressed.

Paragons were just generally all around better than normal, a little smarter, a little stronger, a little faster, better hearing, that kind of thing. And he was still in one piece after more than a decade playing hardball with supers in this town. He could probably fold me into a knot and drop kick me into the river.

"Where is he?" I only had one option, and that was to find him.

"The word in the inside is he spends a lot of time at Handsome Jack's place." I could almost feel the shrug. "It's in the Kages, a real hole in the wall, but a good place to go if you want to hire mercenaries or be hired to be a mercenary."

"Handsome Jack?" I repeated. I knew the Kages pretty well, and I'd never heard of a bar called Handsome Jack.

"I'll get you there. It moves, but I know where it is tonight."

TWO

"How did you find me?" Osprey yelled.

You can draw the dots that got me here. Insert some demeaning jabs from Jackal, a lot of climbing and leaping, then being completely cold-cocked by this jerk. And you're up to speed.

"Tell me!" Osprey demanded again, giving me a little shake. Like the reason I'm not talking is that I'm not paying attention. I'm not talking because I can't breathe.

I was pretty sure I could break his grip. It doesn't matter how strong you are, the thumb is the weakest link. Apply the right amount of pressure and you will pop right out. But the popping was the problem. I still had a hell of a drop.

I tried to see if there was anything I could use to slow my fall. There was a ledge a few feet down. It would be tricky but better than choking.

I applied pressure to his thumb!

Forget what I said about the thumb.

Everything was going a little dark.

"We didn't find you!" Jackal shouted. "You found us, moron."

Good call, J, let's piss off the guy about to drop me.

Osprey was surprised that my back pouch was talking. It was enough. I tried to pop his thumb and slipped his grip.

Hurray!

And started to plummet to my death.

Boo!

I bent, twisted, and got one hand on the lip of the roof. It was a nice roof, good hard square edges. In all honesty it was just a summer thing, but I fell in love with those strong hard edges. It held my weight, and I used my momentum to flip up onto the roof.

"Who was that?" Osprey barked. "Who are you working with?"

I didn't want to tell him anyway, so I was all stoic and silent. Also, I couldn't talk yet. I coughed.

He came at me fast, but I'm faster scared than he is mad. I flipped out of his grasp and ended up on top of an industrial air conditioner so I was looking down on him.

On a long enough timeline he had the edge, what with the real superpowers. He could turn his body into something dense like steel. The more he solidified the slower he moved. Unfortunately, he also had mad kung fu skills, too. How's that for God giving with both hands?

"You've asked a lot of questions. If you would give me a second, I'll answer some of them." I held up my hands, palms out.

"Fine," he lied. He totally did a truce thing in the middle of a fight and it was a total lie. Who does that? He jumped right at me. He can make himself light, too. He jumped light and then went solid in mid-air.

I leapt straight up, not the best move, but I just did it on instinct. Osprey destroyed the A/C unit on impact. There wasn't a good place for me to land on Osprey and the wreckage, so I landed and rolled. Not gracefully, but I rolled. "I'm not here for you!" I got to my feet before he did.

Osprey was still solid and moving sluggishly as he pulled himself away from the wreckage. I had a totally clean shot at his back, and if I took it, he might notice. Probably not, but he might.

"Liar!" He turned around, kicking a compressor pump that was wrapped around his forearm. "Why else would you be here?"

"Why would I be at the number one dive bar known for information?" I found it helps negotiations to use a condescending tone. It's a sign of respect or something. "You think you're the only one who needs information?" I was assuming he was here for the same reason I was here. It seemed like a good bet.

He kicked the last piece of air conditioner out of his way and lumbered around to face me like he was the black and white Frankenstein's monster. "It seems like I'm the only one doing anything."

I found that hurtful.

"This town is falling apart. The cops stay away from actual crime, too scared they might find a super, and the Feds only show up if they're sure they'll find a super." His movements became graceful again.

So now if I punched him he might feel it. He might solidify and break my hand before I landed a punch, but them's the chances we take to defend goodness and stuff. "So what are you doing about it?"

We were having a moment, and he ruined it by attacking me again! This guy's just rude.

He came in fast. I'd seen him do this before. I had to

keep out of his reach. If I tried to block him he might go super solid on me and break my arm. I backstepped and he missed, then I closed. I got two strikes on his chest. The third felt like I'd picked a fight with a gater.

I stopped the momentum of his attack and he went back to patiently circling me. I circled back, getting some A/C debris between me and him.

"Do you even know what's going on in this town?" he asked.

"On a scale of one to ten, I'd say a six." I knew some stuff. Some really cool need-to-know eyes-only stuff.

"You're a child. There's a serial killer--"

Two can play the not truce game. I vaulted over a chunk of the most intact part of the air conditioner and dropped both feet into his stomach.

He rolled with it a little. Instead of the money shot, he was able to take the momentum, spin himself around, and stomp right where I'd landed.

I caught his foot before he contacted me and tried to turn it.

And failed. Boy, howdy, did I fail. He solidified and drove his heel down toward my chest.

"There's a serial killer preying on women in this town," he continued as if he hadn't been so rudely interrupted. "There's a new designer drug hitting the streets, and they're connected. I'm going to find this killer and end him."

Foot getting closer.

I kicked my legs around and spun out from underneath his foot. His leg crashed down and cracked the pavement on the roof.

I waited a heartbeat for him to soften enough to recover his balance, then kicked his leg out from under him.

He landed like a cat, but that meant he was soft and squishy and I unloaded on him with kicks, punches and spinning back fists. He blocked some, but not all, and I dropped him to one knee.

That was fun.

Then the fun ended.

I swung a back kick into him and hit a big jerk-shaped solid rock.

Now it was my turn to backpedal. "So, what's this new drug like?"

He dropped the solidification to keep up with me, but he still had all those mad ninja skills. He moved in a blur and only my armor and luck saved me from a cracked rib or a broken arm. I don't even know how he did it, but all of a sudden he had me in an arm bar then a head lock.

I tried to break out, but he solidified again.

At least this time I could talk. "A serial killer you say? Tell me more. I haven't heard anything about a serial killer."

"Of course not, you're little more than a puppy."

Not sure name calling was needed.

"The drug is called Stardust, glowing blue rocks. The killer goes back years. No one cared. Only Orion tried to do anything about it." His voice changed, the way it does when your vocal cords become iron, I suppose.

"Orion?"

"It was Orion's pet project, but even Raptor couldn't be bothered. The same killer is killing again, if he ever stopped. I'm going to save the city from this threat."

"Well, don't let me slow you down."

"You aren't slowing me down." Osprey had a lot of condescension in his voice now, totally uncalled for in this situation. I mean, let's be civil.

"Okay, well I'm here on a completely unrelated thing." I twisted. If he hadn't been solid and slow it wouldn't have worked but I wriggled free.

Before I could stand he got a shot in my back that knocked the air out of me. I sprawled on the concrete roof.

I was only immobile for a second, but that was all a person like Osprey would need to turn me into paste. I'm not sure if he really wanted to kill me. I don't think he knew what to do with me. But before he could put me out of his misery, I heard a whistle of air and an impact.

Osprey went bouncing on his back into some other part of the air conditioning system we hadn't managed to wreck.

"Peregrine," Osprey cursed.

He was right, Peregrine was hovering in the air, poised to strike again.

Osprey flipped himself up and assumed a combat stance. "I knew you would show up."

He did? I didn't.

Let's talk about Peregrine. I'd decoded Raptor's note, then put a call out to the entire team. And the guy who could fly a bizzilion miles per hour had gotten there last.

I mean, I was the last-last one to get there, but ... I don't really have a point here. Let's focus on the important stuff.

I'd met up with the former team at Rally Point Beta, a rooftop on a deteriorating factory in the bad area of the Kages district. There was plenty of factory- grade machinery, air conditioners, exhaust stacks, and other things that I didn't know what they were. All provided great cover for a band of baseless superheroes to meet and chat. And I'd hoped to plan, but by the look of things, not the planning thing.

"You called us, we showed up. What is it?" Peregrine asked. Not with his nice voice, either. He was all demandy.

I'd looked at the other two apprentices. Flare was uncharacteristically not looking at me. Her arms were wrapped around herself and she was looking down.

Butterfly sat on a ledge that circled an exhaust stack. Why would they build a ledge around an exhaust stack? What purpose did that serve?

"Raven? Why are we here?" Peregrine was hovering above us, rubbing his effortless flight thing in our faces. What a tool.

I held up the letter I'd just decoded. "I know what Raptor's last order was."

That got Peregrine's attention. Even Flare finally looked at me.

"What is it?" Butterfly's voice was distorted, like all our voices were, but I could tell she was fully human and not leaning into her computer-like intellect that drained emotion from her voice and empathy from her soul.

"Read it," Peregrine ordered.

I had a whole "Ask nicely" thing lined up. You know, a teaching opportunity for the social graces impaired.

"Please, Raven. Just read it." Flare wasn't looking at me again, and I heard her exhaustion through her vocal distortion.

"Warn Caesar, the Legacy is coming. He is the only one who can stop them," I read and dropped my hand with the note.

"What is that supposed to mean?" Peregrine asked.

I looked at the other two. "Do you know?"

Flare shook her head.

"I've no recollection of any group or individual that

used that moniker." Butterfly pressed a little into her robot mode to be sure of perfect recall.

"Well, we can't warn Caesar of anything," Peregrine said. "So what do you want us to do about it?"

Not the reaction I'd been hoping for. "There is no Caesar. We have to figure out what this means. It's up to us to stop these guys."

Crickets.

"Or gals," I amended.

Crickets.

"Or individual."

"No, we don't," Flare said. She rubbed her shoulders against the cold that didn't exist. "We don't have to do anything. We shouldn't do anything."

"What are you talking about?" I waved the note at her. "This is the last thing Raptor told us to do."

"I don't care!" she shot back. Then a little more calmly. "I don't care. I don't." She turned away from me. "I came here to tell you all I'm out. For good this time."

"We all want out," I said. "But we can't just let the Legacy..." I ran out of steam there.

"Do what?" she asked. At least she was looking at me again. "Well, do what?"

"I don't know, but if Raptor was willing to team up with Caesar, it must have been for a good reason."

"You don't know that," Peregrine said. "Were you paying attention? We didn't know anything about Raptor. Red Knight said--"

"Red Knight was a liar, manipulating us so he could get his hands on the Phoenix." I still had no real idea what the Phoenix was. I was glad it blew up with Red Knight.

"Red Knight was just the last person to manipulate us,"

Flare said. "Before him it was Clockwork, and before him it was Raptor."

I didn't like the idea of Raptor being put on the same level as those killers. "But--"

"But nothing," Peregrine said. "Raptor didn't give *us* a last order. He gave his favorite an order. So you deal with it."

"His favorite?" What was he talking about? Peregrine was Raptor's golden boy.

"If there's nothing else, I've got things to do." Peregrine didn't wait for an answer and shot off into the dark.

"Flare." I took a step toward her, but she stopped me with a raised hand.

"No, this isn't our fight." She shook her head as she lowered her hand.

"What about Ballista?" This was a Hail Mary pass, but I had to play all the cards I had.

"What about him?"

"He made it through one surge. He's going to surge again. If he doesn't learn to control his powers he could..." We all knew what could happen if a parahuman as powerful as Ballista didn't learn to use his powers. He could die. His body could become wrecked and twisted. Or, he could go insane or explode and take out a city block or two.

"He doesn't need to run around fighting parahumans to get control of his power. I will help him. When he surges next, he'll be ready." She sounded sure, but that was crap. If you couldn't control your powers, it would definitely end badly, but you could have your powers on lock and still die in a surge. Die, go insane, twist into a monster, or you could just explode and kill the people around you. It was the only advantage of being a parahuman level 1. When I surged, I might get a fever.

"A few weeks ago we sat on a building like this one, and you told me you would never want to go back to a normal life." I pointed in the general direction of that spot.

"A few weeks ago?" She laughed without any humor. "That was a lifetime ago. That was before the Guard died, and Ballista was taken prisoner and almost killed." She started off sad but ended mad. "I have so much power." She looked at her hands and green light ignited into green fire. "So much power, and I couldn't do a thing to help him. I couldn't do a thing to help myself."

She was not being fair. "The device they used to capture you? Clockwork used it to kill ALL the Guard. You're still the most powerful super I know." Ballista had more voltage, but she had the control.

"You don't know me." She pointed at her mask. "Raptor made sure of that. We don't know each other. It's better that way." The fire around her hands turned into a nimbus all around her.

"Flare." I recognized the aura she used to fly.

"There's no mission for us here." Flare pointed at the paper in my hand. "If Raptor thought Caesar was needed to deal with this, what do you think we can do?" She looked at Butterfly. "Can I fly you somewhere?"

Butterfly nodded and stood. "I'll look into it, Raven. But I can't risk using my power. You know what I become if I push too far, what Clockwork became when he pushed too far into his power."

"But..." I had nothing else to say. I understood Butterfly's resistance to using her powers. Clockwork was her mentor in the Guard, and was a cognit like her. He'd lost his soul to the power, and in the end when the real Clockwork was able to take control for a second, he'd shot himself rather than returning to being a slave to his power.

The aura circled both women. That was a new trick. Just last week Flare had needed any hitchhiker to jump as the aura formed.

I didn't say anything as they went into the air. Flare had to hug the building as she flew, to avoid being seen.

And now it was just me and a vague note of vagueness being vague.

THREE

Looking back on it, it surprises me that I never considered whether Flare and Peregrine were right. Giving up didn't even occur to me, even though this wasn't my fight. I was just a kid, I didn't need to take on this mission. Raptor hadn't even expected me to. He'd just wanted me to deliver a message.

Nope, my next thought was: I have to ask Jackal.

"Why are you two fighting me?" Osprey had taken a position where he could see us both. Not that it would matter with Peregrine. He was just too fast and he could fly.

I slowly walked to the left, and Peregrine hovered a little to the right, forcing him to split his focus.

"Was that a rhetorical question or a for-real nut-bar ask?" I can't tell sometimes.

"I'm doing what this city needs, what Raptor was never willing to do," Osprey said.

"You mean blowing up Red Knight?" In all fairness, that was a solid for me personally. "You're a psycho."

Osprey pointed at me. "I freed us both of that monster."

True.

"Your methods don't work," he continued. "This city is more corrupt, more violent, more of a hell than when Raptor and his merry men started playing dress-up."

"So your answer..." I had a whole might-doesn't-make-right thing, and only light can chase out darkness monologue prepped. Some seriously moving stuff. But Peregrine made his move, so it was on.

For a year and a half Raptor forced me to spar with Peregrine. I knew a lot of his moves and I knew when he was going to attack. It was just nice that he wasn't going to attack me this time.

He shot in with his patent-pending flying spin kick, really a crowd pleaser. I've been on the receiving end of that move so I can vouch for the power.

Osprey didn't have the hours of experience sparring with Peregrine, so to him one second Peregrine was hovering and the next he was a bullet with judo skills.

Osprey went solid, but not soon enough. Peregrine's strike landed on his side and kicked him into the air.

I was on Osprey before he stopped bouncing. I landed strikes to his face, a knife hand to his neck, anything. Peregrine joined in and we were able to keep up the pressure and stop him from solidifying.

When I pulled back to get room for a punch, Peregrine swept in with a kick, then was gone by the time I landed my strike. It was a thing of teamwork beauty.

Osprey wasn't just about his powers, though. He also had mad ninja skills. Even though we kept him distracted enough that he couldn't power up, he fell back on his martial arts and was able to twist his hips, knock me off him, and roll up, missing Peregrine's following strike. One-on-one he totally owned me, but there were two of us now!

I blocked a strike and wrapped his arms. Peregrine flew in and delivered a series of blows then I spun him to the floor.

Osprey dodged me before I could land a kick, then he rolled away from another strike from Peregrine. With a spin he tried to knock me off my feet. I leapt back, but that allowed him to kip up and jump.

He shot up with zero density, then amped his density to steel as he collided with Peregrine. They both hit the roof and slid. I thought they would stop before they went over the edge.

I was wrong.

At that moment a timer went off in my helmet. I'd set it to remind me that I needed to start heading back right now if I was going to make it home on time. Well, to my dad's place.

Let's talk about my dad's place.

I've seen places as nice as my dad's penthouse. Not in real life. Mostly in movies. Okay, no I haven't. I haven't seen any place like this, ever.

The elevator went up, up, and up and... still going up and then up a little more before opening. This place was huge, and I was just in the elevator lobby. A large area with an assortment of chairs could be used to host tasteful gatherings. The view was breathtaking. A massive window bigger than my house overlooked a few of the buildings between this one and the ocean. The docks were even classy and beautiful. When I think of docks I think of shipping container wastelands. These docks were more for yachts and supplying people with yachts.

Then there was just horizon. Horizon and water.

"Ryan."

My eyes parted with the view of awesomeness and went to my dad. I hadn't even realized he was there until he spoke. He was sitting on a huge leather couch in the elevator lobby. He gave me a wave and pointed to a small bluetooth headset in his ear. "I've got to go, Chris. We'll talk tomorrow."

Whoever Chris was, she had a few more things to say to him. He nodded along, like you do even though Chris couldn't see him. "You've given a lot of power to this, more power than you need to." My side of the conversation paused as Chris weighed in on the correct level of power she was giving it. "Chris, we'll talk tomorrow." He begged my indulgence with a grimace.

I waved. Take all the time you need. I went back to the view. I didn't know the city could look this good. This high up you couldn't see what I'd walked through to get here. We were on the Island, so it was way nicer than the Kages or Flat Stones, but wow.

I set my duffel down and looked out the window, searching for landmarks. Even I got a touch of vertigo, thinking how I would scale this building. That would be hard.

"Like it?" Dad had walked up behind me. I didn't hear him with the thick carpet.

"Who's Chris?" I asked.

"A sponsey. With my move, he needs to get a new sponsor, and he's having a tough time with it." Dad had sympathy for the guy.

My mental picture realigned Chris to male. "So where's

your place?" Now no longer dazzled with the view, I took in the lobby a little more. Four doors led from the lobby, one into a hallway.

Dad seemed confused for a second. "This is my place."

I mentally realigned my head to crazy town.

"This is the living room," he said.

"For what county?" Now that I looked at it, it did look less like a lobby and more like a personal space. I noticed photos on the wall of my half-sister and brother.

Dad laughed. "Yeah, it's a little different from what you're used to." He seemed a little embarrassed.

He should be. This place was insane.

With a head jerk he led me to one of the doors. "Dinner will be at seven. We would love it if you could join us."

"Will I be able to walk to the dining room by seven?" Honest question. "Or is there a trolly?"

He smiled. "It's not that big." He took a step. "No, you're right, it is that big." He pointed at a door marked with a unicorn poster. "This is Helen's bedroom." The next door down. "That's the nanny." He pointed at the room down on the same side of the hall. "This is you."

The room was huge, of course. At this point, if there wasn't enough room for a musical production of *Les Miserables* I would have been disappointed. The view was the same awesome view of the harbor and ocean. The bed was some dark wood four-poster thing that was a little intimidating.

"Closet through here." The closet was only twice as big as my bedroom back home.

I put my rucksack in the center, just out of blue-collar irony. It looked sad and alone.

"Your mom said something about a cat?" Dad asked.

I shook my head. "Wandered off. He might turn up." I hoped so.

"Well, we can make it happen. Our last place wouldn't let us have pets, so Helen would be over the moon to have a cat." Dad smiled.

I tried to picture Feral, fifteen pounds of matted grey and black fur, as either a pet or in this room. It was just too much of a leap for my brain. "We'll see. He turns up when you least expect it."

"Have a seat. I have something I want to talk to you about." Dad gave the same head motion that he'd used to lead me to my new room to direct me to a tasteful collection of chairs around a faux antique table.

I sat. In the history of the Blackwater family, this scenario had never ended with a happy Ryan. Not once.

Dad touched the table. "I know this place looks like a hotel, but you can make it your own. Different furniture, paint color."

I didn't plan on staying long enough to decorate. I was going to prove to Mom I was doing school and then I would be back home. "It's fine. I like it." At least it didn't cause me much pain. Wait, just saw the painting over the bed of Amish people harvesting wheat. That hurt.

Dad smiled. He knew I wasn't being honest. "Shar wanted to put you in a different room, but Helen wanted you close to her."

Shar was my stepmom.

"The view alone is worth the rest." I waved at the Amish painting. Nope, that was a different Amish painting. Good God, there was quite the simple folk motif going here.

"The view is amazing," he agreed.

And the reason we were sitting looking at each other? Each other and peasant farmers?

"We need to talk about school." He said it like that was a surprise.

"I'm going to do it this year. You don't need to worry about that." The public schools on the Island were called the Cake Eaters by the Kages. The cheers got kind of nasty at sporting events. Not that I'd caught a basketball game since my sophomore year. "Next week when classes start I'm going to be the most dedicated student on the Island."

"About that." He seemed a little excited. "I have good news."

In no way did he have good news. It might not be horrible news, it might be wet your pants terrifying news, but it wasn't going to be good news.

"I've enrolled you in a better school."

"Oh," I said, all neutral and open.

"It turns out that one of the best private schools in Darhaven has an opening. Now classes started last week so you'll have to catch up, but they have great support staff." Again with the excitement.

"Oh," said the Zen master of openness and neutrality.

"You meet with the headmaster tomorrow morning and start classes bright and early." My dad looked like Santa Claus and the child getting the presents rolled into one. "It's such an amazing opportunity. I didn't even think to look into it. It's really exclusive and a top notch education."

"Exclusive," I said. But what I meant was "Sumre Island public school was going to look down on a kid from the Kages. Rich, rich exclusive guys are going to freak." But I actually added, "Top notch."

"I was having drinks with a colleague and he mentioned his nephew's school had an opening. I jumped at it. It happened so quickly, I didn't have time to run it by you." Dad's tone was a little apologetic.

"No, it's cool." The problem with wearing a mask in all your stressful situations is your poker face atrophies.

"You don't like the idea." Dad read my face well.

"It's just a lot to get used to." I smiled and shook my head.

"If you graduate from Hellington, any school would be open to you. You could go anywhere."

One, that is a big IF. That is the IF that ate Darhaven, and started on the rest to the east coast size of IF. Two, go anywhere? I hadn't even thought about going somewhere, never mind anywhere.

"I know it's a lot. If it doesn't work out, we can try a different school," Dad offered.

There was so much wrapped up in that statement. His hope he could offer something to his son that I would want. Hope that he could fix almost a decade of screw ups. Hope he could undo the two bad years of drinking. And they were bad years.

"No, it'll be great." Not enough. "I mean, thanks. I'm just surprised. It will be really great." Big smile. I'd like to thank the Academy.

Big smiles all around. "What about dinner?"

"Um, I actually have a couple of errands I have to run."

His face fell. Maybe reading more into the invite refusal than there was.

"I mean, I'll try to get back in time. But I don't want to commit." I had to dig up a bag full of money, bring it to a widow, and finish decoding Raptor's letter. "But then I'll be a homebody. You'll get sick of me being around so much."

He stood, and I stood. Part of my superpower is I can slow down time. Not really slow time, but it seems like things slow down. It's one of those adrenaline things that can happen to normals in a firefight, but I can turn it on or off.

I wish I'd turned it on then. Dad went in for a hug.

Not ready for that at all. An awkward man hug ensued.

Before he let me go. "I know we can make this work."

I nodded into his shoulder. "Yeah, this will work." And I'm doing this for Mom, to make up for what I did to her. Not to make you feel better about abandoning me. Okay, seems I still have some issues to work out.

FOUR

We were, like, nine stories up. No way was I going to survive that in a straight jump, no matter how well I roll.

This was a little trick Cat showed me. You drop to the first windowsill and stop your momentum then drop to the next. If you have time, you stop your momentum. I just slowed it down.

Cat drilled me on this move FOREVER! He forced me to do it again and again until he was sure I had it on lock. We must have been at it for thirty minutes at least. Boy, what a drag.

I miss Cat.

My hands automatically did the work as my mind was elsewhere and I landed in a three story roll and run.

Peregrine had gotten free but was still wobbly. I'm guessing he got free in midair, because a Buick had an Osprey shape in the hood.

Osprey got up, too, his movements sluggish. I couldn't tell if it was his solidification power or because he'd just dropped off a nine-story building. Only one way to be sure.

I double kicked him in the head.

He rolled with the strike and flipped off the Buick.

I landed right by him and delivered a few more strikes that he was able to block, but I had him on the run. If he didn't have a second to breathe, Peregrine would join and we would have this guy.

"What do you plan on doing if you beat me? You can't arrest me. The cops in this town would rather arrest you than me." Don't let the banter fool you. He was just trying to distract me. Also, he had a point.

Why was I fighting him? At first it was to not get killed, but if I beat him it wasn't like I was going to cuff him and read him his rights. "Haven't you heard? The Superhuman Suppression Agency is crawling all over this town. I'll leave you for them." Small ethical concern about the life in prison without trial. I mean, that's the fate I face as a parahuman using powers as a vigilante. But I am a small v vigilante. Osprey here is a big killing-people V vigilante. So I don't feel good about leaving him to do that, either.

I forget if my new class schedule has ethics. I could use a little help in that area.

Screw it, I'll just punch him.

"How did you find me?" I know, sick of hearing that. But it wasn't from Osprey.

"Slicer!" I yelled.

He was in just as nice a suit as the last time he almost killed me. Wow, that was like three weeks ago, seems like a year. He came out the back door, which could have been the only door to Handsome Jack's place. He must have heard the ruckus of Osprey's impact with quality American engineering.

Osprey didn't seem to know who Slicer was, or he was too exhausted to move fast enough.

I slowed time.

Slicer didn't have extra time to react to the situation, but I did. He moved slowly, everything moved slowly when I was in the zone. He raised his hand toward Osprey. Slicer could manifest a shotgun pattern of energy razors from his hand. He might be able to do other things, but that was the only one I cared about.

Osprey might have been able to endure a volley from Slicer if he'd been fully solidified, but he wasn't. He was just a guy in some light body armor.

I ran toward the Buick and jumped off a still-intact fender. Or at least it was intact until I kicked off it. That changed my trajectory so when I collided with Osprey, it moved us both closer to Slicer and outside the blast pattern of the slices.

The Buick took all the glowing orange half moons. Man, did we do a number on that poor car.

I sprung off Osprey and got close enough to connect with Slicer. He was already aiming at me. At this close range there wouldn't be enough of me left to mail home.

Slicer suddenly jerked as Peregrine clotheslined him from the other side.

That bought me enough time to deliver the kick to his stomach that flipped him out of the stairwell and into the Buick.

Poor hard-working Buick, just trying to make a living.

Osprey stood. All the signs indicated he'd solidified, at least to some level. He brought his foot up, then down towards Slicer's head.

"No!" My scream stretched out in my own ears since things were still slow. I would pay for that later. Don't know why, but man, do I have nightmares when I use this power. The longer I use it, the worse the nightmares are.

I grabbed Slicer's belt and yanked him away. Somehow he slid twenty feet on broken Buick safety glass.

Osprey's foot landed on asphalt and spider webbed five feet of parking lot.

"Moron!" Osprey yelled. He might have meant me, but he could have been talking about Peregrine. Peregrine had taken advantage of the distraction to propel himself into Osprey's back. Osprey twisted, solidified, and Peregrine hit an arm like a lead pole. He bounced off Osprey and piled right into, you guessed it, the Buick.

"That's Slicer! He deserves death a hundred times!" I guess Osprey was talking to me. "It wasn't why I came here, but I'll do what needs to be done."

My back itched like crazy. I had to turn on Slicer and face Osprey. "You know that's not going to happen. Raptor trained you, too. You know the cost of killing people. We're not judge--" I was going to add the jury-execution thing, too, but Osprey didn't let me. Rude. What was the point of getting all dressed up if you can't moralize?

"I am his judge. I judge the City. Men like him rule with fear! It's time they feel fear!" Osprey yelled.

In my list of things labeled "A Thousand Things That Might Happen Tonight", a three-way fight for my life was about twelve on the list. Under hippopotamus stampede, number nine-hundred-and-eighty-four was what happened next. A cop showed up.

The siren rolled and red and blue strobe painted everything. The wheels squealed and a blue and white squad car whipped off the street and into the little parking lot.

The shock of that knocked me out of the slow zone. I could only keep it going for a few seconds in the best of times, anyway.

The cop looked young, maybe five years older than me. Maybe not even that old. "Freeze!" he yelled, pulling his gun and pointing it at Osprey and me.

He wasn't full of bravado -- he was terrified -- but he kept his gun level and stayed behind his car.

Osprey solidified. "Shoot your little pop gun."

That's all fun and games for Osprey, but I am in no way bulletproof. I'm not even bullet resistant. I have some armor that might save me, but it might not. "Whoa. Everyone calm down." I held up my hand, palm out.

"You are under arrest for violating the proper use of parahuman ability Act." The cop's voice trembled.

"That's not happening, Junior." Osprey did not calm down as I'd asked.

This was going to get ugly. I would have to jump behind Osprey if the cop fired, then get the cop out of the way before Osprey crushed him, and me, like a zit. Why did this guy show up? He must have known supers were involved. Why couldn't he "wait for backup" for twenty minutes and collect witness statements? Then everyone goes home and lives to wait for backup another day.

Slicer stood up.

No, no, no.

"On the ground!" the cop yelled at Slicer.

He was dressed in a suit, not a damn costume. I don't know if the cop understood he was a super.

"You've got to help me." Slicer took a few steps toward the cop with his hands up.

"No, he's a super!" I yelled and started running toward Slicer.

Time slowed. Not in a fun superhero-now-I-have-time-to-act way. This was slow in a nightmare. There was nothing I could do but remember every moment to replay again and again.

Slicer looked at me and smirked. He knew I was too far to do anything. He pointed one palm at me and one palm at the cop.

I saw the glow of orange energy bubble up from his outstretched hand. One bubble detached itself and was instantly joined by more and more. I changed my trajectory, flinging myself out of the way. I landed on my left shoulder so I was still able to see the second stream of spinning orange crescents first rip into the cop's car, safety glass spider webbing and exploding.

The cop moved like he was swimming in mud. He tried to rotate himself down behind the car, but slices not absorbed by the car hit him in the shoulder, the head, the arm.

There was a moment when he registered the pain, then all expression left his face, and another slice caught him right in the neck.

Time started going again. At least, it started going for everyone else. I stopped. I couldn't move, couldn't react, couldn't think.

For how long it took in my mind for the cop to drop, everything after that moment happened on fast forward.

Slicer pumped a few more showers of sparks, but was running and didn't come close to hitting me or Osprey.

Osprey didn't risk lowering his density, so he couldn't keep up with Slicer.

Slicer dove into the back a car that seemed to appear out of nowhere, and the car sped off.

Peregrine's arms were around me and getting me on my feet. "We have to go!"

I didn't recognize the sound of sirens until he

mentioned them. Not cop sirens. This was the louder jaring ra-ta-ta-ta of the SSA.

I knew he was right, we did have to go. Why couldn't I move? I just saw the mess that was the officer.

"You did this, White Hat!" Osprey pointed at the body. "I could have stopped this. A mother is mourning her son because of you. That blood is on your hands!"

That blood was on my hands.

I felt pressure as Peregrine held me closer, then a jolt as the ground stopped doing what ground normally did.

Peregrine was flying me out of there. That was what was happening. That made sense.

Nothing made sense.

Another alarm went off in my helmet. Oh, yeah, it was a school night.

"Just hanging out with friends?" the headmaster asked. I think he'd said it a second time.

"Um, yeah." I wiped my hand over my face and it came back wet with cold sweat. "Nothing really worth talking about."

"Well, it looks like you were out late and didn't get enough sleep."

"I didn't sleep well." Nightmares on nightmares. A cop dying, a man shooting his face off, Red Knight exploding again and again. All the while the words "That blood is on your hands!" repeated over and over. Sometimes by Osprey, sometimes in Raptor's distorted voice. "That blood is on your hands!"

Dr. Paris rocked back in his magnificent leather chair a couple of times. "I want to be honest with you, Mr. Blackwater. You're going to find Hellington very challenging. And this is not a school where you can just fail classes and be passed on. You're starting on academic probation. If we don't see some progress, then we'll have to examine if this place is right for you. I think it would be a good first step to examine how important your future is and how important 'hanging out with friends' is."

"I've already decided." I said it too quickly. "I'm not doing... what I did last night again. Like you said, it isn't more important than my future."

The headmaster probably thought I was coming down off some drugs. I looked and felt hungover. "That's good to hear, Mr. Blackwater." I thought he might say something else, but he straightened up and handed me a folder that was nested in the folder he was reviewing. "Your advisor and English teacher is Mr. Clancy. He's expecting you after this meeting. Have a good first day at Hellington Preparatory school, Mr. Blackwater."

All the Mr. Blackwater stuff threw me off. Were we supposed to shake hands? The headmaster was already focused on whatever stuff headmasters did. Maybe not. I mumbled a thanks and took the folder as I left the office.

FIVE

I asked for directions to Mr. Clancy's from the secretary. She did not approve of me. I don't know if it was the way I looked, the way I wasn't seven generations of rich snob, or maybe she couldn't fathom how I planned to graduate if I didn't even know where Mr. Clancy was.

I got out from the headmaster's office into something approximating a school. It was like the same guy who'd decorated my bedroom was given a lot of oak paneling and let loose with no adult supervision.

There were kids, lots of kids. Lots and lots of white kids. It was like the population ratio had flipped. I saw a few East Asian and Asian faces, and one black girl. But it was disorientingly pale in here.

And every student had the same blazer. The girls had the same knee-length skirts with the same plaid pattern and boys in navy pants and deep blue shirts, just like me.

And I stuck out like the freak show had just come into town.

A lot of the students just looked at me, blank faces as they passed me.

Oh, this was so much worse than I'd thought it would be.

Five steps from the office I realized the Secretary Judgment's directions were worthless, and I had no idea where I was supposed to go.

"Excuse me." Someone stepped out of the crowd of blonde hair and blazers. He was a little taller than me, probably a senior. His face had a little bit of a sneer and he held out his hand. "Hello, I'm Thurston Hillgrave. I'm sure you've heard of the Hillgraves."

"Ah, no." I took his hand.

He gave me a limp-wristed up and down motion. It made me want to recoil and boil my hand.

"This is your first day at Hellington?" He wasn't really asking me.

I noticed a group of five boys looking at the interaction and snickering. Oh, this was going great. Sorry, I'm with the upper crust now. It was going smashingly, simply smashingly.

"Hellington is absolutely the best school. My family has attended for generations."

"When do they graduate?" I asked.

His eyes flared at the little insult, then he broke into a grin and started laughing. "I can't do it, I can't."

The group of boys started laughing, too.

"I'm sorry." The faint British accent was gone, as was the sneer. He held out his hand again.

I took it again because that's what you do?

This time he shook it firmly. "I am Thurston Hillgrave, but call me Tor."

The show over, the group of boys pointed at Tor, laughed again, and dispersed into the streams of blazers.

"I lost a bet. I was sure the Tornados would win. I had

to give all the new kids the 'Rich Boy Welcome.'" His faint British accent and sneer returned. "You should have seen your face when we shook hands."

Funny. On any other day, maybe funny?

He noticed the folder. "Who's your advisor?"

"Clancy."

"Come on, I'll take you there." He nodded in the opposite direction that I'd been wandering.

So he could still be screwing with me and trying to make sure I was late, but if I wandered around this tasteful hall by myself, I would be late, anyway. So a lateral shift at best.

I stepped into pace at his shoulder.

"So where did you transfer from?" Tor asked.

"Jefferson."

He looked a little confused. "Haven't heard of that one. Is that upper west coast?"

"No, it's the Kages, north side." I looked for his reaction. I didn't want to be a pariah, but I wasn't going to pretend to be someone I wasn't. I was not going to hide behind some kind of made up identity. I mean, who does that?

"Wow, Kages." The question "Then how in all the trust funds of Sumatra Island can you afford to come here?" wasn't spoken but I could see it dance in his eyes.

"My dad has a superpower," I explained.

He got more confused.

"He fails up." I had no idea how far up he'd failed until I'd seen the apartment last night. "He didn't start out rich, but he managed to marry it."

His face cleared up. "Oh, well, welcome across the river. When you said your father had a superpower, I thought for a second you meant a parahuman thing. Which would explain your presence here, too."

We walked a few more halls. Tor waved at a couple groups, and pointed out the different rooms we passed.

And my brain caught up with the conversation. "What do you mean?"

"Spanish? That's where you will learn to express yourself and understand Spanish." Tor was pointing out a room that looked like every other door in the wood and marble hallways.

"No, what parahuman thing?"

A beat of confusion then he tracked. "You know, Mr. Clancy's thing."

When I stopped walking, he did, too.

"You don't know about the Mr. Clancy thing?" Tor wasn't really asking. "Oh boy, sorry. Living in the Hellington bubble you forget normal people don't hang on every breakup and staff issue."

I thought I was going to have to dig harder, but he continued.

"I don't like to gossip, and I like Mr. C." It didn't stop him from talking. "First day of school a family brought a toddler when they picked up their daughter. The toddler was so excited, she ran into the middle of the street. She would have been dead, but Mr. Clancy is a parahuman. He can run at like a hundred miles per hour or something. In front of the entire student body he saved the girl's life, and the stuff hit the fan."

"No one knew he was a super?" Then why was he my advisor and not in the custody of the SSA?

"Oh, he's totally legal. He has his documentation from the SSA and everything. He served on the SSA for five years and was honorably discharged. The headmaster, some staff and trustees knew. But not the parents. So they flipped and pulled their students."

Which was why there was a place for me in the rich school at literally the last minute.

"You didn't know?" he asked.

"Dad didn't go into details."

"I mean, Mr. Clancy is totally cool. He's like thirty-five so it isn't like he's going to surge and blow up or anything." Tor tried to calm me.

"What?" It took me a second to track what he was saying. "If he can run, he might not even be a PL 2.3." If the SSA let him go, he wasn't higher than a two-nine. "Even if he did surge, he might puke. But he isn't blowing up."

Tor relaxed a little. "There was a big push to get Clancy out, but Dr. Paris hung in there for him. He just has a lot of seats to fill now."

I couldn't say I had warm fuzzies from the good doctor, but my estimation of him went up. "So Mr. Clancy was part of the SSA?"

"Yep, for like five years. He arrested illegal supers. Cool, right?" Tor said.

Or horrifying. My English teacher had arrested people like me for a living. That is... awful. "Yeah, super cool," I said with enthusiasm. "Super cool."

The bell rang.

"Nuts. Mr. Clancy is right there." He pointed at a door three doors down. "Just knock and you're home." The movement in the hallway picked up as other students raced to class. "I'll find you in the lunchroom after third period," he promised and melted into the river of plaid and tweed.

Well, there was a chance that the speedy Mr. Clancy had a secondary power of spotting supers. I know Raptor had that ability. Maybe I should just make a run for it and embrace my destiny in the growing profession of janitorial sciences? I mean, better safe than sorry.

The realist in me pointed out that Raptor's ability was rare. And should the SSA find a parahuman sniffer, that sniffer would not be teaching Robert Frost. He or she, would be working for the SSA for life.

Stupid realist, getting in the way of my career dreams.

I walked to the appropriate door and knocked.

"Enter."

So I did. This was a classroom? Where was all the soul-crushing fluorescent lighting? Where were all the decade-old desks with graffiti that commemorated generations of bored children? How could I know "who was here" if all the desks were shiny warm wood with chairs that didn't look like torture devices welded to plastic?

There were even banks of large flatscreen computers with spinning logos that matched my blazer emblem dancing on the screens.

It smelled nice.

"Are you okay?" Mr. Clancy asked. He was at his desk in the far corner.

"I guess." I walked around a cluster of desks, not in rows but positioned to be in groups of four.

"Ryan?" Mr. Clancy asked.

"Yes, sir." I sir'd him. Is that what we do here?

"Have a seat." He pointed at the chair right by his desk. "Are you sure you're okay? You look a little pasty." Mr. Clancy was one to talk. He would get a sunburn walking under a heat lamp. He was physically fit, and the goatee was probably an English teacher regulation thing.

"Rough night, a day before a new school and all." I didn't exactly lie, just misled.

That seemed to cover it. "I have your schedule."

He passed me a paper.

"And a map of the building."

Another paper.

That went on until I had a book of stuff. Some stuff I didn't need, other stuff I did need. The stuff I did need I had to do something with, so something else wouldn't happen to other stuff. I think.

"Listen, I've seen your grades," he finally said. "You're going to find this a very challenging year. Do you plan on graduating from Hellington?"

"I plan on it, sir." I was still sir-ing, not sure how to stop now. I was in a sir-ing death spiral.

"You have already missed a week of my class, so I'll tell you what I'll do. I'll exempt you from all the work you missed and the unit final at the end of the week if you submit a five page paper on Macbeth." He turned and plucked a thin paperback from a row of identical paperbacks.

"Macbeth?" I looked at the cover.

"Shakespeare's Macbeth."

"Ah, okay. But I don't know anything about Macbeth." Or Shakespeare.

"I'll give you a hint. They're in kilts, and first you make your choices then your choices make you. Get that to me by the end of the week, and you can consider yourself caught up in my class."

I blinked. Five pages! Of paper! With words on it! Words that I needed to provide! About something! I should have run for the sweet, sweet bosom of the architectural sanitation industry when I'd had the chance.

SIX

I found my locker. It was kind of a letdown. It was just a locker. I thought maybe I would have a locker valet or something. But it was a sturdy metal box with air vent slits and a combination lock. It was a nice sturdy metal box, but nothing special. I deposited all the stuff Mr. Clancy had given me onto the only shelf and shut the door.

Then I swore under my breath and opened the locker again. Midway through the pile I pulled out my schedule then shut the locker again. Took three steps, swore louder, opened the locker AGAIN and fished out the building map. The pile of papers had been in a kind of order before, with the important stuff on top. Now it was a mess. I swore a little louder and shut the damn locker.

This sucked. I mean, school always sucked, but this freshman-all-turned-around crap sucked. I could find my way around the Kages in the dark, jumping from rooftop to rooftop. But Algebra and Statistics might as well have had a cloaking field and be stored in a bunker.

I tried to orient myself with the crappy glossy full-color

map. And my eye caught a bottlebrush brown tail ducking around a corner.

Was that Feral? The color was right, but I hadn't seen him in days.

I turned the corner, did a quick look around, and there was Feral on top of a row of lockers.

Something in me unclenched. I didn't really believe that Osprey had killed Feral. Sofia had told me that she'd seen him a couple of times after the fight. But he had disappeared on me.

"Oh, am I glad to see you." I got just under him and outstretched my hands. "Come on."

He looked at me, stood, and did that total body arch that cats do, then leapt a second before I was ready, like cats do.

It was good to see him. "Where have you been?"

He nuzzled my head with his forehead and started purring. I don't think I'd heard him purr like that since before Cat was killed.

"Raven!" The female voice scared the ever-loving crap out of me.

I turned, instinctively keeping the cat covering a little of my face.

Sofia had turned the corner and was walking right at me. She was in the Hellington female dress code of blazer and skirt, but she made it look good.

The last time I'd seen Sofia she'd begged me to save her father. I had no idea how I'd done on that. I'd lost track of the Confessor, arch villain wannabe with some mental powers, during the fight.

"Raven, where have you been?" she asked me.

I knew Sofia was psychic, but I'd hoped my uniform would have protected my identity. She'd seen me out of uniform once, but I'd disguised my identity by wearing my shirt as a ninja mask.

Trust me, it made sense at the time.

"Raven, you had me so worried." She scolded me in a small voice. Kinda like you would use on a child.

"Sorry," I ventured. Her tone didn't line up with exposing my secret Identity and destroying my life. Sofia put her hands on Feral.

Oh, that could be bad. Feral could rip a person's throat out if he didn't know them.

Feral was a great big pile of butter and purred louder.

"Raven, you had mommy all frightened," she said in baby talk to the tomcat.

"Raven's the cat?" My stomach did the same flip it does when I get missed by a bullet.

"Yes, he is." More baby talk. "Raven's a pretty kitty."

He's not. He is really not a pretty kitty.

"I'm surprised he let you hold him." She hadn't even looked at me yet. "He can be a bit skittish around strangers."

"Sofia." I might as well find out how much she knew.

She looked at me and blinked. "You know my name?" Then realization crossed her face. "Of course, I'm sure everyone knows the new girl."

I shook my head and held up the glossy map as proof. "New kid here, too." I gave her a second more. "We met a couple days ago at the Golden View hotel." That was stupid. Why didn't I just walk away? I didn't need to connect her thinking of me with the hotel where a loon in underoos got his ass kicked.

She looked at me confused, then with recognition. She reached out and pushed me right on my chest. "You're Ryan."

I didn't see the contact coming, something I needed to avoid from a psychic. "Um, yeah."

"Oh, my gosh. You look so different."

I wasn't in the wrinkled button-up and jeans anymore. "I clean up good."

"That's not what I meant." But that's what she meant.

"So was today bring your cat to school day?" I asked. "I'm going to feel silly if I'm the only one without a cat."

Her attention went back to the fifteen pounds of purring in her hands. "Oh, no. I don't know how he does it. He always gets out and follows me around."

Same old Feral. I reached in and gave his head a rubbing. "I had a cat like that once." There was a little more sadness in my voice than I'd thought there would be.

"He certainly likes you. He can be very protective of me." She smiled at how easy Feral was under my hand.

"Have you had him long?" I asked.

"Just a week or so." She seemed to be considering how much to tell me. "I was having a pretty tough week. I was scared and sad. And Raven showed up to help me. He's been my protector ever since." She buried her face in his fur.

"Raven's a good name." What else was I going to say? Start yelling about gimmick infringement?

She went a little pink at that. "Um, thanks. It just seemed right."

"You better get him out of here. I can't imagine they have a pet policy." I took in the school with a tap on the blazer.

"You're right," she said with a smile. "It was nice seeing you again." She gave a furtive look both ways.

I held up my hand to make sure she stopped and took a couple steps back. The coast was clear. "You're good, go."

She gave a little giggle and rushed around the corner.

I caught Feral's eye as he bumped along. I can't explain it, but I knew that a piece of Feral that had broken when Cat died, wasn't healed exactly, but was mending.

"Feral, you lucky bastard," I whispered. He got the girl and my name. "Simply no justice in this world."

And now I was covered in cat hair. Even for Feral, a shedding machine, this was a crazy amount of cat hair.

"Thanks, Raven." I put an emphasis on MY name, to no one.

Down the way was a bathroom. Might as well try to get some of this off me. I was going to miss first period.

I opened the bathroom door.

I recognized two of the kids instantly, guys Tor had lost his bet to. The other kid I did not know, but he was holding out a small zip-locked bag of glowing green rocks and Tor's friend was holding out a roll of a few twenties.

Aw hell, at least in the hood we had the decency to post a lookout or just put the stuff in a paper bag. "Sorry, I'll try a different john." I turned around to exit.

But another member of the group was standing behind the door and moved in front of me. For a second I thought maybe he really had to use the bathroom, but then it dawned on me -- he was being intimidating.

Aw, hell.

In the bathroom mirrors I saw two of the other kids come up behind me. If this had happened on the street, both those twerps would have been on the ground calling for their mommies' lawyers. But I wasn't on the job. I didn't want a reputation as a fighter, not in normal life. I certainly didn't want to do it with Sofia in the same student body. The less I had to do with violence in her mind was the less she would connect me to Raven. Not cat Raven, but me Raven.

"Guys, it's cool. I don't want any trouble." I let them drag me away from the door. "Seriously, whatever you guys are into is your business." I'd never seen it before, but glowing green rocks had to be Stardust.

"You're damn right it's our business," the kid with the bag of rocks told me. He finished his transaction. "Beat it."

The kid who'd paid the money didn't have to be told twice. Maybe he was off to get help, but probably not.

"What am I going to do with the nosy new kid?" The guy was obviously in charge. He counted the money and put it in his pocket.

"Why would you need to sell drugs?" That question just came out. I mean, his hair product allowance alone exceeded what he could turn for some rocks.

"You have a lot of questions." He took a small pipe the length of a roll and a half of quarters out of his pocket.

I didn't know how you even used Stardust, but that seemed to be a really strange delivery system.

He made a fist around the pipe.

Oh, it was a roll of quarters in the PayPal generation.

He punched my stomach.

That didn't feel good, but let's just say I've had better. A second later I realized that this would go on a lot longer if I didn't play along. "Ah," I yelled.

He did it again.

This time my yell of pain was better timed. That's when I saw it in his eyes. He liked it. He liked the power of inflicting pain. That was why he was selling drugs, not for the money. He did it to get off on the power. He got to be the big scary fish in a homogenized placid pond. I'd seen that look on much scarier people, but I also knew that the breaks were off on this kid. He wasn't going to stop until someone stopped him. Maybe not here in the school bathroom, but there was going to be a time when he thought "I could get away with it" and he would do it.

I rolled with the next strike a little, but made a louder yell.

"Do you understand who's in charge here?" he asked.

"Yes." I tried for a whimper. I've read about whimpers, but you don't really know if you're doing it right without feedback.

"Who's in charge?"

And another shot to the gut.

"You are."

And another shot to the gut. "That is damn right." He grabbed my hair. "Now, if you go whine to a teacher, I will know, and they might give me a stern talking to. Daddy might even take my car for the weekend. But you are going to be coming to school in a wheelchair. Do you understand?"

The bathroom door opened.

Really people, set a lookout. It can't be that hard.

I could see the newcomer in the reflection of the mirror. Tor. First he looked confused, then pissed. "Brian, what the hell?"

"Stay out of this Thurston." Brian pronounced Thurston like an insult.

"Let him go." Tor pulled at one of the guys holding me and my arm was free.

The other guy let my arm go. I tried to look like I was flailing around, got a foot out, and tripped the duffus who had held me. Tor pushed him and they all ended up in a heap in front of the sinks.

I looked back at Brian. His vein was popping out of his

neck and his hand was tight on the quarter pipe. I thought he was going to swing for it, but instead he said, "I'm done here. I think I've made my point clear."

I had to bite my tongue. I did not want to egg this guy on. It would be my word against his. I was a problem kid from the Kages and Brian was a fine upstanding rich sociopath. It hurt, but I didn't say anything. I mean, I said, "I don't want any trouble." But I didn't say what I wanted to say. I'm growing as a person.

He pushed past me, bumping me into the sink as he passed. His two minions had managed to get up. "You watch yourself, Thurston. All your friends graduated or got scared off by Clancy. You must be pretty lonely right now."

Tor didn't say anything, and he didn't back down.

"I'll be seeing you around." Brian walked out of the bathroom without looking back.

The other two walked out backwards, again with that constipated intimidation look they'd given me earlier.

"You all right?" Tor asked.

I looked in the mirror and straighten up a bit. "Yeah, you stepped in before they got going," I exaggerated. "I thought they were your boys." I ran my hand through my hair. Nothing really to be done.

"Let's just say I was trying." He straightened his own shirt and blazer. "Brian wasn't wrong. All my friends were part of the great Clancy Exodus. My dad wanted to pull me, too, but my girlfriend is the headmaster's daughter."

"Well, that's romantic."

"And I like Clancy. It was a big deal about nothing."

"Parahumans don't freak you out?" I was still coated in cat hair.

"Of course they freak me out. I'm not an idiot. Some of

those guys are scary as hell. But it's not all of them." He shrugged.

We were both convinced that we'd repaired what we could and left the bathroom. To be fair, I waited for Tor to use the toilet. That's why he went in there in the first place. For me, a lot of the cat hair had been rubbed off on Tweedle Dee and Tweedle Dumb, so win-win.

Tor directed me to my second period class and the rest of the morning went on without incident.

I mean, I was totally lost in Biology, and American history was pretty confusing. And this is why I hadn't applied myself. It was just too hard.

As promised, Tor found me outside the cafeteria. And holy crap the rich have a better cafeteria. The pudding looked like pudding. And the fries were the thick cut ones with some kind of seasoning sprinkled on them -- amazing!

We picked a table, an actual table with chairs and not a long foldable thing with attached benches. I was so engrossed by the content of the tray I didn't realize a person had approached.

"Ah, Ryan, I would like to introduce you to my girlfriend." Tor was all smiles now, looking at whoever was walking up behind me.

I turned.

She stood out, not just because she was two percent of the brown kids I'd seen that day, but because she was beautiful. And East Asian. I remembered the picture of the little girl in Dr. Paris's office. I could kind of see the resemblance.

But I'm burying the lead here. I knew her. I knew her well. I'd only seen her face once, but I would never forget it.

I was staring at Flare.

SEVEN

Tor stood up, but I was too stunned. Maybe that's what you're supposed to do on the rich side of the river. My etiquette class wasn't this semester.

The last time I'd seen her outside of her uniform she'd been drugged unconscious with a piece of technology called a cuff. It was the most-used device to subdue parahumans. Basically, a really potent drug to knock you out and a device to monitor the dosage to ensure the super didn't wake up or die.

I rescued her from the clutches of Clockwork. Well, technically it went down on my stats as an assist. I rescued Peregrine and Peregrine rescued Flare. Then Peregrine turned around and rescued me.

Just like last night.

I did not want to think about last night.

Tor went in for a kiss, but Flare pulled away. "We're in the school cafeteria!" she scolded him, but it was playful.

He didn't try harder for the kiss and sat down, making room for her tray by moving his. "Ryan, I would like you to meet Jasmin."

Jasmin looked at me and hit me with a smile. Wow.

"Hi, Ryan." That was a trip, hearing her voice, her actual voice. I'd never heard that. It was sweet and a little high. Not the robotic distortion that I was accustomed to. I had to give it to Raptor. If I hadn't seen her, I would have no idea that it was her. Just like she would have no idea that it was me.

"Nice to meet you, Jasmin." I kind of stammered over Jasmin. I almost blew everything and called her Flare. I had to live a double life with my parents, but I wasn't ready to do it here, too.

Flare had never seen my face or heard my real voice. Would she see through my disguise? Did I care? Should I just tell her?

"Are you okay?" Tor asked.

I'd let the thread of the conversation go by me. "Sorry, what? It's already been a long day."

"I asked if you need a tutor? Jasmin's the best in the biz." Tor easily put his arm on the back of her chair.

She did not pull away from that.

"Oh?" That wouldn't be weird or anything.

"Yeah, she helps out kids in the Kages and everything," Tor said.

She looked a little uncomfortable at that. Smelled like a cover story to me. She probably "tutored" while she was on patrol or had been working with her mentor, Orion.

"Well, I'm quitting that," she said.

Yeah, that was her cover story alright. She would have a lot more boyfriend time.

Tor picked up on the possibility as well. A big grin cracked his face. "Really? That means I might actually see you on a weekend or something?"

She gave him a mischievous look over her shoulder that

made my heart skip a beat, and I was just collateral damage. Tor took it full force and was jelly. "I might have a few more minutes here and there." She winked.

Tor went in for another kiss, but was met by the palm of her hand as she pushed him away. "So Ryan, how are you liking Hellington?" She turned to me.

I've had a crush on her since we met, even though I didn't know what she actually looked like. It wasn't like her uniform gave that much to the imagination. The waist-length blond wig was a nice touch, though. Until I saw her, I wouldn't have guessed East Asian.

If you added all the time we took breaks on patrol and just sat and looked at the skyline together, she was the longest female relationship I'd had in the past year. Now, I had to act like I didn't know her. If she had known it was me, she wouldn't have been happy and swooned into my arms. Our relationship had gone frosty since the Guard died. Now every time the team met, we were on opposite sides of every issue.

There was also the issue of her identity. With villains like the Confessor out there, I could be forced to reveal her name, her dad's name, and her boyfriend's, now that I knew them. She would not be happy to know who I am.

"Ryan?" Well, speaking of the Confessor, his psychic daughter had just walked up to our table.

"Sofia." I straightened.

"Can I..." She pointed at the empty seat right next to me.

"Of course." My face said yes. My guts said, "Run, run and don't look back! Why are you not running? Try running, you might like it."

She put down her tray. "I'll be right back."

Tor looked at me, jaw open.

"What?" Was my inner fear showing?

"You've been here three hours and you're on a first name basis with the new girl?" He pushed his chair back from the table and elaborately bowed. "Teach me your ways, o master."

"Stop it, she's coming back." Jasmin slapped him and he stopped.

Sofia returned with a glass of soda.

Let's just live in that for a second. Yes, you can just walk up and get a glass of fountain soda and return to your table. Wow.

I introduced her to Jasmin -- almost called her Flare again -- and Tor.

And we spent the lunch period just talking. Just talking about school stuff.

Sofia talked me up in my little part of rescuing her cat. Tor gave me a wink and a big thumbs up.

There was no debate about our responsibility in a possible city-or-world-changing event. No plans concocted to desperately save someone we cared about before they were killed. We didn't even talk politics.

We just talked. I made with the funny and got warm female laughter. That was a very good moment. Even Brian, giving me scowly eyes as he passed us, didn't ruin it.

"Tor, paper?" Some kid passed by the table and dropped the already read Darhaven Times on our table at Tor's nod.

Tor took the sports section, the piece that had already been read by the other student.

The front page was underneath it, with a picture of a police officer. A staged, official picture of a young smiling man in a crisp, dark blue and white uniform, light blue background, and an American flag in the corner.

"Are you okay?" Sofia had noticed something different about me. She didn't need to be psychic.

I wanted to say I was fine, but I couldn't say anything until I could speak.

It was the cop from last night.

Fallen Hero read the big bold black letters. I'd read the article, when I could think again. That would be a good idea.

My nest, a kind of secret base away from a secret base, was originally an offsite locker room and study carrel, but with the destruction of the Clubhouse -- sorry, Gamma Base -- it was also my total base.

Raptor had set it up for me when I first started my training. It was in an abandoned factory but had power and the Internet. I'd even been playing with the idea of just living here when Mom kicked me out. It had everything a growing boy needs: a cot, shower, toilet, washing machine, computer. But eventually someone would ask to see where I was living or talk to these "friends" I was staying with. Or I would need food.

It was the food thing that got me to take Dad up on his offer.

I finished patching the gambeson and checked my work. I don't know if it really was a gambeson, but it was what Raptor had called it. I guess a gambeson was supposed to provide some added protection to medieval knights. This thing absorbed the buckets of sweat when I was in uniform. I had five and washed them after each use. But sometimes they ripped. All my gear needed little maintenance stuff. I had two helmets and three uniforms. And each of them had nicks and scrapes I had to patch. One uniform had a big burn on the chest because Flare had shot me. How much longer could I patch and not need new material?

Raptor hadn't shared his supplier with us. With him gone I was eventually going to run out of gear. This time next year I would be running around in a biker jacket and ski helmet. Ridiculous.

I folded the gambeson and placed it on top of the five duplicates with sharp military corners. I learned that from Raptor, but with my power I only had to do it once and my fingers remembered how to do it.

I looked at them, piles of glorified underwear waiting for an inspection that would never come.

My eyes went to my backpack.

I had the burn marks to buff out and I needed to see if I could replace the chest piece. Flare had done a number on it.

My eyes went back to my backpack.

When was the last time I'd cleaned the toilet? It had been a busy week.

My eyes went back to my backpack.

I didn't choose to pick my backpack up off the cot, I stopped choosing not to. I didn't want to remove the paper, but I did.

His name was Damon Wilson. The cop I'd let die. Did it make it better or worse knowing his name? He was married with one child. Of course he was. Shit doesn't happen to assholes who no one loves.

I suddenly found my nicely folded full body underwear just too offensive for words. I knocked all of them off the shelf. Screw it. Screw all of this. I was done. I watched a man get killed. And not only did I not do enough to stop it, if I hadn't been there, he wouldn't be dead. Osprey would have done the world and the Wilson family a hell of a favor. Slicer would be dead. Couldn't happen to a nicer guy. Officer Wilson would be home with his son right now!

I pulled back my hand to knock something else over, but I didn't.

What was the point? What was the point of any of it?

I was out. I wasn't gonna risk my life or anyone else's life for some stupid quest that Raptor didn't even give me. The others were right, this stupid note wasn't anything other than a stupid note. I had to make things up to Mom, not flunk out of school again, and not disappoint Dad. Well to be fair, I didn't care much if I disappointed Dad. He was still in the dog house as far as my Christmas card list was concerned.

I picked up one of the gambesons and started to pull it on. There wouldn't be any more Damon Wilsons. There just wouldn't be. I should have just locked the door and walked away, but I felt like I owed an explanation to Jackal.

Funny, right? I didn't think I owed anything to my dad but a convicted killer and ex-gang boss, him I owed an explanation. Last time I'd disappeared on him, he'd gotten a few people to fake an armed robbery until I came to the "rescue."

If anything, I could spare the actors an evening of their time.

I was geared up and out the door in minutes. And running along the edge of the rooftops.

I would miss this. I don't think I felt any more free than when doing a run I'd memorized. I barely had to think about it as I ran, leapt, landed and rolled to where I'd hidden the statue.

"Jackal."

This time the statue glowed yellow and burst into life

right away. "Raven?" He seemed surprised to hear from me. "I'm surprised to hear from you."

See?

"I'm just here to say goodbye. After last night... let's just say I learned my lesson."

"Did you? What lesson did you learn?"

"That I can't do this. Whatever the Legacy is, whether it's coming or not, the world would be better off if I let someone else deal with it."

"And this is because of that police officer." Jackal didn't ask.

"His name was Damon Wilson."

The glow died down to just a glimmer around the statue of Anubis.

"I just didn't want you to think something happened to me or that I was out there somewhere and you needed to find me," I said. "Thanks for your help. I don't know why you did it, but you got me farther than I could have gotten alone." That was hard to say.

"I don't know what to say, kid. Part of me thinks you should walk. And if this Legacy is coming, well get away from Darhaven. Pack your bags and leave and don't look back." The statue flared a little more.

I couldn't leave like that, I had family in this town. I'd never even left this town. I'd never been south of the Flat Stones district. "Yeah, maybe I will."

"I mean, you don't owe this city anything," Jackal continued. "You already stopped Simon from killing half of the SSA, never mind what you did to stop Red Knight and the Confessor."

"Not sure I really did much to stop Red Knight." He was one step ahead of me until Osprey blew him up.

"You already did enough. More than your share. You

don't owe that Raptor guy anything." Jackal was getting a good head of steam. "I mean, if he wanted you to actually be effective he would have made you partners, not dependents. If this Legacy comes and people get killed, it wouldn't be on you. You did all you could."

Well, I guess.

"If this Legacy is bad enough to unite both Ceasar and Raptor, then it must be super deadly. I mean, people are going to get killed when this thing pops, and Raptor doesn't bother to give you enough tools to do anything about it? You should let this city burn. It will all be on Raptor. I mean, I spent all day tracking down this Zed guy, but I don't even want you to talk to him now. Serves this city right."

There was a weight I hadn't been really able to kick off, but I'd felt it lightening. Now it dropped back on me with an extra fifty pounds.

"I see what you did there. You're not even pretending anymore with that reverse psychology crap," I said.

"No, not really."

"The guy's name was Damon Wilson. He's dead now because of what I did." Images of the man jerking as orange disks cut into him danced in my head.

"No, kid, he's dead because Slicer is a psycho and a rookie cop thought he was a superhero. The only thing you did was the next right thing. That's what you signed on for. That's why you aren't done. That's why you're going to track Zed down and see if you can get an angle on Legacy before it's too late." The statue light almost went out. "I'm glad I'm not you. Seems exhausting."

"Yeah, it's exhausting." I picked up the statue and slipped it in the pouch at my belt. This close to me he could talk directly into my head -- so awesome! "Where's Zed?"

EIGHT

The second you walk into the Kages district in Darhaven you've walked into a rough part of town. I mean, different districts have their issues. Flat Stones has its Fish street, a great place to pick up anything illegal or a knife to your back. And Corbyn's 9th Ring is a place you go if you're sick of all your stuff and living. But all the Kages is a rough area. The part of the Kages I was now in is even rough for the Kages.

If I didn't have superpowers, and was using the sidewalk, I wouldn't be walking around here at night. There wasn't a lot of crime for me to fight because everyone knew not to actually go into this area after dark. Don't get me wrong, there was plenty of crime. But nothing for me to get involved with.

On the plus side, it was a great spot for a parkour run, plenty of places to jump and climb, so it had that.

Jackal brought me to the back alley behind some restaurant, a greasy spoon diner on the first floor, but part of a seven-story building. The alley was covered in graffiti, illuminated by a lonely bulb over the restaurant's back door stoop, and boxed in by a three-story apartment building that I stood on top of.

"How solid is your intel?" I asked Jackal.

"Not very," Jackal allowed. "I'm in prison, you know that, right? I have to ask people on the inside who talk to people on the outside. It's like a game of telephone. A violent game of telephone."

So there was that. The place didn't have action. "Is this some kind of underground bar like Handsome Jack's?"

"No, this is just one of his fallback hangouts."

"So how long do I wait? Do I need to break in?" Not sure I was really on board to do that.

"Zed smokes, so at the most you got two hours," Jackal said.

"Really? A very seasoned killer's smoke break is what we got? He kills people. You think he might just smoke inside?"

"No, this is his mom's place." Jackal was not concerned.

"So I wait up here until a nic fit." This did not seem so much like a plan as hanging out and boredom. "I should be writing a paper," I complained and instantly regretted it. I didn't need Jackal knowing anything about me. He must have known I'm young enough to still be in school, but I didn't need to confirm it.

He probably didn't care, but he didn't mention it. "So did you hear my new trial is set for early October?" he asked.

Yeah, I knew about that. He'd manipulated me and my team earlier this month. That was almost the first thing he'd done. He'd tricked us into releasing proof that the judge on his case had been blackmailed. "Got a good lawyer?"

"I do, thank you for asking."

“There’s no way you’re getting out of prison. There’s not a jury in Darhaven that would let you walk.”

“I think you’re right,” he agreed. “That’s why we’re moving the trial upstate.”

Whatever. “Well, good luck.” I said it but I didn’t mean it.

“Thank you.” He wasn’t trying to rub my face in it. “You know, a character reference would go a long way. Maybe send an open letter in the Darhaven Times.”

The back door opened and a mountain of a biker guy walked out, letting the door slam. He bumped out a cigarette and lit it with a lighter.

“We have a bite,” I told Jackal. And ignored the character reference thing.

“Is he almost seven feet tall, black hair that goes all the way down to his butt, and a grey beard that goes to his belly?”

“Too dark. I don’t know what his hair color is, but the rest fits.” The one pathetic bulb that lit his smoking area was just enough to glare my infrared.

“Time to go talk. Don’t try to intimidate this guy. Just ask nicely.”

“Is that going to work?” Why would that work?

“No, but then we’ll see what happens.” Jackal seemed pleased with his clever plan.

I dropped the three stories and came up from my roll with my hands exposed.

Zed, assuming this was Zed and not someone with the same barber and smoking habit, had a gun out and leveled at me before I hit the ground.

I didn’t even see his hand move. He was fast.

“You come for me?” He was keeping one eye on me, but was looking up, too.

"What are you talking about?" Coming for him? "I'm with the Guard."

"Yeah, I heard you guys have gone capital V now. Offing us poor middle management types."

"No. Not here to kill anyone." I kept my hands open and walked a little closer.

With his non-gun hand he took another puff on his cigarette. This guy was cold. He would pop me in a second. He might just shoot me if he couldn't think of anything better to do.

"You got until I finish my smoke," Zed finally said. "If you want to talk. If you want to fight, we can go now."

"I just came to talk." It was nice to work with professionals.

"I don't know where Caesar is." He must have gotten asked that a lot. "I haven't been part of his inner circle for years. But the Caesar I knew would need to be dead to let what happened happen."

"I'm not here to talk about Caesar. Not exactly, anyway."

He took another drag, but his eyebrow raised. "Then why would a Guard," he pointed to me with his cigarette, "want to talk to a has-been like me?"

"It's about when you worked for him. When you were part of the inner circle."

"Usually I get drinks to talk about the bad old days." Another long puff.

"I want to know about the Legacy." Why be coy?

He put his gun away and leaned against the wall. At the speed he pulled his weapon, that wasn't much of a good will gesture. "What do you know about those Euro-trash pieces of crap?"

"They're from Europe?" I ventured.

He laughed. "Well, everything I know Raptor should know. People don't believe me, but Raptor and Caesar worked hand in hand to get rid of them."

Whoa, this was dangerous. "Raptor doesn't know I'm here." Which was true.

He grunted a laugh. "What? You think tangling with the Legacy will prove you're ready for the big leagues?"

I didn't even know what that sentence meant. "Maybe."

"Well, I'll give you some ancient history, but you need to give me some current events." He took another puff from his cigarette.

I couldn't let this guy know that the Guard were dead. I didn't have any other current information. "What do you want to know?"

"Stardust."

I know a guy who could hook you up after third period. "What about it?"

"I work for Midas now, and he's pissed. Someone's peddling this new drug and not giving him a cut. It's my job to hunt down the source."

"It originated in the Kages." If Osprey could be believed. "Now it's on the Island."

"You sure it's on the Island?" Zed's shoulders drooped a little.

"I'm sure."

"That's just great. Midas is going to crap a toaster." He pulled a drag and looked at the burning orange of his cigarette. "Do you know who's distributing it?"

I shook my head. "We're looking into it." And by we, I mean Osprey, but whatever.

"Well, if you find out, maybe we can cut a deal," he offered.

"You tell me everything about the Legacy and I'll tell

you anything I learn about Stardust." It was an empty promise.

He seemed to know it was an empty promise, but either the information Stardust was on the Island was valuable to him or he just liked talking about being a big shot. "Like I said, Raptor would know more. They showed up about fifteen, no seventeen years ago. Somehow they flipped one of Caesar's inner circle. The guy was a Para 2 who could make bone spikes and impale people. Out of nowhere he flips out and tries to run Ceaser through."

"You stopped him?"

"No, Caesar ripped the guy's throat out before I realized what was going on." He shivered a little at that. "This black goop spilled out of the wound and his head."

Black goop. Clockwork's mask had been filled with black goop right before he'd killed himself.

"Never seen a parahuman ability like it, they could influence what people did with this black goo stuff. You could punch them in the gut or deliver any sudden pain and they'd get free of it for a second or two. But they always turned on you in the end." He shrugged like he didn't regret killing them.

"What did they want?" This was about a billion percent more than I'd had on the Legacy five minutes ago.

"Take over the city, I suppose." He shrugged again. "Really wanted Caesar dead. They tried again and again. Eventually Raptor found where they were operating out of, and we hit the place. Man, there were tough guys. Never seen anything like it."

"They had supers?"

"Yeah, but it was weird. They were all the same type of supers. Strong, moving fast, seeing in the dark. Didn't bleed nearly enough when you shot them. There were three of them and a couple of these big dogs." He shook his head. "And a bunch of humans with the Legacy's seven-sided emblem branded on their foreheads. They kept throwing themselves in the way of the bullets to save the supers." He flicked the butt of his smoke into a pool of darkness. "I've been in worse fights, but that one was bad, and just weird."

Okay, a couple different levels there. One, he'd just admitted to gunning people down as he was trying to kill someone else. Two, killing a bunch of people was just "weird." Three, big dogs, really?

"That was the last I saw of them. We had to burn the place down. They must have had dozens of bodies frozen down there. Weird, weird guys."

Do I tell this guy that they're back? Sure, why not? "They're back."

His eyebrow rose then lowered. "Let me guess, you think they're back but Raptor thinks you're making things up. Listen, we destroyed them. Every one of the seven-sided tattooed freaks were dusted. They aren't coming back. That is one monster not under your bed."

Well, at least he hadn't assumed that Raptor was dead, and I was on a fool's mission to do something that Caesar's top assassins had to do last time.

"What else do you--" Then everything got complicated.

A guy about half of Zed's size came out the back door, already with a cig hanging from his lips but not lit. "Zed, these kids are all saying the same thing. They don't know who was under the hood." Then he realized Zed wasn't alone.

So not great, but not the problem. The problem was right behind him. From the alley I could see into the restaurant. The door opened into a storage facility. Suspended from the roof, rotating slightly, were four boys, maybe older than me but probably not. They were shirtless and bleeding, covered in cuts and yellow marks that would be purple in a matter of hours.

One dangled and slowly spun. I recognized him. *Isaiah.*

I'd grown up with him. He lived in an apartment building down the road from my mom's place. I hadn't seen him around school lately, but we'd grown apart. I was spending all my time with the Guard, and he was getting more and more into drugs. Even if he hadn't been battered and bloodied, he still would have looked like crap. He'd always been a rail but now he looked emaciated.

Zed collided with me before I realized we were fighting. He'd done the math faster than I had. Of course we were going to fight. I was with the Guard, I wasn't going to let that stand. That's how Zed was still in the business after all this time.

"I would have let you just walk away, but you self-righteous types aren't going to let that go." He kicked me far enough away that he could have a gun on me, but I wasn't close enough to him to land a punch.

"Ah, is everything okay?" Jackal asked in my head.

I let the gunshot answer that question and rolled out of the direct path behind a dumpster.

"Is that Raptor?" the new guy asked. He pulled his weapon, too.

"No." Zed's tone said "moron." He was moving to get an angle on me with his gun, but still too far for me to touch him.

I kicked the dumpster where I thought the new guy was and was rewarded with a nice collision. I used the moving dumpster as a barrier between me and Zed. He pumped shots into the dumpster and I have a clear memory of a bullet hole opening up between my fingers.

I couldn't see Zed, and he couldn't see me, as I wheeled the dumpster between the two of us.

The new guy started to get to his feet. I hopped over and mule kicked him in the head then returned to the relative safety of the dumpster.

Zed didn't let a good distraction go to waste. He leapt over the dumpster. At the crest of his jump he started shooting at me.

I rolled away to a standing position and jumped backward from where he was going to land.

He stuck the landing, and would have killed me if he'd had any more bullets, but I collided with him as I heard the gun click on empty.

Wow, that's a wonderful sound. I landed a shot to his chin, but he rolled with it and turned the movement into a kick. I landed on my butt, and he pulled another gun.

My hand closed around a bottle and I tossed it at him.

He dodged the bottle, and that gave me enough time to close and start delivering some physical beat down. He was fast and tough. He was able to roll with a lot of my punches and even swerved out of the way of some, but I had him on the ropes. He wasn't keeping up, and I knocked him solid twice.

Then the door opened again.

Three more thugs were outlined in the light from their interrogation room. One was blue with scales, the other two had guns.

Assuming the blue guy's power was more than turning blue, I was in deep trouble. I was in deep, deep trouble. I had to get out of there, but if I did, Isaiah was dead. Same with the other kids.

I got another shot into Zed and bent him around with a

hold, using him as a meat shield between me and the three new gunmen.

"Zed, what's going on?" Mr. Blue asked.

"Guard," Zed grunted.

They all looked up for some reason. Okay, I can't blame them. I would look up, too, if I thought the Guard were here for me.

"He here to kill you, boss?" Mr. Blue asked.

"What's that all about? The Guard doesn't kill." I found that slander offensive.

"That isn't what I heard," Mr. Blue said.

And then Zed did this crazy double-jointed Judo crap, and I was in the air. I landed on my feet, but I did not have anything between me and bullets.

"Shoot him!" Zed yelled.

NINE

And then there was this crazy, crazy bright light. Flare can do something like that, which is why I have special protection in my helmet against blinding attacks.

My first thought was they were trying to blind me to make me an easy shot. But no, they were all blind and screaming in pain as they covered their eyes from the glare.

Not sure how that happened, but I moved. I jumped at the middle guy because he was close and blue. As a rule I go for the known supers first.

An elbow to Mr. Blue's collarbone dropped him like a sack of flour. I jumped on him, then to the door.

"What are you doing?" a woman's voice cried out.

She blended so well into the dark that I didn't see her right away. And she was flying.

"Who are you?" and "What are you doing?" I shot back.

"I'm saving your life! Let's get out of here." She waved toward the entrance to the alley.

"I can't! There are people in there." I pulled open the door and slipped through.

She followed and pulled the door shut behind us,

slamming the dead bolt. "You can't save anyone if you're dead!"

A boot hit the door with a thud.

I used my utility blade to hack at the ropes of the first person I came to. I wanted to run to Isaiah, but didn't dare. Whoever this woman was, I didn't want to tip my hand.

I got the first one down and moved to the second.

"What are you doing?" she yelled over the thudding from the door.

Like I had a clue. I was making this up as I went along.

"I would like an answer, too," Jackal said in my head.

"I'm getting these kids out of here." There were four. How was I going to get four kids out of here?

"I'll check up front," the super said.

"What can you do?" I got the second one down faster.

"I can't fly you or them out of here." She rolled her eyes. "Fine. I can do light tricks. The flash thing was as offensive as I get. I'm just a spy."

She started walking through the kitchen.

"Who are you?" Third one down.

"Pixel," she said after a hesitation.

"What are you doing here?" I got Isaiah down.

"Spying." She peeked out the door. "It's clear. We've got to go before that guy gets through the door."

A self-professed spy spying seemed logical. "Why these guys? Why were you spying on Zed?"

I didn't think Pixel was going to answer, but she came back and helped one of the kids stand. The kid could barely keep upright and put a lot of his weight on her. "Everyone wants to know where this Stardust is coming from. Everyone wants a piece. I knew Zed was looking into it. Thought I'd find out what he knew."

Didn't seem like Zed had known anything about Stardust.

"How many people are trying to break the door down?" Jackal asked.

He was making a hell of a racket, but it couldn't have been more than one. "Just one."

"They're coming around the corner. You need to duck out the back." Jackal was urgent.

"Are you sure?" I asked.

"Sure of what?" Pixel asked. "I know for a fact that Zed is working for Midas."

"Positive. Or they'd have that door open by now," Jackal said.

I looked at the door. "It looks pretty solid."

"They have a key, this is their place." Jackal had a knack for strategy.

It was possible that every one of them had forgotten their back door key. Or in all the excitement they hadn't thought of it. Or they were waiting around the corner to gun us down the second we left through the front door.

"We're going out the back," I told Pixel. Jackal could be wrong, or he could finally see a way just to kill me. Both were a possibility.

"But the men with the shooty things are out there." She had started towards the front door.

"They're trying to flush us out like grose."

"Do you mean grouse?" Pixel asked, but started moving her guy toward the back door.

"I might. Is that the bird thing?" I put my hand on the doorknob. "I thought it was grose."

"It's grouse," Pixel said.

"Huh." I twisted the doorknob and the guy kicking the

door fell in when the door was no longer there to resist his kicking.

He wasn't Zed or the Blue one so I punched him. He was off his footing and an easy hit.

The guy behind him raised his gun.

A bright flash bulb popped right in front of him. He jerked in pain and covered his eyes.

Easy money.

The back alley was empty except for the van.

"They'll realize we doubled back," Pixel said.

"Can you hotwire that van?" Might as well ask. If she was a "spy" maybe she had some spy skills.

She chuckled. "I haven't boosted a car since I learned how to fly." She leaned the guy she was helping against the wall. "How hard can it be?" A slight distortion field went around her and she flew to the van. The door was open.

I didn't wait to see what else she did. I threw Isaiah over one shoulder and hauled him over to the van. This was probably the vehicle used to get the four boys here in the first place. It was empty except for a jerry rigged bench seat.

I went back for the others.

The one conscious kid thought he would be better off on his own and made a run for it for three steps, then he collapsed. He didn't move again.

I got the runner and everyone else in the van and slammed the door.

"They're back here!" someone shouted.

"They figured it out!" I told Pixel from the back. "We need to go now!"

"I've almost got it." Her head was underneath the steering wheel and muffled. "I haven't done this for a while."

People were running, boots slapping asphalt as they

abandoned their ambush. If the van wasn't going to happen, I was going to have to fight. If I had a chance, which I did not, I had to get up close and personal.

"Almost," she said. The engine sprang to life. "Here we go!"

The van ripped backwards and I lost my footing. I dropped on the cluster of people I was trying to rescue. Then we were all jolted to the back of the van in a pile as she gassed it. I felt another jar as she turned out of the alley way too fast.

I risked a look out the rear door window. Zed was running around the corner, but slowing. He wasn't going to catch us and we were already too far for a pot shot.

"We're out!" I said.

"Good job!" I could almost hear a little golf clap from Jackal's mental link. "I never doubted you for a minute," he lied.

I carefully crawled over Isaiah and his friends and took the passenger seat. "Thanks."

She was looking in the rearview and all around, but she was driving the speed limit now. "You're welcome."

"How much did you hear?" I asked, but she didn't seem to understand what I meant. "My conversation with Zed."

"I was there for all of it. From when you flipped that tight little butt of yours into the alley to when you were going to get shot."

"Thanks for that again." I felt a little uncomfortable about the butt comment. I mean, she was in her late twenties, maybe thirty-something. I couldn't tell with her mask.

She gave a little shrug. "I should have just stayed invisible, but..." She didn't give me a reason why she hadn't stayed invisible.

"That's a neat trick, invisibility."

"It pays the bills," she agreed.

"Did you hear us talking about the Legacy?"

"I heard that crazy story Zed fed you. A bunch of supers with the same power and scary big dogs with cult followers. That's not how para powers work. No one has the exact same kind of power."

Not normally. Shale and Landslide had had the same powers and a connection, but they were twins. And Shale had murdered his brother, so there was that.

"I don't suppose you know anything about the Legacy?" Couldn't hurt. She'd already magically appeared and saved my life. Maybe she was my guardian angel.

She shook her head. "Sorry, hot stuff. Never heard of them. With Ceasar dead or gone, there are so many new groups popping up. I can't keep track of them all."

It was a long shot.

"Where are we going anyway?" she asked.

"Mercy General. These guys need medical help." They were still an awkward mess of bodies in the back, but they'd given the faintest of groans. "I don't know what those guys did to them."

"Zed didn't do that," Pixel said. "I mean, he beat the crap out of them, but they're unconscious because they're coming off Stardust. And they're coming off hard."

Now that I was thinking *drug withdrawal,* I recognized the pasty skin and cold sweats.

"The withdrawal is like heroin," she said. "It started to show up two weeks ago, and the high is the same every time. That's the only thing I know about Stardust." She shrugged.

"But you're trying to find out more about it. Why?" It was easy to think of her as walking on the same side of the line as I did -- she had saved my life after all. But she wasn't trying to stop these people. She was trying to sell information.

"I told you, everyone wants a piece of this new drug pie. If I can get the dirt first, there are a lot of people that would pay really good money." She had no shame.

"I'm going to check on our passengers." I crawled back and tried to move them apart. I could see what she meant. They weren't unconscious the way a beating would make them unconscious. They mumbled and started to shiver when they were moved. "How easy is it to overdose on this stuff?" I couldn't check for a pulse very well with my gloves. They were thin enough to let me climb, but too thick to pick up a pulse.

"Don't know. No fatalities have been reported yet. But this stuff is so new that doctors and cops might not even know what they're looking at and conclude death was caused by heroin." Pixel obviously had given this a lot of thought.

"Hurry." They seemed stable, just miserable, like in a bad dream they couldn't wake up from. But for all I knew, they had seconds to live, and I was watching my childhood friend slowly die.

"About that. We have a problem," Pixel said. "We've picked up some heat."

The ra-ta-ta-ta siren of the SSA blared. Man, that sound sends my belly right out my ears.

Pixel started swearing.

"We've got to run for it," I said. The SSA operatives would make sure that Isaiah and the others got to a hospital. But I would be going to jail if they caught me.

She slowed the van and pulled over.

"Not running enough!" Through the back window I could see two SSA SUV/tank assault vehicles. One pulled behind us and the second pulled in front of us at an angle. The van was effectively blocked off.

I moved for the back door.

"Don't. I've got this," Pixel said.

Screw that.

"Listen to her, kid. It's your only play," Jackal said.

So I didn't jump out of the van and lead whatever parahuman neutralizing forces had found us on a breakneck chase through our fair city.

I wanted to, boy did I want to, but what kept me in the van more than Pixel and Jackal was the knowledge of just how screwed I was if I tried that. I'd gone up against the SSA twice last week and barely got away once. The second time, I got caught. Osprey had busted me out on Red Knight's orders. I doubted the Section 5 story would work this time.

"Well, do something!" If she "had this" she'd better do something quick. Like a lot quicker than she was doing something now.

She gave me a wink, and before her eye opened, she shimmered and looked different. No longer in costume, she was blonde and a lot more endowed than she had been just a second ago.

"Out of the vehicle!" someone shouted.

I couldn't see out that door, so I just crouched like a runner at the starting block of a sprint.

Pixel wound down the window and bent out, exposing her new... endowments to the SSA agents. "What the hell? My friend is going into labor. I need to get to the hospital now!" Her voice had more than a little southern accent. "Now!"

The same flickering occurred around the passenger seat and a very pregnant woman writhing in pain appeared.

I only saw it for a second, then another shimmer put me in a wooden box. I could see the interior and I touched the box. My hand passed through it like air. I pulled my arm back.

I heard someone approach the door. "This your van, ma'am?"

"No, it's my jackass boyfriend Zebulon's. He wanted us to get a cab. Like hell!" Southern belle Pixel said. "Can we go?"

The agent said something into the radio. "The van is clear, just some crates. The lady driving says she's borrowing the van. No super activity. Seems like a false report."

Zed might have let us go, but instead of losing gracefully, he'd called the SSA on us. What a jerk.

"Okay, miss."

"Can you give me an escort?" I almost could hear her eyelashes flutter.

"I'm afraid not, miss. Drive the speed limit." The SSA didn't ask for her license and registration because they didn't care. If you couldn't fart fire balls they did not care in the least.

In seconds the SSA pulled out and Pixel got the van going again.

TEN

My heart was still pounding when the boxes disappeared. The southern slut was replaced with Pixel and her pregnant friend wasn't calling shotgun anymore. "You did it."

"I told you I had this," Pixel said.

I went from a crouch to an exhausted lump. I couldn't believe I'd gotten that close to getting caught again. How many times did I want to press my luck? Maybe if the SSA weren't thick in this town right now it wouldn't be as stupid to suit up.

"To summarize," I whispered to Jackal, "I burnt almost all the karma I had getting out of that and I came no closer to figuring anything out."

"I can't hear you," Pixel said.

"So we find other leads. It'll be fun," Jackal said.

"Hey, Pixel. Do you want to blow off whatever you're doing and hunt down a possible existential citywide threat?" I asked.

"How much does it pay?"

"I got six bucks on me, and there's six more in like a week." I thought about it. "Maybe two."

"Um, no."

"Well, think about it, you don't have to answer now." I banged my head against the van. "I've got no backup and I've got no direction," I whispered. "This is stupid. If it wasn't for Pixel just happening by, I would have been shot or arrested."

"Still can't hear you, honey," Pixel said.

"Screw this. Screw it all."

Jackal didn't say anything for a second. "Yeah, screw it, kid. You did more with less, time to hang it up. All the problems of this city can't be yours."

"Yeah, all these problems can't be mine."

The hospital transfer was easy since I was with someone who could make me look like anyone. I was her pregnant friend, just not as pregnant. We dropped off the van and disappeared. Literally. We turned invisible so the cop on duty lost us as we rounded the corner.

Pixel gave me a peck on the cheek then she vanished.

I went back to my nest the long way and through all kinds of tunnels and decoy routes. Pixel was my best lucky charm ever, but if she could turn invisible and sell information to the highest bidder, I wasn't going to risk her following me home.

Jackal didn't say anything as I stashed him. I didn't say goodbye. I didn't say anything else, either.

It took me forever to take the tunnel back to the Island. I had to change trains twice once I got onto the Island, but there was a station right by my dad's apartment. The doorman let me in -- he didn't even look disapproving -- and I rode our elevator up to our apartment.

My dad was waiting for me in one of the overstuffed chairs again. He was looking at some papers, a can of soda on a table beside him and his daughter, my half-sister, asleep on his lap.

"Ryan." Dad smiled.

"I'm sorry I'm so late."

"Helen," Dad whispered. "Ryan's here."

It took a little work, but Helen raised her head, looked at me through blurry eyes, and smiled. Her face explodes in dimples when she smiles. "Ryan." It sounded more like Rye-in, but close enough.

"Yeah, Helen?" I feel like I should have a nickname for her. Something that indicates we have more of a relationship than... well, none.

"Look what I have." She held up a small brown teddy bear in a skirt and hat. I'm pretty sure the skirt and hat were not part of the original packaging. She crawled out of my dad's lap and ran over to show me.

"She wanted to show you her new bear." Dad smiled indulgently.

"Wow, that's pretty great." I got down on one knee and admired the bear.

"His name is Pogs." She held him up like a ventriloquist dummy.

"Hello, Pods." I gave the bear an ear rub.

"Pogs," she corrected.

"You're a nice looking bear, Pogs. I like your hat." I emphasized the name.

"Okay, you've shown Ryan your bear. Give him a hug and off to bed," Dad said.

She took her time about it, but she did pad off to her bedroom.

"Do you have a second to talk?" Dad asked.

"It's late." I did not want another talk.

"It will just take a second." He motioned to the chair right across from his, almost as if he'd staged it.

What do you do, run past him, slam the door, and blare rock music?

"Yeah, okay." I dropped my bookbag and took a seat.

He sat across from me. I don't think he knew how to start.

"Listen, if this is the birds and bees thing, we have health class now," I offered.

He smiled, but no laugh. "Look, I know I don't have the right to talk to you as your father. So, I'm not. There's no threat here, no punishment."

I wanted to snap at him. Damn right he had no right to talk to me as a father. But I didn't. I almost did, though.

"When I lost..." He started again. "When Mindy died."

I stood up like I'd been goosed. "Oh God, I am not up for this conversation." Not tonight.

He held out his hand to stop me. "I lost myself. I failed your sister. I couldn't keep her safe." His eyes welled up with tears.

And mine did, too.

"I couldn't handle it." He blinked back the tears and looked away. "No, that isn't true. I *didn't* handle it."

"Dad, stop." I didn't need to hear some kind of apology. I needed to sleep, that was it. I just needed to sleep.

"This isn't an apology. I got into alcohol, then drugs, and it took the pain away. Then it took everything else."

I motioned to the huge living room/auditorium we were in. "Seems you did okay."

He wiped his face. "What I'm saying is that drugs will kill you, Ryan. It will kill you long before your heart stops beating."

What the what? With a side of what?

"The going out and staying out late? Not telling anyone who your friends are, pulling away from your family? This is all just the start. You don't have to live like this."

I was still standing, and I blinked. "What, you think I'm using drugs?"

He didn't say anything, but his face said, "Well, what else could it be?"

I picked up my bookbag. "No, Dad, it's nothing like that."

"Then what is it? What's twisting you up so much inside?" he asked. "I see it. You try to put on this wise-cracking face, but I can see it."

How? How could he see anything? He didn't know me. A lot had changed since I was nine.

"Forget about it!" Did I have a way to blare rock music? "If you don't want me here, I can find a different place to live."

Dad didn't react to my threat, or stand. "Ryan, what is it? What's going on?"

"They're dead! That's what's going on!" If he hadn't brought up Mindy, and abandoning me, and if it wasn't so late, I would have just soldiered on. "They're all dead. The guy who didn't need to die." I didn't say *cop*. "The one person who gave a damn about me died." Tears were streaming down my face. "And I can't do it, what he wanted me to do. What he wanted me to do, I can't do it."

Dad was standing now and his arms were around me in a way that they hadn't been in nine years. He pulled me close and hugged me so that my bones cracked.

"I have to do everything now, and I can't. He's dead and I can't do it. I'm not strong enough, I'm not fast enough, I'm not smart enough." I don't know if he could understand me through my sobs. "It would have been me, not just Isaiah. It would have been me, too."

"Isaiah?" Dad knew the name. "Your friend?"

"He overdosed. I don't know how bad. He's in the hospital, got beat up. That could have been me. Should've been me." But Raptor had saved me. "I couldn't protect him."

"Isaiah?" Dad was floundering for coordinates.

"No. I tried to do the right thing, what he taught me, but it just got someone else hurt." I couldn't stop talking, I couldn't stop crying, but at least I had the presence of mind to say hurt and not killed. The cop twisting under Slicer's attack, Isaiah gaunt and beaten, Simon blowing his own head off. "It's too much, it's just too much. I can't carry it all. I can't."

"You don't have to. Not tonight." He hugged me harder. I think he was crying, too.

"It's just too much. I couldn't protect him." I don't know what I was saying. "I couldn't protect Mindy."

"You were nine," Dad said.

"But I covered for her. She snuck out of the house and I helped her." I was as guilty as Dad.

"Mindy was going to do what she wanted to do." Was Dad speaking to me? "We can't control others. We just get to do the next right thing. That's all we've got, even when we lose everything."

"The next right thing," I repeated and hugged him harder. My head kind of spun. "Somebody just told me that."

"It's not all on you. On us."

It didn't stop there. I balled. I cried for Raptor, for the other members of the Guard. For police officer Damon Wilson, for my sister, and for what I couldn't do. I didn't even know how to start.

ELEVEN

School was still bizarre and surreal, but it also grounded me a little after the previous night. The bustle and structure of something to do, something I didn't have to think about. I just had to do it.

There was a moment in there when Brian and his gang tried to intimidate me, but nothing that was notable happened. Autopilot carried me halfway through lunch. Tor, Jasmin, and Sofia joined me at the same table we'd had yesterday.

"Ryan, are you okay?" Sofia finally asked.

I looked at her, then Jasmin. "I'm just trying to make a choice." God, I would love to talk about this with Jasmin, with Flare. But I couldn't drop the responsibility of my identity on her. "I feel like I'm caught between two lives."

Jasmin looked uncomfortable and stared at her tray of food.

"What do you mean?" Sofia looked straight at me.

"I have this life." I took in the new school, friends, living in a very, very nice apartment. "But I still have the life that I came from. I feel like I have a responsibility to that, too."

Sofia moved her hand to touch mine.

I acted like I hadn't noticed and used that hand to pick up a French fry. I don't know if psychics have an easier or harder time reading your mind when you're an emotional basket case, but I wasn't going to test it.

"I know what you mean," Sofia said. "I left a whole life when Dad moved here for business." She sounded sad at losing some of it.

"You have to pick one." Jasmin spoke into her tray. "You have to pick a life. Trying to live two just damages everything and you can't do both. One will always put the other one in danger. Before you know it, you're living a lie and don't even know what you want." She realized we were all looking at her in a little shocked silence. She pasted on a smile. "That's why I just have one life."

Tor looked like he believed that cover as much as I did, but he let it drop.

"It's just, I found out that a friend of mine -- we used to be super close -- is in the hospital. He got involved with drugs and overdosed or got beat up or something."

"You should visit him," Sofia said faster than I think she was even ready for. It sounded like she was channeling some of her voodoo. "I mean, it would be good for you." She used her normal voice. "And good for your friend." Now it was her turn to put her face into her food tray.

"It's in the Kages." I was making an excuse. "It's been years since we hung out. I doubt he'd want me dropping in on him."

"Jasmin and I are heading into the Kages tonight. I'll drive. You can come along," Tor offered.

"You should go," Sofia said again, with a little more urgency.

"Yeah, I will, but I can ride the bus." I waved at Tor.

"You don't have to go out of your way for me. Thanks for the offer, though."

I felt a hand close around my upper arm. There was a static charge and it was tight. I almost broke the grip and rolled away from the table.

Sofia's eyes were a little haunted and wide. "You need to go with them. Things will be worse if you go on your own."

The static faded and her eyes went back to normal. At least for a second. Then she looked at me with some confusion.

Tor and Jasmin were looking at her with their collective eyebrows climbing into their hairlines.

"Sorry." She turned pink and realized her hand was on my arm. "Sorry." She awkwardly pulled her hand from my arm and put it in her lap. "Sorry."

"Don't be," I said.

"It's just, I get these feelings sometimes," she mumbled. "Anyway, I have to get to third period early." She stood up, not making eye contact. Whatever juice she'd used had disoriented her a little, and she did not stand properly. But she took her tray.

We all looked at her as she dumped her tray.

"Okay, that was weird," Tor said. "You'd better go talk to her."

Jasmin gave Tor the same confused look that I did.

He shrugged. "I'm just saying, whatever happened, she's embarrassed about it. You let her stew on that..."

"Why me?" Jasmin could girl talk or something, couldn't she? Of course, from what I knew about Flare, that might not be such a good idea, either.

"We're not the reason she sits with us," Tor said.

"What?" Tor wasn't making a lot of sense.

"Go talk to her, dude. You can be the hero just once, can't you?"

Funny thing, I was trying to give that up.

"I've got your tray. Go!" Tor waved his hand.

Jasmin just rolled her eyes. Not sure if it was at me for being stupid, at her boyfriend's matchmaking, or at her disgust with the situation in general.

I stood up. "Be the hero?"

Tor gave me the nod of a wise man.

I moved around a group of freshmen girls that were already lining up to dump their trays, then out past the lunch monitor. I don't think we were supposed to leave the room before lunch was over, but it just wasn't that hard to step out when she looked the other way.

I saw Sofia rounding the corner in the hall, head down, arms tight around her body, and her ears pink. I caught up because she wasn't running.

"Sofia."

She turned with a jump. "Ryan?"

Thanks, Tor. Yes, I should talk to her. But what should I say? "Are you okay?"

"What do you mean?" She looked down and her ears went more pink.

"It just seemed..." Like you had a parahuman incident. "That you had more you wanted to say."

She shook her head. "No, I'm sorry."

"Sorry for what?"

"I just, I just had a weird moment back there."

"And you felt embarrassed." I decided to go with the direct approach. "But there was no reason to be." Except your voice went a little *channeling powers from beyond.*

"Thanks." I got a little smile out of her. "It's just, I get these feelings sometimes."

She'd told me about them before, but she'd been talking to Raven. Me Raven, not the cat Raven.

"And you believe these feelings?" I asked as neutrally as I could.

She nodded. "They might be crazy, but I had one about my dad. And I'm sure he would have ended up dead if I hadn't got some help for him."

"Wow." And about that. "How is your dad?" How is your dad's crime lording going? I mean sure, I was the help she was talking about, and I did save his life. But he was in deep to some mystery guys. Osprey had blown up the thing he had to turn over or die. So how happy could the mystery guys be?

"Great," she said, but didn't sound great.

"Great? You want to say that once more with feeling?"

"No. He came home safe and made whatever big deal he was here to make. So now we're on our way to being rich." She fluttered her hand.

"She says rich, but without the happy."

"What you were saying about a double life? That's my dad. I don't know what kind of work he's been doing. I thought I did, but now I think he's been lying to me."

Because he has been. "Are you sure?" Because I'm sure. I am totally sure. He's a D list criminal trying for the B list.

"No, it's just a feeling." She shrugged. "He's busy doing something. Hardly ever home. When he is home, he's vague about what he's doing. Raven doesn't like him," she added.

"Raven?" My heart skipped. "Oh, your cat." That's probably because he kidnapped and tortured Raptor's widow. I can't believe Feral would be down with that. "Cats are funny like that." I shrugged.

"So what are you going to do about your double life?"

Sure, now she felt okay to look right into my eyes. I was unprepared for the full brunt of those blue eyes. "Well?"

It had been a few seconds. "I guess Jasmin was right. I have to let the other life go." That felt right. "There's no way to sustain trying to be two different people. And I owe it to my mom and dad to grow up." When did dad get on the list of who I owed?

She nodded. "That makes sense."

I didn't know what else to say so there was a little awkward silence. "Do you want to come to the Kages? We can see my friend and I can show you around where I grew up. If you haven't eaten at Pete's, you've never had a burger."

She smiled, but shook her head. "I think you'll be busy. How long have you known Jasmin?"

Weird question, coming from a psychic. "Just this week."

"Really?" She seemed confused. "It seems like you have history."

I shook my head with a shrug. "Nope."

"Okay." She was unconvinced.

"But maybe we can hit up Pete's this weekend." Holy, holy, holy crap! Did I just ask her out? How did that happen?

She smiled. "Maybe."

The bell rang, I looked at the bell and looked back. She took a step closer to me and pecked me on the cheek. "You're sweet. Thanks, Ryan."

There were words, but I didn't have any. Complete blank slate.

She smiled, twirled, and walked down the hall. Now with a little skip to her step instead of hanging her head.

Yep, that's right. I'm the hero.

And she kissed me!

There was another moment when Brian and his group tried to intimate me, but I think it's best for all our dignities to just leave it at that. I didn't push them far enough for them to try to touch me and they didn't know what they were doing. I was willing to call it a draw.

After that non-event I caught up with Tor at his locker.

"Ryan." He smiled. "Word on the street is your little talk with Sofia went well."

And I was red as a beet. "Ah."

Tor pulled out his backpack and shut the door. "I just want to say." He backed up and did a bow at the waist. "I bow to the great and wise master."

I hit him with a zinger that both saved face and restored order. He might remember it differently, that I just said "Ah..." again, but who are you going to believe?

"You still on for a trip across the river?" He stopped bowing and nodded to the parking lot.

"Yeah. Jasmin?"

"She's getting her brother. They do this meditation training thing a couple times a week. I drop them off and then pick them up in a couple of hours and we all grab dinner."

"Jasmin has a brother?" I hadn't seen him in the picture in the headmaster's office. Or hear her ever mention him.

"Yeah, adopted. Good kid, sullen lately."

"So, about dinner. I've been craving Pete's all afternoon," I said as I followed him out to the parking lot.

"Pete's?"

"What? That blank face seems to indicate you don't know what I'm talking about."

"Never heard of it."

"I thought this side of the river was supposed to have culture. Pete's is the perfect burger of perfect burgers. And the Papa Pete! Imagine two huge patties on a perfectly crisp kaiser roll lathered with a secret sauce." I needed a moment.

"What's the secret sauce?" Tor asked.

"No one knows, it's a secret. His grandmother swore Pete to secrecy. He makes the batch for the day in the morning before he lets anyone else into the building. It's amazing."

Tor shrugged. "I guess."

"They have malts bigger than your head." He was not understanding what I was offering.

"Okay, I'll run it by the boss."

In a few more steps we found Jasmin already waiting by Tor's ride, a bright blue Ford Explorer. Because you never know when you'll need all wheel drive on the Island. It was brand new. I have milk older than this vehicle.

"Ryan, this is my brother." She pointed at a blond kid that I hadn't noticed amongst all the other blond kids.

"Hey, David," Tor said.

TWELVE

David. Yes, it was David. *That* David. The David that was also Ballista, most junior but the highest Para Level of the Guard. That David. In a moment of stress a few days ago, Flare had said her "brother" was kidnapped. I'd thought maybe she'd been talking metaphorically, but she'd been talking legally.

Just like Flare, I'd seen David out of his costume a couple of weeks ago. He'd almost surged and blown us all up. He still seemed a little pale, but fully recovered. "Hi, Tor." He looked at me.

"I'm Ryan," I said before Jasmin could introduce me.

"Hey." David smiled a hello, but it was an act. He wasn't happy about something. "Oh, the new kid. Welcome to Hellington." Didn't have much enthusiasm. "There are worse schools."

"I think that was the slogan on the pamphlet," I agreed.

He smiled at that, so Ballista was in there somewhere, but boy, did he seem down.

"Listen, if you guys are going to the hospital, maybe we can go another day," David said.

"No, we need to go tonight," Jasmin said firmly.

David looked like he was going to fight, but shrugged. "I was just thinking of you. I know how much you hate hospitals." He popped the rear door and climbed in.

By laws and customs far stronger and older than I, Jasmin automatically got shotgun, as the girlfriend. I got in on the passenger side.

We passed the time in silence for a while. There seemed to be something between David and Jasmin that was just awkward.

"So, how long have you been family?" Is that a weird question? Felt weird saying it out loud.

"Dr. Paris adopted me three years ago," David said. "After I..." He just left whatever he was going to say drop.

"It's been great having a brother," Jasmin said with forced cheerfulness.

"Just so long as I do what I'm told," David mumbled.

Jasmin didn't say anything.

Well, that conversation was dead on arrival. I guess I should have known better. Not all adoptions start and end with a happy story.

"So, Ryan," David said. "Do you have an older sister that controls everything you do?"

"David," Jasmin growled.

"I wish." I made a silent pact not to expose my tragedy to everyone. Not now at least. "But it didn't work out that way." For fear of more awkward silence, I added, "I have a half-sister, and a half-brother."

Didn't save it. More awkward silence. I looked at Tor. He was flailing around as much as I was. "So David, Ryan grew up in the Kages."

David looked at me with new respect. "But now you're in the Hell school?"

"My dad caught a break." Now I wanted that conversation to die.

"Living in the Kages, did you ever see the Guard?" Tor had no idea the landmine he'd just tap danced onto.

The temperature in the SUV dropped from frosty to frozen. We all looked out the windows, lost in our own thoughts.

"Guys?" Tor seemed to understand something had happened, but had no way of knowing the Guard were dead and they were our friends and mentors.

"Um, yeah. Once I saw Raptor. He saved me when I was stupid and got caught by some thugs."

That got David's interest. "Well, it certainly was a good thing that someone with powers used them to help people."

It wasn't like I was confused. I figured David's issue with Jasmin had something to do with quitting the Guard.

"Yeah, but it's complicated isn't it," I said. "I mean, what kind of life can that be?"

"What would your life have been like if he didn't?" David said.

"Short." I had to give him that.

"Well, it isn't a life for everyone," Jasmin said. "It's a very dangerous life."

"Life is dangerous," David snapped. "My mom and dad didn't have superpowers, but that didn't protect them. And your mom would still be here if she'd had powers."

"David!" Jasmin whipped her head around.

"Whoa, dude. Not cool," Tor whispered. Then in an ill-fated attempt at saving the situation... "So do you think we'll see Raptor flying around if we look?"

"No," both brother and sister said at the same time.

A little more time passed. "I'll drop you two off first," Tor said.

"Yeah, we would hate to have to go to the hospital." David emphasised the word, then added in a stage whisper to me, "Jazz hates hospitals."

"Hospitals are fine," Jasmin said.

David continued in the same stage whisper. "You see, everyone in the Kages was too afraid to help her mother. So when no one helps, horrible things happen."

"DAVID!" She was pissed. Ordinarily when Flare gets pissed green fire erupts around her. Not this time. I was impressed she was able to control it that well. "Shut up!"

David realized he'd gone too far, and did shut up, but he kept his chin out and looked at her defiantly.

It was at that moment I realized that I was sitting in the same car with enough Pissed Off Parahuman to make a crater of this SUV and not even break a sweat.

"Yeah, I just want to throw this out there. For dinner, let's do Pete's," I said.

Two of the most powerful supers I know both turned their gazes of anger on me. I knew they weren't pissed at me, but I also knew they were both loaded guns.

"Do you like malts? Their malts are amazing," I bravely continued.

David looked away from me and out the window.

"Sounds greasy," Jasmin said.

"I could go for a malt," David said.

Both Tor and I strategically withdrew with our tails between our legs for the rest of the drive.

I recognized the location where they were being dropped off. I figured Jasmin's and David's nests were in the area, but not that near. I also assumed that they were going to practice Ballista's powers. Flare was obviously not letting him be a hero, but if he didn't get control, he could still die, go crazy, become physically impaired, or just blow up.

I traded up to shotgun and gave the two a wave.

"Okay, that was tense," I said as Tor pulled into the street.

"David wasn't always like that, but he's gotten really defiant lately. Their uncle died in a car accident a couple of weeks ago, and they haven't been the same since. David took the loss really hard."

"Uncle?" A couple of weeks ago? The timing lined up with when all the Guard were slaughtered.

"Yeah. I don't like speaking ill of the dead, but he was a real asshole. Could not leave anything alone and just kept giving you crap for every little thing."

"An asshole." That was the one description a mask couldn't hide. "Was he the headmaster's brother?"

Tor nodded. "Had to be a closed casket. The wreck trashed him. Hit and run."

So Orion was actually Jasmin's and David's uncle. Well, wow. That explained why Jasmin had taken his death so hard, and why a parahuman level 1.1 archer was the mentor to two of the most powerful parahumans on the team.

"I mean, first her mom dies in a soup kitchen. Can you believe it? She's volunteering at a soup kitchen and gets knifed. She lived long enough to say goodbye to Jasmin and her dad, but that's why Jasmin hates hospitals. And now her uncle. I can't imagine what that's doing to her head."

"Yeah." I had nothing else to say. I had no idea that Flare's mom was murdered.

"She always said that her mother was what inspired her to tutor kids around here." He waved a hand, taking in the Kages. "So it's weird that she's giving it up."

Well if you replaced "tutor" with strapping on a figure-flattering jumpsuit and blasting bad guys, then I knew why.

It got her uncle killed, and it almost got her adopted brother killed.

"And David, man, he has changed so much in the last couple of weeks. He used to be funny."

And my stomach did a flop.

"I mean, he would just keep talking and talking. He wouldn't shut up. Especially about the Guard. How great Raptor was, and Raven."

"Raven?"

"Yeah, I didn't even know the handle of the guy before David started going on about him."

"Huh."

"To be honest, I was a little jealous," Tor said. "I think Jasmin kind of has a thing for Raven, too."

Well, how do you like them apples?

"But recently David is mad at Jasmin all the time and angry at everything. Like a completely different kid."

And that's where the crap meets the fan. I mean, there were all kinds of reasons why Ballista was not his jolly self. One, he's a teenager. Two, he just lost a member of his adopted family. Three, a few weeks ago he was captured and almost killed. That would dampen anyone's spirits.

But what if it's not that? What if it was the surge? Jackal and I had helped him through a bad one, but maybe we hadn't been as successful as we'd thought. Surges could fry people's brains, turn them into psychos. That's what happened with Silhouette. Silhouette had been one of the good guys, a member of the Guard, an apprentice just like me, but he'd surged and went nuts. Ended up killing Osprey's family. If Ballista fried and started killing people, he could do a hell of a lot of damage before someone brought him down.

"You okay? You look like you've seen a ghost," Tor said.

That's an expression people actually use? I guess the rich are different. "I just feel for the kid. Keep an eye on him."

Tor accepted the responsibility with a nod. He was planning on it.

We rode in silence for a while, then Tor turned on the radio. We talked about music and sports, like men do.

THIRTEEN

I hate hospitals. Not on a deep origin of pain level, but on a normal one. No one really likes hospitals.

The place was a maze of white tile and flickering fluorescent lights. I got so turned around I walked by the same break room three times. Tor wasn't any better. He'd insisted on coming with me. But I had to hand it to him. He sweet-talked the nurse on duty into giving us Isaiah's room number with skill that verged on miraculous. Maybe he was a parahuman, too.

We got in the elevator and the door shut.

It was probably because I was thinking how much I hated hospitals, and how Jasmin hated hospitals, but I asked, "Did they ever find out who killed Jasmin's mother?"

Tor shook his head. "Nope. You know Darhaven. I doubt if the cops even looked."

Yeah, that would be Darhaven. "I didn't know."

"Jasmin doesn't want the school to know. It's not a secret, but she doesn't want it dragged into the spotlight." Was he feeling guilty about telling me? "She feels under a microscope enough as the headmaster's daughter."

"I can keep a secret."

When we found the room, it was clear a cop was "guarding" the door. One of Darhaven's finest was sitting on an office chair he'd gotten from somewhere and reading a magazine while eating an apple.

"What do you want?" He didn't look at us as he slurped the juice from the apple.

"I'm here to see Isaiah." I wasn't ready for a police escort.

He looked up from his magazine. "Who?"

The door was open. I peeked in. Rows of beds separated from each other by a drawn curtain. Soft grunting and panting filtered into the hallway. "I was told he was in there."

The cop followed my eye. "If your friend's a dusty, he won't be up to talking. Detoxing off that is a bear." He gave a little shiver. A little empathy for his charges or his own memory? He didn't look that empathetic.

"Could we see?" I asked.

He warred between his orders and not caring enough to stand up. "Whatever." He looked back at his magazine and rotated his apple.

Tor gave me a look of disbelief, but I gave him a shrug. Darhaven cops got worn down by the crap and corruption. Nothing new to me. At least he didn't seem to be the sadistic type.

There were more rows of beds than I'd seen from the hall. They lined both walls with a wide aisle through the center. Every bed was filled with the same situation. The patients were each hooked up to an EKG, so rhythmic beeps played a strange counter beat to the discordant moans. Straps kept the patients in their beds and every "dusty" looked emaciated. Was that an outcome of the

Stardust or the normal demographics of the new drug's early adopters?

I looked at the faces of each addict as I walked down the row, searching for Isaiah. Tor came right behind me. I had to be in the right place. One of the guys I'd rescued yesterday was strapped to a gurney.

One man, maybe in his thirties, but looking closer to eighty, suddenly flared as I passed. "Let me go!" He pulled at his restraint, the EKG started to beep wildly, then he collapsed onto the gurney and stopped moving. His breathing evened out again.

"Ryan?" I recognized Isaiah's voice through slurred speech.

I turned around and saw Isaiah on his gurney, strapped down like the rest, but his cot was slightly elevated. His face was purple and bruised, his cut sewn shut with tight stitches. It looked like his wounds had been cared for.

"Hey man, I heard you were here. I thought I'd come for a visit." What else do you say? Seriously, what else do you say? I want to know. That sounded lame.

He blinked at Tor as we approached. It was clear he didn't recognize Tor and refocused on me. "Ryan, do me a solid. Get me out of these." He looked at his restraints. "I have got to get out of here. There is so, so much money to be made, I'm telling you. Another month and I'll be set."

Okay, that was awkward. I did not loosen his restraints.

"Come on!" He realized I wouldn't help. "Damn it, Ryan. I've got to get back out there. If I'm not selling, he'll move on to someone else and all that money will disappear. This is my break, I finally got some luck."

"You were selling Stardust?" I couldn't believe it. I used to play G.I. Joe with this guy.

"Sell it? I was living it! Dude, it's the answer. It's the

answer." Even through his shakes of withdrawal, a dreamy look went over his face. "You have no idea. It's like being home and loved." Then he refocused. "You've got to get me out of here. I have to find the Man."

"Who is the Man?" I asked, pure reflex. What did I care who this "man" was? I wasn't going to give a tip to narcotics or start a complicated sting operation.

"That's what those troglodytes wanted to know." I'm guessing he was referring to Zed. "They wanted to keep the truth bottled up, but the truth will find a way."

Tor grabbed my shoulder and gestured for us to get out of there. Isaiah was starting to get the other patients excited.

"Let me go, too!" someone begged. "I can pay, I have money."

"But they can't find him because he's a ghost." Isaiah continued to answer my question. "No one knows who he is." He pulled harder on his bindings. "He wears a hood."

What kind of morally bankrupt individual conceals his identity in this town? "Okay, fine, calm down."

"You only need to tell him the truth and he'll give you the answers." Isaiah wasn't even talking to me anymore.

I don't know what I'd expected, but this wasn't it. "Isaiah, I just stopped by to see if you were okay." And you are not any shade of okay. I moved to follow Tor. This wasn't going how I'd hoped.

"Just one touch, and he makes you tell the truth!" Isaiah let go with a shout, then collapsed.

My head whipped back to Isaiah. "The Confessor?" It fit the MO.

"Come on, man." Tor nodded his head toward the exit of the crazy pool.

"Yeah, go. That's what you're good at," Isaiah mumbled, seeming more like himself than just a second ago.

"Isaiah." I almost posed it as a question, not sure if it was Isaiah or some drugged-out version.

"What did you come here for?" he said. "See how messed up I am, so you could feel good about yourself?"

"No." Again, I don't know why I came here.

"Go. Everyone leave me. My mom hasn't even been here to visit. She gave up on me, why not you?" Isaiah said.

I couldn't believe that Isaiah's mom had given up on him. She thought the sun rose and set on him. "It's not like that," I said. "I just got caught up in other things." Also, it wasn't like my phone had been ringing off the hook from him. The last time I'd talked to him I'd told him I wasn't into smoking anymore, and that was it.

"Hey, I see your other things." He looked at Tor. "I heard you kissed your daddy's ass to get into the money. All the crap you used to say about him, but as soon as you could sell out, you did."

I think an unfair interpretation of events.

"So now you're daddy's little boy again and going to the money school. You're finally better than me and came here to prove it! Well, you're not. I never sold out. I'm still the one in charge of my life making my own choices."

I looked at the misshapen, gaunt, and beaten body of my best friend, former best friend. He couldn't see out of one eye, he could barely hold a coherent conversation, and he was in agony from withdrawl from a drug so new there was still only one street name for it. "Yeah, you're living by your choices."

I wanted to vomit.

"Get out of here, sellout." He turned as far away from me as he could in his bindings.

"Do you need anything?" Dumb question, right? "Does your mom know you're here? I could call her."

"She knows." There was so much bitterness in that response that I took a step back and bumped the curtain. "I don't want nothing from you, sellout."

Tor pulled on my shoulder again. "Come on, man."

I let him lead me away.

On our way out a nurse, probably in her late forties and ground down by the same forces that had hit the cop, looked at us. "You're not supposed to be in here."

Now a few of Isaiah's roommates started to get a little loopy and louder.

"Sorry," I started.

"You're getting them all worked up." She was upset that I'd just made her job harder, not that her patients would be more "worked up."

"I'm sorry."

She did not accept my apology as Tor and I went around her.

The cop wasn't at the door. Maybe he needed a new magazine. We started to walk back the way we'd come in.

"Well, I guess that answers one question," Tor said.

"What?"

"Sofia is NOT psychic. I can't imagine that going any worse at any time you came."

"Yeah, he wasn't always like that."

"I know." Tor put his hand on my shoulder. "He didn't mean all that stuff he said. He doesn't know what he's saying."

I didn't have a response to that. Tor wasn't wrong. There wasn't much left of the Isaiah I'd run around with, towels tied around our necks, playing superheroes. I still knew Isaiah. He was calling it exactly like he was seeing it.

I was about to wax philosophically about stuff, when

everything froze in my belly and sweat spiked across my spine and scalp.

"Ryan?" Tor noticed I'd stopped walking.

Getting off the elevator was a man that I'd never thought I would see again. I almost didn't recognize him. He wore a nice suit and leaned on a thick wooden cane. The last time I'd seen him, he'd been dressed as a homeless man and had gotten me arrested by the SSA.

The Worm walked right past me.

FOURTEEN

"Do you know him?" Tor whispered.

I shook my head. "I don't think so." But I did.

The Worm was one of a quadruplet, three with different powers and one normal guy. Together they'd formed a hive mind individual named Wraith, who'd been one of the original Guard. Two of the powered brothers of the Wraith were dead. The one without powers had ended up working for Raptor in more of a supporting role. He'd been injured by Osprey and the Confessor, and was probably still in the hospital, but not this one. Caesar and Mindraker had twisted the remaining brother into the Worm, who'd spent years as Caesar's private informant.

If I let on that I recognized him, it would be a small jump to connect me to Raven. A jump a professional information-gatherer and Guard-hater would make.

But I couldn't just walk away, either. The Worm wasn't handing out fruit baskets. "Tell you what, Tor. I want to check on..." I didn't know what, but I wanted to say villainy.

"Dude, don't do it. This isn't your responsibility." Tor shook his head.

He was right. I mean, it wasn't my responsibility. This city didn't need me running around in body armor trying to save everyone. "I'll just be a second."

I tried to figure out a reason to be walking back the way I'd come, should anyone ask. A bathroom was down the hall. I made that my overt goal.

Ten feet ahead of me, the Worm turned, passed the empty cop chair, and went into the detox room.

Okay, that couldn't be a coincidence. I ran. What was I going to do, arrest him in the name of prep schools? But Isaiah was in there.

The Worm wanted what Zed and Pixel wanted, their supplier. Zed might not recognize the Confessor from Isaiah's description, but the Worm would.

Sofia had mentioned her dad's business was picking up. He'd gone from a lackey to selling THE hottest, newest designer drug.

"You can't be in here." The nurse hit him with the nasal disdain. "Sir, get away from the patient."

I turned the corner.

The nurse stomped over from the far side of the room, annoyed her tone hadn't chased away the trespasser. The Worm stood over a patient who was twisting at his bindings even though he seemed to be in a fitful sleep.

"It's all right." The Worm's voice did not seem all right, it seemed joyfully creepy. "I'm here to help." Again, a big fat, fat lie. He stood straight, no need for the cane.

He turned the big brass knob at the top.

Fun fact: the brass knob had a simple symbol on it. At first, I thought it was a pentagon, but no. It had seven sides.

"Legacy," I whispered. I swear, I whispered. I didn't even mean to say it. I hoped, hoped, hoped he hadn't heard me.

The Worm glanced up, just realizing he had a bigger audience. But I would have gotten a stronger reaction if he'd heard the "L" word. Instead, he gave me a wink, and twisted the cap.

Yellow smoke sprayed from the top and bottom of the cane. He made a face at the smell and tossed the cane to the far side of the detox room.

Job done, he walked right at me.

"Hey." I'm just eloquent. I grabbed him.

Or at least tried. I actually stumbled through him.

He could desolidify. That had been one of the Wraith's powers, but I'd assumed the Worm's power was astral projection. Funny old world.

Our eyes met. "Hellington. Good school," he said.

And that wasn't horribly, horribly ominous at all.

The Worm -- and maybe this is how he got his catchy handle -- faded through the floor.

I thought about chasing him, but the most important thing was getting control of the gas. I looked for the super spy cane he'd discarded.

The nurse was coughing, but conscious.

Let's assume yellow gas is bad. No good gas is yellow. It just doesn't happen.

I held my breath as best I could but still sucked in some of it and burned my lungs.

The cane canister was underneath a bed. I snatched it up and tried to twist the brass knob. It did not move. The yellow haze was thick, blinding me as my eyes watered. I stumbled toward a trash can I remembered seeing when I'd visited Isaiah. I jammed the walking stick in the can and pulled up the liner. Only a stream of the stuff was coming out from where I'd tied it off.

It was then I realized the room had erupted with

shrieks. It didn't take much to rile up the patients, so I wasn't surprised. For a second, I thought it was a good sign. If they were yelling, they weren't dead.

Then one of the patients sat up and roared. Hate and anger drove the sound. He didn't scream or holler. He roared! Veins at the side of his neck bulged.

Other patients answered with roars of their own.

Oh, this was bad.

If the yellow smoke was poison, was I going to go loopy? I looked around the room. None of the patients were sleeping now. They were twisting and pulling at their bindings.

The nurse was horrified. An addict strained against his restraints and snapped at her with his teeth. She jumped back in surprise.

"Stop!" I warned her but she got too close.

The patient behind her broke one hand out of his restraint and grabbed her arm.

She screamed in pain and collapsed.

Her anguished cry was more fuel to the addicts own roars and shrieks.

I gave up holding my breath. If the gas was going to make me a nut bar, I would have felt it by now. I ran to the nurse.

The addict pulled and twisted the nurse's arm as he tried to free his other arm by brute force. He made no attempt to unbuckle his restraint with his free hand.

I popped his grip on the nurse. He was strong, but not Osprey strong.

The strap's buckle took too much concentration for most, but not all of the...let's just call them what they are... zombies.

I looked at Isaiah. Veins bulged up his neck and tapered

off in his cheeks. He had one foot free and was kicking it around with no idea what to do next.

"What is going on?" Tor coughed and sputtered as he inhaled the gas.

I helped the nurse up. She was cradling her arm, which looked broken. I moved her to the door, almost carrying her.

"Tor, get her out of here."

He took hold of her and helped her through the door.

"What did you two idiots do?" The cop walked into the room, too. For a second he focused on the yellow fog in the air and Tor's blazer. Then he realized the patients weren't just making noise and his eyes bugged out of his head.

I ran for the trash bag. I didn't have time to explain. The yellow gas had inflated the bag so it now looked like a ghetto beach ball.

One zombie glared at me with pure rage. His eyes had nothing human. He grabbed my neck with both hands.

One way to keep my superhero ID a secret is not busting out all the sweet kung fu when I'm in my civvies. Screw that! This guy wanted to bend my neck like the nurse's arm.

I broke his grip, quick spun, kicked his legs out from underneath him, and dive rolled over him to a standing position.

Tor and the nurse were gone, yay! The cop had not moved, boo!

"Everyone freeze!" It took a little effort, but he got his gun out.

Oh, come on! I didn't dare move. The cop was panicked and might just shoot me. Another zombie jumped me from off his gurney.

I went spinning onto the floor and the trash bag with the yellow gas and the cane went spinning out of my hands.

I lost track of the cane as I was busy keeping zombie teeth off my throat.

All these guys were strong. I've fought strong, and normal humans could be this strong. These guys weren't PL 2 level strong, but they were stronger than their wasted half-skeletons had any right being.

I flipped the zombie off me but another replaced him. The new zombie took an elbow to the throat.

Another fun fact when facing off against Yellow Gas Zombies, or YGZ if you're in the industry. They don't care about pain. Broken collar bone, not going to impress them.

I kicked my legs out and spun. The zombie wasn't ready for it and lost his grip.

The cop wasn't interested in pointing his weapon at me anymore. He had it directly on Isaiah, who was slowly walking toward him.

"Back, on the ground," the cop ordered.

"No! He doesn't understand you!" I had to stiff-arm a short but feisty zombie, do a roll off the remnant of a gurney, and make a flying tackle a second before the shot went off.

Isaiah and I rolled to the ground. He started scratching at my eyes before we hit the floor.

I don't want to speak ill of the undead, but talk about ungrateful. I rolled him on his stomach and planted his face into the antiseptic tile, then flattened myself again as another YGZ did a fly tackle right over me.

I rolled off Isaiah, stood up, and placed another zombie in an arm bar. My arm bars normally result in a scream of pain. This guy only howled in frustrated rage and snapped his teeth at me. He pushed with his juiced strength, I didn't let go, and crack!

Again, he didn't care. He wanted to kill me, but just in a

general murderous intent to humanity way. It wasn't personal.

I didn't have the leverage anymore now that the arm was broken, so he lunged at me.

I tripped him and spun him into another zombie looking to take a bite out of me. This wasn't working. They would overwhelm me soon. If they'd been coordinated, I would have been their low-carb snack already.

Two zombies blocked the door. One was standing looking at the wall. The second was walking toward the door.

I had to keep them in the room. Keep them in the room and hope the Worm wasn't hitting another ward with his Jamba Juice.

The zombie staring off into space must have realized if he didn't induce mayhem he wasn't getting paid. "Gawwa!" He came right at me.

I flipped him easily. He spun in the air twice before landing on the floor. I ran for the door, doing a dive roll underneath a zombie and popping up right next to the cop.

The cop was waving his gun around, with no idea what he was doing. I guess the older generation isn't trained for zombie survival.

I knew about a billion ways to get the gun out of his hand, so I used one of them. "Come on."

He looked at his weapon, then at me. That's when I saw the veins bulging around his neck. "MY GUN!"

Oh, come on!

The cop was a lot bigger, and I wasn't ready for it. He launched himself at me. I'm not even sure he remembered what a gun was, just that it was his. He collided with me and drove us to the floor. "Kill them all, kill everything."

The cop was special, he could talk. He jammed his knee into my stomach.

"Kill them, kill them!" a few chanted.

Okay, not so special.

The cop brought his fist up to get a good swing.

His office chair collided with his face. Tor had returned to save my ass. This time it wasn't from a bunch of preppy gangster wannabes, but hordes of undead.

I kicked and got the cop off me.

Tor pushed a gurney in front of a couple more undead and gave me the space to get out the door. He came right behind me and pulled the door shut. Almost. A zombie got his foot caught in the door. I hauled off and kicked it and the door slammed shut with a click.

"Freeze!" A new cop on the scene. The new cop's eyes went to the gun in my hand. His partner's gun.

Oh, come on!

I dropped the weapon like it was hot and went to my knees.

Tor did not. "You need to get help. Those people are going crazy."

That's a point. Tor wasn't nuts, and I wasn't nuts. "Brains," I tried. Nope, no interest, I was good.

"No, officer!" the nurse we'd rescued shouted from fifteen feet down the hall at the nurses' station. "You don't understand. Those boys saved my life."

"Tor," I said out of the side of my mouth. "Get down on the ground."

The cop picked up the gun I'd dropped, but still had his weapon pointed at me.

"Where is Officer Lemur?" the new cop asked.

"Kill them ALL!" Well, you feed a zombie a straight line, what do you expect? They tried to open the door, but it was locked. I assumed it was something Tor had done, or maybe it was just standard procedure to set doors to lock people in. Sounded unlikely.

"It's not locked," Tor said. "We should do something."

Oh. They were just too far gone to work a knob.

"Kill them all!" Lemur and his new apocalypse buddies took up the chant. A few scrabbled at the door.

"I don't know what happened," I said. "But they went crazy."

"It's true." The nurse walked halfway back to the detox room.

"Including your partner," Tor said.

But not us. I remembered Lemur's reaction to the Stardust withdrawal comment. He knew detoxing from Stardust from the inside. "It's the Stardust," I said.

Tor got down on his knees. "What?"

"Everyone who used Stardust went loopy when they got dosed with the gas." It was a wild conjecture. It could be blood type or last time they'd had salami. But it fit. And explained why the entire hospital wasn't chanting kill them all.

The cop didn't look that interested in us anymore and walked past us. His partner and a couple of the other addicts were pressed against the small wired glass window in the door.

Remember when I was making a good faith effort to get the canister trash bag out of the room? In retrospect, I should have tried harder.

The brass end with the seven sided polygon -- it has a special name but I don't remember that part of geometry -- came smashing through the little window.

The cop sidestepped the canister, backed up, and

leveled his weapon again. The canister cane was almost empty, but not empty.

"Ah, sir. Did you ever use Stardust?" I asked. The new cop was acting a little off.

"No." He blinked like he'd forgotten what he was doing. "We took some off a guy a couple of days ago." Another blink. "Lemur wanted to try just a little," he murmured.

Oh, come on!

Maybe if he did just a little, he would be fine. I was not going to risk it. I kicked up from my knees to standing, closed the distance to the cop and dropped both feet in his face.

"No, Ryan!" Tor yelled.

I landed, snatched up both guns the new cop had been holding, and stood. The new cop was stunned, trying to understand what had happened to him.

"It's the gas, this is not you." Tor had his hands up, trying to calm me.

What? "What?" I said.

"The gas is making you violent." Tor enunciated each word like he was talking down a psycho first grader.

"I'm not violent." I stood over the cop I'd just drop-kicked in the head. "I mean, I'm not yellow gas violent."

The new cop totally succumbed and grabbed my legs. "Kill them all!" Just so long as he was busy chanting he couldn't be busy biting.

Darhaven police are not good peace officers. No one is confused about that. But two for two with cops who'd used drugs? This was crap. If I wasn't already an illegal vigilante, I'd want to become an illegal vigilante.

He only got a little of my skin through my pants, but he bit me. So not that busy chanting. My hands both had guns and I didn't want to risk firing them.

I wiggled out and spun, running down the hospital hall, still holding the guns. Taken out of context that might look bad.

The new zombie cop clawed his way to his feet, but he didn't follow me. "Kill them all." He didn't have the total committed zeal of his zombie brothers, but he had enough mental capacity to work a door knob.

The hallway had filled with people drawn to the confusion. Again, has Hollywood taught us nothing?

"Go! Go!" I yelled at the spectators. It must have been the tweed. If I'd been running the halls in my torn jeans and hoodie yelling *go* with two guns, people would have gone.

The door opened. Zombies pushed and shoved to get out and get the apocalypse party started. A couple fixated on inanimate objects. One guy vented his anger on Lemur's magazine laying in the hall. One started biting the wall. But most kept focus on job one. "Kill them all!"

"Go! Go!" I yelled again. I didn't have a plan. Unless getting people away was a plan, then I was all about the plan. Yeah, not really a plan.

My guns flew out of my hands. Okay, not *my* guns. My point is, one second the guns were behaving very gun-like and not flying away from me, the next they both flew away from me.

A man in purple and yellow boots rounded the corner with several agents behind him. Oracle and the SSA had arrived.

On an intellectual level, I know it's not all about me. But I whispered, "They found me," anyway. That's where my mind went. The Super Suppression Agency couldn't be here to stop zombies. No, they were here to take down a kid in a blazer.

The lead zombie glowed purple and took to the air. The

floating zombie banged into other zombies and pushing them back into the detox room. Other zombies glowed and started doing the same.

"Boys, get down," Oracle ordered.

When I'd been fighting him last week, he'd seemed a good sort, and plenty powerful. If he'd been trying to kill me, I'd have gotten seven shades of crap kicked out of me. He still sported a shiner, spoiling his good looks. Yeah, that was me.

Tor grabbed me and brought me to the other side of the nurses' station. "Come on, let the professionals handle this."

That sounded like a good plan.

FIFTEEN

The professionals handled it well. The druggies were super-charged, but they didn't have any hope against a telekinetic of Oracle's caliber. One of the shield guys was there. He looked a lot like the one I'd fought, but without a broken jaw, so not the guy I'd fought. You couldn't really tell since they wore grey and blue custom masks and only the lower half of their faces were exposed.

I think Raptor had the right idea. Why go halfway? If you're going to wear a mask you've already sacrificed some of your peripheral vision. Why not go all in and cover your face?

Anyway, these guys ran into the same issues I had. Things like pain weren't that big of a deal to the zombies so the SSA had to use grapple techniques and heavy duty bindings. But these guys took on supers to pay their rent. They had the gear and tactics to get it done.

The problem with ducking behind the nurses' station? There wasn't an easy way out the back. "Come on, we should go now," I told Tor.

The complete takedown didn't last longer than four

minutes, but they were rushing around the hallway so much we didn't dare leave our hideout. With the last zombie completely restrained, we had an opportunity to slip out.

"Don't you think we should stay and give a statement or something?" Tor said.

"Um." Of course we should. That's exactly how they would expect a couple of fine upstanding students from the Island to act. "No, they look busy." Truth was, this was all my worst nightmares rolled up into one. A zombie apocalypse and the place thick with SSA operatives. If I'd suddenly lost all my clothes and needed to go on stage in five, you would've had a clean sweep. "We can come back tomorrow," I offered.

"Boys?" Oracle's deep voice. Boots had seen us break cover. "Did you see what happened here?"

"No, not really." I shrugged.

"Yes, we saw everything," Tor spoke over me.

"I mean, as much as anyone," I agreed.

Oracle looked at me long and hard. "You were running down the hall with guns."

Again, out of context that sounded so bad.

"He took them from the cops before they went psycho killer. It was amazing," Tor gushed.

"Not really. They seemed a bit... out of it. They practically handed them to me. I think they knew something wasn't right," I said with a wave. "Really, we owe those fine officers a debt of gratitude."

"You totally did a mid-air double kick to that guy's face," Tor said. "It was incredible."

Fun fact, a similar move gave Oracle that shiner. Hope no one puts that together.

"I can't really remember what exactly happened, or who did what." I am so bad at the undercover crap.

Oracle looked at both of us, then just at me.

"What happened to your eye?" Tor asked. "Looks like you really got clocked."

"Really? I don't think it looks that bad," I said. "I mean, I'd hate to see the other guy. Am I right? I mean, that guy must be lame." You're not the only one screaming for me to stop talking. I was doing it, too. I just couldn't. "Like probably not even worth your time. He probably just ran. I doubt he's in this county anymore. Am I right?" Somebody please stop me!

"We need you to give a statement," Oracle said.

I think I've done enough damage. "Okay." I'm going to jail. I'm going to jail for a long, long time.

They separated us and put me in the back of their mobile command thing. It wasn't the cell truck they'd used last time, thank God. If they would have tried that I would have gone all Raven on them. That's right, I'm so badass I'm a verb.

Instead, this was the unit that I'd snuck into to talk to Dodger a million years ago. We'd rescued her from Slicer and then she'd turned herself into the feds. She's a heck of a teleporter, so I doubt the feds are ever going to let her go.

I hope they let me go.

I tried the door. It opened. Okay, not a prisoner. I breathed a little easier.

I'm just going to leave. That sounds reasonable, doesn't it? It's not just me. No, that's totally reasonable.

I made it out the door and around the corner. A woman's voice brought me up short. "This is worse than the Cutter Grove incident." She spoke in a low whisper into a phone.

"The Cutter Grove victims did more destruction, but the vector was a drink. A bunch of bums shared the same vodka bottle. This was airborne, and the transformation was faster."

This had happened before? I knew Cutter Grove. A lot of homeless and druggies hang out there. I hadn't heard of any "incident."

"No, it didn't affect everyone. A nurse and two boys were at ground zero. It's got to be the Stardust. It prepares the mind and adrenal glands so when the second element is introduced, things fall apart."

That's how I'd called it.

She listened for a second. "If this is a test, what's the end game?" More listening. "I don't know if the cops tested positive for Stardust. We don't have a test for it yet. They tested positive for pot. I'm about to talk to the second boy now. Oracle gets a weird vibe from him, but anyone would be nervous after what he saw."

And that would be my cue to get my butt back to the van. I turned around and ran right into somebody's waist. "Oh, boy."

I looked up, and up, and up into the face of a giant. I'd met this guy before. Two things. One, he'd put his neck out to help me. Without his help, I never could have saved David, Peregrine, and Jasmin. So two out of three. Another thing is, he can detect supers, just like Raptor could. Or at least something like Raptor could. Raptor's was more a vision thing. This guy had radar.

"Have we met?" He smiled and said that ponderously, like being that tall made it hard for all the thoughts to get where they needed to go.

"Um, I think I would remember."

"Jacob." The woman had finished her phone call and turned the corner.

The giant looked from me to the woman. "Captain, I was about to escort this civilian to see his mother. She's at the perimeter."

The Captain rolled her eyes. "Okay, I'll walk him."

Jacob saluted. "Perhaps we'll meet again under better circumstances, Ryan Blackwater."

"Yeah, that would be..." Horrifying. "Great."

I think he winked at me and walked away.

"Don't give any mind to Jacob. His last surge twisted and fried. Now he's a little slow but still a good person." Captain misinterpreted my apprehension as I looked at the back of the giant.

"Slow." In no way was that true. My ID might be burned by this guy. Depended how well his super detection worked. But I knew his secret, too. He wasn't slow, he was playing these people. Was that good for me, or bad?

The Captain started walking, and I fell into step. "You were quite the hero out there today."

I shook my head.

"You acted fast and kept your head."

"I guess." I shrugged.

"You said you saw a super pass through the floor." She'd heard what I'd told the agent before he'd put me in the trailer.

"Yeah, like a ghost." I nodded. "I've never seen anything like that." That much she could have gotten from the nurse.

"Both your friend and the nurse say you saved a lot of lives today."

"It was Tor that did the heavy lifting." Not me, I'm just a poor defenseless not-super. I certainly didn't break any international agreements regarding the use of superpowers.

"Well, I wanted to talk to you before you left." We must have been close to the perimeter because she stopped. "You're the kind of person the SSA are looking for."

Oh, no, they found me! They figured it out! "Ah."

"Have you ever thought about joining the Superhuman Suppression Agency?" She held up her hand with a card. "This isn't a guarantee, but I would like to talk to you about signing up."

I took the card. It had her name and title, Field Control Captain Susan Brackstan, and her phone and email. "Well, I never thought about joining the SSA." I'd thought about running from them, how best to fight them, but never joining them.

"Think about it."

I don't think I will. "I will." Okay, now or never. I might as well try it. "You know there's one other thing."

She suddenly looked interested. "Yes?"

"When I first came in on the ghost guy..." I wasn't even tempted to say Worm. My undercover skills were improving. "He said something. I'm not sure I heard him right, and it didn't make any sense, but I think he said Legacy." I looked at her face.

If it meant anything to her, she didn't let it show. "I'll make sure it gets in the report, but it's probably nothing."

"You're right." I held up the card. "Thanks. I will think about this."

"Ryan!" I recognized that voice.

"Mom?"

The Captain gave permission with a nod to the agent at the perimeter, and Mom came running to me. And engulfed me in a total mom hug.

"Are you okay?" The question was desperate.

"Your son saved a lot of lives tonight. You should be proud. He's a real hero," the Captain said.

Mom looked from the Captain to me, clearly confused.

"Your son could have run and saved himself, but he rescued people and kept his head in a pretty scary situation." She gave me a nod.

"Wasn't that big of a deal." No hero here.

"Your son is a real hero." The Captain was not a mother. Because if she was, she would have known that what she'd really just said was, "Your son could have died because of the stupid actions he took, and hey, I'm with the SSA so the stupid actions were with and against super-powered individuals that could bend him into a pretzel."

"Hero?" Mom's eyes were wide with fear.

The Captain nodded. "Pleased to meet you. You raised a good man."

"He's a boy," my mom said, but I don't think the Captain heard her. She was already striding away with purpose.

We walked to the other side of the perimeter.

"What does she mean, hero?" She grabbed my face in her hands like she used to do when I'd gotten caught stealing cookies before dinner.

"Mom, it wasn't like that," I tried to say, but it's hard to talk with your face squished.

"You don't do that anymore." She let go of my face and gave me a hug. "Let the professionals deal with this stuff."

"Yeah, I will." Only the professionals have no idea what's going on. They're chasing their tails on this one. I know who's selling the Stardust and who's turning it into a weapon. Somehow the Worm and the Confessor are working together.

But what if the Captain was right? What if this was just

a test? I saw an entire city of Stardust users flipping out and going on killing sprees. The level of chaos that could send through the entire country. That was why Raptor was so frightened of Legacy and willing to work with Ceasar to keep them out of town. They could wipe Darhaven off the map.

"What are you thinking?" Mom asked.

"Mom." God, I was sick of lying to her. "I don't do drugs."

It was a nonsequiteur and it showed on her face. "What? Okay, good."

"But I do have to do something." So vague, it amounted to a lie.

"Is it dangerous?" I don't know why she went there automatically.

"I'm the only one who can do it." Was that true? Yeah, I think it was.

"Is it dangerous?" She doubled down on that.

"I love you." I gave her a peck on the cheek and returned her hug.

"Ah, what are you going to do?" She held onto my hand.

"The next right thing." I gave her hand a squeeze.

SIXTEEN

I finished suiting up. As my helmet clicked and the heads-up information turned on, my stomach churned with fear and regret. I'd left my mom, scared and confused, in front of the SSA crime scene perimeter fence. I hadn't told her anything that wasn't true, but a lie of omission is still a lie. Restoring her confidence was mission one, and I'd just flushed it down the toilet.

I rotated my head in a circle, making sure I had full range of motion, and did the same with my shoulders and legs. Funny how the suit felt more natural than a rich kid blazer. Well, maybe not that funny.

I didn't know what to do with the information from the Captain's card. Last week I'd run around with a letter from Jackal that he'd used to connect with me like he did with the idol. If Jackal could do it, safe to assume the SSA could, too. I'd taken a picture of the card with my phone, left the card on the bus I'd used, then stashed my phone before I got to my nest.

I felt a little guilty about leaving Tor to deal with the SSA at the hospital, but I hadn't known where to find him and hadn't wanted to draw more SSA attention to myself by calling him or walking around poking my head into different vans. I'd make it up to him. Maybe treat him to a burger at Pete's.

For now, I had a job to do. I knew how to find the Confessor, but not without revealing my identity. I knew the Worm was involved but I didn't know how that helped me. I needed to get the team together, then find a way to track the Confessor.

I called the team party line.

No answer. Funny, I'd just assumed that Butterfly lived on that line. I couldn't call Flare, even though getting her number would be easy now. As Ryan, I couldn't very well ask her to come out and fight super villains. I knew Peregrine's home number. He was the only member of the team that knew my real name. And boy, was that a great feeling.

Okay, time to make my other call.

I removed Jackal's idol from its hiding space, and was relieved to see it spring to life at once. "What can I do for you?"

"Really? No crap about me quitting, or what favor I need to do for you?" This was strange.

"Sure, we can do that stuff, but if you're coming to me after you quit, that means the stuff has really hit the fan. So talk to me. What's going on?"

I told him about what had happened at the hospital and the impending zombie apocalypse if they got the yellow gas to enough of the Stardust users.

"Okay, let me clear my calendar. That just bumped my eight o'clock." He paused. Maybe he was actually bumping his eight o'clock. "Let's talk next course of action."

"We've got to find the Confessor." And I did not want

to involve Sofia unless the alternative was a dead city. "Do you have any ideas?"

"We've known each other for a month. Something you should have picked up on by now is that I always have ideas."

"Only a month? Seems longer." It had to be said.

"That's all the quality time," Jackal agreed. "Let's say we know the plan. Stage one, get the primer into as many hands as possible."

"The primer is Stardust."

"Right. Second stage, perfect the activator."

"The yellow gas seemed pretty perfect."

"And the last phase, gas the primed to induce destruction," Jackal continued. "Problem we have is we don't know how they're delivering the activator. Gas is a good step, but you would need to get a lot everywhere."

"The SSA people said it was in a liquid first." Maybe they were going to dose the water supply.

"And if we knew the logistics of the plan, we still wouldn't know the why," Jackal said. "This is some next level chemistry here. Speaking as a former entrepreneur, that's not cheap. Why do it?"

All good questions. "Let's find the Confessor and ask him."

"Love the enthusiasm. We can't go in through the second and third steps but we can go through the first step. Stardust is still super new. They haven't reached the saturation level. Right now the yellow gas would be a tragedy. Let's assume they're shooting for a catastrophe. They need to get Stardust out on the street."

"The Confessor is giving it directly to the dealers." If Isaiah was to be believed.

"That won't be fast enough, and the Confessor isn't

plugged into the city. He'll need to work through some locals. Ordinarily, he would have to go through one of the big bosses, Caesar or Midas. But with Ceasar out of the picture he could go directly to Caesar's pipeline."

"So how do I find one of these pipeline guys?"

Jackal took about ten minutes to get the address of the first guy, Jack Sly.

Jackal knew Sly from his days with Caesar. Sly had staying power, and was up for drug kingpin.

So how would I start these conversations? "Hi, you're a cancer and repulse me, but could you do me a solid?" The direct approach with Zed had yielded colorful results. And we all know how well I do at the undercover crap.

Speaking of crap, this guy's headquarters was a hole for it. This crap hole was what happened when a crap hole suffered a severe personal tragedy and let itself go.

The first floor of the apartment building looked like the zombie apocalypse had already happened. A couple floors of boarded up doors. On the second floor, it looked like a regular apartment.

"This is weird," I told Jackal. "It doesn't look like people could live here."

"He doesn't live here. He has a place in the Haven district. This is where he runs his business," Jackal said. "He should be here tonight."

"So why do you think he'll tell me what I need to know?" This wasn't the first time I'd asked him this little nugget.

"He won't, but let's see if there's any Stardust before we worry about that."

Fine. The building wasn't tough to get into. It was so broken down and beaten up they might as well have had a ladder on the outside. I got in through the second floor. The room beyond was dark and empty.

"I don't think anyone's home."

"That's not right," Jackal said. "Maybe they had to relocate."

If this was a bust, I'd wasted an hour running around after this guy. "Where else would this Jack Sly be?"

I rounded a corner and stopped. "Oh, this is not good."

Two gang members, covered in tattoos, clutching guns, with crushed heads. It was bloody, violent, and familiar. "Osprey was here." This was the same MO he'd used last week when he was working for Red Knight.

"There's another one!" someone yelled up the stairs.

And he was talking about me.

"He killed Jack!" He took a shot at me, but I moved.

"I didn't kill them. They were like this when I got here!" I yelled, but I doubt they could hear me over the gunshots, even if that mattered.

"Wrecker! Get him!" the gunman yelled.

Wrecker? That didn't sound safe.

Part of the ceiling collapsed in a shower of white-blue sparks, concrete, and dust. I'm not sure where the blue sparks came from, but if you've been in the industry as long as I have, you get a feel for these things. I'm going to guess Wrecker.

In the pile of rubble a man stood up. And up. He wasn't like the SSA giant. I mean, he was about as tall and wide, but he didn't seem friendly.

"Wrecker?" I asked.

"You killed the boss!" he bellowed.

"I assume they weren't the boss?" I pointed to the two gunmen.

He looked at Jack's guys and then at me. "You die for that."

I don't like to quibble, but I think his plans for me were already set when he'd dropped down from the ceiling. You don't make an entrance like that and *then* open negotiations or give a strong talking to.

Wrecker slammed his hands together and a white disk twice the size of my head flashed into existence. Okay, so that's where all the sparks came from. Maybe he'd just keep tunneling down.

With a flick of his hips he got his whole body into the toss and the disk came right at me, fast.

I've made a career of dodging, so I didn't even have to think about it. The next thing I knew I was standing up after a roll.

More glowing disks came at me. I rolled and flipped and managed not to come up missing a limb. The wall behind me got the hell kicked out of it. The little ones didn't do as much damage as the big one, but at some point it didn't matter.

I dove through the new hole in the wall, and a few more disks followed me. I couldn't really deal with him so far away. I used to carry some explosive ball bearings with me, but I'd used them all up. I needed to figure something else out.

The new room didn't offer any inspiration. It was empty of people but looked like a low rent opium den. Crappy couches and mattresses lay all around the room. There was nothing like a weapon.

"You Guard think you can start killing us now because Caesar isn't around," Wrecker yelled. "We are not easy to kill!"

Okay, let's live in that for a second. "One, the Guard hasn't killed anyone. It was a vigilante that I'm not a fan of."

Wrecker was closer now. "And two?"

"Your boss, Jack, is dead, so not that difficult to kill." Yes, I was trying to get him pissed. It wouldn't make him want me more dead, but pissed he might make a mistake. Also, you see my point, right? He wasn't making any sense.

I caught a break. Wrecker had to pick the left side of the hole or the right side of the hole. He picked right.

I picked right under the hole.

As he blew through the wall with his burning disk of... I'm going to say wreckage.... I spun out my legs and caught him. He tripped and went sprawling on the floor. The disk he'd used to rip through the wall worked just as well on the floor and he cut through it, lfalling a floor down, then a second floor.

Okay, can't take credit for that as my plan, but that works, too.

The guy who shot at me originally now took a couple more shots.

"I did not kill these guys!" I yelled. This time I think he heard me.

"One of your other Guard did." And he shot at me. The walls were not structural, so bullet holes appeared ten feet from me.

"Osprey is the guy you want. I'm here on a completely unrelated matter."

"Graww!" Wrecker finally got his stuff under control but he sounded like he was three floors down now. I had to start going up before he found the stairs.

"All you Guard are the same." Another shot.

Okay, that's a little hurtful. "I'm just here to talk about Stardust."

"What? We don't have any of that crap." Another shot. The hole was closer. That could just be a coincidence, but I'd had enough.

"Then who does?" I picked up one on the more solid-looking pieces of debris.

"I don't know. We've been trying to find out where the supply is coming from. Everyone is." I figured he was going to shoot after his sentence if the pattern held.

Midway through, I leapt and tossed the piece of debris, catching him in the stomach. I rolled and was up with a chunk of concrete the size of my fist. I wound up and connected with his gun hand. His weapon went spinning.

I'd knocked the air out of him so I was able to approach him without much effort.

He looked at me like a fish out of water.

"Okay, I'm going to say this again. The Guard did not kill anyone. Got that?"

He nodded.

"I don't believe you."

He nodded more vigorously.

"That's better, thank you. Now, if you had to guess, now that your boss is dead, who would the seller of Stardust go to?"

"Earl Chadwick," he spat.

I heard some tromping up the stairs. "Thank you. This didn't need to be so hard." And I punched him out. I mean, he did shoot at me.

If Wrecker was coming up, then I was not going to go down. I ran up the stairs, making sure they didn't have any tricks in reserve.

Wrecker and his pal seemed to be the only ones still alive. There were plenty of others strewn around that Osprey had dealt with.

I followed the bodies to a very expensive and gaudy-looking office. And the body of a large man, both powerful and fat. His chest was caved in. Pockmarks and broken glass were everywhere. There had been a fight that had not impressed Osprey at all. He'd exited through a window, though I don't know why.

The party line finally rung on. "This is Butterfly." She was panting a little. "I got your message, Raven. What do you need?"

"Not a good time, Fly." My head swam a little. I'd seen some pretty gross and violent stuff this last month. This was certainly one of them.

"What's going on?" She was a little concerned now.

"Tell you in a minute." I leapt out the window Osprey had.

SEVENTEEN

"I was late to a crime scene, that's all." I wasn't too broken up about a drug dealer meeting a quick end.

"Oh, no. Was anyone hurt?" Butterfly wasn't dipping into her power at all. She sounded very human.

"I don't think Jack Sly felt a thing."

"Jack Sly." She didn't say that in the tone of voice someone would use if they didn't know Jack. It was more in the tone of, *huh I can't believe I came across that name twice in the same day,* kind of voice.

"Butterfly, what do you know about Jack Sly?" I stopped climbing down the side of the building and waited to get my answer.

"Well, Peregrine is running a case and needed to know where all the free agent drug dealers are located," she said. "Sly was one of the names I gave him."

"What case is he working?"

"He thinks he's found a serial killer case. I think he's right. I've been running the data, and it fits. There was a break of about five years, which would line up with a prison term if the killer was arrested for a different violent crime."

"Serial killer, huh? Wasn't that what Osprey was going on about?" Jackal asked. But he wasn't really asking.

"What's the link between the serial killer and the drug dealers?" I started down the wall again.

"The last victim fought back. Tore some clothes and some Stardust got everywhere. The theory is that this was before Stardust got as widely dispersed as it is now, so whoever had that much product that early is directly connected to the source."

"And they think that one of the free range drug dealers is the source."

"They?" Butterfly did not know who *they* were.

"Peregrine and his new wonder twin, Osprey." Is it still connecting the dots when the dots are jammed that close together?

"No, Peregrine wouldn't..." She thought for a second and finished in a more mechanical voice. "It is possible, and would explain where some of his information came from."

I got down to a neighboring building and started a quick jog. "So pick one, Butterfly. Where are they going next? Where can I go to head them off? Osprey is killing people I need alive to save the city."

Now that I knew what I was looking for, I could tell I was already too late. The second location on the list had an Osprey-shaped hole on top and police tape all around the street-level access.

"I'm going to kill him!" Peregrine was a tool, but he'd crossed a line. He was working with Osprey and helping him kill people. And these were just the guys I knew about.

Their method was simple enough. Peregrine flies Osprey over the building, Osprey does a ten-ton swan dive, kills the guy, and jumps out a window. Zeroes out his mass and Peregrine flies them away.

Perfect little bird of prey-themed kill fest.

"I don't believe Peregrine would go this far," Butterfly said.

"Of course he would go this far. He was just one push from going this far," I said. "All week I've been running into thugs who were saying the Guard were killing people. I guess they were right. In one week, he's undone fifteen years of what the Guard stood for."

"He wouldn't," Butterfly protested.

"Where do I go to find him?"

There was a pause.

"Earl Chadwick. He's the farthest name on the list. But you don't move fast enough. You won't make it in time."

"Peregrine better hope not."

At least I wasn't walking into Earl Chadwick's place blind. I knew that area very well. It had been on one of my regular routes back in the day when I was patrolling. And by back in the day, I mean two months ago.

I was able to make good time on my parkour run because I knew a couple shortcuts, and because I was getting pretty good at this long distance push through the Kages.

Earl was working out of a warehouse that had been built just after Columbus didn't find India. But I wasn't looking for signs of Earl. I was looking for signs of Osprey and his personal chef and valet, Peregrine.

The place seemed calm. There were guards posing as workers. They weren't running around getting their heads smashed in, so maybe I'd beaten them here.

I had not.

Something heavy landed on my back and crushed all the air from my lungs. Peregrine. We'd sparred enough back in the good old days that I'd recognize that paralysing blow anywhere.

I tried to get up, but he flew by and kicked me in the head. Kind of crappy, but with my helmet on, it didn't hurt me.

Normally he followed up with a kick to the kidneys. Maybe he was taking it easy on me. Nope, there it was. Oh, that hurt.

"Why are you here?" Peregrine landed hard enough on my shoulder blade to pin me. He kept flying down, so he got more thrust from the maneuver than just gravity.

I hated that maneuver. "I'm trying to stop Osprey from killing people. People *you* are pointing him at."

"We're trying to catch a killer." Peregrine pushed me a little harder, just to be a dick. And he flew off.

"I could save you some time. Where's Osprey?" I stood up slowly. Not because I had to be slow. Definitely not because I was still wheezing from the first blow. I was just showing him that I wasn't afraid of him and I didn't need to be all nimble. See, it's a head game. Also, it hurt. It hurt so much. "What is your problem, anyway?"

"Osprey was right."

"About what? The serial killer?" If Butterfly says that's legit, I'll buy it.

"About the serial killer, about Slicer. If you'd just let Osprey kill him, that cop wouldn't be dead."

And I have nothing to say to that. Nothing at all.

"I let him do it," Peregrine said.

"When?" I didn't get it.

"That night. I could have stopped him before you

pulled Slicer out. I could have pulled Slicer. And I didn't. I just let him do it."

"Well, then you should have gotten off your ass and protected that cop!" I yelled. What was he talking about, he could have acted? He blocked my first punch, then my second. "A good man is dead and you're telling me you were playing dead?" I set him up for a kick to the gut, but he was ready for it.

He blocked me and started a maneuver that would have ended with me twirling in the air then landing on my head. I did everything I could to break the momentum and managed to get free and start a kick of my own.

He blocked it and fed kicks back to me, but like he was pedaling a bicycle they were coming at me so fast. I couldn't block them all. He was on my back again.

I used the momentum to roll up and tag him in the back as he passed, but I didn't get any good contact. At least I was on my feet again. "Everything Raptor taught us! Everything Raptor taught us--"

"Is a lie," Osprey said from the other side of the building. He leapt and closed the distance.

I jumped out of his way. In midair, Peregrine took that opportunity to collide with me and I spun out, landing wrong on my shoulder.

"You know everything Raptor told you was a lie." Osprey cut his density power and landed like a cat.

I got up, tracking both of them. So, I've lived through a few fights with Osprey, and I knew that Peregrine had always bested me in our sparring matches. So I was outclassed in a big way here. Time to talk my way out. I was so screwed. "Really, Peregrine? Is that how you're justifying your little team-up issue? This is Osprey. Just last week we were working together, stopping him from killing people. Now you've signed with the other team."

"He was forced to follow Red Knight, just like you were," Peregrine said.

"Just like you would have been for the rest of your life if I hadn't stopped him," Osprey said.

"You weren't doing me a favor. That was all for you." It was true, though. Red Knight had me cold.

Osprey didn't deny his motivations, but his shrug indicated that he didn't care one way or the other.

"And now you're going around killing people." I pointed at Osprey. "Or is Red Knight making you do this, too?"

Osprey moved so fast I barely got out of his way as he tried to clothesline me.

He'd solidified to do that little trick, so I went for his legs and tripped him up.

But before he fell Peregrine came in and took me out on my knees, landing me on my back. "Get out, Raven. Let us deal with this."

"Like you dealt with Sly?"

"We needed information they had. They gave it to us," Peregrine said.

"Then why did you kill them?"

Peregrine looked at Osprey when I said that, giving me the opening I needed to flip him off and get to my feet.

It's a pain in the ass fighting someone who can fly. Usually gravity is my friend, but flipping Peregrine off his feet just helps a little with his takeoff.

"What do you mean?" Peregrine didn't press the attack, but flew just out of my reach.

"Your new buddy." I pointed at Osprey. At least I would have pointed at Osprey, but he wasn't where I'd thought he was. He collided with me. This time his clothesline attack worked perfectly.

I spun in the air and landed on my shoulder blades. I tried to roll, but felt the impact of a kick to my side and spun a few feet.

I needed to get up. But I just couldn't get all the limbs to do limb things.

"It was all part of the plan. Whoever is selling Stardust is the serial killer or knows who it is. We needed to make sure we could control who the killer would talk to. We don't have the resources to stake out all four of the drug distributors," Osprey said.

"So you killed the other distributors?" Peregrine said. It was tough to tell if he was shocked or just making a note. It was tough because my head was still spinning and Peregrine's vocal distortion hid his emotions.

"He did. Crushed their heads just like he did to Yaltin." I hadn't seen that crime scene, but Peregrine had.

"You need to shut up now." Osprey lowered his fist. I had a helmet, but I doubt it would have saved me.

What saved me was a sudden familiar green glow between me and Osprey.

"What‘s going on here?" Flare rose up in a glowing green sphere. Butterfly sat on her knees in the green bubble. She must have come in tight to the buildings so she wouldn't be in direct line of sight to the drug distributor building. Osprey's fist bounced off the shield and Flare dropped it.

That gave me enough of a breather to roll out of Osprey's strike zone.

"Oh good, the entire JV squad is here," Osprey said.

"Quick tac update. Peregrine is batting for the other

team." Yeah, I realized how that sounded when I said it. "I mean, he's working with the enemy."

"*I'm* working with the enemy? You've still got Jackal on your shoulder!" Peregrine accused.

"He's got a point," Jackal said. Just to me, at least.

Flare's aura winked out as she landed.

Butterfly fumbled to stand as the sphere support she was sitting on disappeared.

Flare kept walking toward Peregrine.

"What are you two doing here?" Peregrine asked. He sounded petulant through his vocal distortion.

"We were worried about you," Butterfly said.

"And what you two might do to each other." Flare's energy dome was down, but her hand still had a green fire dancing around it, pointed right at Osprey.

"Worried about me?" Peregrine said. "I'm the only one still doing the Work. You all punked out."

Flare's fire got a little brighter and pointed at Peregrine. "I got out because this crap isn't going to kill me. I can't stop you. But teaming up with a killer, both of you." She took me in with that, too. "That goes against everything the Guard stood for."

"What the Guard stood for," Osprey repeated the words as if talking to a child, "was to make this city better. How did that work out? Fifteen years of Raptor making his rules and training his little fan club, and the city is worse than ever. What the Guard needs to stand for is protecting people that can't protect themselves, and stopping these killers."

"Not interested in your little pep talk," Flare said. "Why are you here? To kill some drug dealers?" She was disgusted with the idea.

"No," Peregrine said. "We're trying to catch a serial

killer. A serial killer that the cops won't even admit is real. He just goes about his business. Raven is here to stop us."

"Okay, I know that's how that looked." I raised a finger to interject. "I'm following a completely different case. Trying to stop a zombie apocalypse."

That got everyone's attention.

"Everything is just one big joke to you," Peregrine said. "I'm so sick of your crap."

"No, seriously. I mean, not zombie zombies, but users of Stardust go crazy when a different gas is given to them." Hearing that out loud seemed silly.

"Just keep your mouth shut if you only have jokes," Flare said.

"I believe you," Jackal said.

"Thanks," I mumbled. "Fine, whatever. But I need to talk to the Confessor, too."

And they all looked at me.

"What does the Confessor have to do with this?" Peregrine asked.

"He's the one selling Stardust." Am I really reading that far ahead of the rest of the class? "He's either selling a new drug and making mad bank, or he's planning to bring the city to its knees with a bunch of homicidal drug addicts. I need to know which one."

And if I'd been thinking for half a second, I wouldn't have said that. Osprey had almost killed me and Sofia when he'd been sent to abduct her to get leverage on the Confessor. It was possible that he didn't know why he'd been sent to abduct her. Red Knight hadn't seemed to share that much intel. But it was also possible Osprey knew exactly who Sofia was, and who her father was.

My belly did another flip.

"The Confessor? That guy who was looking for the

Phoenix? Now he's selling drugs? That's a quick turnaround," Osprey said. He didn't sound like he'd put Sofia together with the Confessor.

"I think Raven's right," Butterfly said.

"Why?" Peregrine did not think I was right.

"Because he's right there." Butterfly pointed at the Confessor.

EIGHTEEN

We all looked over the edge of the building.

It was a long way off, and dark, but a man in hooded robes was getting out of a car. Two people at his side. One was a tall man. The Confessor wasn't tall, so anyone might look tall compared to him, but this guy was tall and thick and wore a dark suit. The second was a woman in a white suit.

"It's him." Peregrine's eyesight was better than anyone I'd ever met. "And that's Shell."

He pointed at a person exiting from the building. I could only make out a suit and dark glasses. It could be Shell. "That means Slicer and Homunculus are around, too."

"A problem I would have solved without your moralizing," Osprey said.

"A problem we wouldn't have if you hadn't gone around killing his colleagues. Why do you think Chadwick quickly hired a Merc unit?" I shot back. "He's scared."

"Good call, let's argue some more," Flare said. "This has nothing to do with us."

"I'm going to catch the serial killer," Osprey said.

"I have to stop the end of civilization," I added. Still no one believed me. "I need to talk to the Confessor."

"Fine, we'll wait until they leave and jump just one car of supers." Flare had a good plan there.

"Won't work," Peregrine said.

"They never come out," Osprey finished. "Don't know how they do it, but they go into a building, deliver their product, and then disappear. My guess is a superpower." He walked back from the edge. "I need to talk to the Confessor, so I'm doing it now." He got a running start and leapt.

"Raven?" Butterfly asked.

"I need to talk to the Confessor before Osprey kills him." High stakes here.

Peregrine flew off after his new best buddy. I looked at Flare and Butterfly. "I'm not kidding." I tried to be earnest, which isn't easy through vocal distortion. "This drug is no joke. A lot of people are going to get killed if we can't get to the bottom of this." I didn't have time to walk through everything.

"Fine." Flare landed her hands on her hips. "But when this is over, you'd better have a good explanation."

Butterfly had realized the attention was on her. I could tell she wasn't using her power. Her body language looked like a teenage girl about to risk her life, not an android about to terminate a human insurrection. But she nodded.

"Give me a minute, then follow me over." I couldn't just leap the dead gap like Osprey had. He could beat me on the vertical. But I already had a route picked out. Like I said, I knew this area.

I had to run, drop two buildings, jump alleys, cross a street, then climb a wall. And that would take way too long.

I could already hear fighting. Screw it. I backed a little farther than Osprey had and ran as hard as I could.

I'd started a lot higher than where I'd planned to land, but the gap was a little long for me. I tucked in and somersaulted through the air, then stretched out. I hit the wall of Chadwick's building and scrambled for purchase before I bounced off. My hand closed around the drainage pipe I'd been aiming for, and I used it to climb up the side of the building.

Flare followed, blowing out a window conveniently located near me. She went in first, Butterfly in her aura.

I kept an eye out for Shell. That guy had my number. Last time I'd gone up against him, I'd needed Butterfly to save my ass.

Homunculus was a pain. The longer she had to prepare, the scarier she got. Slicer was a cold-blooded and capable killer. The Confessor didn't seem to get off on killing people, but I had no doubt he would if it came to that. Who knew what the two strong arms that he'd walked in with could do. When I'd last worked against the Confessor, he'd been using rent-a-thugs from Midas. How had he stepped up to his own people in a week? I guess he'd been busy. Also, Midas's guys had turned on him, so I didn't blame him for finding new help.

"This way." Butterfly pointed to the left.

Made as much sense as anything.

Flare turned on her force wall and we stepped out into the hall. A few guys spotted us, but they took one look and ran the other direction.

Smart thugs, clever thugs.

"This is all very exciting, but can I ask a question?" Jackal said to everyone.

"You brought him?" Flare was pissed about that.

Yeah, he's the only one taking my threat seriously. "I'm going to say, yes."

"Did you see the Confessor bring anything in with him?" Jackal asked.

"No," I answered for everyone shaking their heads.

"Then what is he selling to the distributor?" Jackal asked.

I motioned to keep walking. "Maybe they're just meeting. They can work out the deal later."

"Maybe, but I think something more dramatic is happening," Jackal said.

How much more drama did we need? I had that thought right before things got all distracting and violent.

We cleared the hall as it opened up to a second floor overlooking a two-story warehouse space.

In the center was a blue distortion in a half circle large enough for two lanes of traffic. Standing to the side of the distortion was the woman in white, her arms raised and a similar distortion radiating from the palm of her hands to the larger distortion.

The Confessor stood next to her, and the tall guy who'd arrived with them was hauling crates, adding a fourth to the three he'd already brought over.

I didn't know Earl Chadwick from Adam, but the nicely dressed guy about as round as he was tall standing next to Slicer had to be the guy.

"You're right about the drama," I said to Jackal. "Flare, close that hole."

"On it." Flare shot down from the balcony and sent a pulse into the woman in white.

She pulled her punch, but still knocked the woman down. The gate disappeared.

The tall guy tossed his crate at Flare.

She dipped and dodged it. The crate landed with an explosion of small baggies, all containing little glowing green pebbles.

Slicer was a little more accurate, jetting a river of cresents at Flare. Her shield held, but she spun out onto the floor.

I rolled off the catwalk onto a set of crates and kept going, trying to keep something between me and Slicer. If he spotted me, I'd be dead.

I didn't know what Butterfly was doing -- maybe nothing -- too terrified of losing herself to her cold calculating side. She might not risk engaging in the fight. Or if she did turn on her power, her robot self might decide the odds weren't in her favor and just leave.

It wasn't her fault her powers were a little unreliable and risky.

I picked up a pry bar someone had left after opening a crate.

Slicer had not slowed down the pressure, just kept pouring on the laser razor blades. Flare's shield was holding, but she was effectively pinned.

I ran toward him and tossed the pry bar. It went end over end, then was plucked out of the air by a blur. The blur tossed it back at me.

I flipped and dodged the projectile and got to my feet. Homunculus. She didn't look the same as last time, but that was kind of her thing. She'd transformed into a monster, her arms too long, the proportion of a spider monkey, her tail a scorpion hook, and her hands ending in claws. Her face was elongated to a muzzle with fangs dripping saliva.

And she was evolving into something more hideous as I

watched. Didn't change the fact that I had to interrupt Slicer. If I couldn't get Flare in the fight, this would be a short, short struggle.

I sprinted for Slicer.

Homunculus jumped in front of me and landed on a group of ball bearings that had just rolled there. She lost her footing and sprawled. I didn't have time to look around for Butterfly, but I gave her a mental high five wherever she was.

I vaulted over Homunculus before she could stand, dive rolled, and landed a kick to Slicer's knee.

The spray of slices arched up and a green bolt caught Slicer in the chest, throwing him into some crates.

Teamwork!

Out of the corner of my eye, I saw Osprey arching down, right on my position.

Oh, come on!

I rolled away.

Instead of landing right where my head had been, he struck a little farther. The concrete spider webbed on impact. He positioned himself right in front of Homunculus' charge.

She hadn't been ready for a piece of steel to suddenly appear in front of her and bounced off him in a heap.

Okay. "Thanks." I looked around for the actual goal of this escapade.

The Confessor was helping the woman in white up. She looked out of it but not unconscious. I made a move toward him, but Peregrine dropped on him first. He was less than gentle to the woman, and came away with the Confessor.

If we could get out of here with the Confessor, that

would be the best option, but I wasn't sure how much "we" was going around. If Peregrine left with the Confessor, would I ever see him again? Would Sofia ever see him again?

Oh, this sucked.

Peregrine's trajectory abruptly changed into a drunken spin and he did a header into the concrete floor, his body twisting at the last minute to protect the Confessor. I saw a blue flash where the Confessor must have made contact with Peregrine. I had to feel for him. If the Confessor got his hands on you, it was super unpleasant. He could also control your body, and make you answer any of his questions. So, worst in-law ever. You know, should things get serious with Sofia.

Homunculus recovered and attacked Osprey with renewed vigor.

So here's my dilemma. Do I help out Osprey? I mean, he wouldn't be in this situation if he wasn't trying to save my life, but on the other hand, the objective was the Confessor and Osprey was a flaming douche bag.

"Keep on the target." Osprey grabbed Homunculus's tail and tossed her to the ground. "I have the twisted."

She bounced up and slashed at him with her claws.

"Okay, if you're sure." I didn't stay to listen if he was sure or not. Does that make me a bad person?

Not wanting a piece of this, the Confessor ran for cover.

I risked a look at Flare. She was flying around, dropping thugs by the handful and sending blasts into the tall guy. He had transformed and was now even taller, and his skin color had changed. It tugged at my memory, but I only got a second to look at him before I was around the same corner where the Confessor had disappeared.

Two of Chadwick's people had probably been debating what they should do when the Confessor ran around the corner. Now I was there, too. I'd bet if I had been a second later they would have just run. I mean, this is what the boss paid Slicer to deal with.

But they were there and had guns, so they got a fist full of Raven. I knocked their weapons out of their hands, tripped one, and flipped the other with a turn of my hips.

That knocked out what little fight was in them to begin with. I made sure they were staying down, then turned to see if I could locate the Confessor.

And I could. He was a foot behind me.

Both of his palms hit my neck, like he was trying to choke me, but there was no pressure. He must have figured the gorget was the piece of my armor that had the least amount of protection between my skin and him.

Pain coincided with twin white flashes. I dropped to my knees.

"Ah, Raven." The Confessor seemed disappointed. "I am disappointed that we keep meeting like this." See, what did I say? Disappointed.

I was really disappointed to see him, too. Especially like this. The pain dialed back, but I was paralyzed.

"Confession time, Raven." The Confessor seemed to think that turn of phrase was pretty clever. "What is the one thing you don't want me to know?"

The pain that was just localized a second ago suddenly surged in my head, like little icy fingers on fire picking through my thoughts.

At first my real name popped into my head. If any villain figured that out, my entire family would need to run. But his question was not villains in general, it was him specifically, and one thing bubbled up. I had to say something. It was a horrible feeling that I was going to say something. I tried to channel my mind somewhere else. My favorite foods, my least favorite 80's rock band, anything. "I have a date with your daughter this weekend!" I shouted.

And my world flipped upside down. He had it, he had everything. One phone call and he had my name, address, when I had Biology. He had it all. If I survived this fight, I would need to get everybody out of town. Could I go to the SSA? I would spend the rest of my life in prison, but maybe they would protect my family. Poor Helen would never get a free life that was hers.

"Impressive," the Confessor said. "Few people can fight my confession, nevermind insult me."

He didn't think I was telling the truth? He thought I was fighting him! There was nothing stopping me from talking, so let's run with that. "What about your wife, C? With you setting up your little criminal empire, she must be lonely."

White flash and my jaw slammed shut. I just got my tongue out of the way. When the pain eased, I was able to talk again. "Okay, I crossed a line there," I admitted.

"I like you, Raven," the Confessor said. He was probably referring to the time I'd saved his daughter from Osprey. Or the time I'd saved his life from the treachery of Midas' mercenaries. Or he liked adversaries with wit and pluck. "But I still have to know, why are you after me?"

The spikes cut through me. At least this time I didn't care if he knew. "You're my link to Stardust. Stardust is one part of the cocktail that makes people super strong psycho killers. I want to know who's behind Stardust." I kept back any reference to the Worm or Legacy. Not sure if I should have or not. But if he was working with the Worm and I said

I'd seen him drop the yellow gas, then my ID would be broken wide open, too.

"What are you talking about?" the Confessor asked, but the question didn't come with any compulsion. "Stardust isn't a problem, it's a solution to the drug problem."

"Huh?"

"You can't lethally overdose on Stardust. It's also difficult to develop an immunity so even heavy users don't need more and more of the drug," the Confessor said. "Once Stardust replaces heroin and other opiates, the drug world will be safer."

"With you at the center making piles and piles of cash."

"This town needs a leader. I will give it that leadership." The Confessor almost sounded more like he was running for office rather than drug lord of the year.

"Well, where are you getting your stash, dude? Because you're being played. If you want to make this city safer, this ain't going to do it. You're just getting people strung out on a new drug that will turn them into monsters."

So the interesting thing is, he didn't call me an idiot. If he didn't believe his supplier was capable of mind-warping everyone, he would have just blown off what I was saying. Instead, he was serious.

"Do you have proof?" The compulsion hit me.

"Nothing I can show you, but it happened at the hospital in the Kages!" The compulsion made me scream everything, even though I was happy to answer him.

I think he would have hit me with a follow up, but the woman in white ran around the corner, the tall guy right behind her.

The tall guy's suit was in shreds. Some of the destruction was from Flare's burns, but some came from the iron chunks that grew out of his skin.

Now that I was this close, I recognized him. Iron. He was one of the first supers I'd fought solo. Well, for about half a minute until Flare came by and saved my ass. He was strong and impervious to anything I had in my bag of tricks.

And he remembered me.

He saw me and sneered. "You took something from me."

I did? Oh yeah, his kitchen knife. He was going to stab the homeless guy with it. "I can get that for you. Just need ten minutes. I'll be right back."

Iron wound up to smash my head like he was playing Tee ball.

I couldn't move at all.

Then the Confessor let me go and I rolled out of the way.

He stood behind Iron. "We don't have time for this," he snapped. "Transcendence, a gate please."

The woman in white nodded and a smaller distortion opened right behind the Confessor. Both Transcendence and the Confessor stepped through the distortion and into the same warehouse that they'd been unloading the crates from when we'd arrived.

Iron did not look like he was going to cooperate. "We got plenty of time." He lunged for me, but a gate opened up in front of him and his momentum carried him through it. I heard something clunking into something else, but the sound came from the gate Transcendence and the Confessor were still standing in.

"I will look into your accusations." The Confessor removed a flip phone from his pocket and tossed it to me. "I will be in touch."

Should I have tried to jump through the gate? I almost

did, until I heard a vocally modulated scream over the sounds of a fight. Butterfly or Flare was in trouble.

I picked the phone out of the air and let the gate close. Let's be real, there was no way I could handle Iron on my own, and I doubt Transcendence or the Confessor would save my bacon while I was crashing their party. I rounded the corner and dove back into the main show.

NINETEEN

It was a wreck.

Homunculus and Osprey were still at it. Osprey had taken some cuts here and there, but Homunculus looked much the worse for wear. She was more twisted and larger, her tail had a scimitar-like spike, and her arms were cords of veiny muscles. She wasn't using one of her arms. It looked broken and bent at the wrong angle. Her face no longer looked human, closer to some prehistoric beast.

All the vanillas had either fled the scene or were no longer moving. Crates of green glowing pebbles were broken and scattered all over the floor. I hoped just having contact with the stuff wouldn't make us susceptible when the crazy juice hit.

Chadwick was laying in a heap with a Flare energy burn on his chest. I assumed he was still alive. Flare had good control and knew how hard to hit an unprotected normal.

I scanned the area for Flare or Butterfly, but didn't see either.

A stream of slices shot out, and I spotted Peregrine

dodging them in the air. He was trying to get close enough to take out Slicer, but was barely able to keep from getting shredded.

My instinct was to help Peregrine. If I could get close enough to Slicer to distract him, Peregrine could put his lights out in a second. Nice thing about Slicer, he wasn't that tough if you could lay a hand on him.

Then I saw something worse -- a glowing yellow ball very, very small. I recognized Shell's power from when he'd had me in a ball like that. The ball was glowing green. Did he have Flare in there?

Shell was on the other side of the warehouse. I didn't have any cover between him and me. Running for him would take me right into Slicer's field of fire. I looked up. The balcony I'd originally come in on went all around the room. I climbed up, flipped myself onto the balcony, and ran the length, trying to keep down. Now that the gunfire had stopped, the only sounds were Homunculus' weird cry and Slicer's energy blast. Hopefully enough noise to cover my steps.

I risked a quick peek when I approached Shell's original location. He'd moved back a little, now under the ledge. Was he taking cover from Peregrine, or me? If I didn't tag him before he saw me, I'd end up in one of those balls.

I jumped, slid, and popped up right in his face. I connected between his eyes and then just kept the pressure going.

The yellow ball exploded in green fire. Flare tried to get up, but collapsed onto her back.

Not good. If Slicer realized she was free but vulnerable, he might risk a cascade of slices in our direction. I dropped one more crack to Shell's head, ran the few feet to Flare, grabbed her by the heels, and pulled her around some crates.

Peregrine and Slicer were keeping each other busy, seemingly unaware of our little fisticuffs yet.

"Flare?" I shook her.

"Check to see if she's breathing," Jackal told me.

He was right, I should have done that first. I put my ear as close to her vocal modulator as I could and placed one hand on her chest. I mean, not on her *chest* chest. Just right above, close to the neck. Oh, forget it. I wasn't copping a feel.

"Get your hand off my chest," she whispered.

It wasn't on her chest!

"Dude, that is not cool," Jackal told me.

"Are you okay?" I asked.

"No, exhausted. Just need a minute."

"The rest of your team doesn't have a minute. You've got to get in the fight, Romeo," Jackal said.

"I didn't touch... oh, never mind." But he was right. Shell was breathing fine, but not moving. I would have loved to have thrown a bag over his head and tied him up, but I'd already used all the supplies that Raptor had given me to keep in my suit. The supply issues were going to be a bigger and bigger problem if I continued to do this.

I took a peek over the crates. Peregrine was not getting any closer to Slicer, who was forcing him back behind the concrete post on the second floor.

I couldn't take Slicer by myself, not this far away. "I don't suppose Pixel might be around?"

"Are you asking me?" Jackal asked. "How would I know?"

"Yeah, how?" Her showing up last time to save my bacon had seemed like a little more than a coincidence. I was starting to think Jackal had lined it up for me. But I couldn't count on it. And if it was true, and he was able to bring in a super at a moment's notice, that was scary in and of itself.

I risked another look at Slicer. He was closer to getting an angle on Peregrine's hiding place.

"Is anyone on the line?" I tried the party line.

"Butterfly." Her voice was timid, not the confidence and detached robot-voice of her power.

"Peregrine?" I asked.

He didn't respond. Moron. "Okay, Fly. Slicer is about to get an angle on Peregrine while he's catching his breath. We need a distraction or Peregrine is toast. I can't get to him without getting ripped to shreds. I need Slicer looking the other direction for a five count."

"Tell me when." Butterfly tried to sound less timid.

"Are you up for this?" As far as I knew, this was the first time she'd been in the field since our fight with Clockwork.

"Tell me when," she repeated, but not in a way that made me feel any better.

"You've got to power up." That's the only way she'd make it out alive from the full attention of Slicer.

"Tell me when." Now she was just getting pissed.

"On three." I counted off and hit three when Slicer was as close to me as he was going to get before he had a clear shot at Peregrine.

An iron ball bearing dropped from the floor and got right under Slicer's foot as he was running to get into position.

Two more ball bearings followed, hitting Slicer in the shoulder and knee.

The parahuman howled in pain and looked where they'd come from.

I broke cover and sprinted toward him.

Butterfly was up on the balcony, crouched behind a load-bearing column kitty-corner to us.

Slicer fired a wide stream of slices.

If she'd been using her power, she could have avoided every individual spinning razor. Instead, she tried to dodge behind the column. Her movements were very much those of a normal teenage girl, not the robotically efficient movements of a cognit when she's using her power.

The razors sliced into her and her body spun, just like the cop's. My memory transposed the twisting motion of Damon Wilson as he'd dropped behind his squad car. Butterfly did the same thing behind the banister of the balcony.

Someone was yelling "No!" and I realized it was me.

I shouldn't have yelled. I should have just attacked. I'd almost wasted the distraction that had cost Butterfly her life.

"No!" Now that it didn't matter.

"What's going on?" Jackal asked.

I didn't have the bandwidth to answer even if I'd wanted to.

Slicer realized I'd broken cover and turned to disembowel me, letting the golden circles spring from his fingers.

I slowed time. Sometimes I try to do that, and sometimes I don't. It doesn't really slow time, it just speeds up my processing speed so I can see what's happening. I don't get to move any faster, but it seems like I have more time to pick my movements.

I dropped to my knees, then pressed my back to the ground and let my momentum carry me on a slide. The spinning killers passed over me with just inches to spare and my slide got me close enough to Slicer.

I sprang up and delivered a merciless shot right to his junk. That was the best use of my time slow thing. I got to see his face move from anger and malice, to surprise that he'd missed, to the horror of what was coming, and finally to the realization that what had happened was so much worse than he'd thought.

"You killed her!" Time went back to normal, but that didn't save him. As he buckled over from the pain, I caught him with an uppercut to his chin and sent him crashing to the ground as I stood.

"Raven! What's going on?" Jackal screamed in my head. Or maybe he talked normally but everything in my head was screaming.

"He killed her! He killed Butterfly!"

This would have been a good time to make sure Osprey was actually winning the fight with Homunculus. But I didn't even think about it. I couldn't.

I landed on top of Slicer. I remember how angry his suit made me. It was perfect. Even with all the fighting it didn't even have a wrinkle and looked like it was worth more than my mom's house. How dare he... I don't know what, but it infuriated me. Like killing the cop and now Butterfly hadn't even cost him his best-dressed status. I know that's stupid -- as I'm saying it now it doesn't make any sense -- but I hit him. I hit him again, and again. Now there was blood on his suit at least.

"Raven, what are you doing?" Jackal's voice pounded in my head.

"He's a monster. He kills and kills and nobody stops him. He killed the cop, he killed Butterfly, because I didn't stop him." I kept hitting him. "I'm going to stop him now."

"Say it like it is. You're going to kill him," Jackal said.

For some reason, that froze my fist in midair. "He deserves it."

"He does." That was Osprey. He walked over to me and dropped Homunculus' limp form right in front of me. "Do it. If you care about Butterfly, just do it."

I don't think Slicer was conscious enough to understand what was happening, but he coughed up blood in a spray that splashed me.

"And a little water will cleanse you of this deed." Jackal's voice didn't pound anymore.

"What?" That sounded familiar, like something I'd just read.

"I said, kill him," Osprey said. "I'll do it if you don't have the balls to give him justice."

"Is this justice?" Jackal asked.

"You're talking to me about justice?" I yelled at Jackal. "You're the Jackal. You killed people, people less deserving than this piece of trash!"

"Who are you talking to?"

Later, as I played this moment back in my head, I can hear the sudden temperature drop in Osprey's voice. But at the time, it was all about me and murdering a man in a bloody suit.

"He's talking to me." Jackal went full audible. "Jackal. And I did choose who lived and who died. I killed people. Some had it coming, and some were just in my way."

"Like Hawk," Osprey said through grinding teeth.

Jackal had told me he hadn't pulled the trigger, but it was his responsibility. "Like Hawk," he agreed.

"Then what do you have to say about Slicer?" I asked.

"Kill him, don't kill him. I'm not going to lose sleep over

it. If I was where you are now, he'd already be dead," Jackal said to everyone.

"Well?" I closed my fist.

"Do you want to be like me?" Jackal's question was casual. *Do you want cream in your coffee* level of casual, but that was the biggest kick to the gut I'd gotten all month.

I didn't want to be like Jackal, I didn't want to be like Osprey. I didn't even know what it meant to be like Raptor. It seemed everything he'd done had three meanings and four of them were lies. It was time. I had to choose who I wanted to be. What I wanted to be like.

It wasn't this.

I stood. I wasn't gentle. I got off him and kicked him in the stomach, but not hard. Well, not *that* hard.

Homunculus stirred and rolled to one side. The twisted monstrosity had faded quickly into a woman in her early twenties with a tail and deep frown lines.

"She's a tough one. I thought I'd already dealt with her." Osprey raised his foot.

"Stop!" I yelled, but more importantly, so did Flare. And everything took on a green hue as fire danced around her hand. "One more move and we're calling you stumpy."

Osprey did not make another move. He backed off. "Fine. You idiot white hats. The next widows these people make, you should go to them and explain why you're feeling good about yourselves was more important than the lives of their husbands and their childrens' fathers."

"We are the Guard," she said. "That isn't what we do."

Osprey's body language indicated he wanted to say more, but he didn't.

"Help me!" Peregrine yelled.

We all looked at him. He was on the balcony, kneeling over Butterfly.

I swear, I'd seen her die, but maybe? My heart climbed in my chest. I ran up the wall and flipped myself over the banister. Flare and Osprey only beat me by a heartbeat.

Peregrine had his hands pressed over deep cuts to slow the bleeding. "We need to get her to a hospital."

It was true, but we didn't like it. If she lived, she would go to prison. SSA would be all over her, and through her, they might be able to find us. She was a cognit. Who knew what she might have uncovered about each of us.

"No." Her voice was faint, but insistent.

"We don't have a choice," Flare said. "Peregrine, you're the fastest."

"Hospitals will be a mess," Jackal said. "Take her to Grandend and 123rd. There's a guy there. He will be discreet."

Grandend and 123rd was a lot closer than a hospital, but a criminal doctor knowing Butterfly's ID seemed even worse.

"You'll need to stay with her and make sure he doesn't remove her mask, but it's the best bet," Jackal said.

"A patch guy will need money," Flare said.

"I'll meet you with money," Osprey said.

"Fly, what do you want?" I asked.

No response.

"Fly?"

She was unconscious.

I turned to Peregrine. "Do it! Go! I'll be right behind you."

He picked her up. He'd already pressed white gauze on the worst of the cuts. The gauze had turned bloody and moving her body made it worse.

Flare sent a pulse through a skylight and Peregrine disappeared with Butterfly in his arms.

Osprey was next out the door and Flare followed.

It would take me fifteen minutes to reach Grandend and 123rd, so I dropped back to the floor and found the nearest unconscious thug. I grabbed his phone, and when I was a couple blocks away, I called the SSA hotline, reporting the fight and the presence of Slicer and his crew at that address.

My voice was distorted, so I assume they realized it was one of the Guard. I tossed the phone on the bed of a passing truck.

TWENTY

Jackal walked me through how to get into the mob hospital. The guy at the door saw me and opened the door to let me in. The hallway was poorly lit. The place looked like a cellar full of crap people didn't need after a flood had destroyed their dude ranch.

An old woman was scrubbing the floor. She looked up at me, stopped her scrubbing and pointed to the left, then went back to her work -- mopping up Butterfly's blood.

I hadn't even realized the tunnel went that direction. I made sure not to knock over any of the crates of pinball parts and pushed open a door that stuck a little.

"This is a hospital?" I whispered to Jackal.

"No, but he's the best doctor in the area. Plus, he has a few parahuman tricks up his sleeve." Jackal seemed a little tense. "That being said, he's not a friend. Not an enemy, but Morries is for himself first."

I don't think he liked bringing us here. Maybe he didn't want us coming to a dangerous place, or maybe he didn't want to burn any contacts. But he'd done it anyway. That meant... something.

The hallway ended in darkness, but I pushed on the wall and it moved easily. White light poured through from a small operating room. It actually looked clean, except for some smudges of fresh blood. The walls were tiled, but also draped in a clear plastic, and a tarp was on the floor. The beep of medical instruments was faint, and Butterfly was on an operating table.

"Is she going to be alright?" That was Peregrine. I would recognize his voice modulation anywhere.

A bag marked O negative was plugged into her vein as well as a clear bag. She wasn't moving.

Flare was looking over the doctor's shoulder.

He had a mask on, partly standard issue medical like I've seen in all the medical dramas, but also partly identity protection. He was short, wide, and working quickly.

There was a nurse in the room as well. She was either a child or a very short adult. Her hair was long and dark, and she wore the same type of mask as the doctor.

That's when I noticed all the blood covering the doctor's smock and Peregrine.

That couldn't be good.

Flare and Peregrine turned to me when the door slapped shut behind me.

"This is your fault!" Peregrine pointed a finger at me and took the few steps to get right in my face.

"My fault? We were trying to save your ass!" I didn't back down in the least. "You'd gotten pinned by Slicer and in a second he would have ended you."

"You're the reason we had to worry about Slicer in the first place," he shot back.

"Why? Because I didn't kill him like you and your new buddy would have? Is that your plan? Just kill all the people you don't like? That won't leave much of the city."

"You don't know what you're talking about."

"First Sly, then the other guy." Yeah, in the heat of the moment I forgot the other guy's name. If any of the other guy's loved ones are reading this, I apologize.

"What?" He actually seemed confused.

"And then there's all the people who worked for him. How well do you vet your mass murderers? I mean, is there a level that you decide they need to reach before you kill them, or is it good enough that they're standing next to someone who you heard from a guy who said he might be bad?"

"Raven." Jackal spoke just to me. "Perhaps this isn't the room to air all our laundry."

He was right. "Fine, we can talk about this later."

"That would be appreciated," Morries said. He dropped his tools in a metal tub of water on a tray and stood back.

"Is she going to be alright?" Flare asked.

"No, she's going to die," Morries said.

That got us all looking in the same direction.

"What?" Peregrine asked.

"She needs something, something expensive. And I have not seen any money yet." Morries scanned us, looking for who was in charge.

Peregrine moved forward, but I held him back. "Let's not hurt or piss off the only person who can save Butterfly."

He pushed against my grip, but just to get my hands off him.

I let him go, but kept an eye on him. "The money is coming." Probably. If Osprey was legit. "You get nothing if she dies."

The doctor nodded. "It may surprise you, but I have done this before. I do jobs on credit, but your credit's no good, especially now. You're the Guard, but you've turned a lot more violent. I will not put myself out there for no chance of reimbursement."

"You know the Guard has money." I didn't know if he knew anything of the sort.

"Raptor has money, but I don't see Raptor here." Morries looked around.

"Morries," Jackal said in surround sound.

I pulled the idol out.

"You know my credit's good."

I think he was shocked. I know I was. Jackal had just publicly announced to someone he did not trust that he was working with us. That could be dangerous to him.

"Well, well, Jackal." Morries made a clicking noise.

"You owe me," Jackal said. "Do it."

Morries spread his arms expansively. "If this is how you want to cash in your chit."

"Do it."

"Madam K, please." Morries gestured to his nurse.

She set down the instruments she'd been cleaning and approached Butterfly. "This will hurt and be dramatic." Her voice did not sound young and she had an European accent. "If you touch her or me, the process will not work."

"Do what she says," Jackal warned. "We only get one shot at this."

Morries nodded.

Madam K, if that was indeed her name, started to sway and bounce a little on the balls of her feet. Then she slammed both hands on Butterfly's temples. "She is so weak, we may be too late."

Butterfly arched as if electrocuted and Madam K did as well.

Light started to crackle, first from Madame K's eyes, then her hands where they touched Butterfly. The light got brighter and brighter, then snaked around Butterfly's wound. Those lights exploded in light of their own, becoming little fountains.

Butterfly started to hover over the operating table, only moored by Madame K's grip, or she would have started floating around the room.

While the show was going on, Morries removed his operating togs and gloves and dumped them in a plastic dumper like the scene we were witnessing was just another day at the office. After he'd removed his bloody smock, he pulled a couple of energy drinks from a mini-fridge.

The light went out and Butterfly bounced off the operating table.

Madam K stumbled back. I think she swore, but in a language I didn't recognize.

Morries cracked the safety seal on the energy drink and handed it to Madam K.

She turned from us, lifted her mask, and downed the contents.

The marks that Morries had patched up were now pink lines. Even the stitching was gone.

"Well?" I asked.

Morries checked Butterfly's pulse and got out his stethoscope. "She needs rest, and a lot of fluid. But she'll be fine." He seemed to be smiling. "I so much prefer giving good news."

The flap door opened and Osprey entered. He plopped a duffel bag in front of the doctor.

The doctor bent and opened the bag. "Well, this is unnecessary. Jackal has already arranged payment."

The name Jackal got Osprey's attention. He spotted the statue in my hand.

"Keep it," Osprey said. "For the next time any of us need your services."

When did he get to use the term "us"? *We* are not an *us*. We are a few of us and definitely them.

Morries shrugged and picked up the duffel. "Then it is a pleasure doing business." He made a shooing motion. "This is not a long-term care. I do need to clean up this place for other clients."

Flare, being the only one not covered in blood, helped Butterfly stand.

Her uniform was in tatters and she wobbled a little.

Madam K was halfway through the second energy drink, but she retrieved a too large sweater and matching sweatpants. Flare took them and helped Butterfly dress.

I led the way out the way we'd come and into the back alley.

"This was a disaster," Osprey said.

"Not enough people dead for you?" No one called me a diplomat.

Osprey whirled on me. "The only reason your friend ended up on the operating table was because of your white hat bull--"

"No." Butterfly's voice was weak, but steady. "The reason that Slicer was there at all was because a lot of Earl Chadwick's competitors were ending up dead. He was forced to hire more protection." The effort of talking drained a little juice and she leaned more onto Flare.

Yeah, what she said.

"It doesn't matter," Flare said. "We need to get you off the street."

We didn't have a base anymore, not really.

"The Alpha site," Peregrine said.

"Sorry, she was talking to we," I said. "Psycho killers and accomplices need not apply."

"Raven!" Flare snapped. "Alpha site it is."

"I'll meet you there." I had to go hide the direct line to the psycho killer in my pocket. Boy, moral high ground is uneven and shifty.

Flare nodded. An aura went around her and Butterfly and they rose into the sky.

Leaving just me with team nut bar.

"You're not welcome at the Alpha site," I said, just to be a dick.

"So Jackal, can you hear me?" Osprey asked.

I'd stowed the statue already, hoping a little out-of-sight would also be out-of-mind.

"I can hear you," Jackal said at full volume.

Osprey walked toward me. "You've got this white hat all twisted up, working for you."

I didn't back down. There was no way I could out fight both of them, and there was no way I was outrunning Peregrine. So my back was against the wall. I actually started running the numbers. I had to strike first and strike hard. If I handed them the initiative, they would hand me my ass.

"Do you know what he did? What he has done?" Osprey asked me.

"Yep." First I'd have to go for his neck, then for Peregrine. If I could take Peregrine down I could try and outrun Osprey. It wouldn't be a given, Osprey was fast. But I knew this area like the back of my hand.

"And you call me a killer." Osprey's voice was low and dangerous.

"At least he's in prison, where you belong."

"Prison," Osprey repeated. "That won't keep you safe,

Jackal. I have a few things I'm going to take care of, then I'm coming for you."

"Oh, my pretty little birdy." Jackal's voice was honey. "I wouldn't have it any other way."

Osprey pulled away from me. "Peregrine, we have to salvage something out of tonight."

Peregrine didn't look like he'd been paying attention to the conversation, but he snapped to attention when the boss spoke. He took to the air, and Osprey held up his hand. Peregrine swooped down and grabbed him.

Now I was alone.

"I don't know, do you think we could patch things up?" Jackal asked.

Okay, not exactly alone.

I went back to the Alpha base via the place where I hide Jackal's statue.

"You know, Raven," Jackal said when I was slipping the idol into a bag.

"What?"

"You did the right thing with Slicer."

"I almost didn't." There had been murder in my heart. I'd watched Butterfly die right in front of me. It hadn't even occurred to me that she'd lived through that volley by Slicer. Maybe he'd been getting tired, or maybe she'd been just out of range, or maybe she'd used enough of her cognit ability to angle her body to survive. "I almost killed him. If it wasn't for you, I would have killed him." That was hard to say.

"You give me too much credit. You didn't kill him because you'd chosen who you were going to be a long time ago."

I didn't know what to say to that. I didn't know if he was right. I'd been so close to killing Slicer. It had been a coin flip. "Good night, Jackal." I dropped the idol in the bag.

TWENTY-ONE

I hadn't been to the Alpha site recently, but I was right. Ballista and Flare had been using it to train.

Even though it had been abandoned for a week, the place looked more worn, with a few new holes in the training room floor. Ballista's energy ball shaped holes.

Flare came out of the bunk room and shut the door. She seemed surprised to see me and jumped a little, an aura flashing around her arms for just a second.

I apologized for spooking her. "Is she okay?"

She shook her head. "She's pretty shook up. Not just the dying. She takes some responsibility for all those drug dealers being dead, too. She tracked them down for Peregrine."

One more reason Peregrine was a tool. "She had no idea what he was going to do with that information."

"I don't think Peregrine did, either."

"Then he's an idiot." What did he think Osprey would do with that information?

"No argument here." She sighed, clearly exhausted. "She doesn't look it," she used her thumb over her shoulder to indicate Butterfly, "but she's heavy. I don't think I could have carried her much farther."

I knew Butterfly would probably tax the limits of Flare's flight ability. She'd never offered me a ride.

"So what are we going to do about Peregrine? We need to talk to him before he does something stupid." Flare leaned against the wall and folded her arms.

"Really, the moron is so low on my priority list right now he's going to have to take care of himself. I have an apocalypse to stop." And just how was I supposed to do that? I would have to find the Worm, but he was far better at hiding than I was at seeking. Jackal had said he'd look into it, but how could he find him from inside prison? Although that's how I'd found him the first time.

Flare stood up and put a hand on my shoulder., "Wait, that zombie stuff? You're telling the truth? You actually think there's going to be a zombie apocalypse?"

"I said so, didn't I?"

"You say all kinds of stupid stuff."

Fair point.

It kind of surprised me that she didn't know already. I mean, why hadn't Tor filled her in? But I couldn't say that. I couldn't even say how I knew. "I heard it from some SSA I was spying on."

"You spy on SSA?" Her voice sounded like she'd just delivered exhibit one for the "he says stupid stuff, Your Honor" case.

"Yeah, kinda. It doesn't matter. At Mercy General today, there was an incident and I'm afraid it's just the start of many."

"Mercy General?" She'd started to put pieces in place. Her boyfriend and the new kid had been at that hospital.

"It has something to do with Stardust," I said. "Stardust and a yellow gas."

"I… I have to go 511."

A five-eleven was the code we used when we had to deal with real life when we were on patrol.

She looked a little lost. There weren't a lot of places to go in the Alpha base to have a private conversation.

I moved so I was no longer blocking the training room.

She nodded and hurried past me.

Now I was a little lost. I had to get back out there and find the Worm or the Legacy. But Jackal didn't have any information for me to use now that our one lead had burned up.

So I wandered into the main conference room because it had chairs. The room was seventy percent the size of the entire base, but was the same size as the meeting room in the Gamma base. Man, I missed the Clubhouse. Stupid villains and blowing it up and stuff.

As I entered the room a "ding" sounded. The microwave. Ballista removed a noodle cup and shut the door.

"Ballista?" I'd almost said David because he wasn't wearing his mask. But that would have been okay since he'd told me his name the first time I'd seen him without his mask. He just didn't know what I looked like or my name. Or that we now went to the same school. Oh, this double life stuff was a pain in the ass.

"Raven." He was dressed in his uniform, dark purple and light purple. His mask sat on the conference table alongside a lunchbox. He hadn't brought a lunchbox with him on the drive to the Kages forever and a day ago, so it must have been here already. He looked guilty, like he was going to lunge for his mask. It was against regs to be in a common space without a mask.

I held up my hand. “Finish your dinner.” Then I had to pretend that I didn’t know Flare was his adopted sister. “But Flare’s here. Does she know your face?”

His shoulders sunk a little. “Yeah, she knows. Sorry, man.” He removed his cup of noodles.

Boy, did that look good. I hadn’t eaten anything since lunch and my stomach grumbled. But it’s tough to eat in a mask.

His shoulders deflated a little more. “She's not going to be pumped I’m still here. I was supposed to go home.” He took a seat at the conference table with his noodles and a can of soda.

I sat and put my feet up on the table across from him. “Why are you here?”

“I wanted to practice more.” He slurped up some noodles, then waved a hand in front of his mouth and sucked in air when he realized they were too hot.

“And what you wanted to practice wasn’t what Flare wanted you to practice?”

He shrugged. I thought that was all I was going to get out of him, but he continued. “She wants me to control small things and dissipate the energy.”

“Not blow the hell out of things.”

“I should know how to do both.” He picked up the argument he’d had with Flare in mid-anger.

I raised my hands. “I’m on your side here, B.”

He settled down and tried another spoonful of noodles. “It’s just been worse since we found out what Red Knight was.”

“It” was probably his relationship with Jasmin.

"She keeps talking about quitting and hiding our powers."

"It isn't a bad plan." Isn't that what I had chosen to do?

"But we were given these gifts. Shouldn't we use them to help people?"

He didn't sound all fried and psychotic. That was good. That was very good. "It's not that simple."

"I just feel every time I choose to hide, to play it safe, I'm becoming someone who hides, instead of someone like you," he said around another bite.

"Like me?"

"Yeah. I mean, you lost your mentor like Flare and me. But you haven't given up. You're still out there doing what the Guard should do. Just because things are bad you don't want to give up."

"Oh, Ballista. I want to give up every day. I keep trying to give up." I didn't want to say that, but it was the truth.

"Yeah, right."

Fine, I wasn't going to convince him that I was a cheap imitation of the Guard who'd set up this base. "Okay, show me what you can do."

He looked up from his noodles. "What?"

"You've been practicing control. Red Knight was evil, but he seemed like a hell of a coach." While Red Knight had been pretending to be a good guy, he'd taken an interest in getting Ballista up to speed. Probably in an effort to exploit Ballista's powers for some horrible endgame, but how much damage could he do in like three days?

Ballista put down his spoon. "Okay." He limbered up his shoulders.

"Mask." Best to keep in practice. Mask on, power okay, but no mask, no powers. I'm sure that's why Jasmin doesn't glow every time she gets pissed.

Ballista nodded and put his helmet on. "Right." His vocal distortion kicked in and he sounded more like the Ballista I knew. "Okay."

He opened his palms and two spheres appeared in each of them.

I'd never seen him manifest two at the same time. That was pretty cool. Also, he seemed okay for them to be just sitting there in his hands. A month ago they would have jetted off and exploded, either into a puff of harmless nothingness or by blowing a Volkswagen-sized hole in concrete. You didn't know which you were going to get.

The spheres of energy raised from his hands, but just hovering, like glowing and dangerous soap bubbles.

I clapped. "Nice."

"For my next act." He was concentrating and focused. The soap bubbles drifted towards each other until they touched and then they became one big bubble.

"Ah." Could that end all life as we know it?

"And for the grand finale." He twitched his wrists and the bubble split into dozens of pebble-sized bubbles that shot out, popping the second they touched anything solid. It was like a micro firework in the council room.

None of the small explosions did any damage and the ones that touched me I didn't even feel.

"Wow." That was a huge improvement over just last week. "You're learning fast."

For a second he stood a little taller. Then his shoulders slumped. "I'm learning how to do a light show. It takes a lot of focus and control, but it isn't really useful."

"You think Flare's light show isn't useful?" I said. "Her blinding attack has saved my bacon more than once."

"Yeah, I suppose." I think his wheels started spinning.

"If I focus a little more on it." A new sphere appeared, shot up about a foot, and popped in a white light.

If I hadn't had my helmet with my eye shields, I would have been seeing spots.

"Oops." Ballista waved his hand like he'd picked up something hot. "First I think it, then it just happens." He didn't seem very apologetic. He'd just found a tactical use for his parlor trick.

My work here was done.

"Could you train me to fight?" Ballista asked.

"Ah, well." My powers actually make me the worst teacher. I don't have to go through the trouble of practicing stuff. If I'm shown a skill a couple times, I'm ready to go. "I'm not a good teacher. But I'll do what I can." Not sure how that would happen, or if that would fly with Flare.

A phone started ringing.

"That yours?"

Oh, crap. I'd brought a phone that a villain had given me into our secretish base. *You moron.* Here I was giving crap to the kid about putting his mask on. At least it looked like a burner phone. And it wasn't like this place was secure, anyway.

I fished it out of my belt pouch. "Super villain on line one." I held a finger to where my lips would be if I wasn't wearing a mask. "Hello?" I always feel like I should have a better way to start these kinds of conversations. Like something cool, but instead I just say hello. I guess it's better than "What's up?" or "Yo."

"Raven." It was the Confessor's voice. "It seems you are correct." And he was not happy. "I have been used. The person I was able to track down and get a confession out of confirmed what you said. He didn't know why they were doing it, but Stardust is the first ingredient. It primes part of the brain, then Perdition is added. The Perdition triggers prepared brains. Drives them crazy."

Okay, Perdition seemed as good a name for the yellow gas as anything. "Are the effects permanent?" I had no idea what was going on with Isaiah.

"I don't think they've done too much long term testing."

So now what? He believed me. "What are you going to do about it?"

"Me? Nothing. I'm not the hero type. That's your job. But I do know where a shipment is coming in. At the docks, tonight, in mere hours." He rattled off the cargo area. I didn't know what the numbers meant, but I wrote them down on a pad sitting on the conference table.

"So tell the SSA." That's what my next call would be.

"Well, that's an issue. The gentleman I got my confession from was an SSA operative," the Confessor said. "Very curious. I don't think you can trust them. Not all of them at least. If another shipment of Stardust hits the city with a large quantity of Perdition... well, it's a matter of time. Good luck. I like your chances. You seem to have gumption." The line went dead.

I ripped out the battery and plopped both parts in the noodle soup.

"Hey!" Ballista reached out for his soup.

"Flare!" I yelled. We had to get the band back together. I had no idea what we were going to do, but we were it. The Confessor could be wrong about the SSA, but he could be right, and the stakes were too high.

TWENTY-TWO

"What is this guy doing here!" It wasn't really a question, and I yelled it into Osprey's face.

We'd all met a little way over from the actual address. It took me the longest to get there, like always. It was a quarter to midnight. God knows where Dad thought I was.

And where was I? On top of a stack of shipping containers down by the docks in the presence of Flare, Peregrine, and Osprey. I had a question about that. "Seriously, why is this butt nugget here?"

He didn't back down. "Why are you here?" he shot back.

"This is the only lead I have to stop a zombie apocalypse!" Okay, I know there's some armchair righteous indignationing going on here, but you try pulling that sentence off.

"You moron." Osprey shook his head like I was the stupidest person he'd ever seen.

I think he's a complete psychotic tool, but I can't blame him. Again, you try pulling off the apocalypse sentence. "It's true."

"Something happened at the hospital tonight," Flare said. "They aren't really zombies."

"No kidding," Osprey and I said simultaneously. But I said it with irony. He was still in "moron" mode.

"But all the people who'd used Stardust lost their minds and tried to kill everyone else," I said. "And it happened after the Worm sprayed them with yellow gas."

"The Worm?" Now it was Flare's and Osprey's turn to do the unison thing.

"It could have been the Worm." I shouldn't know it was the Worm. "I mean, the description I heard made me think the Worm. I guess I don't know if it was the Worm." Crap. This double life thing sucks.

"The Worm doesn't make sense," Peregrine said. "I thought he worked for Caesar. How would he get to the point of controlling a new street drug?"

Normally Peregrine is the one I'm arguing with, so his calm voice of wisdom threw me. "How do I know? Who cares? Sorry I mentioned the Worm." So very, very sorry. "The main point is, why is this psycho killer here? We have to figure out how to stop a load of drugs and gas from hitting the streets, not slaughter a bunch of defenseless vanillas. If that was the case, I'd have him on speed dial."

I thought Osprey was going to hit me. "They weren't defenseless. They all had guns, and they were drug-dealing pimp scum."

"You asshole, guns are not a defense against a super who's bulletproof." I had to break that down. "And you were not trying to defend--"

"I was trying to finish what the Guard started," Osprey cut in. "Making the city safer."

"Do you think the criminals of this town will wake up and decide to go into the food service industry instead?"

Now who's the moron? "They're going to get bigger and badder weapons and supers. You're not making anyone safe, you're just speeding up the arms race."

"Better than what you did, keep letting them go until your team member winds up dead." Osprey slashed a thumb in the general direction of the Kages.

I was about to skewer him with my wit and cunning, but Peregrine saved him.

"There's something going on." Peregrine had the super hearing and vision thing. He turned his head in the direction of the address the Confessor had given me.

"Check it out," Flare prodded.

Peregrine took to the air, vanishing into the dark.

"Keep out of sight," Flare ordered, taking charge of the situation.

I lifted my hand to ask the question again. No one had told me why Osprey was standing in front of me.

"Because we need his help," Flare answered before I said anything. "Butterfly is out, and there's no one else."

No one besides a one-person prepubescent demolish and light show. But I didn't really want to put Ballista in the field. I'd almost lost him once already when Silhouette grabbed him.

"Peregrine said you had a lead on the Stardust," Osprey said. "That's why I'm here. If this brings me back to the Confessor, the Confessor will lead me back to the serial killer."

"Serial killer?" Flare asked. There was an edge to her voice that I might not have caught if I wasn't accustomed to the vocal distortion.

"He's been killing blond women in the Kages for a decade." Osprey was still looking at me, though I wasn't the dangerous person on the roof. We both knew I could do little more than survive vs Osprey. "Orion was hunting him when I was an apprentice."

"Orion..." Flare's voice trailed off. "The guy who killed... Shannon Paris." I suspect she was about to say "Mom".

"That was one of his early victims. Then he disappeared for about five years, and now he's back at it." Osprey was oblivious to the wreckage he'd just caused.

"Not saying we ignore the serial killer." I wanted Flare to understand that I was on her side, without revealing that I knew who Shannon Paris was to her. "But we've got to stop--"

"Zombie apocalypse." Flare nodded. "That is the mission. Everything else is secondary. If Orion couldn't find him, and he looked for years, then we aren't going to do it tonight."

Wow, what do you say to that, without being able to say anything to it? She was all about the job, and not even her mother's killer was going to distract her. It had happened years ago, but still, I don't know if I would care about Worm and all the Legacy's yellow gas if the person who'd killed my sister was out there.

"Raven's intel looks good." Peregrine's voice came over the radio. "An SSA truck just pulled up. They're taking a shipment of something, and a lot of it."

"For all we know this is a trap," Osprey said. "They could be taking a shipment of SSA issue jockey shorts."

I didn't like the fact that Osprey was on the radio frequency. But of course Osprey and Peregrine were now one great big happy blood-bathing family. What other proprietary info did Osprey have? Thanks to Red Knight, he knew my first name, but only Peregrine knew my full name. Would they keep my secret if I opposed their plans to go big V vigilante?

"They're transporting pallets of propane tanks," Peregrine said.

"There you go," I said. "That's the Perdition, the yellow make-you-crazy gas."

"Still doesn't explain why the SSA would have it," Osprey said. "Where did you get this info?"

"The Confessor." I should have lied, but screw it. Maybe he would leave.

"The Confessor? Did he tell you over a milkshake? You have a way to get in touch with him?"

Yes, I do. "No, I had a burner phone he gave me at the last fight---"

"When you let him get away," Osprey accused.

"Or managed to not die, however you want to characterize it." This guy was such a tool. "I told him about the zombie thing and he tracked this down."

"Tell him about our theory," Jackal said into my head. I'd almost forgotten he was along.

"Jackal thinks this isn't an SSA operation. There's probably a person using the SSA resources to get their poison past customs." Yes, I dropped Jackal's name on purpose.

"Jackal." Osprey swore. "Phone calls from the Confessor, planning sessions with Jackal. Do you even know whose side you're on anymore?"

Coming from this guy, that was rich. "Everyone here who's not a confirmed murderer, raise your hand." I jammed up my arm. "Flare, let's get those hands in the air."

"Moron," Osprey spat.

Again with the moron. I'm not sure he likes me.

I let my arm drop. "I see you kept your arm down," I

told Osprey. "Thanks for playing my little game, psycho killer."

"Man, you really want this guy gone," Jackal said. "Can't blame you. He's kind of Peregrine raised to the next level."

Osprey took a step toward me, his hands balling into fists. "You have no idea what I've done, you little self-righteous white hat."

"Enough!" Fire sparked around Flare. She made sure we were listening. "Get into position. I'll wait here until it's game time, then fly in."

"Okay." I stood straight. I hadn't even realized I'd matched Osprey's combat stance with my own.

Osprey stood, too, giving Flare a nod. "Go. Don't be stupid." She said that like it was inevitable.

"I'll make sure he's fine," Osprey said.

"No, you won't. I'll make sure I'm fine all by myself." Literally a week ago he'd been trying to kill me. Well, injure me. Injure me really badly.

"Guys. If we're going to do something, we need to do something now," Peregrine said.

Osprey didn't bother waiting for me and took off with one of his great big leaps. He landed about sixty feet away without making a sound.

Well, I didn't have anything like that, so I started moving. The shipping yard was a great space for me. A lot of regular-shaped containers stacked close together made for a pretty good parkour run. Downside, it was still dark, and I didn't know the area.

"They're finishing some paperwork and loading up the truck," Peregrine informed us over the radio.

I landed on a shipping cart stacked one container lower, rolled, stood, and ran the length of the container.

"What's the SSA compliment?" Osprey asked, running away from me.

I jumped the gap between container stacks and kept running.

"Five Agents, one of those Shield guys, a girl with a pink mohawk, and an officer," Peregrine reported.

The Agents had a lot of gear and were pretty tough. I'd fought one of the Shield guys before. I came out the better side of that deal. I'd seen the mohawk punk rocker at a distance at the SSA crime scene in front of the Carlton. I didn't know what she could do, but she wouldn't be in the SSA if she wasn't powerful.

"The mohawk girl is Spike," Jackal informed me. "She can manifest these glowing spiky things that hurt and paralyze without leaving a mark."

"How do you know?" I asked Jackal.

"Because I'm looking right at them." Peregrine's tone gave me more of the moron thing.

"Word on the street, a batch of the SSA supers are making a name for themselves," Jackal said. "And by street, I mean lunch room."

Good enough for me. "Mohawk girl is Spike. She can paralyze you with energy spikes." I put on a little extra speed so I could run up a container wall, get my fingers on the top edge, and pull myself over in a roll.

I was making good time. I would be in position in just a minute.

"Now!" Osprey yelled.

"Ah... what? No, not now!" I wasn't ready.

I started running faster.

"What are you going to do when you get there?" Jackal asked.

"You ask that now?" I'd muted the radio so no one

would think I was crazy. Nope, just a completely sane young man in a vaguely bird-themed one piece running on big metal crates. At night.

"I'm just saying, I was kind of caught up in all the team building you were doing back there," Jackal said.

I had to slow into stealth mode now. I could see the headlights of a semi truck with SSA stamped on the side of it.

The agents had the full gear, net guns and everything, but they didn't have their weapons out. "They don't seem ready for a fight."

"That's good. Unless they're trying to lure you into a trap," Jackal said.

"Trap?"

"Sure. The Confessor sets you up and the second you strike, dozens of agents and supers pile out of the truck."

Nice thought. "Peregrine, are you hearing anything in the truck?" Then I took myself off mute and said the same thing again.

There was a pause before he responded. "No, there's nothing."

I didn't know where Osprey or Peregrine were anymore. I hoped Peregrine was seeing everything worth seeing.

I used my vantage to plot a course. I would have to get on the ground. Walking on the containers was just too loud. This was a shipping dock, so it wasn't still and silent, but I didn't want to draw attention.

I dropped to the ground.

"Do you really think the Confessor was so angry at whoever hookwinked him that he turned them over to you?" Jackal asked.

"It seems that way." I didn't have any other ideas.

“Seems like what?” Flare asked.

“Nothing.” I muted my radio again, dropped to the ground in a roll, and started making my way toward the truck. “What if we just tell the SSA that they’re shipping Perdition for the Legacy?”

“If you get them to believe you, then they’ll say thanks and arrest you,” Jackal said. “If you need a character reference, I’m your man.”

“So we steal the truck?” And what?

“And what?”

“We destroy the Perdition. Flare should be able to make short work of some canisters.” That was the only plan I had.

“Assuming Perdition isn’t flammable and explosive. Then we could be talking major explosion here.”

I unmuted. “Okay, guys, what’s our plan?”

“Wreck all their stuff and make our escape,” Osprey said.

“We don’t have any other options,” Flare agreed.

“Just keep in mind we don’t have any idea how flammable this stuff is.” I might as well try to be safe.

“Good point. Let’s find out. Now!” Osprey yelled.

TWENTY-THREE

"What? Not now! So not now!" I wasn't in position. I heard the "Now!" over my radio just as Osprey landed on the truck. He turned up his solid to an eleven and accordioned the engine like he was a cartoon anvil. It sounded like a car crash.

"Huh, I guess we have ourselves a ballgame." I could almost hear Jackal chomping popcorn.

Damn it, I knew it was stupid bringing Osprey.

I started running. Stealth was no longer needed. I saw Flare's green zip overhead and beat me to the scene.

See? We were supposed to wait until we were all ready. That was the plan. Wait until we were *all* ready. It wasn't that complicated, we barely did any planning. And we couldn't even manage that.

I rounded a corner and spotted an agent in full-on riot gear taking aim at Flare with one of his tripped out rifles. At least, I assumed he was aiming at Flare. He was pointing up. It could have been at Peregrine, but he was harder to see and in the fight he didn't stay above the fray.

I ran and slid low like I was going into home plate. I cut

him off at the knees and his shot spun wide. The discharge was a deafening boom. Blue glittering pellets banged and popped off with metal clinks and fizzes as they ricocheted off the metal shipping containers. I continued the momentum and dropped the guy right on his back.

Pro tip: The SSA agents were well armored, but they were kind of like turtles if you could knock them over.

The agent managed to keep hold of his weird space rifle, so I grabbed it and pulled. It was strapped around his shoulder.

"Behind you!" Jackal shouted into my head.

I bent backwards and looked behind me. One of the other agents had put a bead on me with a similar sparkle cannon.

If the shot would have connected, it might have done something to me. I don't know. Instead, I got the first agent's weapon in the way and it crackled with electricity all the way down so he twitched like he was being tasered.

That worked, I guess.

I turned the momentum of my dodge into a flip and did another flip. Agent Two took another shot at me, missed, and I covered enough distance to duck behind a conveniently placed shipping container.

The shot that had missed and another shot hissed and sizzled off a container. I made sure that I was not actually touching the container, just in case the electricity had enough juice to conduct.

Also, sure hoped there wasn't anything combustible in the containers. A spark from those joy buzzer guns could start all kinds of drama.

"How did you know?" I whispered.

"Raven, get out here!" Osprey was in pain and talking through it.

"Who knew what?" Peregrine yelled.

I didn't have time to follow up with Jackal. He'd once told me that if he concentrated he could get vague impressions of what was happening around his focuses, in my case, the idol. The problem was, he was full of crap and I'd suspected he was lying. He'd never proven it before, and it wasn't like this was the worst situation I'd ever been in.

But more importantly, why wasn't I hearing all kinds of green death from above? "Flare?"

"Flare is down!" Osprey said through clenched teeth.

That was not good, She was our big gun and she'd already dropped.

"Get out here!" Osprey yelled before he screamed in rage and pain.

I listened for the SSA agent, but he wasn't following. The shipping container I'd ducked behind wasn't that well placed to provide cover for a run.

I did a quick jump and got my fingers around the edge of the container, pulled myself up, rolled, and ran to the other side. I didn't dare take the time to judge the distance perfectly, but the agent had only moved a little. I was able to clip him with a clothesline as I propelled myself off the container and turned my momentum into a roll and stand with my back to the SSA truck.

I didn't knock the guy out cold or anything, but he was struggling to get off his back. I took a second to survey the battlefield.

Flare was indeed out. She was spread on the pavement face down. A large glowing pink spike stuck out of her head.

"They killed Flare!"

"No, she's just in a lot of pain," Jackal said. "Spike's spikes don't kill, but if she gets a headshot it will put you out."

Good to know. And no one had said anything about a headshot. More proof he could see what was going on.

Spike, the girl with the mohawk and dozens of piercings in her ears, nose, and lip, was facing down Osprey.

Osprey was solid and heavy. The asphalt bent into little indentations under his feet.

There were a couple of footprints behind him. His chest and arms were pincushioned in glowing pink spikes. He looked like a porcupine in drag.

Spike, who looked about my age, was sweating and not looking confident, but not giving ground, either. She kept throwing more spikes into Osprey as he took steps through the pain to get closer to her.

She flicked her hand as I watched and a small slender spike caught Osprey in the thigh.

He groaned in pain and staggered. His bulletproof nature didn't seem to help him with the spikes. Neither did Flare's force field for that matter.

Peregrine was finishing off the last agent standing. Another agent was on the floor and not moving. Probably Peregrine's work. I recognized the brush strokes.

A few of the dock workers had abandoned the pallets of propane containers on a fork lift and were running away from the fight. Smart dock workers, clever dock workers.

A man in a SSA uniform but not all kitted up was not running. A clipboard sat at his feet, and he'd just finished assembling some kind of rifle. He leveled it at Peregrine.

"Peregrine, your six!" I yelled. I think I kicked the agent before he got on his feet, but that was an automatic muscle memory thing. I don't really remember it.

Peregrine used his crazy versatile flight to shoot himself to the left.

The paperwork rifle guy still took the shot. The bullet

fired with a roar and sliced right through the mangled truck's front end and buried itself into a container.

Okay, I missed the Buck Rogers fun guns.

Peregrine didn't waste the opportunity. He streaked back before the gunman could take another shot, grabbed the gun on his way by, and used it for a headshot on the fourth agent, then spun around to strike Spike.

Man, I wish I could fly.

Didn't Peregrine say something about a Shield guy?

No sign of him. Maybe Peregrine or Osprey had already tussled with him before I'd gotten there.

Or maybe he'd had a crazy amount of foresight.

As Peregrine rushed toward Spike, I saw the grey and blue uniform as the Shield bearer jumped from the top of a shipping container.

Shield and Peregrine collided.

There must be something funny about those shields, because Peregrine's impact did not alter the Shield's momentum at all. Peregrine's momentum got impacted all over the place.

They both dropped to the ground, the Shield in a cool three-point landing, his non-shielded arm supporting him, his left arm up, protecting his head.

Peregrine landed like a heap of overripe melons.

I took a quick headcount. Just me and Osprey. And Osprey didn't look like he had much more in him. I wasn't sure if Shield could do anything to him when he was this solid, but Osprey couldn't keep that up forever. The only way he was enduring the pain of those spikes was maxing out his solidification power. If he pushed his power any more, he wouldn't be able to move.

"You have got to take out Spike, now," Jackal said.

"It's a pretty target-rich environment," I pointed out, but

I didn't have a problem with that. Okay, I had a little problem with it. I mean, I didn't want to beat up a girl. I know I've fought female adversaries before, but this close she looked like she was fifteen playing dress up in some tactical gear. Also, she looked terrified. And she wasn't some thug trying to kill me, she was a government agent risking her life to protect people.

"Once she's done with Osprey, she's going to cut you up and you're done," Jackal warned.

Great.

"Or run now," Jackal added.

And condemn Flare, Peregrine, and Osprey to prison. I couldn't do that to Flare. Also, I was no closer to stopping the zombie thing. It wasn't really a debate. I had to go through Spike. I just felt a little bad about it.

I jumped, scaled up the semi-truck, and ran along the roof. The paperwork SSA guy spotted me and yelled, "Shield, up on the truck."

Before I'd run the length, the Shield ran up the broken cab and onto the trailer. These guys were a kind of mysterious subsection of the Agents. They all had the same blue and grey uniform. Their faces were covered in a mask except their mouths. Fun fact that the chin revealed, they're all white guys, every single one of them. You'd think that would be a discrimination problem somewhere. I mean, what's stopping minorities from carrying around a shield? Maybe everyone else knows that a gun is better.

The second he saw me, he didn't hesitate, just ran right for me. Man, this guy looked exactly like the last Shield I'd fought. So either this guy healed up fast, or they really stressed the exact same look.

My objective wasn't to get in a tussle with a Shield, so I ran at him, too, and did a flying kick at his head.

He pulled his shield up to block my strike, like you do when you have a shield. Now I had a platform and used it to leapfrog over him and get a little extra air. I somersaulted and brought my legs out to connect right with Spike's mohawk.

And it would have worked, too, but Shield tackled me in midair and we both crashed onto the asphalt.

I was able to see the Spike/Osprey battle of endurance. Osprey was wracked with pain. I couldn't see his face but I could hear his grunting and the effort he put into each step. Spike was weaving for air, sweat streaming off her face, the spikes that she made getting smaller and smaller and not glowing as much.

The Shield did some Greco-Roman crap on me and got me pinned. I couldn't move.

Osprey gave a yell and took a step closer. He was now in striking distance. Instead of taking a step back, Spike stepped forward at the same time. A huge, bright, glowing pink spike formed in both hands and she stepped in, jamming it up through Osprey's chin and out the back of his head.

He arched and fell backwards.

That was intrinsically badass. I mean, it couldn't have happened to a nicer guy. I'd wanted to hear Osprey make that sound since I'd met him. Downside, if I didn't figure out something quick, I would spend the rest of my life in a parahuman detention facility. But still, good for Spike.

Even though he had leverage on me, about a year ago Raptor and Cat had run me through wrestling moves for like forty minutes. So, I was probably as good at wrestling as anyone. I'd rather be able to fly, but my power has its perks.

I twisted and flipped him off me. He recovered and

dove back, getting me in another hold. Damn, this guy was quick.

"Where's Raptor?" Wow, this Shield had the same voice as the last Shield.

"Well, I'll tell you -- oh wait, you're a crazy government type that wants to arrest him." I got my feet underneath me and tossed him off.

He landed like a cat, and got his shield up to absorb the kicks from my counterattack. "No way would he be okay with the crap you kids are pulling."

I blocked his punch, but had to hop back to avoid his shield punch. "That's not true. Raptor would be all about kicking your ass."

He followed up the shield punch with the hard press. I had to give more ground.

"Don't talk to him, drop him and drop Spike," Jackal ordered.

Like it was that easy. This guy was good. I could tell he'd been taught at the same school as the other Shield guy. Even if they weren't dressed in the same getup and shield, I would have known that this guy fought like the other Shield. "You're one to talk. Do you even know why you're here? Or are you just an idiot?"

"I'm not the one trying to steal sedatives!" he yelled. I think he was getting frustrated. He had the momentum, but couldn't land a good enough strike to take care of business.

The Shield tried too hard, and I was able to lock him in an arm bar. "Sedatives?"

"Bio-Globe is in disarray." He said that like it was my fault.

Technically it was Osprey's fault. He'd killed the second in command guy under Red Knight's orders. The president of the company, a.k.a. Raptor, had died three weeks ago. And Raptor's wife was on the lam. I didn't know who was running things over there.

"We need to get more cuff sedative. We're running low." He twisted -- that must have hurt -- and got out of my arm bar.

I didn't let him keep the momentum and timed a shot to his face when he was using his shield to swing at me.

He staggered, and now I was keeping on the pressure. "This isn't the sedative you use to keep parahumans drugged, you moron. This is Perdition. The same--" Got a little carried away with exposition there. He swept my legs right out from under me, and followed it up with a shot to my stomach.

"Who told you that?" He pointed at Osprey. "Him? He's using you."

"Old news," I hissed through the pain. I tried to get up, but he stopped me and gave me another good kick to the ribs.

"You dumb kid. You think killing all those people makes you a hero? Makes you important?" He pulled a pair of industrial strength handcuffs from his belt and rolled me over. "When did the Guard become murderers?"

"The Guard aren't murderers." I struggled, but got nowhere.

"I got a mountain of bodies with his MO that says otherwise." Again he was talking about Osprey.

"He's not a Guard." I had to move. If I had a chance, I had to move.

He grabbed my wrist.

"Looks like you're on the same team to me. You should have come to us. We could have trained you. You have some skills and ability, you could have been part of something."

"I am part of something." I spun and took his leg out, then axe kicked him in the face.

Lucky shot, Shield was stunned.

I kiped up. "I'm a Guard!"

"Okay, that was just cool," Jackal said. "You can't hear it, but I'm golf clapping."

"Thanks."

"Not just kidding here, lots of punk points," Jackal continued. "So how is Spike doing?"

Good point. I turned to see where she was, and searing pain started in my shoulder.

"So she's doing good then," Jackal noted.

I dropped to a knee and instinctively clutched at the glowing spike sticking out of my shoulder. And I may have done a lot of swearing.

"Get on the ground." She said it so faintly and she was panting so hard I had to ask.

"What?"

"Get ... On... THE GROUND!" Another spike formed, but this one didn't glow like the others.

In fact, the one in me wasn't glowing that brightly, either. Still stung my hands like crazy when I touched it. It hurt a lot as I stood. "No."

She took a couple of steps closer and the spike flew at me.

I was ready for it and bent away from it. Almost blacked out as I jarred the spike in me, but I didn't get stuck twice, so in the official tally I'm calling that a win. Mostly a win.

"You have got to listen to me." My vocal distortion concealed the pain, I hope. "Those canisters aren't what you think they are."

She didn't say anything, but she didn't create festively colored spikes of pain, so I kept talking.

"You've been lied to." Hopefully you've been lied to, and aren't one of the Legacy people in on the plot.

"You're the one who's been lied to." She pointed a trembling hand at Osprey. "Do you have any idea what he's been doing! What your team has been doing?"

"Okay, fun fact, I hate that guy. He's a complete tool. He should be locked up. He's tried to kill me like a bazillion times in the last couple of weeks. He's not part of the team."

"He isn't Osprey, trained by Raptor, to be a member of the Guard?"

"Well, no, that's true." I had to give her that.

"You've got me convinced," Jackal said.

"But that's not all the truth," I said.

"Let's keep on mission: zombie apocalypse," Jackal said. "Or you could just hit her for the love of all that is holy!"

With the spike in my shoulder, my range of motion was in the toilet, but my feet still worked. I took a couple steps toward her. "Just open one of those canisters. It's not sedative for your cuffs. It's the missing ingredient in a great big batch of crazy pie!"

She followed my finger to the racks of propane containers.

That's when I remembered the paperwork guy. He'd been busy. He had one of the unconscious agent's guns out and leveled it at me.

"Come on!" I dived, purely on instinct, and dodged another shot of those blue pebble things that zipped over my head.

And the spike lit my shoulder on fire and my right arm was no longer open for business. It flopped and created more fire. I compensated and got Spike between me and the bureaucrat.

"Are you the one in on it?" I put my left hand around Spike's throat and pulled her back against my hip.

She tried to fight, but she was exhausted. That's when it clicked for me. She wasn't just exhausted because she'd made a bunch of spike things. She was out of it because she was still powering each of those spikes. Just the number in Osprey alone would be enough to keep her winded.

"Surrender or I will fire." The paperwork guy flipped a switch on his weapon.

"Captain." Spike sounded nervous. Not because I had her in a half nelson, but because that switch had gotten flipped. "That level is lethal!"

TWENTY-FOUR

And he fired.

In that split second I realized who the Legacy mole was. This guy was totally cool with frying Spike to get to me.

Yes, of course I got Spike out of the way of the shot. I twisted and flipped both of us to the ground.

The packet of crackling energy glowed white hot and bright as it streamed past me.

But as I was flipping Spike to safety, I also flipped her onto Osprey.

She landed on all of her own spikes. They sizzled right through her body. I'd figured she might be immune to her own power. I was wrong.

She had a second to scream in pain, then she went limp.

The spike in my shoulder disappeared, leaving nothing but a slight ache of a memory.

I thought maybe the rest of the team would be able to get up and at 'em, but Flare was still unconscious. The same with Osprey. Spike was on top of Osprey, not moving, so that was good.

I took in all that in a second, stood, and ran at the Captain in one motion.

The full power charge must have been all the gun had because he threw it away without even trying for a click and ran at me with a dagger.

I think this guy actually knew how to use a blade. He slashed at me when we got in range, but he was still a vanilla. On my worst day I was faster. I hopped over his slash and landed a kick to his face.

He staggered back.

I took the weapon and slugged him hard in the stomach. "Who are the Legacy?" I yelled.

"Ah, kid, not so loud," Jackal warned.

What was he talking about? The SSA had been shooting off uber stun guns. This was not a stealth operation.

Paperwork guy looked at me, took a valiant stab at making a fighting stance, then bent over like he was dry heaving. "They are here." He moaned and spit up a mouth full of black gunk that splattered on the floor. "They are ..." He was trying to talk, but couldn't.

"Carl?" Shield said right behind me.

I hadn't noticed he'd gotten up, but he wasn't attacking me, so good?

"Steven," Carl moaned. "Help me." He dropped to his knees and a torrent of that goo spilled out.

Shield -- this one was Steven I guess -- started toward his side.

"No," I warned.

Carl had another knife. He pulled it and stabbed at Steven.

I don't know if it was my warning, or if Steven was just badass, but he got the shield up easily, blocked the strike, and took the knife. "What's going on?" He was more horrified at the sludge that continued to vomit up and pour out of Carl's eyes like tears of oil than at the attempted murder.

"He's controlled," I said. "Using you, using the SSA to get that stuff in the city." I pointed at the tanks.

"Carl?" Shield asked.

"It's true. You have to hit me. You have to beat it out of me," Carl gargled over the goo that dribbled out of his mouth.

"You're my friend. I can't," Shield said.

I kicked Carl in the groin then in the stomach again, ending with a right cross. I shrugged at the Shield's look. "He's not my friend."

Man, I'm a jerk.

The goop was now streaming out of him, just like Zed had said happened with Caesar's assassin. Just like I'd seen with Clockwork.

"Go check that tank," I said. "See for yourself."

He looked at his friend, then at me, then at the nearest group of propane tanks. He walked over to the first one and put his hand on the tank release.

"You haven't ever used Stardust have you?" I asked.

He gave me a look.

"I'm just saying, if you've used it, you'll go a little loopy." And zombie cops were bad enough.

At that moment, Peregrine woke up and jetted right for Shield.

"No, wait!" I yelled.

Shield didn't need my warning and got his shield up, but didn't need to. Peregrine stopped in midair. Pretty impressive, actually. He killed all his forward momentum in a second and just hung there like a cartoon character about to realize they were over a chasm.

"We have a truce," I said.

"Do you?" Jackal asked.

"Do we?" Shield asked, but didn't make any move to prove me wrong. With one eye on both of us, he twisted the canister a quarter turn. A thin yellow mist escaped before he shut it off again.

"See?" I asked. Come on, you've got to see.

"It looks like the stuff at the hospital." He looked at his friend. The puddle of goop was drying and flaking like dried blood. "I don't understand what happened to Carl. But if they infiltrated our people?" He let that hang in the air.

"They are the Legacy," I said.

"So you said." Shield looked at me. "I need you to tell my people what you know. This could be a threat to the entire country, not just this city."

Whoa, hold the phone there, chief. I was not going anywhere with him. "Yea, maybe I could write it down. Mail it." I backed away.

"Don't you see? This isn't some garden-variety parahuman. This is a complex chemical and biological creation." He waved at the tanks and what was left of the goop. "We have to warn the SSA. Warn the world."

"I think that would be a great thing for YOU to do," I pointed out.

"Listen, if you and your friends come in, I can guarantee amnesty."

"Even for him?" I pointed at Osprey.

"Well, maybe not for him. But he will get an opportunity to explain himself," Shield offered.

"Nice. Your bribe is due process," Peregrine said. "Normals already get that."

Shield didn't deny it.

"As long as we're dealing," I said. "Could you arrest him, too?" I pointed at Peregrine.

Peregrine used dirty words.

"Do we have a deal? You could come in. No sneaking around. Join the SSA, do what you're doing without the fear of prison," Shield offered.

But what about our families? They would be in protection so fast they wouldn't have time to pack.

"I'll do it," Peregrine said.

"Hey, as long as you're dealing, can you get a reference out of him for me? Might go a long way in my retrial," Jackal said.

"Peregrine?" I asked. If he did it, then I might have to. Peregrine knew who I was. If he started waving the SSA flag, would he keep my secret? Would he be able to keep my secret? Red Knight had mentioned a room full of egoists on the SSA payroll.

"It's the best offer we're going to get," Peregrine said. "You were right, Osprey's just a murderer. I thought... I thought it wouldn't be like that."

I didn't know what else to say.

Peregrine wasn't looking at me. Was he disgusted? Ashamed? "Where do I sign?"

It wasn't like he had any of the information that Shield was bargaining for, but I could give it to him.

The big question was, why not take the deal? I couldn't even pass high school. What life did I think I was going to have? Was I really going to college? And then what? The only thing I was good at was not dying when the odds said I should.

"Are you considering this?" Jackal asked.

"Why not?" I said out loud.

"Your family. Are you going to make that choice for them?" Jackal didn't sound like he was judging either way. He was just putting it out there.

"What about my family?" I asked.

"Depends," Shield said. "If you do your work and your identity is secure?" He shrugged. "They don't even need to know. But if you get burned, they will be protected."

That was more than I had now, way more. If I was burned now, they would be in deep trouble.

"This group employed people like Red Knight. You want to give them everything?" Jackal added. "That 'protection' is a double-edged sword."

That was the reason I'd never thought about joining the feds in the past. But Mr. Clancy had demonstrated that they weren't all Red Knight types. He'd served his time and then been allowed to live whatever life he wanted.

"You going to make that choice for Flare, too?" Jackal had all the good points.

"Flare goes free. She's just here to save the city and because I talked her into it," I said.

Shield made a face indicating he wasn't sure.

"That is non-negotiable," Peregrine said. "We go right now if you say no."

Nice that he was speaking for me. "She won't use her powers like this again." I knew she wanted out, and this would be the excuse she'd been looking for. "Let her go. She'll disappear and never return."

I could feel him judging my word.

"Something's wrong." Jackal spoke with a tension I'd never felt before.

"What?" I was looking at Shield, too. If he said no, we

would have ourselves a ballgame. Peregrine couldn't get Flare and me out of here. I would have to deal with Shield on my own while Peregrine got Flare to safety, then hope he would come back for me or I could beat Shield again.

"You need to get out of there," Jackal said. "It feels weird."

"I need a little more than that," I whispered. He'd gotten me looking around though. I didn't see an SSA chopper or hear any attack trucks plowing down the road.

"I'm giving you all I can," Shield said. "Flare can go free. But if she illegally uses her powers again, she's fair game."

"It feels like... Caesar." Jackal wasn't sure about that, but couldn't come up with anything closer.

Caesar was dead.

Shield held out his hand.

I looked at Peregrine.

Peregrine looked at me.

"Deal," I said.

I reached out for his hand and clasped it.

Shield smiled. "You made the right--"

"Run!" Jackal screamed into my head.

I pulled back my hand and looked around.

Peregrine had a second to ask, "What?" Then he went flying.

I don't know the order of things. I have no idea how it happened. I didn't think anything could move that fast. Putting it together, the man, the member of Legacy? The monster? Moved from behind and clobbered Peregrine.

Peregrine flew headfirst into the wreckage that was the SSA cab.

The form dressed in black, which could have been a shadow given life for all I knew at that point, collided with

Shield, hands around his neck. I heard, felt, and saw -- in that order -- Shield's neck break.

The thing discarded Shield and turned on me.

He was tall and muscled like a professional basketball athlete. His skin was pale, almost glowing in the poor streetlights. His hair was thick but combed back, and his eyes were an impossible blue. I don't know how I could tell they were blue. It was dark, maybe I'm remembering it wrong. But that electric blue seemed to penetrate the shadow and glow into my head.

He turned his attention on me.

"Run!" Jackal yelled.

Man, I wanted to. If I'd been gifted with any kind of super speed, jump, flight, crawl, or hop, I would have done it. I didn't know what I was looking at, but whatever it was, it outclassed me by so many levels I couldn't count that high.

"And boy, am I sick of YOU!" the not-Caesar said. He moved. I mean, I assume he moved. He could have teleported. My eye couldn't follow him. He slammed into me and sent me to the ground.

All the air got knocked out of me. I couldn't breathe, couldn't think. Jackal was yammering in my head, but I couldn't hear him.

"You're just a kid." He was right in front of me again. All I could see were glowing eyes. "How are you such a problem?"

I had to talk my way out of this. "I... huh?" Go silver tongue!

I'm going to die.

He picked me up. I thought I was going to get the same neck twisty thing Shield had gotten. "Do you have any idea how much time it takes to make that much voluntatem mortem? And how expensive it is?"

I did not. I didn't even know what he was talking about. He seemed to be looking at Carl in the pool of black goop.

"It has to be perfectly tailored to the subject." He put a finger in the goop and tasted it. "Ruined, completely ruined."

Enough of my senses came back to me. I should try to do something.

Before I came up with a plan, he bashed me against a cargo container. Not the closest container. He wanted to build a head of speed.

Now both Jackal and the not-Caesar were yelling in my ear. I didn't know what either of them were saying.

"Answer me!" That made sense as words. The not-Caesar wanted me to answer him.

"What was the question?" I was so willing to answer.

Something violent happened, and it happened fast. I have got to be remembering this wrong, but he threw me against the cargo container. As I bounced he clotheslined me, then caught me on my first bounce off the pavement and ran me up to the top of a group of cargo containers stacked four high.

By the time I was thinking again, I was suspended over the four-story drop at the end of one arm. He didn't even look like he was struggling to keep me aloft.

"How have you been dogging me every step of the way?" he screamed.

TWENTY-FIVE

"You're the Legacy." I wish I hadn't said that, it just came out.

He squeezed my neck harder. "See, you shouldn't even know that name. If you think the voluntatem mortem is expensive, you have no idea what all that Perdition cost me. I got it all into this city without a bump, then all you... children show up." He was calm until he said "children" then he spasmed with anger.

"Sorry." Might as well try manners, the normal stuff wasn't doing it.

"You're sorry!" Spittle foamed around his lips. "I had a tool that could turn off all you freaks and you stole it."

Who are you calling freak, Freak?

"Then you forced me to... *act*!" He was horrified at that. "Do you have any idea what the Legacy will do if they realize I had to act personally?"

There was more of the Legacy, and he was afraid of them? I give up?

"Ask him why," Jackal said.

"Why?" I wasn't doing what Jackal had asked me to, I

was asking Jackal why I should ask why. But Not-Caesar misunderstood.

"Why? Why what? Why did I want to kill the SSA freaks?" He was disgusted when he said the word freak.

I wasn't tracking, and I knew it. I'd just watched him kill an SSA super with ease. "Freaks?"

"You superhumans. For centuries we didn't have to worry about the servus acting up. They went about their little short lives and we controlled everything that needed controlling."

Wait, if freaks were parahumans... "You wanted to use the nullifier to kill the SSA agents." If the Super Suppression Agency had lost all of its heavy hitters in one night, all of America would have been destabilized. Every half-baked villain with a superpower would have had nothing to fear and cities all over the country would have been buried in super activity. "But why?"

"Why? Why? We're at war, that's why," he spat.

"Ask with who?" Jackal said.

Seriously, I was already there. "With who?"

His face was twisted in disgust and rage, but for a brief second I saw fear flicker. "We don't know. Whoever is giving the servus superpowers."

"No one is 'giving' superpowers." That was ridiculous. "They're a natural biological process." That no one understood and that routinely defied physics.

"There is nothing natural about them. They will rip apart your little societies eventually. Caesar was supposed to stop them, but he went native. Decided he knew best. That he could use the tool of the enemy against the enemy." His face turned in a bigger snarl. "And he used the tools, the freaks, against his own people. For what? So he could be king of this sad little hill." He spun his arms around and took in the entire city.

He shook me with the gesture, as if I was inconsequential.

"He turned on his people for this heap of trash!" Legacy Guy was offended.

"So this guy took control of Simon, and that SSA Captain," Jackal mused, "in an effort to kill more parahumans. How does the Stardust and Perdition thing support that agenda?"

Sure, I'd play go between. I mean, I should try and be useful instead of just hanging around. "Why the zombie drugs?" Did I already use that hanging around joke? Seems familiar.

His face went from full of hate and rage to full of hate and rage and confusion. "Zombies?"

"Perdition crazies," I clarified.

"Because we need to destroy this city."

"Why?" I kinda like the city, but I couldn't argue the point, either. The traffic alone makes me want to blow the place up.

"This is where *it* comes from," he hissed.

"It? It what?" Jackal asked.

"It--" I started, but my window of opportunity evaporated.

Not-Caesar brought me to his face. "You're probably wondering why you're still alive."

"I know I was," Jackal put in.

"Kinda," I answered.

"You were there when that fool Simon killed himself."

"I was." Why lie, especially if it's keeping me alive.

"What else did he tell you?"

"Ah..."

"He told you about the Legacy and the Perdition. What else did he say?"

"Ah..." What do I say?

"Stall, just for a few more minutes," Jackal said.

"He said the Legacy was controlling him," I lied. "That you had a big plan for this city and... he didn't tell me anything."

"Don't lie to me!"

"Close your eyes and get ready to control your fall," Jackal said. "Just a few more seconds."

I didn't have many more seconds. "He told me about Caesar." Caesar seemed to piss him off, so I threw that name out there.

"Yes." His blue eyes sparked. "Where did he say he was?"

"The body?" Caesar was dead. He had to be.

"The head!" He was crazed.

"Ah... uh?" This guy was gross.

"Now!" Jackal said.

A bright light. At first I thought it was Flare, but the light wasn't green. It was a bright flash bulb. The same kind of light that Pixel used.

"Graw!" The Legacy Guy flinched away from me and covered his eyes on instinct.

I was in the air and falling. I tucked in and turned it into a roll, but I didn't have anything to grab. There was just rushing up pavement.

My momentum halted as two arms went around me. Halted is a bit of an exaggeration. It slowed.

"Grr!" Peregrine screamed as he tried to stop me.

I think we both would have survived the impact, but why try? I used Peregrine to twist and redirect my fall, landing on a cargo container. My hands and feet scrambled for purchase. The tips of my toes caught on the lip of a container's base. I arrested my momentum and kicked off, somersaulted, and landed in a backwards roll.

The I-don't-know-what swung his fist in a blur at nothing. Pixel flew in the air about ten feet above him. Legacy Guy wasn't aiming at her, but at empty space. He hit something.

Pixel vanished, an illusion. The real Pixel appeared at the point of impact.

She had tried some sleight-of-hand, but he'd seen through it. Half-blind, he'd still known exactly where she was.

"Peregrine." I pointed at Pixel as she went careening off the cargo containers.

He had better senses than I did so he was already moving.

Legacy Guy -- that's what I'm calling him from now on -- stepped off the container like he was taking a short hop.

To him it was a short hop. His knees gave a little and shed the momentum of the fall when he landed. "Where were we?" he asked me.

I was already on the attack. I could have run, but he was just too fast. I wasn't going anywhere he didn't want me to go.

Right when he landed I went for the leg and swept it. He fell to his back. I think I was more surprised than he was, and then I delivered a couple shots to his genitalia. Assuming whatever it was had genitalia.

If he did, they were well protected. He didn't care that I'd knocked him in the nuts, and stood.

Now, these last couple of weeks I've made it a career to not get hit by people way faster and tougher than me. So I was not where he grabbed as I dodged him again. I slowed down time, hard and as slow as I could push it. He was easier to fight than Silhouette, none of those shadow tendrils. But this guy was faster, so much faster. If he could keep up the speed, there was no way I could win. I was already feeling the burn. I would need like three breaths to recharge. Maybe four. It had been a long day.

I did a backflip to give myself some more room, but he closed the gap.

"Lead him back a few more feet," Jackal said.

Sounded good to me. I needed to get back farther. I could tell Legacy Guy was getting pissed. He probably had never had to try this hard to lay hands on someone before. I bent back, turned it into a reverse somersault, rolled three times, and stood.

I realized the plan just a second before she struck. Spike, pink spike in hand, lay in wait behind a container. Legacy Guy turned the corner, and she jammed her spike into his hip, the closest part of him she could reach.

In the heartbeat it took me to realize what was going to happen, I changed my trajectory. Just because my mind was working faster while time really seemed to slow, I couldn't get any more speed out of my body. And I was screaming to get more speed.

Legacy Guy's leg buckled from the spike, but that didn't stop him. He moved his fist right toward Spike's head. It was a race. Unless she was tougher than she looked, Legacy Guy was about to splatter her between his fist and the cargo container.

I knocked her to the ground and rolled.

Legacy Guy's fist pounded through metal.

He screamed in agony. Not sure if it was from frustration, or pain from the spike in his hip.

Spike probably didn't know either, but she wasn't going

to wait to find out. Still on her back, she started launching more spikes into Legacy Guy. The first hit his back, the second missed.

Legacy Guy twisted and dodged, then pulled his fist out of the cargo container with a massive twist.

"Raven, move!" Flare yelled. She was still on one knee where she'd fallen, but her hands were a furnace of green fire. And she was aiming right through me to Spike.

"No, no, no!" I lost the zone and time sped up. It happens like that. I waved my hand vigorously.

Flare had a perfect line of sight on me and Spike, but Legacy Guy was blocked by a shipping container. Even if she could have seen Legacy Guy, she knew that Spike had just dropped her like a bad habit, and that was not happening again.

"She's on our side now. Shoot that!" I pointed at Legacy Guy.

Flare's fire sputtered out and she threw up her hands. "I've been out of the fight for three minutes, and we've switched sides!"

I started to help Spike up. Screw it! I threw her over my shoulder fireman style and started to run, crossing right through Flare's line of fire, so Legacy Guy would do the same.

He did.

"Holy crap, what is that?" Flare asked, but thankfully didn't need an answer to blast a hole in it.

I didn't bother looking. I was running, but I heard Flare's beam hit something and the something scream.

"Put me down." Spike slapped my back.

This was about as far as I was planning on running anyhow. I had to figure out a way to get back in the fight.

I put her down. "Thanks." She smiled. "For saving my

life, not..." She took in carrying her away like a sack of potatoes. "That was kinda rude." A spike formed in her hand. "Down."

I got out of her line of fire. She threw another spike into Legacy Guy.

Flare was keeping a sustained blast on him, but the energy was shearing off in green sparks from some kind of shield Legacy Guy was making. The spike still in his hip had Legacy Guy on one knee and the effort to make the shield was keeping him pinned.

Spike's spike added another one to his back.

Legacy Guy arched in new pain, but the shield held.

At that moment, Peregrine returned. He had found a wooden pallet somewhere and used it to clothesline Legacy Guy as he raced by. Wood planks shattered into splinters and Legacy Guy spun.

Now his shield was still up, but not facing Flare.

Flare's full blast caught him in the side and Legacy Guy spun through the air, leaving a dent in a cargo container.

I got the Y sound of "Yes!" out before it died on my lips.

Legacy Guy was already up and moving toward Spike and me. I tried to slow time again, but couldn't get into the zone. That happens sometimes if I've just used it.

I noticed the dagger in his hands and got my arms in the way of the strike. He hit me with enough power to push me back ten feet. I managed to turn the movement into a flip and landed on my feet.

But I wasn't Legacy Guy's target. Spike dropped to her knees, clutching a wound in her stomach. The pink spike in her hands and the three already in Legacy Guy disappeared.

"That's better." Legacy Guy threw one on his daggers at Flare. It spun in the air like it was a buzz saw blade.

Flare already had a shield up, and the blade bounced off it, ricocheting sparks from another container.

Without Spike's spikes slowing him down, Legacy Guy moved toward Flare as fast as his knife.

Flare sent streams of green fire, but Legacy just danced around them like he knew where she was going to aim before she did.

"Flare, get in the air!" I yelled. She couldn't hit as hard while she was using her power to fly and keep a shield, but she was going to get ripped apart if she didn't move.

Her flare brightened, and she went straight up. It would have been too little too late.

Legacy Guy jumped in the air. His trajectory would have caught her easily, but Peregrine came out of nowhere and clipped him in midair, angling him into a cargo container. Legacy Guy bounced off the corner of the shipping container and slammed onto the pavement.

Peregrine wasn't alone. He was carrying Osprey in his less dense form. Osprey solidified and dropped right on Legacy Guy.

TWENTY-SIX

I lost interest in the fight at that point and focused on Spike. I applied pressure with my hand to her wound. She was still conscious but scared and cold.

I pulled out a pressure bandage from my ever-decreasing stock of standard Guard gear, and slapped it over the wound. "Peregrine, medical evac!" I had no idea where the closest hospital was. Hopefully Peregrine knew the area better than I did.

It would take him out of the fight. It would also take away my way out of the fight. But I was too heavy for him, anyway. And Spike was dying.

Peregrine landed on Spike's other side. If he hesitated, or thought I was wrong, he didn't second-guess me. He picked up Spike as gently as he could -- not very -- and they were airborne.

"You did your good deed. Now get out of there," Jackal told me.

I looked back at the fight. "How's Pixel?"

"How should I... Oh, fine. She has a broken rib. She's not going to be any use in this fight." Jackal didn't deny

Pixel was working for him, or that he was in contact with her.

Legacy Guy was stunned and Osprey kept punching him. Each fist left an impact crater of broken bone and blood splatter. But before Osprey's fist was raised and falling again, the damage had repaired itself.

"This guy is like Caesar," Jackal said.

"How is that possible? That isn't how parahumans work." I remembered saying the same thing to Zed.

"He isn't a parahuman." Jackal had some fear in his voice. "I don't know what he is. But they're old, older than the first parahuman."

Osprey's arm stopped. Legacy Guy had caught it. In the split second before Osprey went solid enough to resist, he cursed in pain.

Now Osprey wasn't moving. Flare had a shot and she took it. But Legacy Guy was ready. The same shield he'd used before materialized six inches above him and sheared off the green light.

I had to think of something. Maybe I could get one of the loading cranes, figure out how to use it, and drop a cargo pod on him? No, that seemed dumb. Maybe skewer him with a forklift? Not that I had any idea how to weaponize a forklift.

"You heard him, he's here for the Perdition," Jackal said.

Right, I wasn't any use in this fight. I still didn't want him to have the Perdition.

I sprinted to the wreckage of the truck. There were two carts filled with Perdition tanks not yet loaded.

"Check the truck," Jackal warned.

There were two more in the truck. "How can I get rid of it?" I could open the valves, but Legacy Guy would just come over here, break all my bones in three places, then shut the valves. The one set of pallets was still on the forklift. I could drive that into the harbor, but who knew what that would do. Would the Perdition be destroyed or just get wet?

One of the SSA agents caught my eye. They were still out. It seemed like I'd fought them a half-hour ago, but really it might have been only five minutes. Each of them, except the one Carl had hijacked, had one of those electric zap guns. Maybe that would do it.

I didn't even spare a look for the actual fight. I could hear the sounds of Flare shooting and big strong things punching, so it was still going on.

I used my multi-tool to cut away the nylon straps, and I had myself a big gun. I had never fired a normal everyday gun, so this sci-fi thing was outside my comfort zone. I looked for the lever that Carl had used to jack the juice.

The weapon started to hum. Now I had nothing to do but pull the trigger and guess. If I stood too far away I might miss, and it seemed I only had one shot at full power. Ah, hell. For all I knew this wouldn't do anything.

I sprinted around to the opening for the inside of the trailer and fired.

Kaboom!

I was knocked off my feet as geysers of yellow gas caught fire and started cooking off the other canisters with smaller bangs.

"No!" Legacy Guy screamed.

I think he caught me in midair as I was propelled back by the explosion. My body bent in all kinds of ways it was not supposed to bend. He ripped the gun from my hands and crushed it.

"You seem upset," I offered, but maybe not loud enough for him to hear. I was in a lot of pain myself.

"You have no idea what you cost me, you wretch," he snarled.

Flare blasted him in the back. He went spinning and set me free. I landed on my feet and slowed time again.

Legacy Guy caught himself on a cargo pod and turned around. He easily dodged another beam from Flare and started at her.

To get extra power to save my life, Flare had landed.

I slid into him and caught his legs. It was like putting your finger into the spokes of a bike. Boy did that sting.

Legacy Guy tripped and went sprawling, his momentum sliding him along the asphalt. He howled in frustration.

"Flare!" I yelled through the pain. "The tanks." I pointed at the still intact pallet of tanks.

She was already taking to the air, and launched several green streaks into the pallet.

This explosion was even more spectacular. As was Legacy Guy's scream of rage.

"I don't think your plan is working," I told Jackal. "I think we just pissed him off."

"If he's anything like Caesar, he will weigh the cost." Jackal sounded sure, but he wasn't sure.

Either way, we'd kept the Perdition from him for today. Maybe someone else would have to take it from here.

Osprey finally got to the party in one of his jumps. He looked beaten up, and his left arm wasn't moving right, but he was still in the fight.

Legacy Guy looked at Flare, Osprey, then me, and I could see him doing the math. He was still the odds on favorite for coming out of this alive. But it would take time, and it wasn't a guarantee. I also remembered him going on about how much he hated having to "act" himself. Maybe now there wasn't a reason to risk it. He could leave and create anarchy another day.

"How did you know of this shipment?" he yelled at me.

Not sure how he knew I was the driving force here, but his question hit me like a wave. If I hadn't had experience resisting compulsion from the Confessor, maybe I would have answered him. But it wasn't hard resisting him. Maybe distance had something to do with it, or maybe he just wasn't that good at it. No one can be good at everything. That's not a criticism, I'm just saying.

"Fortune cookies," I yelled back. "Turns out I will soon be invited to a karaoke party, too." True story, that was a fortune cookie I got once.

He bared his teeth, possibly at my taunt, or because I'd resisted his compulsion, or because he hates karaoke. Like I said, this guy is evil.

His head twitched, and he seemed to sniff the air. "It was the Confessor," he sneered.

Could he read my mind? Maybe the compulsion thing wasn't what was going on. Maybe he was bringing the information to the front of my mind so it was easier to read. I mean, this guy seemed to be able to do a little of everything.

"While we are here, he is raiding my stores." He pointed at a building about two hundred feet away and in the general direction the forklifts full of Perdition had come from. "Well played, Confessor." He still seemed more pissed at me. Not fair! It was the Confessor who'd screwed him. "I will get more Perdition, and the Confessor will insure I will have thousands for my army." I don't think he was really thinking out loud. He was probably trying to manipulate us to go deal with the Confessor for him. Spoiler alert: totally works. Kinda. So, not totally.

You'll see. "As for you all, Guard of this cesspool. I condemn you to live long enough to see your city burn." Then he spat, but before the spit hit the asphalt, he was gone in a blur.

"You lived through that!" Jackal seemed pleasantly surprised. "Totally another golf clap going on here."

"Let's go!" Osprey said. He may have sounded all ready to take on the next fight, but he looked like hell. He'd fought Spike, and Legacy Guy, all in the last ten minutes. He did not look ready for round three.

If the Confessor was in the warehouse. A big if. Okay not that big of an if. I mean, using us as a distraction so he could get his hands on a duty free supply of Stardust was totally what was going on. Why else would he tell me about the Perdition? Civic responsibility? But okay, Legacy Guy was telling the truth. That meant at bare minimum, the Confessor had his teleporting chick, Transcendence, and Iron in the warehouse. Three legit supers versus two exhausted legit supers and myself, technically a superpower. I was also tired, but by the time I'd run the couple hundred yards to the warehouse, I'd be good to go.

"Let's not go!" I said. "We did what we set out to do, and the SSA can't be that far away." I waved around the disaster zone that was their little convoy and the dead Shield. Hopefully Spike would survive and tell everyone that the Guard didn't kill him. And my chance of going legit. I know, selfish, but it was there.

"I set out to find answers about the Kitchen Knife killer. The Confessor has those answers!" Osprey wasn't going to wait for me. He crouched to jump. "Come or don't."

"Why do you care about the Kitchen Knife killer?" Flare said, before he leapt.

"You wouldn't understand. Go back to planning for

your prom. I'm going to do the work the Guard were starting to do."

"I have more reason to want the Kitchen Knife killer caught than you," Flare snapped. I knew why, but she didn't know I knew and she didn't want Osprey to dwell on it, so she added, "Orion was my mentor a long time, and he wanted the killer caught."

"What is all this Kitchen Knife stuff?" They'd never used that name before.

"It was what Orion called him." Flare didn't take her eyes from Osprey. "He left a kitchen knife from the same knife set with each victim."

"Even the cops in this town couldn't turn a blind eye to that, but a serial killer draws too much national attention. So they swept that fact under the rug," Osprey said.

A kitchen knife? And there was a connection to the sale of Stardust? Oh, crap. It couldn't be. "How did you know it was the same set?"

"It doesn't matter." Flare obviously didn't want to think about it. What kind of memories did this stir up? Her green aura lanced up with fire.

"White pearl handle with a K," Osprey answered. "There isn't any confusion." He finished his crouch. "Come or don't." And he jumped.

That was the exact knife I had sitting in my nest in a Guard-issue evidence bag. "Flare?" Should I tell her? Yes, absolutely. But now, in the field, with no time to process? That could get her killed.

"Don't worry, I'll make sure he doesn't kill anyone." She'd misread me. Her aura ignited, and she shot after him.

And I was left to hoof it.

I wish I could fly.

"You going or not?" Jackal asked.

"I'm going." I sprinted the couple hundred yards to the warehouse. The loading door was still open. When Legacy Guy's loaders had been scared off by our attack, it didn't look like they'd paused to lock up. Which slid into the Confessor's plans perfectly.

Although Transcendence seemed to be a massively powerful teleporter, she had to have limits. Most teleporters either needed to see where they were going, or had to go to a place they knew really well. That was the theory anyway, and it tracked with what we'd seen. Otherwise they wouldn't have had to drive anywhere like the last place we'd fought them. At least I hoped so, or we could just start signing over our taxes to Transcendence now.

Gunfire sounded, answered by the fri-zap of Flare.

Two guys, don't know if they were Legacy Guy's guards or the Confessor's people, walked out backwards, their backs to me, firing their handguns up at something.

That something could be a friend of mine. I launched into them, flipped them on their backs, kicked their weapons out, then sent two swift kicks to the face. I didn't have time to make sure they were out, but I was sure that they were dazed for a little bit.

The warehouse had tons of crates still in it, but also had tons of crates moved to the other side of Transcendence's event horizon.

About six guys, dressed similarly to the two guys I'd dropped but better armed, were shooting blind and up. I might have missed one of Flare's blinding assaults.

It didn't seem to have worked against Iron. Or maybe he didn't need his eyes to choke a guy. He was completely thick with the iron skin that gave him his name and had his arms around Osprey's neck. Osprey was dense enough so that Iron couldn't crush his windpipe, but limber enough to pound his fist into Iron's groin.

Even covered in iron, he was feeling it, and was forced to release Osprey's neck to stop the punishment.

At the wavering arch that connected Legacy Guy's warehouse to the Confessor's, Transcendence was rubbing her eyes, another victim of Flare's blinding. Standing next to her was the Confessor.

Flare had to deal with the gunmen, so it was up to me to deal with the Confessor and Transcendence before she got her vision back.

I scaled up some remaining crates and skirted the outside of the conflict.

I wasn't being stealthy, but it still surprised me when the Confessor looked right at me as I attacked from the flank.

I tried to slide into Transcendence, but the Confessor moved her out of the way.

I sprang up and took another shot at her. If I could drop her, then the Confessor's exit would be cut off, and maybe then I could capture him and turn him over to the SSA. And my not-girlfriend would have a father in prison and be out of my life.

Being a superhero sucks.

The Confessor did the same math, or maybe he just wasn't an epic douche, and stood in front of his teleporter. Both his hands were glowing. He only needed to touch me to send pain through every part of me. I had been there, done that, and it forced me to reset and adjust.

Flare pumped a shot into a gunman and the gunman went down. I could tell the other three were able to see at least a glowing blur now. Their guns were tracking Flare, if poorly, as she zipped around the warehouse.

The Confessor came at me. I dodged him. I could do that all day and finish my paper on Macbeth that I still owed Mr Clancy.

Note to self, finish that paper for Mr Clancy.

The Confessor had some skill as a fighter, but come on. He was not up to Shield, or Legacy Guy, or those guys who'd jumped me in the school bathroom. If a brush of his hand wasn't so devastating, this would be over already.

I spun, took out his knees, and dropped him on his back. I hopped over him, out of his reach, and threw a punch at Transcendence.

The Confessor had done his job. T had recovered enough to see me coming. My fist passed through a circle in the air and connected with the concrete block of the warehouse wall twenty feet away.

Ouch!

Then she made a wave of her hand, and a circle appeared right below my feet. I fell.

Before I knew it, I was on the other end of the warehouse and all the way up.

I scrambled, instinct taking over, and got one hand around a girder.

Transcendence hadn't needed to drop me where I had a hand hold. So either it was a mistake, or she wasn't trying to kill me.

Either way, I was hanging four stories up, by one hand.

I missed Flare dropping two other gunmen but the last guy was saved as a portal formed right over him, gobbled up Flare's shot, and came out another portal above Osprey.

The blast wasn't tough enough for Osprey to feel, but it made him stagger and Iron took advantage of it with a haymaker to the chin that sent him flying.

I hand-over-handed it directly above a high stack of

crates and dropped, turning the momentum into a roll that sent me off the highest crate to another five feet below. I jumped to another stack. From there it was just a little hop to the floor.

I had to get back into the fight and draw some attention away from Flare so she could end these guys. And by end, I mean knock them unconscious so they could have their day in court. And by "in court" I mean to disappear into the back of an SSA truck and never be seen again.

So there was that.

I dodged a hole that opened in front of me and a Flare blast that was probably meant for a gunman or Transcendence.

Flare was moving too fast for the gunman to get a couple of shots to ricochet off her forcefield. But while he was looking up, I clobbered him from behind. All the gunmen were down. Now just the supers.

I caught a glimpse of Osprey getting a good shot into Iron, but I don't know if he cared or not.

Flare dropped closer to where Transcendence and the Confessor were standing. Maybe trying to shorten the range so Transcendence didn't have time to put up her portal. But as she dropped a portal appeared in her force bubble. The Confessor's hand came out and touched her for a second on the neck.

TWENTY-SEVEN

Flare didn't even scream, she arched. Her aura went out like someone had blown out a candle. The portal disappeared and she fell to the ground.

I didn't give my fears voice. I just ran at Transcendence, right into a portal and hand of my own.

I could see the portal in front of the Confessor, and his arm poking through it. Pain shot up my spine as he got a solid grip on the back of my neck.

Every part of me twisted in agony like I was nailed to my own invisible cross.

A second later Osprey did the same.

Pieces of Iron had been knocked off, but with the second reprieve, he started to heal, exposed flesh gaining a sheen that became solid iron again.

"Well, isn't this a pickle." The Confessor was chastising children. "Let's put the kiddies to bed, and the adults will discuss your punishments."

Pain drove me to my knees.

I was aware of Jackal yelling into my mind, trying to get

me to think, to move. He was afraid and so was I. But more than afraid, I was in agony.

"But before we do that, it's time for confession." The Confessor's voice ticked up now that he was getting to play his favorite game. "Raven."

Crap.

"You resisted me before, so let's see how well you do now."

Only I hadn't resisted him, I'd fooled him like... too much pain for similes. I'd just fooled like a fooling thing.

The Confessor seemed to think for a second. "I know. What is the one thing you don't want your team to know?"

My name. That I knew who Flare was. Both rattled around in my head but the one thing that I didn't want them to know, not right now at least, shouted out of my mouth. "Iron killed..." I avoided saying Jasmin's mother. "Shannon Paris. He's the Kitchen Knife killer!" The last part pulled out of me on a scream.

Maybe the other two wouldn't hear. Flare had just crashed, and Osprey was in as much pain as I was.

"What?" The Confessor did not seem happy about this news.

"He's the serial killer," my voice said before I had any thought of stopping it or saying something else. "I just figured it out."

Iron was standing now, his fist pulled back, ready to deliver a strike that would kill Osprey if he wasn't ready for it. And he was not ready for it.

"What?" Flare said. It was a whisper, and I wouldn't have heard it except she transmitted over our channel.

The Confessor pulled his hand off Osprey, who collapsed backwards. "Transcendence, please."

"Boss, this is crap," Iron said.

A portal appeared right above Iron's head and the Confessor's hand dropped on the iron-covered skull. The white light arced.

"Tell me Iron, have you been killing these women?" Apparently the Confessor knew more about the serial killings than I did. I guess if you want to be a gang leader you need to know what's going on in the area. Or maybe the Confessor had a psychosis of his own and needed to know a confession if it was just sitting there.

"Boss, I..." I knew what it felt like for the compulsion to take hold, and I saw it even on his warped, metal-encrusted face. "I killed them all. I had to. She kept coming back. The things she did to me when I was small. I killed her, but then I would see her again. She kept coming back! I had to kill her, I had to kill them all."

"You killed Shannon Paris?" Flare yelled. She was glowing brightly and fire was around her hands.

"No!" I almost said Jasmin. "Flare, don't!"

"Answer the question, Iron," the Confessor ordered.

"She gave me *the* Smile." Whatever *the* smile was, it meant a lot to Iron. "A cup of soup and *the* Smile. Like I didn't know what she was thinking. It felt so good to stop that smile. Make her feel what life was really like, just for a second, just at the end!" he shouted. "I wasn't the one screaming, she was!"

If I had to guess, I'd say it wasn't the admission that did it. That was bad enough, so I could be wrong, but it was the look on his face. His face was stitched-together plates of iron, his expression cast in changing metal. The memory of inflicting pain, of killing, brought such ecstasy to his face, such awe of a wonderful moment.

I was horrified. I was disgusted. I was infuriated. But he was not talking about my mother.

Flare's aura went out. The green light just stopped. My first thought was that she had lost focus, her grief making her lose her powers. Silly, really. I should have known why her aura dropped. But he was not talking about my mother.

My visor protected my eyes from the blinding light of a thin, concentrated beam of green energy. Every scrap of power Flare had at her command was poured through the grief of a child.

The beam hit Iron in the center of his forehead. The Confessor's hand and the portal vanished, but he kept smiling his crazed grin, the iron on his face glowing red, until the smile melted into a scream. Before any sound escaped, all his features melted away. His entire head became a glowing mass of red, then a hole opened up. The beam cut through, and all the molten metal poured in. God, I hope he was already dead.

The Confessor released me, and I could move. Well, my body was under my control again. But I couldn't move.

"Stay out of my way, Raven," the Confessor warned. "And you'd better run. I think I hear sirens."

Transcendence, the Confessor, and a well-stocked warehouse disappeared as Transcendence's portal vanished.

"He's right. SSA are on their way." Osprey stood up. "Good work, Flare. We gotta go!"

Her hand had no aura left. She was just staring at Iron. There was no skull or flesh left. It was just nothing, a headless statue, his arms frozen in a swing meant for Osprey that he would never deliver.

Then parts of the iron started to flake off.

"You have got to go now," Jackal told me.

"She killed him," I said.

"And she did the world a favor. Now do yourself one and get the hell out of here!" Jackal ordered.

A large fragment sloughed off and dropped to the floor. A chest -- tattooed, muscled, and human -- was exposed.

"Oh, God," Flare said.

Osprey got to her first. "Come on, let's go."

"I..."

"You've got to get out of here," I said into the radio. "What would your family do if you got caught?"

That snapped her out. "We've got to go." Green flame started to spark then ignite around her.

"Go!" I yelled.

She looked at me. I couldn't see her face, I didn't know what she was thinking, but it was a long look. Then she was up and through the hole in the skylight she'd used to get in.

"Good work," Osprey told me. "You'll have to tell me how you figured out who he was." He motioned to the headless corpse.

"Good work?" Was he serious? "You sick, bloody, son of a bitch!" He wasn't close enough for me to hit him, and I could barely get my legs under me. "A man is dead, and WE killed him."

"A monster won't kill anyone else, so win-win," Osprey shot back, rubbing his palms together like he was knocking dust off after a good day's work.

I wanted to hit him, I wanted to kick him, I wanted to scream. But I dropped to my knees. So, I must have stood up at some point. "You don't understand." He didn't. He was little better than Iron, both trying to silence screaming children hurt by a monster. "You think you did something today, but you didn't. You didn't accomplish anything."

"Whatever, white hat. Keep out of my way." Osprey made a leap and was out the skylight.

"Raven." Jackal's voice was urgent. "You're out of time. You need to go now."

I got my feet underneath me somehow. The post-combat fatigue was starting, which was crap because it wasn't post-combat yet.

I sprinted for the door, got out.

And I was too late.

Oracle, a platoon of geared out SSA, and a Shield all landed at the combat site. I could hear the wail of sirens from the main road, and a helicopter with the SSA three-headed dog logo was right overhead. The spotlight went right on me.

And kept going.

"Boss said you'd need my help," Pixel said from behind me. She was leaning against the side of the building.

The spotlight kept sweeping. There were no cries, no net-gun fire, or telekinetic grabs by Oracle.

"They can't see us?" My belly did a flop and shake.

"Nope." Jackal seemed to be letting out a breath. "Thanks, Pixel." Jackal was saying it into my head, but she gave a two fingered wave like it was no big deal.

"You have an idol," I said.

She nodded.

"Don't worry, I wasn't cheating on you," Jackal said. "It won't change the thing we have."

Whatever. "Let's go." I took a step, but realized Pixel wasn't following me. Then I really looked at her face. She was in pain.

"I'm not really going anywhere," she said through gritted teeth.

"Legacy Guy did a number on you."

"Legacy Guy? Sure, whatever. Saw right through my invisibility as if I had a neon sign." She stood. Without the wall's support, she began to sway.

"You need each other," Jackal said. "She can keep--"

"Yeah, I'm already there." If she could keep us invisible, we could get out of this without incarceration.

"I have a car that way." She pointed deeper into the harbor.

I didn't like the idea, but I wasn't going to leap from rooftop to rooftop holding her.

She sneezed in pain when I picked her up. "I'm fine, go!" She was not fine, but I didn't know how much time I had before she passed out.

Stealth was the most important thing, and I kept to the shadows. I didn't know how well she obscured us and I didn't know how long she would be able to keep us covered. "Thanks for saving my life again," I told her.

She had her hands around my neck and her face pressed into my shoulder, stopping her from yelping in pain. "If I don't, who will?" she muttered through her pain.

"It couldn't have been easy coming back for me." I didn't know where Peregrine had dropped her, but it wasn't at the warehouse door.

"You've got that right," she agreed.

"Well, thanks."

There was nothing else to say. I got her to her car, she drove, and I got in the trunk. It sounded like a good idea at the time, but in the confined space I had no way to fight the adrenaline fatigue. I was asleep before the car started moving.

TWENTY-EIGHT

I sat down next to Sofia at the lunch table that had become our usual spot. Usual as of two days ago.

She jumped at the little clang of the tray.

"Sorry." I hadn't meant to startle her.

"No, I'm sorry." She looked horrible. I mean, she looked hot, but also exhausted. She made room for me to sit next to her. "I didn't sleep well last night."

Last night for me had been never-ending nightmares, the side effect of using my time slow power. All I saw was Iron's headless body. Or whatever Legacy Guy had used to slice Spike's guts open. And thanks to the adrenaline fatigue, I couldn't stay awake, returning again and again to my nightmares. Dad had literally poured a glass of ice water on me to get me up this morning. I hadn't even touched base with Peregrine. I didn't know what he knew, or if Spike had made it to safety. I didn't dare use the radio, just in case the SSA had figured out our channel or were just scanning for encrypted signals. Paranoid? Maybe I just didn't want to know. I wanted to think that we'd at least done something.

"Why not?" I asked after too long a pause.

"Why?" She'd lost the thread of the conversation.

"You didn't sleep?"

"Oh, it was Raven."

My heart skipped a beat before I realized she was talking about Feral, not me. Like I said, exhausted.

"He totally flipped out around eleven-thirty and I couldn't calm him down."

That was about the time we'd gone head-to-head with the SSA, then Legacy Guy, then the Confessor. I got more worn out just thinking about it.

"How 'bout you? You look like you pulled an all-nighter, too," she said.

"Paper for Mr. Clancy. It's due Friday, but I couldn't sleep, so I just got it done."

"That's great." Tor sat down across from us. I hadn't seen him all day. He was sporting an impressive shiner and a newspaper that he put in front of me.

"What happened to you?" Sofia asked.

"The same thing that happened to him." Tor pointed at me.

As God is my witness, I had no idea what he was talking about.

"The major freak show that was our hospital visit last night," Tor said like I was the biggest lamo. "You should have seen this guy."

Oh yeah, that hospital thing was last night. It seemed forever ago, and was not the most important thing that had happened last night.

"I'm just glad you're alright." Jasmin took her seat beside him. "You must have been terrified."

I almost jumped. I wanted to say something. What? Accuse her? Ask her if she was all right? Rage at her for killing someone? What I did was stare at her in shock.

"Ryan saved my life," Tor said.

I blinked and tapped down my flipping stomach. "That isn't how I remember it," I said. "I seem to remember you pulling me out of the fire." That was the truth.

He pointed at the paper. The hospital incident was on the front page. Not the part about Perdition making people nuts. Just some addicts getting away and going crazy. Luckily, our heroics were just down to a line. "Visitors called the SSA."

"Wow, you're heroes," Sofia said to both of us.

"Yes, he is." Jasmin leaned over and gave a bruise-free portion of Tor's face a kiss.

"I'm just glad the SSA showed when they did," I said. "A lot of those guys were crazy."

"Weird there's no mention of the yellow gas," Tor said.

I just shrugged.

"We're going out to celebrate," Jasmin said. "You two should come with us."

Sofia got a little uncomfortable. We were not at the double-dating phase.

"Celebrate?" What was there to celebrate?

"Our victory." Tor pointed at the paper.

Victory? I didn't feel victorious.

"I need a fork." Jasmin gave Tor another peck on the cheek and went to the silverware caddy.

"She seems..." Sofia watched her walk away. "Lighter."

Tor nodded, looking fondly at his girlfriend. "I know. She said last night she did something she'd wanted to do for a long time, and a weight is off her shoulders."

"Oh," I said. That was so much worse.

Tor stuffed a fork full of pasta in his mouth. "So you got your paper finished. What angle did you take?"

I kept looking at Jasmin. She selected a fork and returned to our table with a huge smile on her face.

I hadn't written a word, but I knew exactly what I was going to say. "Nothing revolutionary. Just went with what Mr. Clancy suggested. First, you make your choices, then your choices make you."

TWENTY-NINE

The Worm paced back and forth in the little underground room. The large dog looked at him, tracking him as he paced. Others came and went, their vacant stares unnerving, and not one of them acknowledged his presence.

One of the others placed a file marked with "Phoenix composition" on the desk. The Worm asked about it, but was ignored.

He tried to read it, but it was in a language he couldn't even recognize. It could have been a code, but it wasn't even in letters.

A rush of air and Malice filled the chair. A squeak of protest as he rocked a little.

He looked haggard, his clothes ripped and torn.

"My lord, the truck did not arrive." The Worm hated not knowing what was happening. He knew he should be silent, but he had to know.

"I know!" Malice pounded the desk. "The remnants of the Guard destroyed it." So much hate was tied up in the word Guard. "Why couldn't they have just been blown up when they were supposed to?"

The Worm didn't know when that was, but he didn't care. "All the Perdition?" This was a disaster.

"All of it." Malice nodded.

"How long will it take to get more?" The Stardust wouldn't stay in the junkies' systems forever. They only had a couple of weeks, maybe a month before it lost potency.

"A while. The good news is, Stardust will continue to be supplied to the streets. It gives us time."

"But how long? Can you get more Perdition?"

"You have no idea the cost." Malice shook his head. "I will have to go to the Legacy Council, and they are not forgiving." He picked up the file on his desk and paged through it, out of pure instinct. "But I will accept their punishment, and this city will still burn." He stood. "Leave me. I need to contact the Council..." Realization flickered over his face and he looked back at the file he'd discarded. He snatched it up and took his chair again. "Oh, my." The anger vanished in a second. "Oh my, my, my." He laughed. "Look what you did, you naughty, naughty boys."

"Sir?" Sir seemed safe.

"I think we can go to the Council with much better news," Malice said.

"But the city..."

"Oh, the city will burn. It will take a little more time, but with a much hotter fire." Malice looked at the Worm with a city ablaze dancing in his eyes. "Also, what is left of the Guard must die. Especially that Raven child."

"I will see to it, sir." The Worm bowed and left the room.

. . .

From the author, Arthur Mayor.

I hope you enjoyed my story. Get a FREE SHORT STORY, *Origin,* when you join my newsletter. Origin tells the story of when Ryan's powers first manifested, how he met Raptor, and became Raven. The Dark Shadowy Cabal newsletter will also give you updates and new releases from Dark Shadowy Cabal, cover reveals, deep dives into characters, and other "blu-ray" extras.

Become a member of the Cabal today: https://www.subscribepage.com/b5v7p6

Continue following Raven's thrilling adventures in *Villains, Superpower Chronicles book 4.*

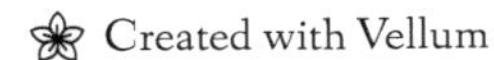
Created with Vellum

ACKNOWLEDGMENTS

Special thanks to my editor Audrey Sharpe

Cover Design by Nicole Montgomery at Significant Cover
https://significantcover.com/

Dedicated to my Wife.

She is always my inspiration and her support made these books possible.

Made in the USA
Middletown, DE
07 June 2021

Human Resource Development:

The Theory and Practice of Need Assessment

Francis L. Ulschak

Reston Publishing Company, Inc.
A Prentice-Hall Company
Reston, Virginia

Library of Congress Cataloging in Publication Data

Ulschak, Francis L.
Human resource development.

1. Personnel management. 2. Assessment centers (Personnel management procedure) I. Title.
HF5549.U416 1983 658.3'01 82-16163
ISBN 0-8359-2996-5
ISBN 0-8359-2997-3 (pbk.)

A Prentice-Hall Company
Reston, Virginia 22090

10 9 8 7 6 5 4 3 2 1

Printed in the United States of America

Contributors

The author wishes to give special thanks to the following contributors:

Beck, Larry. Training and Development Officer, Personnel Department, State of South Dakota, Pierre, South Dakota.

Fisher, Phillip, Ph.D. Associate Professor of Management, School of Business, University of South Dakota, Vermillion, South Dakota.

Gepson, Jim. Management Consultant, Omaha, Nebraska.

Johnson, Steve. Human Resources Officer, Northwestern Bank, Sioux Falls, South Dakota.

Martinko, Mark, Ph.D. Associate Professor of Management, Florida State University, Tallahassee, Florida.

Rath, Gustave, Ph.D. Professor of Industrial Engineering/Management Sciences, Northwestern University, Evanston, Illinois.

Roegiers, Charles, Ph.D. Associate Professor of Management, School of Business, University of South Dakota, Vermillion, South Dakota.

Sargent, Alice, Ed.D. Organizational Consultant and Trainer, Washington, D.C.

Schneider, Mary. Acting Director of Health Services Administration Program, University of South Dakota, Vermillion, South Dakota.

Stoyanoff, Karen, Ph.D. Castle, Rath, and Stoyanoff Consulting Firm, Evanston, Illinois.

Table of Contents

PART III: THE ASSESSMENT SUPPORT SYSTEM

Acknowledgments

Acknowledgments provide me with an opportunity to mention some special people and their influence on my book.

Deserving special attention are Karen Bihlmeyer and Kathy Nordstrom; they put in countless hours typing and retyping drafts of the final product.

Also deserving attention are the contributors to this book. They willingly gave of their time and energy to share their expertise. Their contributions are greatly appreciated.

Last, a group deserving very special attention is my family—Glennys, Michael and Heather. Together we have learned how important it is that assessment precede action. I thank them for their tolerance and patience during this project.

Introduction

. . . It is a capital mistake to theorize before one has the data. Insensibly one begins to twist facts to suit theories, instead of theories to suit facts.

Sherlock Holmes

INTRODUCTION

The telephone rings. The caller has been asked by her company to design a training program for first line supervisors. Her series of questions to me are "Where do I begin?" "How do I find out what the training needs are?" "What is a good way to assess training needs?" This scene depicts an area in which I often am asked for assistance: designing needs assessments for training programs. It is out of experiences such as these that this book developed. The purpose of this book is to provide resources that not only focus on various methods of needs assessment, but that also discuss the milieu in which those methods are found.

The need for this book is clear. While almost any book on training, human resource development, or personnel will have an overview of needs assessment, finding an indepth discussion on the topic is relatively rare. Materials are frequently scattered in a wide variety of journals and books. The best that might be done for persons seeking information regarding assessment is to provide them with a set of general readings. This book is designed to be a guide to the total assessment process. It provides an overview of a variety of techniques that are useful in assessing needs. The book pulls together thoughts from many information sources—psychology, sociology, training and development, management, and organizational behavior. Usefulness was the key consideration in selecting the sources to be used. The question asked was "Does this source provide information useful to the design and implementation of a needs assessment process?" Underlying the material contained in this book is the author's own experience in conducting assessments. The information sources have been filtered through the author's experiences. The result is a blending of theory and practice.

Whenever the reader sees the term "training" in this book, he should assume it includes "training and development." The author has expanded the meaning of the term in order to deal with developmental concerns that may not normally be included in a discussion of training. This reflects the author's belief that training and development go hand in hand, as well as his background in organizational development.

Nadler (*Designing Training Programs: The Critical Events Model*, 1982, p. 7) identifies three types of learning programs. The first is training; training is learning related to the present job of the employee. Second is education; education is learning related to a job for which a person is being prepared. Third is development, which is learning related to the general growth of the individual and to the organization. While this book addresses all three of these learning levels, the second and third levels are emphasized.

DEFINING NEEDS ASSESSMENT

Webster's Dictionary defines assessment as setting an estimated value on property, e.g., for taxation. Training needs assessments attempt to place a value on the variety of needs that potentially can be satisfied through training. Needs assessment is an attempt to look at a given set of needs and to identify those that are the target needs. Assessment is a diagnostic process. A useful analogy: If I am not feeling well, I go to my physician. She does not prescribe whatever medication is in vogue—"Here, try this. It had great results with the last person here." Rather, the first step is diagnostic: What are the symptoms? Where is the hurt? And, after a thorough evaluation, a prognosis is given along with a therapy process. Before a treatment is prescribed, a diagnosis is made.

A training needs assessment has the same function as that diagnosis. Before any training (treatment) is prescribed, some type of diagnosis must be made. The major theme of this book is that the prerequisite to effective and efficient training is a needs assessment process.

Kaufman and English (*Needs Assessment: Concept and Application*, p. 31) define needs assessment this way:

> . . . needs assessment. It is a tool for determining valid and useful problems which are philosophically as well as practically sound. It keeps us from running down more blind educational (training) alleys, from using time, dollars, and people in attempted solutions which do not work. It is a tool for problem identification and justification. . . . Needs assessment is a humanizing process to help make sure that we are using our time and the learner's time in the most effective and efficient manner possible.

Kaufman and English continue their discussion of needs assessment by identifying six types of needs assessment. These assessment processes parallel stages in planning and problem solving. They are

- Type 1: Alpha assessment. Alpha assessment assumes few givens, assumptions, or ground rules. Rather, the questions are "What problem are we addressing?" "How is it a problem?" If asked to design a supervisory training program, the "Alpha" trainer will ask "What problem is trying to be corrected?" "Who sees it as a problem?"

- Type 2: Beta assessment. Beta assessment assumes the goals and objectives given to be valid. The assessment proceeds from those goals and objectives. The Beta trainer will ask questions about content, frequency, methodology, but will not ask if supervisory training is needed.

- Type 3: Gamma assessment. Gamma assessment determines the discrepancies between the methods of resolving a particular problem. The problem and methods are assumed—now it is a question of weighing the methods.

- Type 4: Delta assessment. Delta assessment focuses on performance. Are there specific performance gaps? If so, this is the target of the Delta trainer.

- Type 5: Epsilon assessment. Epsilon assessment looks at the gaps between the outcomes of a particular event and the objectives of that event.

- Type 6: Zeta assessment. Zeta assessment is an ongoing evaluation process. The feedback from the Zeta assessment allows for ongoing changes and corrections.

While defining needs assessment and identifying types of assessments may be relatively straightforward, defining a training need is not. Moore and Dutton ("Training Need Analysis: Review and Critique," p. 538) identify the standard definition of a training need:

Desired Performance − Present Performance = Training Need

The gap between the desired performance and the present performance becomes the training need to be addressed.

However, Moore and Dutton and others raise a question about this formula. The major concern is that the gap between the desired performance and the present performance may not be a training need but rather some other type of need.

Gilbert (*Praxeonomy: A Systematic Approach to Identifying Training Needs*, pp. 20ff) provides the classic discussion of training needs. His "Rule 1" defines deficiency:

Deficiency = Mastery − Initial Repertory

He identifies two types of deficiencies. The first is deficiency of skills (DS). The second is a deficiency of execution (DE). Deficiencies of skills are training targets. When skill is the need, a training intervention is appropriate. However, deficiencies of execution are not effectively addressed by training interventions. Deficiencies of execution are

1. Inadequate feedback about performance.

2. Task interference, i.e., interruptions that interfere with the task being done.

3. Punishment, i.e., in the process of doing the work, the reward structure is such that the individual is "punished."

4. Lack of motivation.

Gilbert suggests that if you are unsure if a particular need is a DE or a DS, ask him/her one question: "Could this person do this task if his/her life depended on it?" If the response is "yes," the deficiency is DE; if the response is "no," the deficiency is a DS.

Laird (*Approaches to Training and Development*) provides a flow chart as a means of determining training needs (see Figure P-1).

Laird's model revolves around three decision questions: (1) Is there a deficiency, (2) Is the deficiency important, and (3) Do the workers know how to do the job properly?

Perhaps one of the most useful models addressing the issue of a training need derives from Mager and Pipe (*Analyzing Performance Problems*). The model raises several major questions:

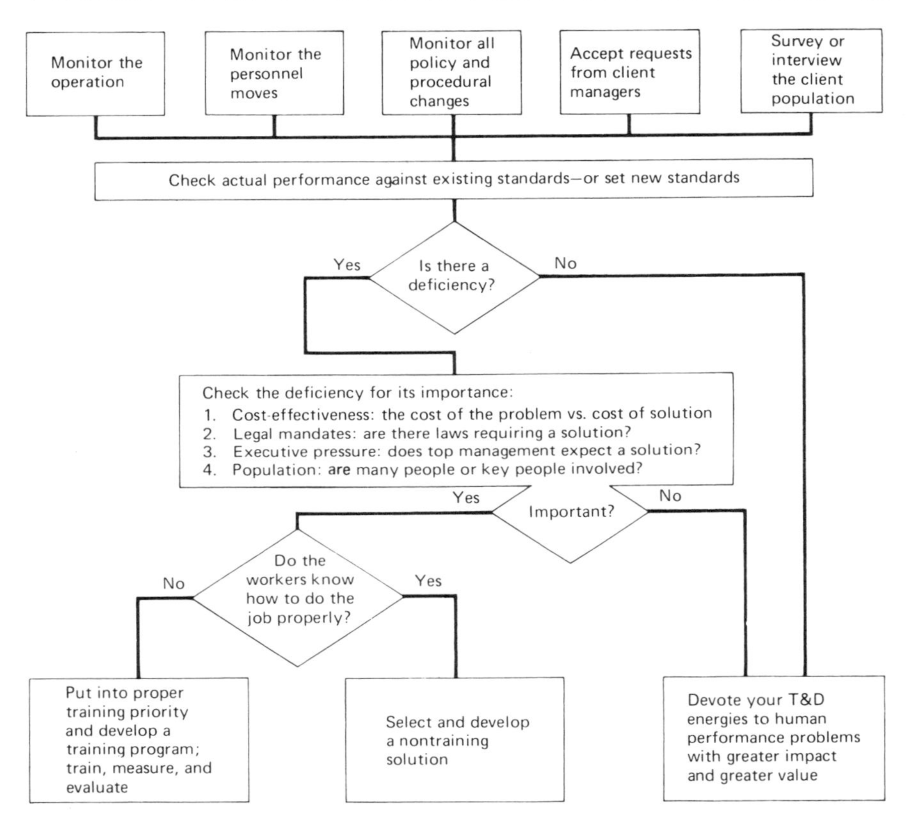

Figure P-1. Laird's model. From *Approaches to Training and Development*, 1978, p. 60.

1. What is the performance discrepancy? The discrepancy is discussed in detail.

2. Is the performance discrepancy important? If not, go no further. This is a key screening question. If the discrepancy is not important, it is not worth the energy to pursue correcting it.

3. Is the performance discrepancy a skill deficiency? If yes, then begin to explore such questions as "Has this person done this in the past?" "Is this a new skill for the person?" "Is the person getting feedback?" If it is a skill discrepancy, training might be arranged, practice might be arranged, or other interventions may be used. If it is not a skill deficiency, then begin to explore questions such as: "Is the performance being punished?" "Is nonperformance being rewarded?" "Are there obstacles in the way of performance?" Mager and Pipe's flow chart is illustrated in Figure P-2.

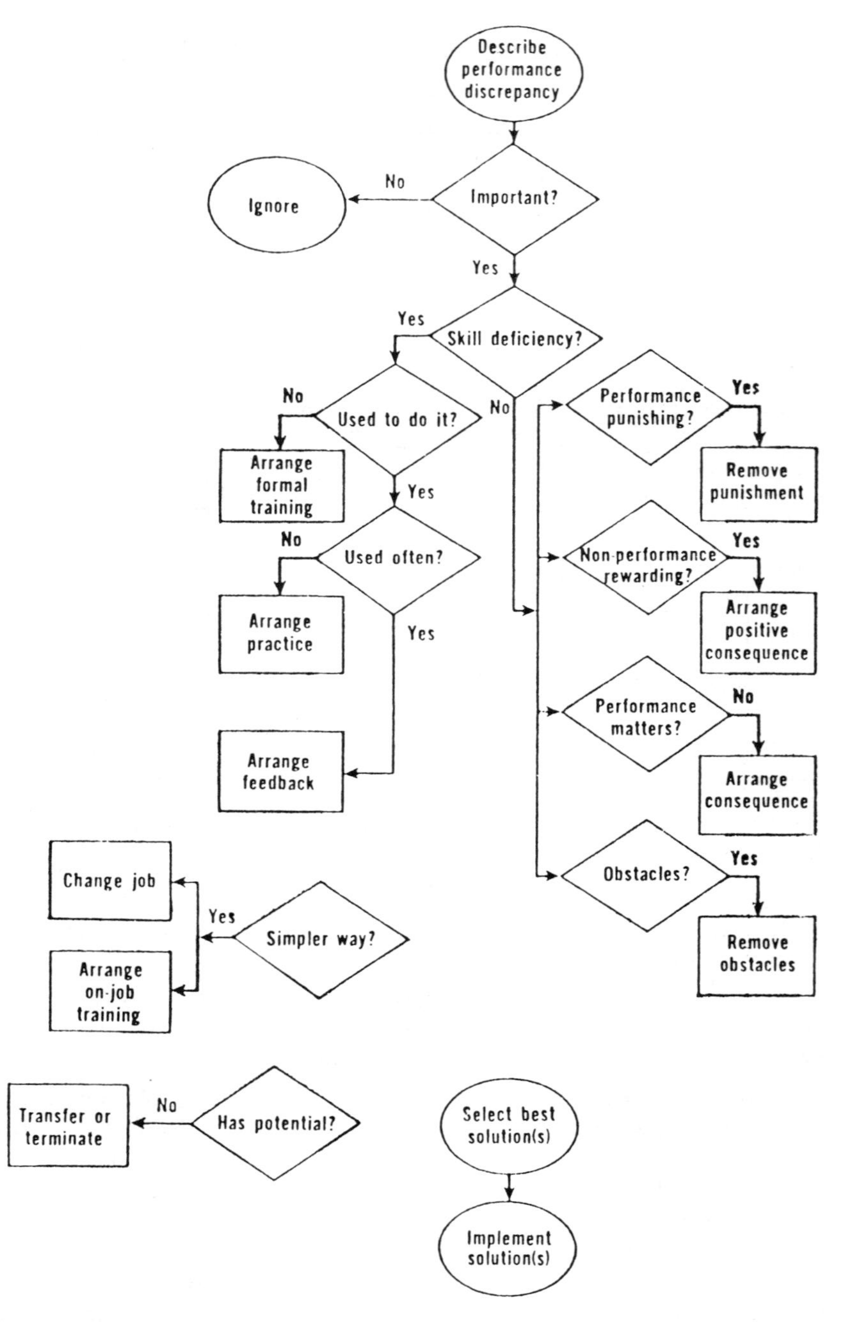

Figure P-2. Mager and Pipe's flow chart. From *Analyzing Performance Problems*, by Robert F. Mager and Peter Pipe. Copyright 1970 by Pitman Learning, Inc., Belmont, Calif. Reprinted by permission.

Nadler also identifies several questions that are important to the assessment process:

1. Is there agreement on the problem?
2. Is there agreement that training is the solution?
3. Is there a specific decision to start the design?
4. Who says it is a need?

Most of the above discussion may be summarized in the following A → B model (Ulschak, "Contracting: A Process for Defining Tasks and Relationships").

Assume for a moment we are assessing a training program. Point A in the model is the present condition or situation of the training program. What type of training is there (if any)? What is the frequency? How effective is it? Who is involved? What are the facilities available? What assessment is being done? Point B is the desired future conditions of these various components. Two parts of a needs assessment are (1) present conditions, and (2) desired future conditions.

A Present	B Desired Future
Human Resources	Human Resources
Training Program	Training Program
Facilities	Facilities
Assessment Process	Assessment Process
Etc.	Etc.

An example of this model: a typist involved in a needs assessment. Step A is to find her speed and error rate and compare it to step B, the desired rate. If a significant gap exists, then step three, a plan for correcting the gap, is proposed. Note that the gap is not assumed to be a training need. Rather, a plan is formed to correct the gap.

This book stresses the concept of identifying gaps between what is and what is desired. However, the discrepancy identified in that process is not assumed to be one that needs to be addressed by training. Indeed, the only assumption is that there is a "gap" (a discrepancy). The next step (step three) is to determine the most effective way of intervening to correct the "gap."

The three overall steps of the needs assessment process are

1. Identify present conditions.
2. Identify desired conditions.

3. Develop strategies for moving from present conditions to desired conditions.

The third step raises the question of training as an appropriate intervention. The third step is deciding on an intervention strategy. Argyris (*Intervention Theory and Method*, p. 15) defines intervention as "... (coming) between or among persons, groups, or objects for the purpose of helping them." Argyris continues on to identify three key elements of an intervention. They are (1) valid information—the intervention is based on valid information, (2) free choice—the intervention needs to be a "free choice," and (3) internal commitment—the intervention needs internal commitment. A multitude of interventions may be made in step three. Hornstein, Bunker, Burke, Gindes, and Lewick (*Social Intervention*) identify a multitude of intervention possibilities. It is with step three that some of the intervention controversies arise. Mager and Pipe, Gilbert, and others stress the point that training is not the only intervention available.

The essence of this book is built around steps one and two. Step three is left for the trainer to decide about. In one organization, the trainer may be strictly that—she is a person who only has responsibility for training. In another organization, she will have responsibilities for a variety of training and development interventions. Consequently, the assumption is that the processes discussed in this book will result in "needs identified." The next determination is if those needs are to be addressed via training or by some other means.

TRAINING AND DEVELOPMENT: THE INTERSECTION OF THE INDIVIDUAL AND THE ORGANIZATION

> Perhaps one way to dramatize this is to say that we may, within another 10 years, become far less concerned with managers development as a means of adapting the individual to the demands of the organization and far more with management development to adapt the organization to the needs, aspirations, and potential of the individual.
>
> (Drucker, 1973, p. 35)

Note the emphasis here: the organization and the individual. This statement represents a part of the author's value system. Training and development efforts will have their greatest impact when they happen at the intersection of organizational and individual needs. This is illustrated in the following diagram:

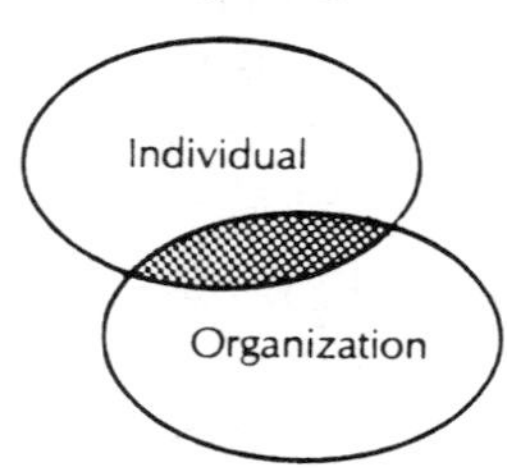

For training to be effective and efficient, both sets of needs must be recognized. Obviously, if only the individual's needs are recognized, the organization will be inefficient because training will not further the organization's purpose. On the other hand, when only the organization's needs are targeted, the individual will find little motivation to achieve those needs. Only when the individual's needs are met, as well as the organization's needs, will there be motivation.

An individual in training who does not see this relationship probably will carry back very little of his/her training to the job. During the training session itself, motivation will be a problem. Training is "adult learning," and a key principle of adult learning is that adults learn because they see a relationship between the learning and a goal that is important to them. Perhaps the goal is a sense of satisfaction in being able to do a job better, or perhaps more money. Whatever the outcome, the individual sees that meeting the organizational need is also meeting some of his/her needs.

Park (*Management Training*) discusses the relationship between company objectives and individual objectives. For example, the individual and company both have objectives relating to growth and survival. However, the company is interested in efficiency, profits, responses to consumers, and social responses, while the individual is interested in effectiveness, stability, self-actualization, and self-worth. Park's point is while the two go hand in hand, their uniqueness must also be seen.

The training target, then, is the intersection of the individual's needs and the organization's needs.

AN ASSESSMENT IS NOT . . .

These are some things that a needs assessment program is not. *A needs assessment is not magic.* It is only as productive and useful as the information invested in it. For example, if an organization has a high level of distrust, an assessment process may track down some fairly useless information. It is the "garbage in—garbage out" syndrome. Assessments at best will provide direction. If you are looking for an answer "for all time," you will be disappointed. There is no magic, but a good assessment can save considerable time chasing training "red herrings."

A needs assessment is not static. Organizations and persons are open systems, i.e., they are dynamic and changing. What was an important need this week may shift next week. Consequently, change needs to be taken into consideration in the assessment process. What was useful information this time may not be useful a month from now. That means assessment must be a continuous process. Maslow ("Theory of Human Motivation") pointed out that we are constantly being motivated by unfulfilled needs. As soon as one need is met, another emerges to take its place. This is certainly true in training. Training is an ongoing process rather than an end point.

A needs assessment is not an end in itself. It is a means to an end; consequently, it requires monitoring. A recent meeting with several trainers discussing needs assessment was stagnating fast. Whenever the word "need" was stated, each trainer became very serious and racked his or her brain with the question "What do I need?" The result was a very boring, dead-end session. Then, one of the trainers said "Let's stop talking about needs and instead talk about things we would like to see happen." All of a sudden there was a spurt of energy, and in a few minutes, a list of "wants" was identified. The "wants" were evaluated for the "needs" implied in them. The result: a highly productive meeting. If the formal concept of needs assessment gets in the way, throw it out. What is significant is that we develop ways to assess "gaps." It is not important to do it a "certain way."

Sauer and Holland (*Planning In-House Training*, p. 61) provide an interesting comment. Their advice is that if assessments have not worked for you, shift away from asking about needs. Instead, talk with the people with whom you are working about what they do—what are their problems? What are their operations? Out of those discussions will come needs. Argyris and Schon (*Theory and Practice: Increasing Professional Effectiveness*) discuss theories-in-use versus espoused theories. When you ask someone what they would do, you get an "espoused theory." When you see what they do in a certain setting, you get "theory-in-use." Asking for needs directly may get "espoused needs." Talking about problems may produce "needs-in-use."

Assessment is a tool. A recent article in *Training* (Zemke, 1981) points out that at one time training assessment was a simple process. The world of that time was a simple world where jobs were stable, well defined, and unchanging. Today, that is the exception rather than the rule. Jobs may be ill defined or under defined. Change is a constant. And, the simple models of assessment may not work as they once did. By keeping assessment in the "tool" perspective, it is possible to see the methodologies of the past as useful places to begin a study of the modern organization.

OVERVIEW OF TEXT

This book deals with assessment of training needs. The processes described are appropriate regardless of whether the training program is part of a company in the private sector or part of an organization in the public sector. The processes will be useful for business organizations as well as for voluntary organizations. The applications presented are general and need to be adapted to a particular organizational setting. The intention of the book is to provide a "smorgasbord" of ideas and processes that may be adapted to a variety of settings. The key question for the reader is "How might I apply this to my setting?"

There are four audiences for this book: (1) the novice trainer who is just beginning to be involved in training needs assessment; (2) the professional trainer who would like to have a book of methods and options available; (3) the "duel hat" trainer, i.e., the person who has several roles to play in the organization, one of which happens to be the training role; and (4) the student of human resource management. In essence, it will be useful for anyone who has some responsibility for training design.

This book is analogous to a "tool box" for needs assessment. In it are a variety of tools that may readily be used in all areas of assessment. There are tools for assessing climate, developing criteria, conducting assessment, and evaluation. The reader selects the tools that best fit his/her organization.

The book is divided into three parts. Part I directs its attention to the needs assessment environment. Assessments happen in an environment and that environment requires understanding. The chapters in Part I include

Chapter 1: A model for viewing the overall training and assessment function. This chapter is designed to give an overview of what is to come. It provides a road map of what to expect. The training function is laid out in sequential stages with a discussion of each stage. Later chapters are built around the model presented. The intention of this chapter is to provide an overview of the author's model for training.

Chapter 2: The environment. Training programs happen in a context. They are not independent of their surroundings, but rather are initimately caught up and dependent on what is happening around them. To not realize the constraints and opportunities of that environment could be fatal to the training venture (and the person in the training seat). A key concept proposed for the trainer is the recognition of "power bases." Trainers need to be sensitive to the "political environment" in which training exists and happens. Several practical exercises are included to assist the trainer in diagnosing the training environment. The important point is to recognize the training function within the organization and to understand the political connotations of the training role.

Chapter 3: Criteria. There are many possible needs assessment tools. One of the problems might well be a "tyranny of options," i.e., too many possibilities from which to select. By developing criteria in advance, there is a higher probability of selecting those methods most useful to your current setting. Several exercises are included to focus on specific criteria applicable to your particular setting. The goal of the chapter is to help the reader identify and develop criteria for conducting needs assessment in his or her own context.

Part II specifically focuses on assessment methods. The intention is to provide an overview of the traditional method of assessment as well as current methodologies. Part II is divided into two parts. The first is a discussion of "generic methods" and the second a discussion of some "composite methods." The composite method chapters have been contributed by a number of persons who have done considerable work in their particular area.

Chapter 4: Generic methods. Generic methods are the traditional assessment methods offered in most discussions of needs assessment. Observation, interviewing, and questionnaires are examples of generic methods. Generic methods also refer to the components that comprise some of the more current assessment methodologies. For example, assessment centers involve the use of observations, questionnaires, interviews. Generic, then, refers to those methods that are the traditional methods as well as those that form the components of most current methods.

Chapter 5: Nominal group therapy. Nominal group theory is a group method for assessing training needs. It involves leading the members of a group through a series of structured steps designed to target a set of training needs. NGT has a wide variety of applications for problem solving and need identification.

Chapter 6: Delphi technique. The Delphi technique is especially useful when the group being surveyed represents a cross section of an organization and there is concern that certain members will exert a biasing influence. It involves the use of written questionnaires given out to a respondent group. The responses to each questionnaire are tabulated and the next questionnaire is composed from these tabulated results.

Chapter 7: Critical incident. Critical incident is a technique for assessing training needs. It focuses on incidents that happen in the work setting. These incidents are collected and categorized for training needs.

The specific methods are

Chapter 5—Nominal Group

Chapter 6—Delphi

Chapter 7—Critical Incident

Chapter 8—Competency Models

Chapter 9—Assessment Center

Chapter 10—Performance Appraisal

Chapter 11—Career Development

Chapter 12—Exit Interviews

Chapters 10, 11, and 12 do not contain specific needs assessment methods; rather, they are included as possible sources of needs assessment information. The main purpose of each of these processes is not needs assessment. However, in the process of carrying out their intention, they do collect information that may be useful for the trainer.

Various levels of assessment may be identified throughout the chapters. McGehee and Thayer (*Training in Business and Industry*) provide the classic model for viewing needs assessments. The three major levels are

1. Organizational Analysis
2. Operations Data
3. Individual Analysis

Chapter 8: Competency models. Competency models begin with the question "How do we identify the competencies which are needed in this particular job?" The goal is to identify specific competencies needed for a specific job.

Chapter 9: Assessment centers. There is probably no other assessment method that has received more attention than the assessment center. This chapter will focus on some of the theory behind assessment centers and will present actual examples.

Chapter 10: Performance appraisal. Performance appraisals are a rich source of needs assessment data. While appraisals may be used in a variety of ways, the focus of this particular chapter will be on their use in the training and development of employees. A variety of examples will illustrate their use.

Chapter 11: Career development. Career planning is a vital source of assessment material. As with appraisals, career planning may already exist within an organization. This chapter will discuss how information that is found within career planning may be readily used by the trainer as a source of needs assessment.

Chapter 12: Exit interviews. When an individual leaves an organization, many organizations have an exit interview. The interview is designed to assess the individual's reasons for leaving the organization. As such, it can provide the trainer with hints about possible training needs.

Part III is a support section. It contains material designed to be supportive of the assessment process. The chapters include

Chapter 13: Survey design. Since most assessments involve some type of survey, i.e., an interview or questionnaire (or both), this chapter focuses on the design of surveys. A major discussion in the chapter relates to planning the assessment. Two other important parts are (1) a discussion of interviews and questionnaires, and (2) a discussion of types of questions that may be used. The goal of this chapter is to assist the training practitioner in the design of effective surveys. Many of the tips in the chapter are pulled from social psychology and organizational field research. However, they are put in a form that is readily usable by the trainer who wants to design a questionnaire that will provide valid information on training needs. The chapter has useful advice for the novice trainer and confirms what the experienced trainer has learned.

Chapter 14: Evaluation. No discussion of the needs assessment process is complete without an evaluation of that process. How effective was the needs assessment? Did it do what it was supposed to do within the resources and constraints of the process? If it broke down, where did it break down? What parts? And, was it adequate for our needs or do we need to restructure it? The evaluation chapter presents specific evaluation questions the trainer may use to determine the effectiveness and efficiency of the assessment process. The model presented may be useful to evaluate not only assessment but the actual training program itself.

Appendices: Several case studies are presented in the appendices at the end of the book. They illustrate some of the concepts in the text—both what should and should not have been done. They also provide practical illustrations of assessment processes based on the author's experience.

One last comment about the organization of the chapters. At the end of most chapters are exercises and questions that attempt to assist the reader in applying the chapter content to his/her organization. The intent of these exercises is to provide a means of grounding the chapter's lessons.

This book, then, contains a number of "tools" useful for the assessment of training needs. As with any "set of tools," the user is ultimately responsible for selecting and using those tools appropriate to his or her situation. The chapters contain many suggestions and tips about the selection of a needs assessment process as well as evaluative comments about the processes. The reader is the final judge as to what may work best in his or her setting. In harmony with the opening quote, the reader is invited to view needs assessment as "detective work."

REFERENCES

Argyris, C. *Intervention Theory and Method.* Reading, Mass.: Addison-Wesley, 1973.

Argyris, C., and Schon, D. *Theory in Practice: Increasing Professional Effectiveness.* San Francisco: Jossey Bass Pub., 1974.

Drucker, P. *Management.* New York: Harper & Row, 1974.

Gilbert, T. "Praxeonomy: A Systematic Approach to Identifying Training Needs." *Management of Personnel Quarterly,* Fall, 1967, p. 20ff.

Hornstein, G.; Bunker, B.; Burke, W.; Gindes, M.; and Lewick, R. *Social Intervention.* New York: Free Press, 1971.

Kaufman, R., and English, F. *Needs Assessment: Concept and Application.* Englewood Cliffs, N.J.: Educational Technology, 1979.

Laird, D. *Approaches to Training and Development.* Reading, Mass.: Addison-Wesley, 1978.

Mager, R., and Pipe, P. *Analyzing Performance Problems.* Belmont, Calif.: Fearon Pub., 1970.

Maslow, A. H. "Theory of Human Motivation." *Psychological Review,* Vol. 50, July 1943, p. 370–396.

Moore, M., and Dutton, P. "Training Need Analysis: Review and Critique." *Academy of Management Review,* July 1978, p. 532ff.

Nadler, L. *Designing Training Programs: The Critical Events Model.* Reading, Mass.: Addison-Wesley, 1982.

Park, C. *Management Braining.* Basking Ridge, N.J.: Walliker Pub., 1977.

Sauer, S., and Holland, R. *Planning In-House Training.* Austin, Tex.: Learning Concepts, 1981.

Ulschak, F. "Contracting: A Process for Defining Tasks and Relationships." In J. Jones and J. Pheiffer. *The 1978 Annual Handbook for Group Facilitators.* La Jolla, Calif.: University Associates, 1978.

Zemke, R. "Needs Analysis: A Concept in Search of Content." *Training,* February 1981, p. 22ff.

Part I

The Assessment Background

Part I provides the foundation for performing needs assessment. An important aspect of any assessment is understanding the environment in which it takes place.

Using the categories of Kaufman and English (*Needs Assessment: Concept and Application*), this becomes the "Alpha" assessment because the intention of these chapters is to explore the assumptions being made about training and needs assessment. In doing so, some of the assumptions being made about assessment may surface and be addressed.

Chapter 2 directs its attention to understanding a general model of training and how that model corresponds with assessment. The chapter provides a road map with which to view the training function.

Chapter 3 focuses on the question "How valued is the training function in the eyes of the formal and informal organization?" The more valued the training function, the greater the potential impact on the development of employees. An important dimension of this chapter is the concept of "power." Various trainer power bases are discussed.

Chapter 4 is concerned with criteria that the assessment process must take into account. Any assessment must adapt itself to certain boundaries and limitations, such as time constraints and personnel constraints.

REFERENCE

Kaufman, R., and English, F. *Needs Assessment: Concept and Application*. Englewood Cliffs, N.J.: Educational Technology, 1979.

1

The Training Cycle Overview

There is nothing so practical as a good theory.

Kurt Lewin

INTRODUCTION

The function of a theory or a model is to provide an accurate representation of some empirical phenomena. For example, a good theory of behavior is immensely useful because it allows us to understand the "whys" behind certain behavior and, in some cases, allows us to predict behavior and to intervene in determining it. A practitioner confronted with a problem between two subordinates may find that a theory of conflict is extremely useful. The example of a road map is an appropriate analogy.

Have you ever taken a trip without a road map? If so, you know the value of having a guide to help you make decisions through the maze of highways. In fact, without a map you may find yourself hopelessly lost. Maps provide a representation of reality. They are not equivalent to reality, but rather provide a compact, though approximate, picture of reality. This is the shortcoming of a map (or model)—by design they are simplistic. If you have used a dated map, i.e., one which no longer is current, you know the problems that can arise—

turns that no longer exist (or do exist but do not appear on the map), dead ends, etc. The dated map no longer provides an accurate reading of empirical facts. Current maps are important in helping us to get from one point to another. Their value is determined by how accurately they represent reality.

This chapter provides a "map" of the book and a model for viewing needs assessment. Its purpose is to provide a model for viewing the assessment process in the context of the training program. The "map" will let you know what to expect as you progress from chapter to chapter. And, like most maps, it is designed to provide information not only about the specific area you are looking at but about the surrounding area as well, i.e., not only will you be looking at needs assessment but at a general training cycle as well. The major concern of this book is for needs assessment methodologies. A companion concern is understanding the context in which the assessment takes place. Like all models, the one presented in this chapter is simplistic. That is its purpose—to take a complexity and simplify it. If it did not simplify it, we would be left with trying to analyze a chaos of undifferentiated facts.

An important concept here is that of systems. In its simplest form, a system is an attempt to look at the total picture—to see the whole—instead of one aspect. By viewing assessment from this perspective, we are able to identify how a change in administrators or new equipment impacts the assessment process itself. Systems theory allows us to understand more clearly how change in one dimension of the training system impacts and carries over to other dimensions. The chapter will begin with a general systems view of training and then move to the specific model for this book.

SYSTEMS MODEL

Seiler (*Systems Analysis in Organizational Behavior*, p. 23) provides a model focusing on input-output analysis of social and technical elements of organizations. While his original focus is on organizations, the model can be readily applied to a training system. Seiler's model is illustrated in the following table:

Inputs	Transforming System	Outputs
Social	Activities	Productivity
Technical	Interaction	Satisfaction
Human	Sentiments	Development
Organization		

The "inputs" are

1. Social structure—here are the norms, the values, etc., of the organization. Training will function differently in an organization where human resources management is valued than in one where human resources management is seen as a waste of time and money.

2. Human—quite simply, this refers to the people who are involved in a particular organization—those who constitute the human resources. For the trainer, this is the basic material he must work with. He must analyze human skills and deficiencies.

3. Technical—every organization or system has a technical environment that includes the physical environment as well as the technical resources, e.g., word processors, computers, etc. With computers, trainers have new training options.

4. Organizational—the final input is the way the social, human, and technical structures are interrelated. One place where this relationship is evident is in the organizational chart. Whether the training function is located close to the chief executive officer (CEO) or not will affect its potential effectiveness.

The inputs to the organization pass through the transforming system and become "outputs." Productivity, organizational growth and development, and job satisfaction on the part of employees comprise the major outputs.

Seiler's model provides a foundation for viewing training as a system. The system has inputs, transformations, and outputs. Figure 1-1 illustrates the specific applications of Seiler's model to the training environment. The components of a training system shown in Figure 1-1 are not inclusive; other specific inputs may be identified as the model is applied to a training program.

A second way of viewing the training system is to view it as a process via a flow chart. Parker ("Statistical Methods for Measuring Training Results," p. 19) provides a process model for viewing training systems (see Figure 1-2).

Parker's model provides a specific road map to follow in training design and evaluation. The need analysis leads to training objectives. Training objectives become the basis for designing curriculums and selecting training methods. The evaluation is designed on the basis of the curriculum and training methods; the program is implemented and the results measured. The model is a step-by-step process. The flow is cyclical in nature.

Laird's model (*Approaches to Training and Development*) for the training and development process takes in a broader perspective (see Figure 1-3). The model begins with the decision to hire and is followed by a variety of questions:

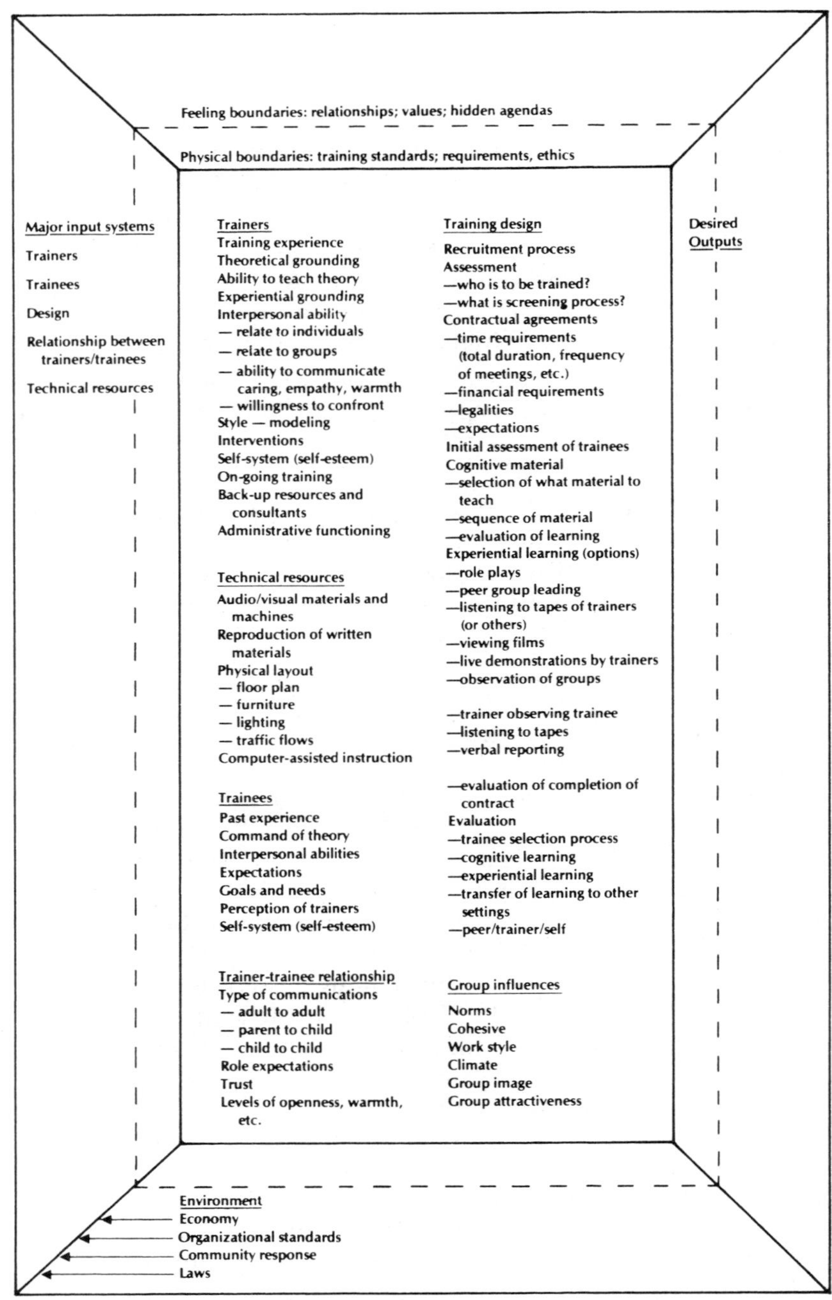

Figure 1-1. Components of a training system. Francis Ulschak.

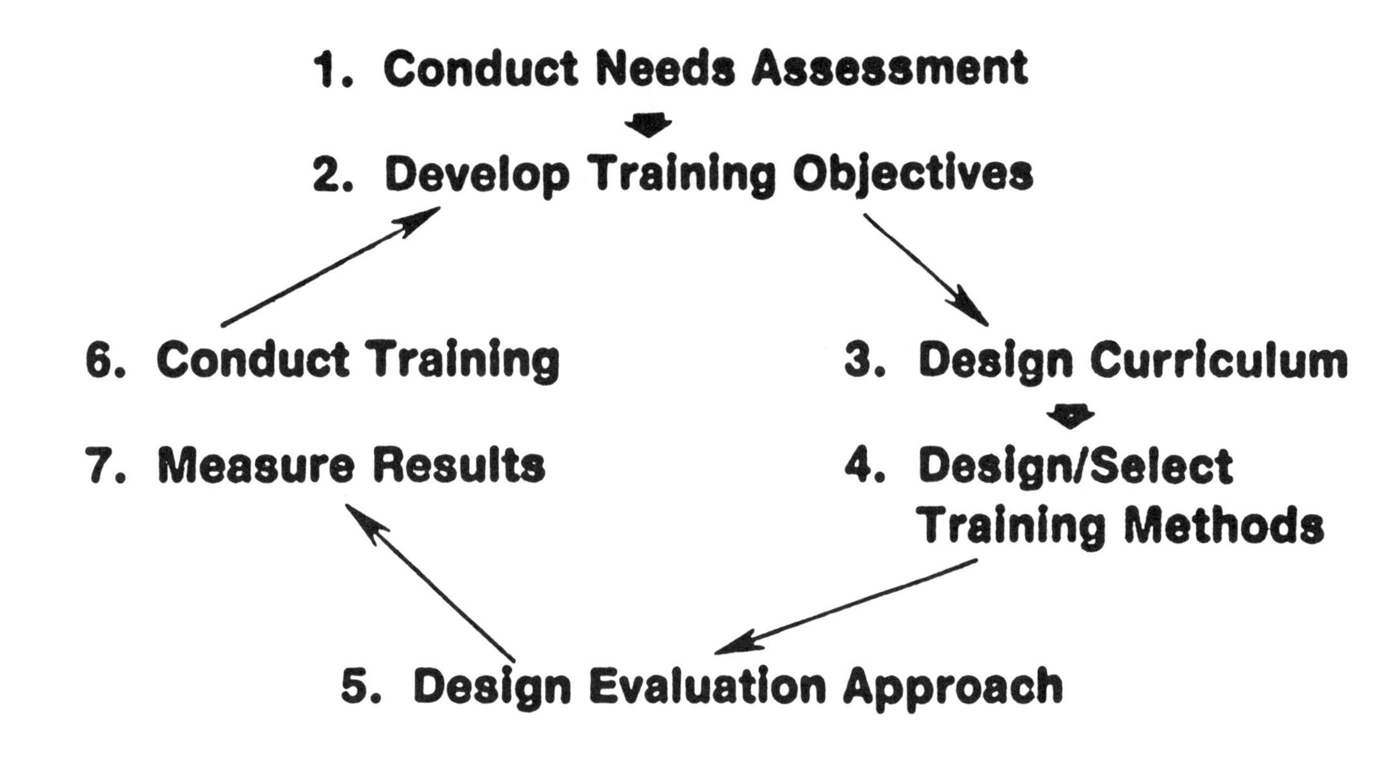

Figure 1–2. Parker's model. Material taken from R. Craig, *Training and Development Handbook*, 2nd edition. New York: McGraw-Hill, 1976. Reprinted with permission.

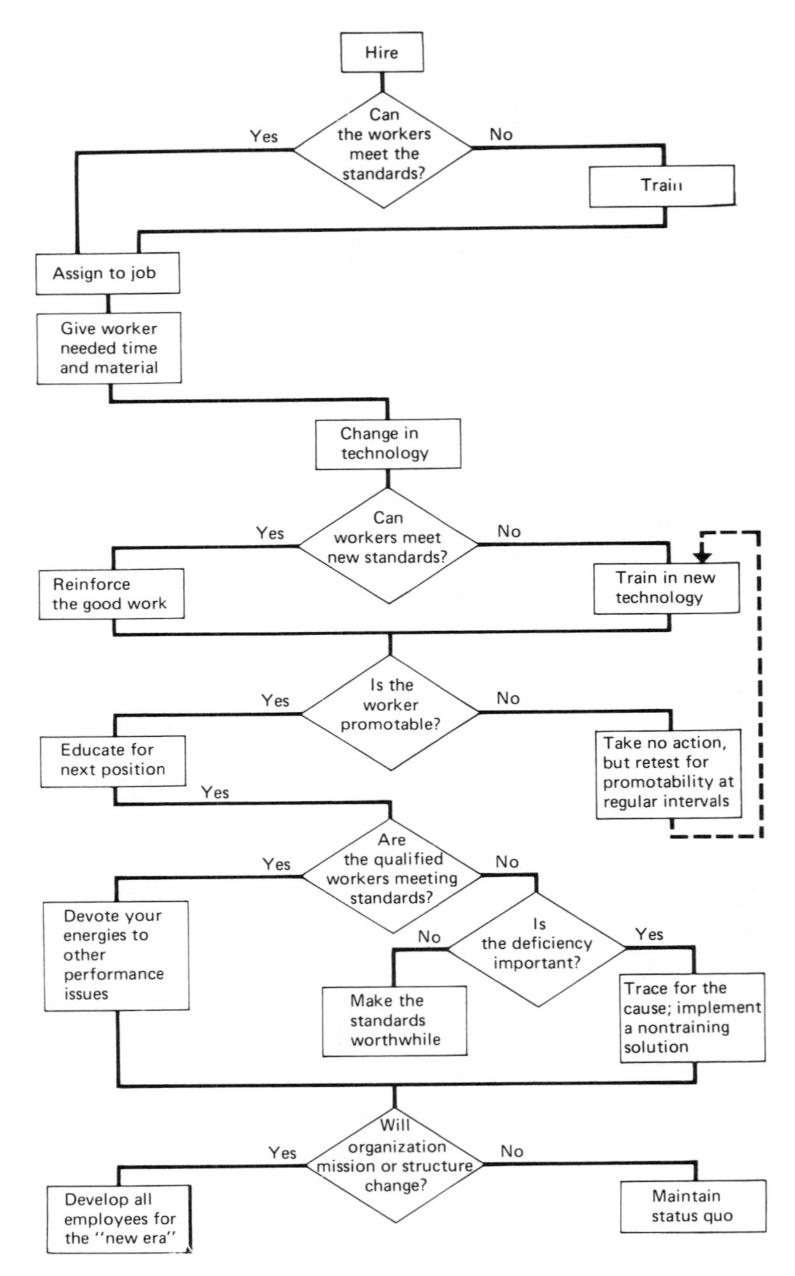

Figure 1-3. Laird's model for training and development. From *Approaches to Training and Development*, Dugan Laird, 1978, with permission of Addison Wesley Publishing Co., Reading, Mass.

1. Can workers meet standards?

2. If there is a change in technology, can workers meet these changes?

3. Is the worker promotable?

4. Are standards being met?

5. Will the organization mission or structure change?

The model provides a series of questions to be asked that have implications for training design.

The author's model for training and development represents still another approach (see Figure 1-4). The model is cyclic and is presented in a flow chart manner. It will be discussed in detail.

Figure 1-4. Ulschak's training cycle model.

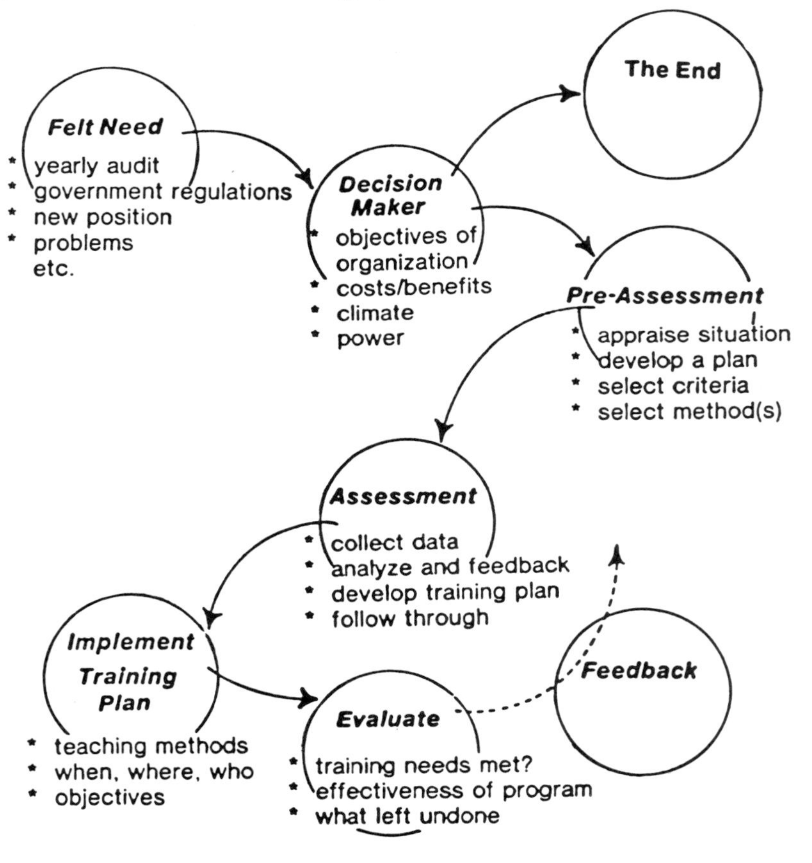

Felt Needs

Training of any kind begins because there is a felt or perceived need. The felt need may arise in many ways:

- Financial statements that indicate a drop in productivity.
- Market analysis that shows a drop in the market shares.
- Quality control finding that indicates an increase in rejections.
- Rapid employee turnover (retention of "good employees" is difficult).
- Exit interviews that indicate employees did not feel they were able to develop their skills or that they were not trained properly.
- Government regulations indicating a program that must be developed, i.e., safety training or EEO training.
- New positions within the firm that demand training, i.e., a new computerized record-keeping system that demands information be stored in a specific way.
- The "boss" says so. Perhaps one of the decision-makers has been to a conference where a colleague from another company has talked about the effectiveness of a certain motivational training program. Returning to his own company, the decision-maker proposes, "We will try this new training package."
- Customer complaints increase significantly.
- An attitudinal survey or problem survey identifies a problem to be corrected.
- Performance appraisals indicate a need for certain training.
- A supervisor observes employees performing an activity incorrectly.
- Employee accidents and the morbidity associated with them apparently increase.
- A formal needs assessment.

These situations represent a few ways in which the initial training need becomes "felt." The needs may be divided into two different categories. The first of these is internal to the company. Examples would include morale problems, establishment of new positions, exit interviews, etc. The second of these is external to the company. Examples involve such matters as government regulations, the availability of new technology, competitors, a shift in values by the larger society, etc. For example, a major construction project is required to put its field supervisors through training in government regulations affecting their job safety. Before the project is entitled to government permits, an external source determines the kind of training the field supervisors receive.

Both the internal and external sources of need awareness result in change that is related to

- Technical changes
- Human changes
- Product or service changes

The following diagram represents these changes:

External	Internal
Human Changes Technical Changes Product/Service Changes	Human Changes Technical Changes Product/Service Changes

An example of a technical change is the addition of a new piece of equipment. Some level of training is needed in order to operate it correctly. Human change may be seen in a shift in the work force via demographics, e.g., an older work force requiring a different kind of training. Product or service change relates to the organizational outputs—some change has occurred that requires attention; perhaps a new product or a new way of producing it has effected the change.

While the two sources of need—external and internal—in an environment are identified for the sake of analysis, one must recognize that there is constant interaction between the internal and external. The mini-computer is a good example. The technology for the mini-computer has been developed and the price has become competitive. Consequently, a firm may see the cost benefit from acquiring this tool as highly favorable. A change (new technology) occurs in the business environment affecting the firm. New ways of recording and storing information become necessary, persons trained in its operations are needed, and information collection and storage become necessary. A change in the external technology brings about new training needs.

Another example may be seen in a totally different area. Recently, much has been written about sexual harassment in organizations. One way of identifying this problem has been through internal surveys ("Sexual Harassment: Is Training the Key"). Since the need has been identified, there have been various social pressures to develop problem-solving responses to it. Today, some organizations under external pressures, e.g., threats of law suits, are developing internal training to address the issue. The point: the internal and the external interact.

Training assessment, then, begins with an awareness that there is some problem or potential problem that needs to be addressed.

Example. XYZ Penitentiary contacts a consultant to provide them with communication training for the guards. The stated intent is to create a "better climate" within the penitentiary.

The consultant asks the question "How is it you reached the decision to begin the training now?"

The response was that the number of altercations between the guards and prisoners is increasing very rapidly. In the first half of the year, the number of altercations almost equaled what happened in the past year. The result: the decision to do something.

The awareness came about because of the increase in "write ups."

The Decision-Maker

A need is felt. The next question is "for whom is the felt need a problem?" Somewhere the data is changed from facts and figures about employee retention to the information: "We have a problem with retention." The question of who makes that move is secondary to the question, "Is he or she a decision-maker?" If the answer is "no," the next question is "Does he/she have the ability to influence the decision-maker(s)?" Whyte, Wilson, and Wilson (*Hierarchical Structures*, p. 219), in a discussion of systems, use the following analogy about the decision-maker:

> It's a bit like the umpires discussing their efforts. The first one said with some satisfaction, "Balls and strikes, I call them as I see them." The second, a little more arrogant, said, "Balls and strikes, I call them as they are." The third one, of greater experience and wisdom, said, "Balls and strikes, they ain't nothing until I call them."

Who is the decision-maker? A decision-maker is the person who has the power to say "yes" or "no" to the proposition of exploring the felt need. He/she is that person who has the authority to say "Go ahead" or "Forget it." The decision-maker is the one who determines if it is a strike or not. The decision-maker has "organizational clout."

If the decision-maker says "No," the process comes to a halt. The need may still exist, but the process is formally terminated. The person who has the "felt need" may decide to (1) forget it, (2) put it on the back burner, or (3) figure out ways to influence the decision-maker, e.g., find a higher level decision-maker to intervene on his/her behalf. Depending on the situation, any of these may be effective courses of action.

"Forget it" is equivalent to "avoiding the problem." The person involved decides that there are other more important uses of his/her time. A training person may have an indication that stress management would be useful for a group of employees. But her boss vetoes it. The trainer sets it aside and proceeds to work on other training programs.

"Put it on the back burner" means that the program is not forgotten. Rather it is set aside temporarily, but the person involved keeps a mental note of the program and watches for changes that may signal a time for raising the issue again. Gathering more information on the need for the program might be a useful tactic.

"Figuring out ways to influence" the decision-maker actively engages the person involved in a "selling" process. She feels strongly about a need and actively pursues it. She pursues the politics of the organization, which may mean enlisting the aid of other decision-makers, or it may mean collecting more information. It also may mean getting others to talk to the decision-maker about the need. The person involved makes a commitment to pursue the need against the current of the primary negative response. Chapter 2 discusses this issue of "power" and environment. It is a neglected topic in training literature and is of critical importance. Without it, the best laid training plans may not be developed.

However, the decision-maker may also say "yes" to the request. Permission is given to explore further, and a variety of factors come into play.

Some of these include

- The organizational objectives. How does the "felt need" accommodate organizational objectives? A person may identify a training need as relaxation or well being. However, if the decision-maker does not see how these apply to the organizational objectives, they will be dismissed. Accommodating organizational objectives is an important consideration.

- Cost-benefits. These relate to objectives. A decision is made about the cost and benefits associated with pursuing the "felt need." Is it worth it? A need may fit with the organizational objectives and simply not be worth pursuing. Once the question of accommodating objectives is settled, the next question is about worth or value.

- Organizational climate. An important factor to consider is the general climate of the organization. A rigid and "hard core" organization influences decisions one way; an organization concerned about the "quality of work life" influences them in quite another way. Webster's Dictionary summarizes the meaning of climate in the following definition: "any prevailing conditions affecting life, activity, etc." Obviously, if the climate is "closed," this may implicitly affect the decision-maker. Perhaps a decision to proceed is made, but everyone involved knows that it is futile.

• Power. Another consideration is power. This refers to the political conditions of the organization. The decision-maker by definition has the authority to make things happen but may choose not to because of internal politics. Or a decision to proceed may be made on the basis of politics. As mentioned earlier, power is a fact of organizational life that the trainer must acknowledge.

• Training mission. Still another consideration is the training mission involved. What is the intent and purpose of training within the organization, and is a particular need relevant to that intent and purpose? Thus far, the needs being identified have been referred to as "training need." However, that determination is yet to be made.

The above considerations will influence the decision-maker toward a resolution of "go" or "no go." Remember, the decision being discussed is one of exploring a need further. The "go" or "no-go" decision will determine the prospects for further exploration. This is the initial period for deciding whether a program merits exploring and developing.

Something is "felt" as a need. Now, a decision to explore it has been made.

Example. As mentioned earlier, the decision was made to address this increase in altercations. The decision-maker (clinical director) decided that communication was needed. Discussions with other officials seemed to confirm the decision.

The consultant found the decision-makers ready to move. However, he also sensed that the treatment would not get what the penitentiary was after. A problem had been partially defined—now an assessment needed to be done to identify clearly the nature of the problem and possible courses of action.

The decision-makers agreed to consider options other than a training intervention.

Pre-Assessment

Either through a formal or informal process the decision has been made to proceed with the assessment. When the decision-maker has given his/her sanction, it is time for pre-assessment.

The first step is to actually plan for the assessment process. A little exploring reveals that there are a multitude of assessment methods from which to choose. Thus, a plan for approaching the assessment process itself is required.

As with other planning processes, there is a temptation to jump over a formal planning process into actual performance ("Let's forget about planning and ask some people what they need"). It is frequently the case that the error is not a consequence of too much planning or assessment but too little planning. The tendency may be to jump into assessment without giving adequate thought to what method may work best. To paraphrase Kurt Lewin—"There is nothing so practical as a good plan."

An important part of the plan is an identification of the criteria that will be used to select an assessment method. We all have criteria from which we work. It is not uncommon to use implicit criteria, but it is much more valuable to make them explicit. "Budget" is a criterion that is normally very explicit.

If financial resources are abundant, the potential for an assessment expands accordingly. Questionnaires may be validated to a highly significant degree, outside experts may be used, interviewing may take place in exotic retreat centers, etc. However, it is rare to find such abundance of resources.

There are a multitude of other criteria that could be mentioned and these are discussed in a later chapter. The important element here is to recognize that part of the planning process involves identification of the major criteria that need to be considered.

After the criteria are identified and listed, the next issue is one of weighing the criteria. Are some criteria vital and others of minor importance? One criterion may be critical; another may be nice but not necessary. For example, in one organization, confidentiality of the assessment process may be critical, and in another organization it may be a minor consideration.

Finally, we are ready for a decision about an assessment method. Considering the many possibilities, we may simply check them off against the criteria listed. A sample matrix such as the following may be sufficient.

	Method 1	Method 2	Method 3	Method 4
Criterion 1	______	______	______	______
Criterion 2	______	______	______	______
Criterion 3	______	______	______	______
Criterion 4	______	______	______	______
Criterion 5	______	______	______	______

The method that satisfies the greatest number of criteria "wins." Actually, there may not be a clear winner, but the table provides good clues about the method having the best probability.

Example. One of the first steps was to identify the criteria for the assessment methods. Several important criteria surfaced:

- Time. The problem was one demanding immediate action; a time limit of two weeks was decided on.
- Money. A definite limited budget was given to the project.
- People. A total of sixty-plus people were to be assessed. It was decided to do a sampling of prison officials as well as guards.

Several other criteria were discussed. After developing a matrix, it was decided that a group interview combined with questionnaires would provide the information needed.

Assessment

With the pre-assessment work behind us, the assessment process can now move forward. The information is collected in the manner that has been selected and is analyzed according to identifiable training needs.

An important aspect of the assessment process is survey feedback, i.e., the respondents are given an opportunity to respond to the analyzed information. The case studies at the end of the book provide some examples of the feedback method. The method becomes a way of not only checking the analysis, but of gaining support for the decisions.

Once the training needs have been established, the training objectives are put together in a training plan. The questions become:

- Who will do the training? Insider? Outsider?
- When will the training be done?
- What will be the duration of the training?
- Where will the training be?
- Who will be involved in the training?
- What will the budget be?
- What will be the training methodologies?
- What resources will be used?

The following illustration reflects these questions:

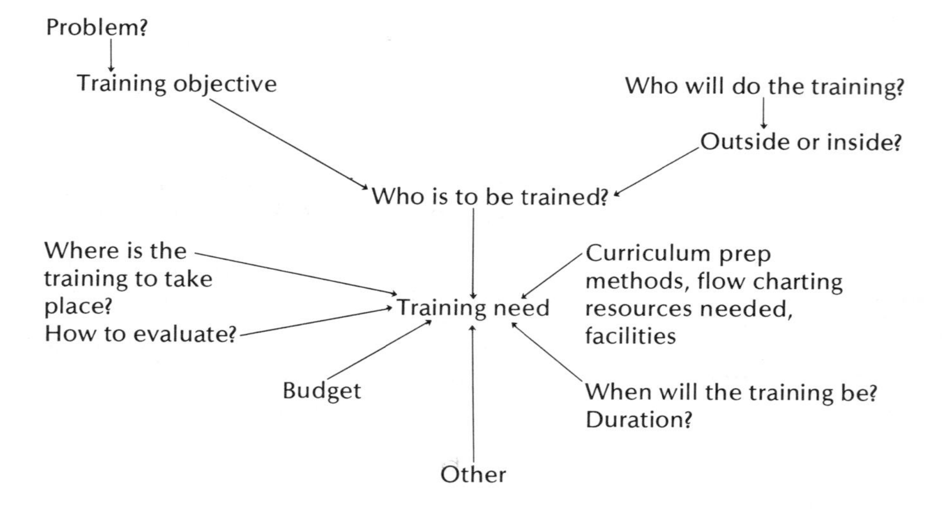

These questions interact with one another. It is not important in what order the questions are asked; it *is* important that the questions are asked.

Thus, during assessment, the information is collected, analyzed, and a training plan established. This is all a part of the input phase.

Example. With the method selected, the assessment proceeded. Group interviews were held at which questionnaires were also filled out.

The theme of the questionnaires was on how the problem of contacts might be dealt with. In this way it was a "Beta" assessment since the objective was given.

The results of the assessment clearly indicated that training was a questionable intervention. While it could be done quickly, it would be relatively ineffective.

Implementation

Implementation is simply putting the plan into action. The training now takes place. Very little will be said in this book about implementation, because the major focus is on the needs assessment process itself.

Example. Priorities shifted and it was decided that some communications would be useful as a way of saying to the guards, "You are important." However, future interventions were targeted as being the crucial agendas.

Evaluation

With the training (or at least a segment of it) complete, the time is ripe for an "end evaluation." The most important question is "Within the constraints set forth, did the assessment do what we wanted it to do? Did we get the information we were after?" The outputs of the assessment are evaluated.

Here, it becomes necessary to discuss evaluation at two levels. The first level is an evaluation of the needs assessment: Did it actually get the information that it set out to get? It may be that, at the end of the evaluation, we find that we have obtained good information, but the cost of the assessment was disproportionate to the cost of the training—we spent more money on assessment than the final training warranted. In other words, the assessment was not efficient.

The second level is the training program itself. Did the training program (a) do what it was designed to do? (b) meets the needs only partially? (c) miss the mark? If it did what it was supposed to do, we can celebrate. If it has been partially successful, we need to identify the parts left undone and decide whether to redesign a program for them or simply to dismiss them. And, if the training missed the point, we can either rework it or leave it alone.

An important consideration in evaluation is "spillover" from the training. For example, a supervisory training session was not very successful in teaching a specific skill, but a positive spillover was that people got to know one another and shared ideas and problems, i.e., "networking." The primary goal was partially met, but most important, something unintended but even more significant occurred.

The spillovers may be either positive or negative. The example above is positive. At a poorly designed training program people may leave saying, "Boy, I never want to come to another training program here," or persons may leave with incorrect information resulting in damage to people or machines.

Evaluation is a critical step for the training cycle and the assessment process. If the assessment was accurate, it will be reflected in the evaluations.

Example. The general consensus was that the assessment was vital and effective in identifying courses of action that more adequately addressed the needs identified.

The evaluation process was done informally with the decision-makers involved.

Feedback

Feedback is continually happening in the training cycle. It is included in the flow chart simply to index its presence and importance.

Specifically, at the end of the evaluation, feedback needs to be circulated back to the decision-makers and others involved in the training cycle. Via feedback, additional needs are discovered and the effectiveness of the assessment process is maintained.

Again, feedback and assessment are a continuous process. Assessment begins with the initial felt need which is the result of feedback, which in turn results in assessment, and the cycle continues.

Example. Feedback was fairly continuous through the entire project. When the initial questionnaire was being developed, various individuals were sought out to critique the questionnaires. Also, one of the questions during the interview had to do with evaluation of the assessment process—did they understand the questions? Did they think the right questions were being asked, etc?

SUMMARY

This chapter has presented several models for viewing the training function. The author's general model for training has been discussed in detail. The parts of the training cycle include

1. Felt needs: Coming from internal and external sources.

2. Decision-maker: Deciding whether to pursue the need or not.

3. Pre-assessment: Identifying criteria and assessment methods.

4. Assessment: Collecting and analyzing data and developing a training plan.

5. Implementation.

6. Evaluation: Did it do what it was supposed to do?

7. Continuous feedback.

REFERENCES

Laird, P. *Approaches to Training and Development.* Reading, Mass.: Addison-Wesley, 1978.

Marrow, A. *The Practical Theorist.* New York: Basic Books, 1969.

Parker, T. "Statistical Methods for Measuring Training Results." *Training and Development Handbook.* 2nd ed. New York: McGraw-Hill, 1976.

Seiler, J. *Systems Analysis in Organizational Behavior.* Homewood, Ill.: Irwin, Inc., 1967.

Whyte, L.; Wilson, A.; and Wilson, D. *Hierarchical Structures.* New York: American Elsevier, 1969.

Zemke, R. "Sexual Harassment: Is Training the Key?" *Training,* February 1981, p. 22ff.

2

The Needs Assessment Environment: How Valued Is Training?

INTRODUCTION

Assessment is not done in a vacuum. Rather, it happens in an organizational context. The purpose of this chapter is to provide an understanding of some of the dimensions of the organizational context. Consider the following illustration.

Some time ago a social service agency invited me to conduct a needs assessment that would lead to a staff development workshop. As usual, I requested a meeting with representatives of the staff to facilitate the study, i.e., to find out what they would like to have take place at the workshop. During the assessment, my questions focused on their perception of organizational and personal training needs. One of the questions I asked them was to identify organizational problem areas.

However, after a few interviews, I began to question the information I was getting. A typical interview revealed that the agency was a wonderful place and that there was nothing to improve upon. I decided that either I was in "organizational heaven" or that there was a hidden agenda that I was missing.

Finally, one staff person (who happened to be moving to another agency) made a disclosure. In the past few months, some sensitive material about the agency had been leaked to various persons in the community, resulting in bad publicity. In the wake of that publicity, the director called together the total staff. In this meeting, she made it clear that anyone who talked about the internal workings of the agency or made critical remarks about it to outsiders would be dismissed. The meeting was extremely emotional, and the message left little room for ambiguity.

Three weeks after that very intense meeting, I reappeared to ask questions about problem areas in the agency. Even though I was there with the sanction of the director and the agency's governing body, distrust and doubt about the assessment questions permeated the entire meeting.

The context in which the assessment is done has a significant impact on the assessment process itself. This chapter will discuss several aspects of the assessment context. An important theme throughout is that the more training is valued within the organization, the more effective the assessment will be. First, we will look at the formal organizational structure and the placement of training. The intent will be to discover how training is formally viewed within the organization. Then we will discuss the informal role of training. The power bases of the trainer, along with trainer "roles," will be examined next, and finally some of the negative spillovers from assessment will be identified and discussed.

TRAINING: THE FORMAL IMAGE

The essential question in this section is "How valuable is training in the eyes of the formal organization?" Several indicators of the value placed on training will be discussed.

A good place to begin our discussion about the impact that the context of training has on assessment is to look at the formal placement of training in the organizational chart. How the training function is viewed is critical to understanding whether assessment will be useful or not. If training does not have management support, the assessment process may be a useless exercise. A fairly typical organizational chart may be similar to the diagram on p. 23.

This traditional type of organizational chart shows the authority structure of a particular organization, i.e., the chain-of-command. The training personnel report to the personnel manager who, in turn, reports to the vice president of human resources who, in turn, reports to the chief executive officer (CEO). The training function becomes quite removed from the CEO.

Normally, training will be found in the personnel function or

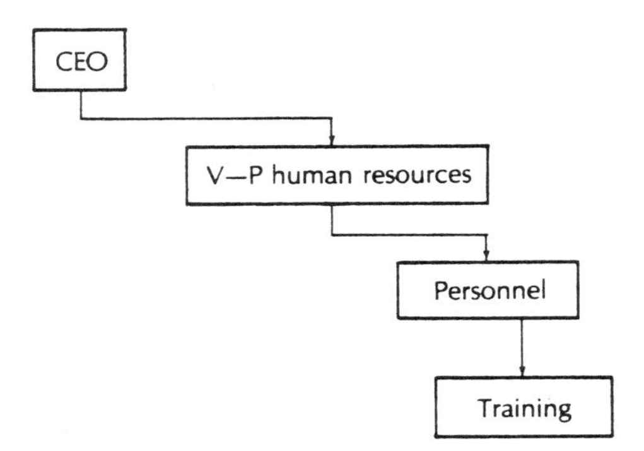

within its immediate vicinity. The reason is quite simple: personnel has a good deal to do with the human factor in the organization—human resource planning, recruiting, selecting, hiring, exit interviews, job descriptions, safety programs, affirmative action. Consequently, training is an appropriate "bedfellow."

Depending on the size of the organization and its training needs, the personnel manager may (1) be the trainer via the "multiple hat" routine; (2) supervise the trainers; (3) have training delegated to other personnel. With increasing government regulations, specifically in the area of safety (OSHA) and affirmative action programs (EEO), there is a good probability that some training functions will be found in personnel.

Another structure that might be seen is the following:

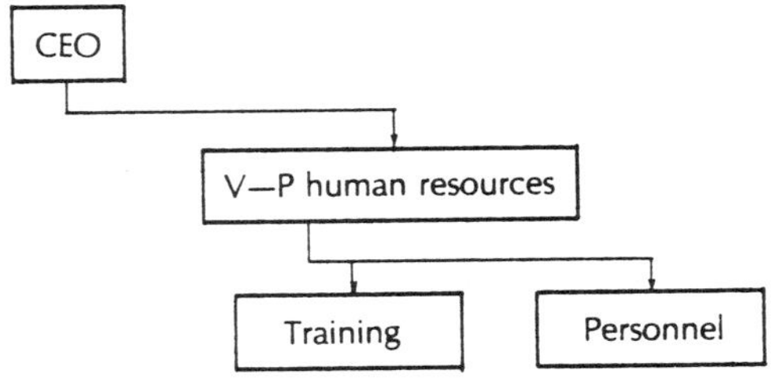

The new position of training in this structure indicates that training has taken on a significantly new role in the organization. Training has only one layer of management before it has access to the top level of decision-making in the organization. The new position indicates that training is seen by the organization as a more vital function than in the first chart.

Still another structure is shown in the following diagram:

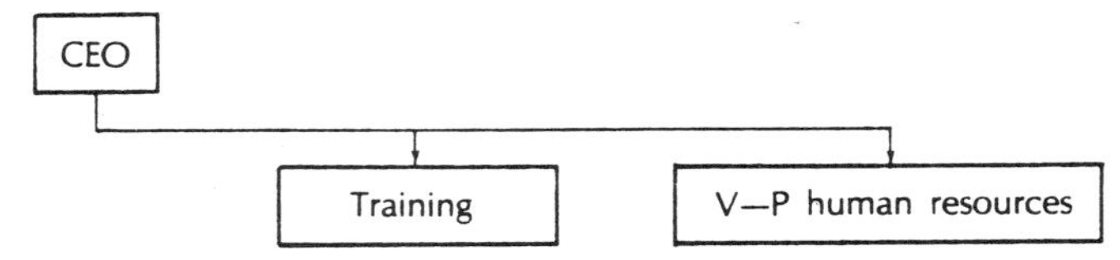

Here, training takes on an even greater role in the organization. Instead of having to penetrate one layer of the organization, training has direct access to the highest level of management. Its organizational structure has increased substantially. Of the three structures, training would have the greatest organizational clout in the third structure. Laird (*Approaches to Training and Development*, p. 41) suggests that this is the ideal training position. "Everyone knows" that the trainer has direct access to the CEO. The result—an expanded power base for the trainer.

A good place to begin assessing the role of the training function in an organization is to look at the formal structure of the organization and to raise the question "How close is the training function to the top decision-makers?" A general rule is that the closer the training function is to top management, the more "clout" it will have within the organization. The actual organizational structure, then, may be a useful starting point when assessing the organizational climate of training.

Thus far, we have been considering only the organizational structure as an indicator of the value of training. There are other clues that may be used to assess how valuable training may be within a particular organization.

Another way to look at the context of training is to view the physical settings of training. Steele (*Physical Settings and Organizational Development*, p. 3) states that one purpose of his book is

> . . . to make readers aware of an environmental crisis in our culture. This is not a crisis of pollution. . . It is a much more subtle crisis, arising from the fact that people always exist within an environment, and that usually they are in surroundings which are unhelpful or detrimental to what they are trying to do. The crisis here is a lack of fit between needs and setting. . . .

Steele's book is an exploration of the importance of the physical setting on the organization. Physical dimensions not only influence work patterns, social contacts, etc., but also make a statement about how the organization views that particular position or department. Where is the training department located physically with respect to the rest of the firm? Is it a "back burner" location, i.e., out of everyone's way? Or is it in a location that provides access to significant decision-makers? Simply stepping back to view the physical setup will provide some insights into the position of the training program in the organizational context.

Pfeffer (*Power in Organizations*, p. 222), in a discussion of power within organizations, refers to the "space" a department has within the organization as a symbol of power. He states:

> The competition for power and status within organizations becomes evidenced in and reflected by physical settings. In the case of at least two major banks in the San Francisco area, the personnel and executive development departments are located in separate buildings; in both cases they are located in older, smaller, and less lavishly appointed spaces than the principal administrative offices. The physical separation makes contact with important operating units on a regular basis more difficult. And the physical separation and condition of the buildings provides a continual, visual reminder of the relative status of the various functions.

Later, Pfeffer provides the following quote from J. Wright's 1979 book *On a Clear Day You Can See General Motors*:

> In General Motors the words "the fourteenth floor" are spoken with reverence. This is Executive Row . . . To most GM employees, rising to the fourteenth floor is the final scene in their Horatio Alger dream. . . . The atmosphere on the fourteenth floor is awesomely quiet . . . The omnipresent quiet projects an aura of great power. The reason it is so quiet must be that General Motors' powerful executives are hard at work in their offices . . . It is electrically locked and is opened by a receptionist who actuates a switch under her desk in a large, plain waiting room outside the door . . . GM executives usually arrive at and leave their offices by a private elevator located just inside Executive Row.
>
> Across from the elevator are several bedrooms used by visiting executives or those too tired to go home. To the right, inside of the entrance, is the executive dining room. Straight ahead . . . are executive offices opening on either side. They are arranged in order of importance . . . There is great jealousy among some executives about how close their offices are to the chairman and president . . . The decor of the fourteenth floor is almost nondescript—blue-green carpeting and beige, faded oak paneling . . . The executive offices are arranged in pairs, separated by a central office occupied by a private secretary for each executive . . . Doors . . . open to a single, spacious executive office. All were uniformly decorated in blue carpet, beige walls, faded oak paneling and aged furniture . . . except for those of a few uppermost executives, who could choose their own office decoration. . .
>
> One rule on the fourteenth floor was that we should frequently use the executive dining room especially at lunch. GM wants its managers to eat together whenever possible . . . As in the offices outside, there was a pecking order even in the executive dining room. To the left of the main dining area was the "Executive Committee Dining Room" where the top corporate officers met every day for lunch.

There is no empirical data that the closer the training offices are to the decision-makers, the greater the influence of training will be within the organization. However, there is some intuitive data. While there may be a variety of factors mediating the relationship between the physical location of training offices and facilities and the esteem or status of training within the organization, location still remains an indicator.

A recent consulting example illustrates this point. In visiting a previous client, I found that the physical location of the offices had been changed. Formerly, training had been assigned to an "out of the way" first floor office. The space was limited and conditions were crowded. Training's new office space was located on the third floor. The offices had been decorated and there was plenty of room for privacy as well as interaction. Significantly, the third floor was also the floor that held the offices of the CEO and the top vice presidents. The change in office arrangement reflected a new role for training in that organization. A new CEO was recently hired who had a strong commitment to the training function.

Physical location of offices is yet another formal indication of the importance of training.

The budget is a more delicate and difficult indicator. The training budget (or lack of it) indicates the organizational position of training. Is the budget adequate for the training needs? Does training have its own budget or is it a line item on another department's budget? Is training one of the first budgets to be cut? These questions provide clues to the value of training.

Pfeffer (p. 232) discusses budgets and their meanings within the organization. Citing the works of Cyert and March (*A Behavioral Theory of a Firm*) and Wildavsky ("Budgeting as a Political Process"), he builds the case for budgets as symbols of decisions made and outcomes of political processes establishing priorities. As such, budgets are indicators of power and status within organizations. And as such, they have implications for trainers.

Still another way to get a view of the context of training is by looking at the persons who are in charge of the training function. In the past, one of the criticisms of the personnel function was that it was the "dumping ground" for incompetent managers whom the organization decided to keep around rather than terminate (Byars and Rue, p. 23). Personnel was seen as a relatively safe place for an incompetent because he or she could do only minimal damage there. However, times have changed and a firm that continues this practice today could be in serious trouble. Government regulations are one force that has caused personnel functions to expand considerably.

Training may be the new "dumping ground." A quick way to discover this is simply by asking "Who have been the persons involved in the past in the training function?" "What is their background in training?" "What was their organizational experience?" As you consider those persons, you may quickly get a sense of the organizational context. For example, if the "dumping ground" practice has been in effect, you may find persons who have little or no training background, experience, or interest. Perhaps they came to training via marketing, finance, management, or some other area, and their track records may well be below "par."

Or you may find the opposite. There may be persons in the department who are actively involved in the training profession regardless of their previous positions. Walking through their office, copies of various professional training journals may be seen; their interest in the training profession is expressed through familiarity with current developments. By determining who is in the training seat, a good deal can be discovered about the organization's outlook on training.

To summarize this section, then, there are many organizational indicators that provide clues as to the value placed on training within the organization. Some of the more significant ones include

1. The location on the formal organizational chart. Where is training located in relation to the other organizational functions?

2. Physical location of offices. Again, where are training offices located in relation to other offices?

3. Budget. Does training have its own budget? Or are its functions dependent on another budget? If there is a budget, how are budget requests responded to in relation to other departments?

4. Training director. What is his/her experience and how did he/she get into this position? Does he/she show a concern and interest in the training function?

TRAINING: THE "INFORMAL" LOCATION

The formal context of training is fairly easy to identify through the use of organizational charts, physical location, an examination of who gets into the formal position, etc. However, equally important is the "eye of the beholder," i.e., the perception in which training is held by various groups within the firm. Four major groups include: superiors (those to whom trainees report), trainer's peers (a trainer's colleagues), supervisors (those supervising the persons being trained), and, of course, the trainees (those who are the subjects of the training). These four groups will be discussed in detail later.

The informal context of training deals with the perceptions of these various groups concerned with the training function. Their perceptions are as important as the formal aspects. Why? Because people act on their perceptions. If the general feeling is—"Training gets in the way of my being an effective supervisor. I mean, here I am at a training program on time management. But who is going to take care of that pile of stuff on my desk? Training around here is useless."—that will definitely influence behavior during training sessions and attitudes toward training in general. If the general attitude is that training is a waste of time, the probability is that it will be a waste of time. The emphasis here is on the image of training.

The general point is that training will be significantly influenced by how people perceive it—whether they see it as an important, useful function or not.

One aspect of this is the history of the training. How do the various interest groups view the usefulness of the training that has taken place? What is the training's track record? Consider for a moment the four major groups mentioned earlier.

First to be considered are the "superiors." Some of the formal aspects just discussed indicate their perception of training, i.e., the training budget, physical structures, its location on the organizational chart. However, there is also the "off-the-record" view of training. Perhaps formal training is regarded as a valuable function but, "off the record," it is seen as a stumbling block to management operations. Imagine how the superiors would respond to some of the following questions:

- Do you see training as contributing to or detracting from the "bottcm line"?
- If you were to describe training as a person, what kind of person would it be?
- How highly valued is training here?

Responses to questions like these earmark the superiors' view of the training function. Obviously, these responses have a significant impact on the way training will be viewed in the organization.

Second, the supervisors must be considered. Supervisors are those persons who manage and oversee the persons involved in training. They are the "front line" of the organization and have the immediate impact on the supervisee in the day-to-day relationship. Potentially, they may be training's greatest friend or worst enemy. Consider the following two scenarios:

1. A skills training program has been set up for a specific department. Joe is going to participate and he asks his supervisor about it. The supervisor says, "These programs are a waste of time. All they do is create problems. Who is going to be working while you're gone tomorrow? And, you will forget everything by the time you get back anyway. What a waste."

2. The scene is the same as above except the supervisor says, "Good for you. I'm glad you are going to be involved in that training. You show initiative. When you get back we will do some talking about how what you have learned may be useful to the rest of us."

Which of these two descriptions do you think provides the greatest incentive for the training program? Probably the second scenario. The supervisor sets the tone for training and has an immediate impact on the training environment. The supervisor is a critical person for the trainee; if he/she is supportive, the training has excellent potential. If the supervisor is not supportive, the training has questionable potential. The important point here is that the supervisor's perception of the training program is a social element. If the perceptions are negative, this becomes an important issue for those in the training function.

Nadler (*Designing Training Programs*, p. 227ff) provides an excellent discussion of the need for a training support system and the key role the supervisor plays in that support system. The supervisor is involved in pretraining preparation (actively participates in design, helps select employees, arranges for trainees to attend, etc.), during-training backup (helps cover work assignments, avoids interrupting them at the session, etc.), and followup support (provides reinforcement, identifies new needs, gives feedback, etc.). The supervisor is a vital part of the support system.

Third, and most important (for trainee-centered training), are the trainees' perceptions. It is useful to begin training sessions with questions that extract these perceptions. Questions such as "What do you expect to gain from this training?" or "Why are you here? What do you hope to gain from being here?" provide clues as to how training is viewed. Ulschak ("Contracting: A Process for Defining Tasks and Relationships") discusses the concept of contracts. The initial time in any training event is a time of defining roles and expectations. If responses to questions about expectations include, "I have no expectations for learning," "I've got to be here because I was told to," or "Nothing," then the trainer needs to alert himself to this. Again, a key element of adult learning is that if the learner does not see a purpose or reason for learning, he/she won't learn. If the responses reflect a negative view of the training function, these need to be explored.

The responses to these early questions, then, may indicate how the trainees view the training function. In some companies, it is an honor to be selected for training, and the groups reflect that attitude in their approach to the training session—they are eager and ready to work.

When people attend a training session only out of a sense of obligation, it quickly becomes evident that they feel it will be a "useless session." The group is slow to arrive, resistant to involve themselves, and the resistance becomes an issue to be dealt with early on in the training program.

The trainees are "the bottom line." The training ultimately succeeds or fails according to how the trainees apply and use the training. Knowing the trainees' perception of training, then, is an important piece of information for the trainer. In the needs assessment process, this becomes significant because groups that feel that training is useless and a waste of time may not be open to sharing information on training needs. This attitude may need to be addressed prior to assessment.

Yet another group comes into the picture—the trainer's colleagues. How do they see the training function? What are their beliefs about its place in the organization, and how do they view the trainer? We are familiar with peer pressure and how it may influence behavior. The way the trainer's colleagues look on his function and respond to him may have a significant impact on his views.

Lastly, the trainers themselves must be considered. How do they view their role? Are they waiting to "move ahead"? Do they view themselves as competent and their function as significant? Do they keep up with new events in training, attend conferences, read journals, share with other trainers? Obviously, the kind of attitude they hold toward their work will have a significant impact on how others will view their work and outputs.

The "informal image" of training then may be said to be an intersecting of the perceptions of these various groups. While there will probably not be a consensus (although there might be), the sum of the group's images will give a plus or minus to how training is viewed within the organization. The following diagram represents that summation.

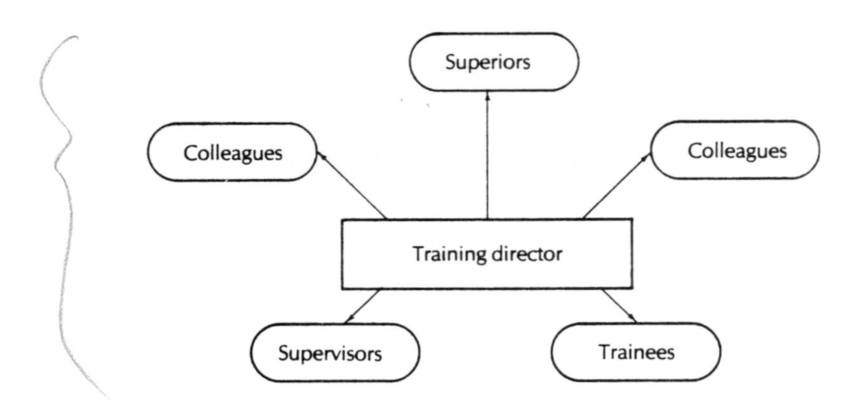

So far, the discussion of the "formal" and the "informal" image has been in relation to the general training function. The relationship to the needs assessment process is obvious. If training is not a valued function (but rather a necessary evil), obtaining the information needed for the assessment may be extremely difficult. Information given may be inaccurate, misleading, or incomplete. If training is valued, the persons involved will be motivated to provide accurate data and adequate time necessary for the interviews, etc. This chapter's opening illustration provides an excellent example of how the context impinges on the assessment process.

The implication of this chapter thus far is obvious: the power position of the training function needs to be assessed as part of a needs assessment strategy. While some shirk at the word *power* and others welcome it, here it is used neutrally, i.e., having neither a good nor a bad connotation. Power is simply the ability to influence another's actions. It is the ability to get something done. Power is an important topic to consider in a book on needs assessment because without an understanding of it, the assessment process may be ineffective and inefficient. Assessment implies some actions will be taken. If training has little power in the organization, the ability to influence actions, e.g., to do an assessment, will also be minimal. Power is the topic of the next section: trainer power bases.

TRAINER POWER BASES

Regardless of the organization, trainers do have a variety of power bases from which to work (Wydra, "Power and the HRD PRO"). The classical listing of power sources by Raven and Kruglanski ("Conflict and Power") has been expanded by Hersey and Natemeyer ("Power Perception Profiles"). These are:

1. Coercive Power—"Based on fear." A leader who uses coercive power forces compliance from his staff through threat of punishment. Failure to comply with the leader will lead to punishments such as undesirable work assignments, reprimands, or dismissals.

2. Connection Power—"Based on the leader's connections with influential or important persons inside or outside the organization." The leader using connection power gains compliance from others because of his connections. Others know that the leader has connections.

3. Expert Power—"Based on the leader's possession of expertise, skill, and knowledge, which gain the respect of others." The leader with expert power is seen as having the necessary expertise to help others get the work done. Their behavior is influential because they see his expertise.

4. Information Power—"Based on the leader's possession of or access to information that is perceived as valuable to others." Since others value the information the leader has, he gains power in their eyes.

5. Legitimate Power—"Based on the position held by the leader." The key word with legitimate power is authority. The person has authority given to him or her by the organization. Generally, the higher the position a person holds in the organization, the greater is his/her legitimate power.

6. Referent Power—"Based on the leader's personal traits." The leader gains power because of personal traits that are liked and admired by others. They identify with the leader and allow the leader to influence them.

7. Reward Power—"Based on the leader's ability to provide rewards for other people." The leader has power because others believe he has the ability to reward them in some way, e.g., pay, recognition, promotion.

Note: An important point to make leading into this discussion is that power is based on the perceptions others have of the trainer. Power that is not so perceived is useless. It is only when a person is perceived to be powerful that others behave appropriately. A key concept, then, is recognizing that power is within others' perceptions.

Coercive power denotes the trainer's capacity to have someone do something via threat. For example, training may be required for a certain position, without which one simply will not be considered for the position. Training takes on considerable power in this context. The trainer can say "Yes, this person has successfully completed the training," or "No, this person has not," and in that evaluation, significantly influence the person's career. An example is doing "well" or "poorly" in an assessment center context. In this sense, he/she has the capacity to use the threat of punishment. The trainer is perceived as having the power to say "yes" or "no" to an advancement. An assessment may carry with it the implications of punishment. The persons involved may feel that they will be punished.

Connectional power is power the trainer has because of his/her connections. Perhaps the trainer has ready access to the CEO or is a member of the top management team. Or the training offices themselves may be prestigious. In this case, training may have clout through the people with whom it associates. An example is the trainer who is close to the personnel manager. If a trainee wants something from the personnel manager, he may carefully "groom" his relationship with the trainer; the trainer is perceived as powerful because of his/her connections. The assessment process may facilitate the building of a trainer's connectional power. In the process of talking with people and assessing their needs, the trainer accumulates connectional power. The manager may reason, "After she talks with me, she will be talking with my boss. . . ." An active trainer will probably have a good deal of connectional power because he/she circulates throughout the organization.

Another source of power is expertise. Perhaps the trainer is not an expert on all the topics the training is designed for, but he or she is an expert on how to design training events. In fact, the crux of expertise may well be a matter of getting others (who are experts in what they do) to share their information. Expertise comes from competence. Competence is not an end in itself; rather, it is an ongoing process. Assessment increases the level of competence. It provides the trainer with even more competence and information about needs, resulting in more effective training.

Informational power is similar to expert power, but it has a different twist. The trainer may have access to information that others would like to have. If so, there is a perception of power. Perhaps the trainer has been privy to discussions regarding plant expansion. Others may look to him as someone who has information about hiring or contracts to be let. The trainer has the power of information. I recently made this point to a group of trainees by casually mentioning that I knew the identity of someone in the group who was being considered for a very prominent position. After a little more discussion, I asked them to reflect on how my comment had affected them. The response was overwhelming: My power had grown substantially and the crucial factor was the information I possessed. The information here may have to do with which individuals or departments are effective and which are not. Information about what people consider to be "needs" may be seen as vital and important, i.e., as powerful. It may be for this reason that some top management groups will watch assessments closely. Assessments may result in the shifting of power bases.

Legitimate power derives from the organization. It is simply the authority the organization assigns to the trainer. As the discussion on organizational charts indicated, this varies from setting to setting. The distinction between line and staff is a major one in this case. Since training is primarily a staff function, its authority may be minimal. The major exception to this is in the area of federal regulations. The safety trainer may have a good deal of clout—if he or she does not, the organization may face trouble. In this way, training is similar to personnel; the more its functions are seen as vital to the organization, the greater is its increase in legitimate power.

An important distinction should be made between power and authority. Authority is derived from the organizational position of the individual. Power represents the individual's ability to get something done. A trainer may have little authority and yet may exert significant power. An excellent discussion of the trainer's authority and power is found in Wydra's article, "Power and the HRD PRO."

Referent power refers to the trainer's own charisma. Watching a "Zig Ziggler," for example, is a good example of charisma. The mannerisms and style are such that people get excited. This may be referred to as the "cheerleading style." The trainer's excitement, enthusiasm, and entertainment are so great as to be infectious. The charismatic trainer has power because he is perceived to be exciting, dynamic, and entertaining.

Reward power is the inverse of coercive power. The trainer is perceived as someone who can authorize a reward. Instead of losing an employee his job, the trainer is seen as having the potential to pass on rewards, such as a promotion. Since the trainer has the option of handing out "goodies," he is perceived as powerful.

The above sources of power represent the major power bases a trainer may have. It is important to note that some have a purely personal basis. Regardless of the organization's endorsement of training, a trainer may still have referent or expert power. The implication is that even in the most thwarted situation, a trainer has potential power bases from which to work.

Power is an organizational given. It is neither "right" nor "wrong," but is a reality to be reckoned and dealt with. For the trainer, it is an important organizational reality to assess. An excellent reference for further reading is Pfeffer.

One way a trainer may begin to assess his power bases is through the use of the "Power Perception Profile." It is a very useful tool in identifying present power bases and developing plans for future power bases.

Another way is to begin to be aware of and assess the roles the trainer has in the organization. Suddenly, a trainer may discover a multitude of ways to increase power bases and, consequently, the effectiveness of training.

TRAINER ROLES

What is a role? It is a set of behaviors that is associated with a position. Trainers have a variety of roles associated with their position. Sauer and Holland (*Planning In-House Training*, p. 2) talk about trainer roles as data collector, data analyst, designer, resource planner, scheduler, supervisor, proposal writer, host, and evaluator. Their particular approach to roles emphasizes tasks and functions.

Mintzberg (*The Nature of Managerial Work*) provides another set of roles for trainers. While his work focuses on general management, an application of his roles to trainers can be very useful. The roles defined by Mintzberg are

I. Interpersonal Roles. Interpersonal roles relate to the interpersonal elements of a trainer's job. Three categories under this heading are

A. Figurehead. The figurehead role is composed of the symbolic jobs. A trainer attending a retirement party in a department or attending the wedding of someone in the organization is an example. Symbolic functions are not required and yet they are important.

B. Leader. The leader role involves getting things done through people. This may mean a task force that the trainer is part of or a person the trainer supervises within the training department.

C. Liaison. The liaison role is the linking pin role. The trainer links up with various persons and groups throughout the organization. Perhaps the trainer makes a point to meet with the industrial engineer or a corporate planner. The role is one of linking.

II. Information Roles. Information roles relate to the gathering and dissemination of information. Some of the roles here are

D. Monitor. The trainer is a monitor of a good deal of information within the organization. The trainer gathers information about problems and needs, workshops and training events, local and regional resources.

E. Disseminator. Not only does the trainer monitor information, but he passes that information around the organization. All types of training information are disseminated to members of the organization, e.g., upcoming training events. Indeed, with so much information coming across a trainer's desk, a key element is deciding what to pass along.

F. Spokesperson. When the trainer is speaking on behalf of the training department, he is a spokesperson for training. Perhaps it is a report session about training activities. Or it may be a presentation of training's view on a topic.

III. Decision Roles. The last category of roles deals with decision-making. They include

G. Entrepreneur. The trainer is concerned with the development of the training function—this is the entrepreneur role. He is concerned about development and growth of personnel, equipment, etc., which help training to do a more effective job.

H. Disturbance Handler. Both within the training department and within training events, the trainer is making decisions about how to handle a particular disturbance. The disturbance may be as simple as a noisy group in the next room or a person within a training session creating a disturbance.

I. Resource Allocator. There are three major resources to be allocated by the trainer—people, time, and money. The trainer is constantly looking at decisions about the use of resources—should we devote staff time to developing this training or that training? Should we have three people work on the project or two? Do we need co-facilitators?

J. Negotiator. The trainer is also a negotiator for resources. Regardless of the structure, the trainer will be negotiating with someone about money, people, etc.

Needs assessments influence these various roles. One part of the assessment may well result in building interpersonal roles. As the trainer collects various information in departments, relationships and links are made. Another obvious outcome is that an assessment process will result in gathering and disseminating information. The result of the assessment will be new information concerning needs and problems. Finally, assessment will also influence decision-making roles. Without proper assessment, there simply will not be the information needed to look at resource allocation or to negotiate for resources.

Trainers, then, need to be aware of the roles that they have within the organization. By so doing, they may assess what areas they are weak in and develop plans for self-development.

POTENTIAL PROBLEMS

Thus far, this chapter has been concerned with how the organizational environment affects training in general and assessments in particular. We have been looking at the organizational factors that overlap and affect assessment. However, assessment in turn overlaps and affects the organization. Many of the positive spillovers have been indicated already. This section will briefly consider some of the problems associated with a needs analysis.

Moore and Dutton ("Training Needs Analysis: Review and Critique," p. 544) identify three major problems associated with the current state of assessments: (1) Assessments are not made periodically, i.e., they occur whenever they appear to someone as a good idea; (2) Assessments are conducted only on a crisis management basis, i.e., when an existing problem needs to be addressed, an assessment suddenly becomes necessary; (3) Assessments are not coordinated with other functions, e.g., human resource planning.

Leach ("Organizational Needs Analysis," p. 58) provides another listing of possible problems. The assessment problems he identifies include (1) failing to distinguish between needs and wants; (2) uncritical acceptance of management's perceptions of needs; (3) failing to correlate needs with organizational plans and objectives; (4) assuming all needs can be met through training; (5) underutilizing needs in program selection and development; (6) depending on intuition and the literature alone to explain the meaning of expressed and demonstrated needs; and (7) the tendency of needs assessment to be reactive rather than future oriented.

The two authors do not provide mutually exclusive lists. Both lists identify common problems, and taken together, they provide a useful backdrop to this section on assessment problems.

From the author's experience, one of the major problems in any assessment process is not using the information that is gathered. Assume that a company decides to do an organization audit but does not act on the material collected. They have launched a "fishing expedition," i.e., they were simply casting around in hopes that something would develop. However, they have no explicit goals for the audit nor any commitment to act on the findings.

The result may be a shattering of employees' expectations raised on the basis of inquiries made. If people are asked to identify training needs, an expectation is created that something will be done with the results. If nothing happens, expectations are unfulfilled and the organization may be confronted with a worse situation than if no questions had been asked. When an assessment process is thwarted, the results are negative, giving rise to more problems and conflicts. There is no such thing as a neutral inquiry. The mere fact of asking questions is a form of organizational intervention: It affects the organization. More will be said about this in a later chapter.

Another problem involves getting information that may be sensitive to the greater organization. I once worked in a setting where the need assessment resulted in a major indictment of a department head. We collected information that created some political problems within the organization. The problems identified were real, and they were eventually dealt with. However, during the information accumulation process, what was obtained was not what was expected. A second problem is obtaining sensitive unanticipated information. An important question is "Will we get information that we don't want, and if we do, how will we handle it?"

Yet another problem occurs in the search for the "perfect assessment." This typically happens in an organization that is continually running assessments. More energy is going into the assessment than into the training. The assessments become a way of avoiding the training program itself—a means has become the end.

Information growing out of assessment may be misused, and that creates further problems. A person may design and use the assessment to prove a point, and in proving the point, may enhance his/her organizational position. Information may be used in a way that is inappropriate to the original intent and design.

Finally, and related to the above, is a simple category of "waste." When not designed properly, the assessment is a waste of the time and energy of the persons involved. A training program's foundation may have been built on faulty information. The result: a waste of people, time, and resources.

The above are some potential problems facing an assessment process. They are not blocks to assessment, but they are problems the trainer needs to be aware of.

SUMMARY

Potential assessment problems include

- Raising expectations and not responding to them.
- Obtaining unexpected sensitive information.
- Putting inappropriate energy and resources into assessment.
- Misusing information from the assessment.
- Crisis management approach.
- Not having periodic assessments.
- Not coordinating with other functions.
- Failing to distinguish needs and wants.
- Assuming all needs can be met through training.
- Uncritically accepting management's perceptions.
- Depending on intuition.
- Underutilizing needs in program selection.

The purpose of this chapter has been to explore the relation of assessment (and, indeed, training) to the organization. Attention has focused on the formal and informal (or perceived) image of training within the organization. A central concern has been power. A major theme is that assessment is not a value-free process—it may alter the power bases within an organization significantly.

The appendices immediately following this chapter are designed to help you think about your organization in light of the chapter's discussion. Take some time to assess training in your setting before moving on to the next chapter.

WORKBOOK: EXERCISES RELATING TRAINING TO ITS ENVIRONMENT

1. Draw your formal organizational chart, noting the location of training.

A. As you reflect on the chart, what status does training hold?

B. How accurate do you perceive your response to (A) to be?

2. Take some time to find out the history of training in your organization. Talk to a few persons about its past history. Note below some of the major points brought up.
Major Points:

A. What are the implications of the history for the present training program?

B. What have you learned from exploring the history of training in your organization?

3. Take a few moments and develop a floor plan indicating where training is located in relation to other departments and top management's offices.

A. As you reflect on the drawings, what implications do they have for your view of training?

B. How significant do you feel the physical location is in your setting?

4. Ask the following question of at least one person in the categories listed below: "If you were to describe the training department as a person, what kind of person would he/she be?"

Top Management Person

Supervisor

Colleague

Trainee

A. What kinds of persons were described? How do they fit with your view?

B. What are the implications of these views for training?

5. Political Analysis. Pfeffer (p. 38) suggests developing a matrix to look at issues of power in organizations. Across the top of the matrix put the political actors. Down the side identify current issues affecting training in your organization. Across the top, indicate the decision-makers involved and, finally, your perception of their stance. Fill in the matrix with (+) in favor of, (−) opposed to, or (0) neutral.

	Political Actors			
	Person A	Person B	Person C	Person D
Issues	______	______	______	______
______1.				
______2.				
______3.				
______4.				
______5.				
______6.				
______7.				
______8.				
______9.				

REFERENCES

Byars, L., and Rue, L. *Personnel Management: Concepts and Applications.* Philadelphia: Saunders, 1979.

Cyert, R., and March, J. *A Behavioral Theory of a Firm.* Englewood Cliffs, N.J.: Prentice-Hall, 1963.

Hersey, P., and Natemeyer, W. *Power Perception Profiles.* Center for Leadership Studies, 1979. Obtained from University Associates, 8517 Production Ave., San Diego, CA 92126.

Laird, P. *Approaches to Training and Development.* Reading, Mass.: Addison-Wesley, 1978.

Leach, J. "Organizational Needs Analysis." *Training and Development Journal,* September 1979, pp. 66–69.

Levinson, H. *Organizational Diagnosis.* Cambridge, Mass.: Harvard Press, 1972.

Mintzberg, H. *The Nature of Managerial Work.* New York: Harper and Row, 1973.

Moore, M., and Dutton, P. "Training Needs Analysis: Review and Critique." *Academy of Management Review,* July 1978, pp. 532ff.

Nadler, L. *Designing Training Programs.* Reading, Mass.; Addison-Wesley, 1982.

Pfeffer, J. *Power in Organizations.* Marshfield, Mass.: Pitman Pub., 1981.

Raven, R., and Kruglanski, W. "Conflict and Power" in P. Swingle *The Structure of Conflict.* New York: Academic Press, 1975, pp. 177ff.

Sauer, S., and Holland, R. *Planning In-House Training.* Austin, Tex.: Learning Concepts, 1981.

Steele, F. *Physical Settings and Organizational Development.* Reading, Mass.: Addison-Wesley, 1973.

Ulschak, F. "Contracting: A Process for Defining Tasks and Relationships" in J. Jones and W. Pfeiffer, *The 1978 Annual Handbook for Group Facilitators.* La Jolla, Calif.: University Associates, 1978.

Wildavsky, A. "Budgeting as a Political Process" in the *International Encyclopedia of the Social Sciences* 2nd ed. New York: Cromwell, Collier, and Macmillan, 1968, p. 192.

Wydra, F. "Power and the HRD PRO." *Training,* August 1981, pp. 26ff.

3

Criteria for Selection: How to Choose From Alternatives

INTRODUCTION

The last chapter discussed the formal and informal images of training and how they impinge on assessment. This chapter focuses on criteria for making decisions. How is a decision made?

Think back to the last time you bought an automobile. How did you make the selection? There were big cars, small cars, multiple colors, multiple interiors, foreign imports, and chrome linings. The different combinations were nearly endless.

One possibility might be that you did not give it much thought, but simply said, "I'll take that one." Even in an innocent statement like that, some criterion was used. Perhaps it was the color, or the particular design, or the interior. Or maybe the only criterion was: Get anything with four wheels that works.

For another person, the question of criteria may be paramount and explicitly stated. For example, during my last purchase, I had several criteria that needed to be met: (1) fuel efficiency (25 MPG minimum); (2) cost; (3) comfort enough for two adults and two children; and (4) front wheel drive. For me and my family, defining the criteria gave us a greater margin of probability that the final selection would meet our needs. And in that definition lies an important aspect—objectives. Criteria are discerned when objectives are defined.

While objectives and criteria are two-way streets, this chapter will begin with objectives and then talk about criteria. The objectives a person has for a particular purchase highly influence the criteria selected. An overall objective to find a vehicle that will allow a person to travel 5,000 miles per year is quite different from an objective to find a vehicle that will travel 60,000 miles per year. Criteria also tend to shift. Perhaps the concern for mileage lessens as the number of miles driven per year decreases. And, as more time is spent in the vehicle, the concern for comfort may increase.

As objectives change, criteria change. Again, criteria only make sense in light of something else. However, the emphasis on the two-way street needs to be reinforced. While the major flow of influence is from objectives to criteria, criteria also influence objectives. Let's look again at the cost factor mentioned in the car decision. If we have a fixed amount of money to spend, our objectives may change.

Enough of the analogy. The purpose of the analogy is to highlight the need for explicit criteria in the selection of a needs assessment method. Note the word "explicit." We all use some sort of criteria in any selection process. However, some of the criteria will be implicit and others will be explicit. Implicit refers to what we have not thought through but still influences us; perhaps it is the manufacturer's name, the color coordination, the recommendation of a friend. The important part of implicit criteria is that we have not consciously identified what it is that we will base our decision upon. And, when we have plenty of resources that is perhaps a minor problem. But, as our resources narrow, criteria become exceedingly important.

Explicit criteria are those conditions we consciously identify that our final assessment must meet. We say "The criteria are. . . ."

1. Criterion
2. Criterion
3. Criterion

Explicit conditions are stated. In conducting a needs assessment, a trainer may have the following criteria for the assessment methodology:

- Must be confidential
- Must cost less than $300 to implement
- Must result in quantitative data

- Must be completed in two weeks

Implicit criteria that accompany these may be

- Must be done by existing staff
- Must produce an agenda for supervisory training

Thus, there are two types of criteria:

1. Implicit—implied assumptions, unstated
2. Explicit—specifically identified and stated

This chapter looks at objectives and criteria. The first consideration in a needs assessment is objectives: What is the assessment going to do? And what is it we desire it to do? A second consideration is that of criteria: What conditions have to be met? Again, these considerations obviously interact: They inform and influence each other.

OBJECTIVES

"Would you tell me, please which way I ought to go from here?" "That depends a good deal on where you want to get to," said the cat. "I don't much care where—so long as I get somewhere," Alice added as an explanation. "Oh, you're sure to do that," said the cat. "If you only walk long enough."

Alice's Adventures in Wonderland

As the cat says, if our objective is simply to get somewhere, we are sure to do that by walking long enough. If our objective is to get to a specific place, then we need to identify that place. There are plenty of persons around who will tell us which way we "ought" to go. There are fewer people with the wisdom of the cat, saying, "That depends on where you want to go."

"Where we want to go,"—a question of objectives. In the Preface, the A→B model was presented. Essentially, the model involves a simple process for setting objectives: Point A is where we presently are; Point B is where we would like to be at some future time; and the lines from A to B are the methods or strategies for achieving that movement.

The model, repeated here, is

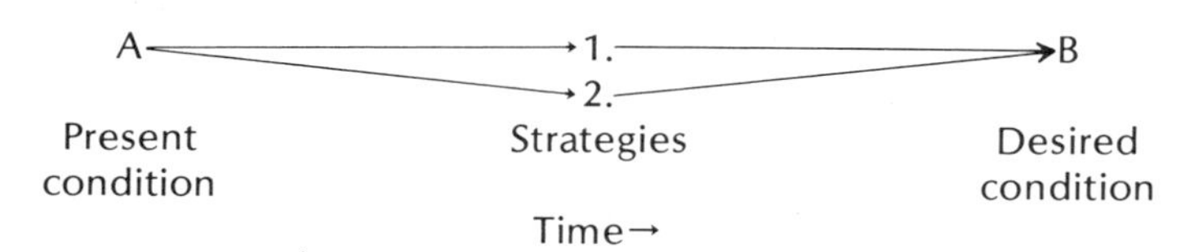

A basic assumption of this chapter is that human beings are goal-oriented. We function continually in a goal-oriented manner. At times we may have difficulty in understanding how another person's behavior (or even our own) could possibly be goal-oriented. However, if we begin to examine the behavior from that person's rationale, we will begin to see the goal directedness.*

A second assumption is that individuals and organizations do not have singular objectives but rather multiple objectives. To conceive of individuals or organizations as being "uni-goal"-oriented is wrong. As individuals and organizations, we have multi-objectives interacting at multi-levels (Mesaronic, "Foundations for a General Systems Theory"). Using the persons identified in Chapter 2 as categories, we will look at the multiple objectives they might have in a needs assessment process.

Objectives for Needs Assessment

Persons	
Management	?
Supervisors	?
Colleagues	?
Trainees	?
Trainer	?

Management's objectives for a needs assessment may be to increase the effectiveness of the training program, or to collect information about the functioning of the organization. Or, there may be an individual manager who wants certain kinds of information to be used for future political tactics. Still another manager may be counting on a feather in his cap: Assessment makes training look good and that will reflect on his managerial capabilities. Within this one grouping of people exists a multitude of objectives.

Supervisors' objectives may be to identify weak areas in the supervisees. Again, there may be other considerations. One supervisor may want to disclose an individual's incompetency. Another may see that training his workers is important for his own advancement. Another may be a firm believer in training. A multitude of objectives will be involved.

Trainees also have multiple objectives. One objective may be self-improvement—learning areas of weaknesses and strengths and

*Throughout this discussion, the term *objective* will be used. While some authors have distinct definitions for "goal" and "objective," I do not. The terms goal and objections may be used interchangeably. In this I agree with Nadler (p. 105) that the important point is not to engage in a semantic debate but rather to understand what the term means.

deciding on a plan for improvement. Or the goal may be to impress the supervisors and prove the trainee's initiative. Still another objective may be to involve themselves in the training venture in order to get away from their jobs for a while (earn a paid vacation).

Colleagues' objectives in a needs assessment will also be diverse. One may promote an assessment program in order to further his program. Another may do it because that is "the thing to do." Still another may be involved because management has said, "You will do assessment." They may talk in terms of effectiveness—increasing the employees' effectiveness and, by better training, enhancing their functions.

A look at the trainers themselves reveals some obvious statements about objectives: to increase effectiveness ... to identify current needs ..., etc. These are not insignificant objectives. However, other objectives also may be involved, i.e., learning how to conduct an assessment, enhancing the status of training, increasing the impact of training, being recognized as having important organizational information, and personal accomplishments.

Park (*Management Training*, p. 56) identifies a number of pulls on the trainer in a training design that may influence objectives:

1. Training program content required by the company.
2. Training content that appeals to individual participants.
3. Allocation of time to training.
4. Participant time investments—is it enriching?
5. Questions of amount of time to cover parts of curriculum.

It is important to recognize the variety and multitude of objectives. Setting objectives becomes continuous as it is applied to managing conflicts and pulling together a variety of objectives within a single sphere.

A second important lesson from multiple objectives is avoiding the assumption that the actors involved share the same assessment objectives. They may have objectives intrinsic to themselves; that is normal and to be expected. By understanding the multitude of objectives involved, it is possible to plan strategies that allow many of the objectives to be met at the same time.

Some common objectives that might be identified are

1. To develop an effective training program. Needs assessment is a means of identifying specific training that will result in a more effective program.

2. To develop a training plan. Perhaps the training program has been drifting and you decide upon an objective and develop a plan to guide the program.

3. To collect data on needs for selling purposes. Recently a person was in my office discussing needs assessment in order to sell a program to top management. She felt that a well-designed needs assessment would appeal to top management.

4. To "keep up with the Joneses." This is the fad element of needs assessment. Everyone is susceptible to it. The objective is to stay abreast of what others are doing.

5. To prove or disprove a point. The needs assessment may be a means of collecting information in order to incriminate another person or group. The accumulation of data validates one set of assumptions and discredits others.

6. To solve an operational problem which will increase organizational effectiveness.

Implicit in Alice's quote is the belief that the more specific the objectives are, the easier they are to achieve. The broader they are, the more difficult to achieve. Broad objectives are fishing ventures—the trainer does some general casting around to see what he/she might catch. At times, the general objectives are useful; at other times, they waste resources. Let's look at the objectives as stated above.

1. To Develop an Effective Training Program.

This objective is very broad and ambiguous. The key to making the objective useful is to specify the conditions. Using the A→B model, we can begin to tighten up the objective.

Condition A (Present)	Condition B (Future)
Training happens when problems arise. Training happens about once a month.	A regular schedule. The 3rd of each month is a training event. Training to anticipate problems, not just react to them.
Training reactive. Something happens and people react.	Training development oriented toward the future; "proactive."
Training responsibilities rotate among several managers. No one is really sure who is responsible.	Designate one manager in charge of training.
Supervisors (4 out of 5) indicate training is a waste of time and do not support it.	Supervisors (4 out of 5) feel training is useful and support it.
Training programs instigated by anyone delegated the responsibility for that month.	Training programs developed via assessment.
No cost-benefit analysis of training.	Training evaluated in terms of specific cost/benefits.

By beginning to focus on specific conditions of A and B, the broadly stated objectives take on measurable characteristics. In essence, effective training is being defined. Actions become clearer. The important move is to make the objectives specific. A specific objective statement that can be derived from this operation might be: "Within two weeks to have the personnel manager designated as responsible for training and for scheduling a set time each month in which training can take place."

Suddenly, the objective becomes very clear and we have established control over it. We have a clear sense of when, what, and who is involved. Cook (*Developing Learning Outcomes*), in a discussion of learning objectives, identifies four parts of a well-stated objective: (1) the who, (2) an observable action or product of an action, (3) conditions under which an assessment will take place, and (4) minimum level of acceptable response. These four aspects of an objective can be very useful in obtaining a measurable, clearly defined target.

The above objective contains most of these parts.

1. Who—Personnel Manager

2. Observable action/outcome—Be designated responsible for scheduling a set time each month.

3. Conditions for assessment—None.

4. Acceptable level—This is a "yes/no" response. The acceptable condition is "yes."

Note that objectives can also be directed toward feelings and attitudes. A target objective may be the ability to change or modify a supervisor's attitudes. Attitude change may be difficult to measure. Consequently, when we work with attitudes and feelings, we begin to use indicators that reflect change.

2. To Develop a Training Plan.

This is implicit in the first objective. And, indeed, after examining the first statement, we may decide that this is what we are really seeking. Again, a useful approach is to use the A→B model:

A (Present)	B (Future)
No consistent plan	A plan outlining who, what, where, when, why, and how much

Other items may be listed under A and B but this is sufficient for now. A indicates that at present, things are simply floating. B indicates the desired goal is a plan.

The way to begin shaping a definite objective is to include Cook's conditions: "The objective is that the training director develop a training plan consisting of an assessment process, a regular schedule for training, training responsibilities, and the location where training will take place. This operation must be completed in two months."

Though we could continue listing other objectives, we will stop at this point. The important concept is that the A → B model is an excellent tool to help create objectives that are useful. Once we have defined A and B, we can begin to look at strategies used to move from A to B.

The important points to remember in this section are

1. There will be multi-objectives and multi-levels involved in a needs assessment.

2. Different "actors" will have different objectives.

3. The A→B model is very useful in shaping a definite objective-setting process.

4. At the very minimum, objectives should reflect who, what, and when.

CRITERIA

The next consideration is criteria. Anything that is deemed to be an important condition for objectives can be considered a criterion.

Newstrom and Lillyquist ("Selecting Need Assessment Methods," p. 52ff) and Steadham ("Learning to Select a Needs Assessment Strategy," 1980 pp., 56ff) provide a useful listing of criteria for consideration. This section will focus mainly on Steadham's work. His list is used as a starting point. However, before we approach that list, we must be aware that this is a "smorgasborg of ideas." Some of these criteria may be appropriate for you and your organization and some may not. It is hoped that the list will sensitize you to the variety of options that exist and provide you with ideas from which to build.

Steadham's criteria include the following:

1. Resources (time, money, people)
2. Health of organization
3. Relation of consultant to client
4. Persons to be involved
5. Desired outcomes
6. Extent to which needs are already known
7. Decision-makers' preference
8. Time lag between collection/action
9. Degree of reliability and validity needed
10. Confidentiality
11. Facilitators' favorite tool

1. *Resources (time, money, people).* Perhaps one major criterion that will be used to select a method will be the availability of resources. Time is an obvious criterion. How much time is available? Do we have days, weeks, or months? When does it have to be completed?

The factor of time has a number of impacts. Some examples include (A) Questionnaire construction. Developing a questionnaire with high reliability and validity takes a fair amount of time. On the other hand, a "quick and dirty" type of questionnaire may be developed in a couple of hours (and, in some cases, get the desired information). (B) Choice of interviews versus questionnaires. An interview process may take longer than the use of a questionnaire. (C) Time constraints may mean that it is more efficient to bring in an experienced external person rather than to try developing material internally. Time is a significant consideration.

Money is another factor. Many would say that in this day and age, money is the criterion: "Give me enough money and I will produce the most brilliant, perfect assessment needed." Given that money is available, other criteria can work in terms of it, e.g., designing for reliability and validity, hiring more people, conducting intensive interviews, using the latest technology. Money needs to be kept in line with the overall training budget. Probably 8–10 percent of the training budget is a maximum guideline for assessment purposes. (There are many figures that might be used here. Laird (p. 23) cites Malcolm Warren's figure of 20 percent for analysis and another figure of 30 percent for task analysis. What is unclear is what these terms mean. They may include a good deal more than what we are discussing here by way of assessment.)

People are another obvious resource. People constitute the power to get done what needs to be done; people who possess the necessary skills to do a particular job are a valuable resource. Will we have to go outside of the firm to get the people we need? Will we have to train people to understand our goals and values?

Resources of time, money, and people are key criteria for assessment.

2. *Health of the Organization.* If the organization is not healthy, it may resist certain types of questions or a particular methodology. If the organization is fairly distrustful, more time and energy may need to be spent in selecting a method(s) that will be able to circumvent the mistrust. For example, instead of only using a questionnaire, a combination of questionnaires and interviews may be used.

The example about the environment at the beginning of Chapter 2 is a good example of an organization with a health problem. If the organization is paranoid, asking questions that reflect on the organization or its members may create inaccuracies and misleading results. The fact is that a healthy organization may be willing to further its health via evaluation and assessment. The unhealthy organization, which really needs the help, may be the most resistive to the very help it needs. An analogy to a family illustrates this point: The healthy family may be the one most willing to seek help and assistance; the family with problems may be the one most resistive to help.

The health of an organization is an intangible—it is hard to determine what healthy or unhealthy is. Yet, at an intuitive level, the difference may be very clear to those who work within a particular organization. Asking people within the organization, "If this organization were a person, what kind of person would it be?", is an excellent way to get at the question of health.

3. Relation of consultant to client. If an outside consultant is being used, the consultant's past relationship to the organization needs to be considered. Will his/her past performance hinder or facilitate the assessment process?

The first part of this is the selection of an internal or an external person to actually design and do the work (or bear the responsibility for getting it done). If the person is internal, he knows the organization and the organization knows him. What do people think of him? Is he a respected part of the organization? Or is he seen as an opportunist who will use anything discovered to his advantage? How do the decision-makers view him? How do supervisors view him? If the person has the respect of his colleagues, that will be very favorable. If not, there may be problems.

The major advantage of the external consultant is neutrality. Precisely because he/she does not know the internal workings, the person may present a less biased survey. As an outsider, he/she brings in the atmosphere of the outside expert. The old adage—"They will take the word of an outside expert, but won't listen to what we say"—is alive and well in many organizations. The obvious disadvantage is that the outside person may fall into organizational traps which an inside person is usually aware of. And the external person may be rationalized away—"What does she know about our business?"

It is wise to be aware of the reputation that a person brings into the organization. The question to ask is "How will that reputation affect the assessment?"

4. Who will be involved? This is an important criterion for a number of reasons. The first one concerns numbers. An assessment involving 600 persons is quite different from an assessment involving 30. The former uses more resources for data collection, analysis, etc. Numbers may dictate the type of method to be used, e.g., with large populations, questionnaires are used as opposed to interviews. One major value of questionnaires is that they may be readily used with a great number of persons.

Another factor is power. What power position do the persons involved in the assessment have in the organization, i.e., legitimate power? If we look at a vertical slice representing a sample of people, whom do we see in control at the various levels? For example, if you are using a group interview format, what do you do if the group is composed of supervisees, supervisors, and management? Or if managers feel that one type of need is more important than their subordinates feel it to be, how should that be factored into the final analysis?

The question of who is involved deals not only with numbers but the character of people as well. Organizational positions, i.e., the level at which a person functions in the hierarchy, need to be examined. Also, some groups may have difficulty with written questionnaires. One setting in which I worked involved persons who did not read. Questionnaires were quickly set aside in favor of other methods.

Simply stated—what characteristics of the persons involved need to be considered in the selection of an assessment process?

5. *What will be done with the outcome?* This is another obvious consideration. Who will use the outcome and for what purpose? If the outcome is to be used to design more relevant training, then the process can be fairly straightforward. If, however, the outcome needs to be "sold" to a decision-maker, then a rigorous, exacting method must be selected. In the first case, the trainer is working with a client in order to identify needs for the next quarter's training programs. The needs are identified and one proceeds to develop the training program. This is quite different from another setting in which one works with a skeptical management team that needs to be convinced of the effectiveness of the assessment process.

6. *To what extent are the needs already known?* Some needs may be fairly obvious. And, as they are discussed informally with various persons, it is clear that they are "needs." Perhaps the training need involves learning how to run a specific machine that has been creating problems for the operators. Everyone knows what the problem is; it is simply a matter of doing something about it. The general rule is that if it is clear and common knowledge what the training need(s) is, don't reinvent the wheel—do the necessary training.

If, on the other hand, there is organizational confusion and chaos, then an extensive assessment may be in order. A company may have gone through significant growth and may have simply lost touch with the training needs. Investment in the assessment process may be significant.

The vast majorities of companies fall somewhere between chaos and recognition. The "common knowledge" is present in an elementary way. Everyone says, "We have a need for supervisory training."

However, the specificity of what that means is missing. Organizational chaos has not occurred, but neither has clarity. The organization is fairly cognizant of its training needs and opportunities and needs a little more clarification.

7. *Decision-makers' preference.* Again, the decision-maker theme comes through. If the decision-makers have a preference for a particular type of method, that becomes a significant criterion. Recently, I was in a setting where the decision-maker was trained and schooled in survey feedback. The type of method he wanted to use was survey feedback. We responded with a survey feedback approach.

Some decision-makers will have a special preference for quantitative data. They would like an analysis showing how serious needs rank in relation to each other, and want to develop a questionnaire resulting in quantitative data and statistics. The final report may have averages, medians, frequencies, or even more sophisticated statistics.

Another decision-maker may lean toward qualitative data—"Go out and talk with people and let me know what they say." The emphasis is not on numbers, but on meeting with people and having open discussions. In a recent project, when a sophisticated assessment plan was suggested to the decision-maker, he simply said, "Just take time to talk to the supervisors. Just ask them what is needed."

An important question to be asked of the decision-maker is "Do you have preferences about how the assessment is done?"

8. *Time lag between collection and action.* Another consideration pertinent to this resource is the time gap between when the information is collected and when action is needed. If there is very little time, a short questionnaire format or a group interview may be best. On the other hand, if the time gap is sufficient, a complex process such as Delphi might be used to conduct the assessment. How immediate is the need?

The greater the amount of time, the greater the number of options. Any study that involves some type of feedback will need to have a response time built into it. Otherwise, if the process is fairly simple, e.g., "Respond to these questions and return the form to me by Tuesday," the time span is short.

A common training situation involves the short time span: "We need a training program next Friday." That makes significant assessment difficult. In this case, the most effective method is sampling a few people to get a sense of their perceptions and then continuing assessment at the training itself.

9. *Degree of reliability and validity needed.* Validity refers to the accuracy of the material. How accurately does it represent the views of the participants? Reliability refers to replicability of the material—if other questions were asked at other places and in different ways,

would the same results turn up? If we think in terms of the following continuum, our question becomes "At what junction do we reach the point of acceptability regarding reliability and validity?"

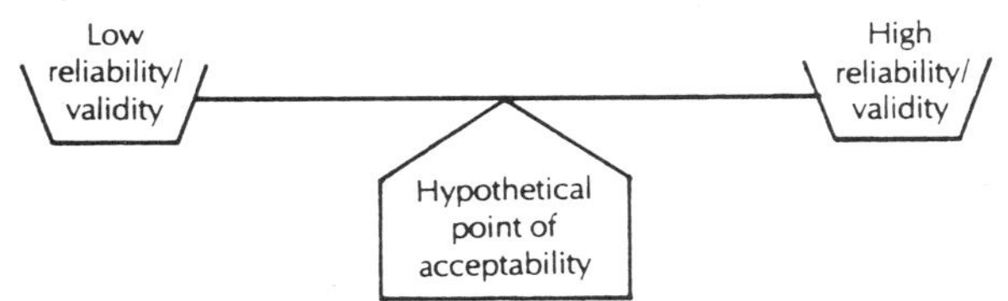

The "point of acceptability" is that juncture at which our needs for validity and reliability are satisfied and where greater reliability and validity become a luxury.

Designing a two-day seminar for first-line supervisors probably does not require the same "point of acceptability" as an expansive training program that needs to be promoted to top management. The general rule is that the greater the need for reliability and validity, the greater will be the number of resources for the assessment. High levels of acceptability may require industrial psychologists to design testing and validation, as well as significant resources of money and time.

10. Confidentiality. How confidential does the information need to be? If confidentiality is a concern, it must be planned for in the pre-assessment time.

The major issue is how much confidentiality should one strive for, or guarantee. It is not unusual for a manager to look through a list of responses to a particular question from which the names have been removed but nevertheless be able to identify their author. "This response here must be old George. It fits him perfectly," thinks the manager. If an assessment is billed "confidential," the trainer needs to do all he or she can to make sure that it is confidential. Otherwise, future confidential assessments will be thinly veiled.

When confidentiality is a concern, the assessment needs to be thoroughly conceptualized and designed with confidentiality in mind.

11. Facilitators' favorite tool. Facilitators, the persons conducting the assessment, frequently use favorite tools. I favor a process that involves the use of both questionnaire and interviews and is built on a survey research model. When a client talks to me about assessment, there is a good chance that, at least initially, this will be the model I propose. As more information is gathered about the organization, another model may replace it, but the first tendency is to use the favorite.

We all have a favorite tool that we like to use, and we become very proficient with it. But a problem arises when the chosen method ıt appropriate to the current situation. This is where the riteria becomes relevant and vital. By using criteria, we ense if our particular tool is going to expedite what needs to be done, or if it is going to get in the way.

An additional criterion that is not part of the list thus far is "What was done last time?" Sauer and Holland (*Planning In-House Training*, p. 37) point out there has always been a last time, whether the last time was in this organization or some other organization. The "last time" influence is important. Regardless of whether the experience was productive or unproductive, "last time" provides material for consideration for this time.

The above, then, represent some criteria to begin thinking about. Your unique setting will demand that you consider criteria peculiar to it. Perhaps an issue will be the availability of excellent training facilities, or the unavailability of training facilities. Perhaps your people are geographically scattered. The list is only a beginning—adapt it for your particular organization.

SUMMARY

This chapter has discussed objectives and criteria. They are linked together in important pre-assessment exploration. While they are very interactive, criteria make sense in light of objectives. Without objectives, criteria are simply random, drifting facts and figures—they have no substance or direction.

Proceed to the appendices. They will provide you with exercises highlighting objectives and criteria relevant to your specific setting.

APPENDICES: OBJECTIVES AND CRITERIA

1. Imagine yourself beginning an assessment process. You are to develop a set of objectives for the assessment. List three objectives:

A.

B.

C.

Now, with each objective, fill in "present conditions" and "desired conditions."

Objective A	Present Conditions	Desired Conditions

Objective B	Present Conditions	Desired Conditions

Objective C	Present Conditions	Desired Conditions

Now, return to the original objective statements. Rewrite them, being sure to include who, observable actions, conditions for assessment (optional), and minimum level of acceptable response.

Objective A:

Objective B:

Objective C:

2. Think back to a past assessment you have completed. What were the

A. Implicit criteria?

B. Explicit criteria?

C. How were the implicit criteria discovered?

3. Take one of the objectives from question 1 and write it in A below:

A. Objective statement (include who, when, and what):

B. As you think about the objective identified in A, identify which of the following criteria are relevant to it. Next, rate each of the criteria identified as relevant on a 1–5 scale with 1 being relatively unimportant and 5 being very important.

Criteria	Rating
Money	______
Time	______
People	______
Organizational health	______

Your relation to client	______
People to be involved	______
Desired outcomes	______
Extent to which needs are known	______
Decision makers' preference	______
Time between collection and action	______
Degree of reliability/validity	______
Confidentiality	______
Your favorite tool	______
(Others)	______

C. List of top five criteria that are important to the objective you have identified. List them according to priority, with number 1 as the most important.

(1)

(2)

(3)

(4)

(5)

REFERENCES

Cook, J. *Developing Learning Outcomes*. Columbia, Md.: Council for Advancement of Experimental Learning, 1978.

Mesaronic, M. "Foundations for a General Systems Theory," in M. Mesarovic (ed), "Views on General Systems Theory." New York: John Wiley and Sons, 1964.

Nadler, L. *Designing Training Programs*. Reading, Mass.: Addison-Wesley, 1982.

Newstrom, J., and Lillyquist, J. "Selecting Need Assessment Methods." *Training and Development Journal*, October 1979, pp. 52ff.

Park, C. *Management Braining*. Basking Ridge, N.J.: Walliker, 1977.

Sauer, S., and Holland, R. *Planning In-House Training*. Austin, Tex.: Learning Concepts, 1981.

Part II

Assessment Methodology

Part II is about the specific methodologies of needs assessment. Chapter 4 is concerned with the traditional categories of assessment, e.g., observations, skill tests, questionnaires, and interviews. Indeed, Chapter 4 is the "generic chapter" for this section. Almost every needs assessment process can be derived from it.

Subsequent chapters focus on areas of contemporary assessment. These chapters are designed to reach beyond generic methods into specific tools that might be used. These chapters have been contributed by persons knowledgeable and experienced in their particular area. They might well be called "composite methods," since they are combinations of generic methods.

The specific methods are:

Chapter 5—Nominal Group

Chapter 6—Delphi

Chapter 7—Competency Models

Chapter 8—Critical Incident

Chapter 9—Assessment Center

Chapter 10—Performance Appraisal

Chapter 11—Career Development

Chapter 12—Exit Interviews.

Note Chapters 10, 11, and 12. These chapters do not contain specific needs assessment methods; they are included as possible sources of needs assessment information. The main purpose of each of these processes is not needs assessment. However, in the process of carrying out their intention, they do collect information which may be useful for the trainer.

Various levels of assessment may be identified throughout the chapters. McGehee and Thayer (*Training in Business and Industry*) provide the classic model for viewing needs assessments. The three major levels are:

1. Organizational Analysis
2. Operating Data
3. Individual Analysis

Moore and Dutton ("Training Need Analysis: Review and Critique," p. 532) provide an excellent overview and critique of needs assessment training based on these levels. One of the features of their work is a list of sources from which organizational needs can be assessed according to the levels discussed by McGehee and Thayer. The following three tables identify the assessment level and some of the possible data sources for needs assessment.

Organizational Data Sources

Organizational Objectives and Objectives	Analysis of Efficiency Indices
Manpower Inventory	Cost of Labor
Skills Inventory	Cost of Materials
Organizational Climate	Quality of Materials
Labor Management Data	Equipment Utilization
Grievances	Cost of Distribution
Turnover	Waste
Absenteeism	Down Time
Suggestions	Late Deliveries
Productivity	Repairs
Accidents	Changes in the System
Short-Term Sickness	Management Requests
Observations of Employees	Exit Interviews
Attitude Surveys	MBO or Other Work Planning
Customer Complaints	

Operations or Job Data Sources

Job Descriptions	Ask Questions About Job
Job Specifications	Of Job Holder
Performance Standards	Of Supervisor
Perform the Job	Of Upper Management
Observe the Work	Training Committees
Review Literature Concerning Job	Analysis of Operation Problems
Other Industries	Down Time Reports
Professional Journals	Waste
Documents	Repairs
Government Sources	Late Deliveries
Ph.D. Dissertations	Quality Control
	Card Sort Method

Individual Analysis Sources

Performance Indicators Showing Problems	Tests
Productivity	Job Knowledge
Absenteeism/Tardiness	Skills
Accidents	Achievement
Short-Term Sickness	Attitude Surveys
Grievances	Training Progress Charts
Waste	Rating Scales
Late Deliveries	Diaries
Product Quality	Critical Incidents
Down Time	Devised Situations
Repairs	Role Play
Equipment Utilization	Case Study
Customer Complaints	In-Basket
Work Samples—Observation	Diagnostic Ratings
Interviews	Assessment Centers
Questionnaires	Coaching
	MBO

Source: M. Moore and P. Dutton in Academy of Management *Review*, 7/78; with permission.

The above list of possible data sources is provided to show the many options available. Needs assessment methods may deal with any one or more of these levels. The organizational analysis is concerned with such things as the organizational climate and objectives. Methods here focus on the total organization, e.g., communications audits, problem audits, and surveys of various organizational concerns. Some resources for organizational assessment are Levinson (*Organizational Diagnosis*), Leach ("Organizational Needs Analysis") and Weisbord (*Organizational Diagnosis: A Work Book of Theory and Practice*).

Organizational analysis is the broadest level of needs assessment. It tries to identify organizational training needs as distinguished from job or individual needs. The sources listed under the previous table reflect the level of information to be obtained.

Next are the operations data. Assessment methods here deal with the actual jobs being performed, e.g., job analysis. Job analysis is composed of two parts. The first part is the job description. The job description includes a written description of the job, organizational relationships (who reports to whom), machine operations, etc. The job description looks at what the job actually entails. The second part is the job specification, which focuses on the person who is to do the job, i.e., the qualifications necessary to perform it. Such things as education, experience, and training are pertinent considerations.

Obviously, as changes occur in the job description, changes also occur in the job specifications. If a new machine is added, the job specifications will have to reflect the requirements necessary to operate it. If the job is expanded, new responsibilities in the job specifications may mean additional training. Job analysis may be seen as a classical place to start needs assessments. The first question is "What are the skills needed to do the job described?" The next question is "Do the persons have those skills?"

This leads to level number three, an analysis of the people performing the job. Using job analysis as a measuring rod, a person's actual abilities to do the job are assessed. Perhaps a skills test of some sort is designed, e.g., a typing test requiring a certain rate of speed and a minimum rate of errors. Or maybe a time motion study is conducted assessing both the persons involved and the task they are expected to do.

At the individual level, four subgroups of assessments may be used (University Associates, 1981). The first one involves the theory a person has or needs to have. Supervisors, for example, may need to have a theory of motivation for working with employees. The theory is the model from which they work when faced with a motivational issue. Perhaps it will be as straightforward as a Theory X–Theory Y model or as complex as a psychoanalytical model. The question becomes "What theoretical frameworks are needed by the individuals in their positions?"

The next subgroup of personal assessment is *technique*—does the person have an understanding of techniques that conform with that theory? Assume a transactional analysis theory of motivation which states that a stroke provides a unit of motivation (Jongeward, *Choosing Success*, p. 77). The person understands the theory. The next question is "Is he/she knowledgeable about the techniques involved in stroking? Is he/she familiar with assessing the stroke economy? Does he/she know how to give positive conditional strokes?" Techniques refer to the way the theory is applied.

The third subgroup of personal assessment is skill—how skilled is the person in using a particular technique? He/she knows how to use a stroke economy with a person. Now the question is "How competently does he/she do it?" People may know the theory and understand the techniques but simply do not have the skills needed.

The last subgroup is frequently overlooked—personal power. He/she may know the theory and the techniques and be perfectly skilled, but for psychological reasons, cuts back his/her own power. The individual may discount his/her ability to perform—"I can't do it." The result: poor performance in a specific area.

The level (or levels) of assessment, then, is important to keep in mind when considering methods. Different levels involve different approaches. And if the assessment is done at an inappropriate level, e.g., at the operational level when the problem areas are at the organizational level, the end result of the assessment may be a waste of time and energy.

Finally, the levels interact. Truskie ("Getting the Most from Management Development Programs") discusses the importance of this interaction and suggests that training needs analysis be done in concert with organizational needs analysis. While it is useful for discussion purposes to see them as distinct, in reality, shifts and changes in one level will affect, in varying degrees, the others.

In summary, the Levels of Assessment are

1. Organizational Analysis
2. Operations Data
3. People Analysis
   - Theory
   - Technique
   - Skill
   - Personal

Thus, assessment may be conducted with a wide variety of data sources. The methodologies discussed in the chapters in this section merely skim the surface of possibilities. The reader is encouraged to use his or her creativity in exploring those methodologies that best fit his or her situation.

REFERENCES

Jongeward, D., and Seyer, P. *Choosing Success.* New York: John Wiley, 1978.

Leach, J. "Organizational Needs Analysis," *Training and Development Journal*, September 1979, pp. 66ff.

Levinson, H. *Organizational Diagnosis.* Cambridge, Mass.: Harvard University Press, 1972.

McGehee, W., and Thayer, P. *Training in Business and Industry.* New York: John Wiley, 1961.

Moore, M., and Dutton, P. "Training Need Analysis: Review and Critique." *Academy of Management Review*, July 1978, p. 532ff.

Truskie, S. "Getting the Most from Management Development Programs." *Personnel Journal*, January 1982, p. 66ff.

University Associates. Material given as part of Laboratory Education Intern Program, Denver, Colo., 1981.

Weisbord, M. *Organizational Diagnosis: A Workbook of Theory and Practice*, Reading, Mass.: Addison-Wesley, 1978.

4

Assessment: The Generic Methods

INTRODUCTION

The purpose of this chapter is to present the "classical" or "generic" approaches to needs assessment. They are classical in the sense that they have fairly well dominated the assessment literature. They are generic in the sense that they are the ones from which composite assessment methods are derived, i.e., they are the building blocks from which most assessments are built. For example, assessment centers are built from the generic methods of questionnaires, interviews, observations, etc.

The methods in this chapter, then, are the ones that are most commonly written about. Such authors as Steadham ("Learning to Select a Need Assessment Strategy"), Kirkpatrick ("Determining Supervisory Training Needs and Setting Objectives"), Moore and Dutton ("Training Need Analysis: Review and Critique"), Nadler (*Feedback and Organizational Development*), and Zemke and Kramlinger (*Figuring Things Out*) have discussed them in various ways. While the methods are not to be seen as exclusive, they cover most possibilities.

The concept of "obtrusive" versus "non-obtrusive" will be used in this chapter as a way of organizing the methods. The concept being referred to here is one discussed by Webb, Campbell, Schwartz, and Sechrest (*Unobtrusive Measures: Non-Reactive Research in Social Sciences*). Essentially, obtrusive measures directly intervene in the organization. A questionnaire is one example. The questioning process affects the organization and the persons being questioned. People's activities and interactions are disrupted for a period of time while they focus on the assessment: A direct intervention has taken place. Unobtrusive measures result in a minimal disruption of activities and interactions within the organization. For example, a reference to certain employment statistics such as "turnover" offers information but is relatively free from disrupting the activities and interactions within the organization. Unobtrusive measures result in minimal disruption in the immediate working routine of the persons within the organization. Most assessment methods may be used in ways that are either obtrusive or unobtrusive. For example, an observation may be made in a way which is relatively unobtrusive, e.g., a supervisor makes an observation while walking through a work area. Or an observation may be made in such a way that it is intrusive, e.g., the observer who stands around with a stop watch recording the workers' every movement.

The concept of "obtrusive" or "unobtrusive" is a useful organizing concept. Any assessment will have some sort of impact on an organization. Even the collection of statistics may cause someone to think "Why is he doing that?" and, thus, have an impact. Levinson (*Organizational Diagnosis*, p. 12) points out how the mere asking of diagnostic questions becomes an intervention. It is important for the trainer to think about the probable impact of a particular method on the organization. By doing so, some problems resulting from the assessment may be avoided or minimized.

The following table lists the methods we will consider:

Unobtrusive
Observation
Print Media
Records, Reports
Work Samples

Obtrusive
Questionnaires
Key Consultations
Interviews
Skill Tests

Gunkler (1981, p. 57) identifies a taxonomy of three distinct types of needs assessment. Type O is a pseudo needs assessment; examples might be market survey and consumer demand analysis. The assessment is a spinoff. Type 1 is a primary data source assessment. This type includes methods that collect data directly from the persons involved and those that collect information about the persons involved from a third source (e.g., collecting supervisory training needs from the supervisor's supervisor). Type 2 views secondary sources. These include methods that perform analyses and make interpretations about the population being assessed. They take type 1 assessment material and interpret and analyze it.

Gunkler's taxonomy provides an intriguing backdrop for this chapter. It provides cognition of not only the type of method selected but the relation of that method to the primary data source. All three types provide needs assessment material and, as such, are useful. All three may readily be used within an assessment strategy as a means of cross verification.

One last comment by way of introductory comments: DiLauro ("Training Need Assessment: Current Practices and New Directions," p. 351) makes a very important point when discussing needs assessment. The purpose of the needs assessment is what dictates the type of data *needed*. The type of data needed is what dictates the *data-gathering instrument*. And the data-gathering instrument will dictate the *data gathered*. The important point is that the method selected needs to be in harmony with the purpose of the assessment.

The chapter will be organized as follows. First, the method will be discussed; second, the use of that type of method will be discussed; third, the method will be evaluated. Three major sources for evaluation concepts are Steadham, Newstrom/Lillyquist ("Selecting Need Assessment Methods"), and Nadler. Finally, there will be a general discussion about the methods.

OBSERVATION: STRUCTURED AND UNSTRUCTURED

Observation seems simple enough—it is merely a matter of observing the work being done, and making decisions regarding training needs accordingly. A supervisor, for example, may observe the workers on an assembly line. As she makes her rounds, she notices that one worker is not performing a special function in the prescribed way. She makes note of this and then checks to determine if the problem is one of skill or attitude. After the analysis, a decision is made about an appropriate intervention.

Another example is a store manager who on his regular rounds notices that clerks are not using the magic words "Thank you,"

"Hello," "How are you today," etc. As he notes this, he decides that the time is right for a seminar on customer relations. Or, perhaps the safety person making rounds notices that safety rules are being violated and thus decides some type of intervention is needed.

These are simple examples of unstructured observations which lead to the identification of a potential training need. The result—a discovered need. First-line supervisors are constantly making this kind of discovery. The needs assessment is made through the observation of day-to-day events. It is unobtrusive and, for the most part, unstructured.

A second kind of observation is structured. A structured observation means that there is a deliberate observation taking place. The observation does not occur at random, but deliberately. Perhaps the supervisor decides that she will observe the workers performing specific functions. She selects specific functions to observe and proceeds to make an observation. Or, perhaps a problem has arisen and the observation focuses on its causation.

Time motion studies are an example of a highly structured observation. A traditional time motion study (Chapanis, *Research Techniques in Human Engineering*) involves:

1. Establish categories of observation.
   - Do the categories exhaust all the activities?
   - Are the categories observable?
   - Are the activities sufficiently limited?
2. Develop data sheets to record observations.
3. Select sampling duration.
   - Will the activity be observed for a specific period of time, e.g., five minutes?
   - Or, will the activity be observed based on a unity of activity, e.g., observe the total activity or simply a part of it.
4. Decide on the interval between observations.
   - What should be the time length between observations?
5. Select the persons to be observed.
6. Make observations.

The result of the time/motion approach is a highly structured observation.

Example 1: The Travel Agency

A travel agency was experiencing problems with customer relations. During the peak hours of customer contact, there was a tendency for the employees to be short and irritable with customers. The manager decided that there was a problem with stress management.

A consultant was hired to work with the employees to develop more effective ways of dealing with workaday stress.

The manager identified the problem through observing the employees' work performance. It was decided that it would also be useful for the consultant to observe the work setting during a typical stressful day. The employees were informed of the observations that were planned to take place.

The consultant's observations were unstructured. He simply noted the employees' responses at times of high stress during the day. After several hours of observation, the manager and the consultant compared notes.

A major outcome was a stress management event that focused on dealing with telephone conversations. The observations also resulted in the consultant and the manager developing a coaching relationship about employee expectations. One key source of stress did not have anything to do with the customers, but had a great deal to do with how the manager scheduled the employees' workload and what expectations he had of them.

The observation process leads to identification of not only the employees' training needs but also those of the manager.

Example 2: The Pipeline Problem

A pipeline company was having a quality control problem with welding creaks. One segment of the pipeline had an inappropriate number of welding cracks. This problem resulted in a team of eight persons being selected to go to the site and make welding observations.

The observations that were made were highly specific. Such factors as the welding temperature, the welding rod material, the number of welders involved, the time of weld, moisture conditions of the pipe, and pipe alignment were recorded. Various team members observed specific aspects of the welding process and recorded observations on predesigned forms.

The result of this highly structured observation was an identification of the cause of the creaks. The cause was related to the quality of the pipe and not the welding process itself.

When the problem was initially discovered, it was assumed to be a welding problem. However, as the observations revealed, the problem was a structural defect.

The above, then, are examples of observation. Still another example is that of process consultation (Schien, *Process Consultation: Its Role in Organizational Development*). Process consultation focuses on the process by which a decision is made or a meeting is run. An observer observes what is happening during the process of a meeting and at the end of the meeting, and shares his observations about how the group is working together. The process consultant is an observer whose role is to report what he sees taking place. The group then discusses the observation. Example 3 gives one view of this.

Example 3: The Nonparticipant Meeting

The director of a social service agency called on a consultant to work with his management team. The problem: lack of participation in meetings and lack of commitment to decisions made during the meeting. The director complained: "I don't understand what's happening. They just sit there and agree to what I suggest but then don't carry through with the decisions."

It was agreed that the consultant would observe the next meeting. At the meeting the director acknowledged the consultant's presence and mentioned that he would be working with the agency for a period of time. Then the meeting began.

The director's opening remark captured the tone of the management meeting: "Here is what we will do in the coming week and here is how we will do it . . ." It became clear to the consultant that the style of leadership was preempting team functioning. Toward the close of the meeting the consultant was asked to share his observations. The consultant first had the participants note their level of involvement in the meeting on a five-point scale. The consultant summarized the group responses. The result showed low involvement and satisfaction. The consultant asked for reflections from the group about some causes they saw for this and shared his own observations as well. The final step was a discussion about what they learned from this and how they could apply it at future meetings.

As a result of this process, the director became involved with the consultant in assessing leadership style and its impact on the participants. The consultant established a coaching relationship with the director.

Example 3 shows process consultation as a form of observation. Observations may be structured and intentional, or they may be unstructured. Generally, the more an observation is structured, the greater is the impact and the obtrusiveness. This brings us to the pluses and minuses of observation.

Observation intrinsically has some important strengths. (1) It generally is not disruptive to the work process. The work continues while the observations are being made. Observations also focus directly on the work being done. (2) It does not rely on secondhand reports; it directs itself to the source of the problem. In the case of the travel agency, had the consultant been satisfied with the manager's judgment alone, he would have missed another significant problem area. No spoken words or dialogue need interfere with the process of observation; the observer simply watches. (3) Management involvement may also be minimal. (4) Observations may not necessitate major commitments. (5) Observations may be inexpensive. However, as observations become more structured, costs may increase. And if an expert is brought in to observe, the costs may increase substantially.

The above represent the major strengths of observation. Some of the weaknesses are (1) The possible need for a training process for the observers in order to establish observation credibility. (2) The possibility that the observations are highly subjective. Accuracy depends on the observer and how accurate his or her observations are; personal bias, misunderstanding, misinformation, etc., all may obstruct accurate observations. (3) Observers may unintentionally intervene in the work process. In the welding example, the welders may work harder and become very conscientious because of the person with a stop watch observing them. The act of observation may affect the observed ("Hawthorne effect"). (4) If observation is limited to only the work being observed, the information may be restricted. Observation alone may be limited; it requires other sources of information to validate it. Take the example where the observable behavior of the person doing the job is not as significant as what the person is thinking as they do the job. Observation relies too heavily on the assumption that the observable behavior is all that is needed.

PRINT MEDIA

Another way of determining needs is through professional journals and workshop announcements. Print media is broadened here to include professional training publications, journals and periodicals specific to industry, brochures announcing workshop sessions, and those workshops presented at conferences and trade shows. Any type of media that reports on a particular training possibility is informative. By keeping up with professional journals, e.g., *Training, Training and Development, Personnel*, and industry publications, a number of needs may be identified. Sources such as these provide information about what other trainers are doing in the training area and are an index to potential training needs. For example, a trainer going through a particular in-house trade magazine may find a number of articles dealing with a particular selling technique, e.g., transactional analysis. From that, she may decide to explore developing a training program that uses TA as a selling technique.

Or, a trainer may see a number of articles beginning to appear on the topic of sexual harassment and the organizational responsibilities. After pondering the material, he may decide that this is training his company should develop. In both cases, the needs come out of literature pertinent to the area.

While there may be problems with this approach—the material in the text may not be applicable to a specific organization—it is still an extremely useful way to glean information about current training trends. What other companies discover about training needs may be very similar to what your own needs are.

The following examples illustrate the use of print media.

Example 1: Use of the Printed Word

The Training and Development Journal (Jones, "A Caution Signal for HRD," p. 44) reports on a survey conducted with a sample of its membership. The survey is related to types of training they are currently involved in, types they expect to discontinue, and those they expect to increase. The summary table is shown in Figure 4-1.

By looking at this table, a trainer may readily get a sense of what is happening in other companies and also get a sense of what programs may be important additions to his own. A note of caution: The key is to see them as sources of potential training needs. The trainer still needs to use other methods to determine if they fit in his organization.

Example 2: A Management Training Program

An XY university is in the process of developing an external management/supervisory training program. As one part of the process of assessing its market needs, it has singled out universities of a similar size and geographic location which currently have successful programs. It requests to be put on the mailing list for those universities and each year keeps track of the types of programs being offered. If there appears to be a program that several other universities are offering but which it lacks, XY then takes steps to explore the feasibility of offering that program in their area.

Record-keeping is done by means of a simple matrix. Each time a brochure comes across the director's desk, she simply fills in another row and column in the matrix. A sample matrix is given below: (A,B,C, etc., across the top of the matrix represent university A,B,C, etc.)

	A	B	C	D	E	Etc.
Assertiveness Training	X		X		X	
Behavioral Modeling						
Quality Circles	X	X	X	X		
Productivity		X	X	X		
Leadership Styles	X				X	
Etc.						

Figure 4–1. Jones's table. Copyright 1981, *Training and Development Journal,* American Society of Training and Development.

			More	Same	Less
1.	14*	Assertiveness Training	24	21	18
2.	2	Behavior Modeling	19	12	15
3.	8	Behavior Modification	29	12	18
4.	8	Body Language	10	21	15
5.	10	Burn Out Syndrome	18	11	17
6.	1	Business Ethics	12	12	23
7.	19	Career Development	48	1	16
8.	6	Change Management	30	4	17
9.	18	Coaching/Counseling	22	5	25
10.	6	Correspondence/HS	7	19	24
11.	7	Disadvantaged/Minorities	19	16	16
12.	1	Dual Career	20	11	9
13.	13	Executive Devel. (Top 5%)	24	3	19
14.	2	Handicapped	18	4	22
15.	37	Management Devel. (Mid Level)	31	1	25
16.	10	Meeting Effectiveness	12	9	26
17.	11	Organization Development	26	8	22
18.	20	Personal Growth	24	7	18
19.	6	Power (In the Organiz.)	9	10	23
20.	18	Problem-Solving	23	5	31
21.	11	Productivity	43	4	12
22.	13	Professional Updating	14	5	24
23.	6	Programmed Instruction	13	19	17
24.	7	Quality of Work Life	34	2	10
25.	19	Retirement/Pre-Retirement	29	3	17
26.	15	Safety	9	6	37
27.	11	Sales	13	8	31
28.	23	Skills	12	3	29
29.	24	Stress Management	12	3	29
30.	33	Supervisory Development	26	3	23
31.	14	Team Building	29	5	21
32.	13	Technical or Scientific	15	7	23
33.	30	Time Management	13	6	32
34.	15	Train the Trainer	11	7	28
35.	10	Transactional Analysis	7	36	19
36.	12	Upgrading Skills	19	4	21
37.	7	Values	15	10	16
38.	5	Women	24	13	11
39.	4	Work Redesign	21	8	15
40.	10	Writing Skills	16	6	21

*Figures to the left of the program indicate percentage of respondents who initiated that type of program for the first time in the last 12 months.

Keeping the matrix up-to-date provides a handy record of workshops that are being offered. The result is new ideas for program development.

Some of the strengths of print media are (1) They provide a good idea of what is taking place in similar firms. If there is some equivalency with firms of similar size and situation, some very good comparisons may be drawn. (2) They are inexpensive (most trainers get more than they like through the mail). (3) They are easily and readily categorized by an individual. (4) They present no organizational intrusions. Items are tabulated as the mail comes in.

There are also some major expenses with print media. (1) The first and most obvious weakness is that the information may not be applicable to your firm. (2) Consequently, the information may not be useful. That is the overriding consideration. (3) Related to the first, fads may be passed on along with training needs. "Since everyone is doing stress management, we will do stress management." The result is a waste of time, money, and resources.

RECORDS AND REPORTS

Records and reports are still another way of assessing training needs. Consider for a moment the number of reports that may be kept by an organization. The following is a brief listing of some of that material:

- Employee work records
- Tardiness
- Turnover
- Quality control
- Performance appraisal
- Grievance files
- Career development information
- Organizational development plans
- Human resource plans
- Exit interviews

The list could continue. Most organizations will keep a wide variety of records. The first question is "What kinds of reports and records are kept in a particular company?" Second question: "Will these records provide useful information for the trainer?" Third question: "Does the trainer have access to these records in some way?" If for some reason the trainer does not have access to the information, the records will not be useful. Chapters 10, 11, and 12 discuss three types of records the trainer may find valuable.

The reports and records are of two types. The first type are reports that infer or imply that problems exist. An example is turnover. If turnover within a particular industry exceeds the norm, the inference is that there is some kind of problem. This may lead to a needs assessment to determine the nature of the problem and the possible actions to be taken.

The second type of report is direct training information. This encompasses such things as performance appraisals, human resource plans, and career development material. Let's assume that a certain supervisor consistently receives low performance appraisal ratings for his inability to cope with a conflict situation. When conflict arises, he simply "blows his top." Some training in conflict management might be useful. And if there are several individuals who score low, a general workshop may be indicated. Direct training needs have been identified. Most performance appraisal forms will have a section referring to "plans for development."

Example A: General Motors' Tarrytown Plant

Guest ("Quality of Work Life—Learning from Tarrytown," pp. 76–88) provides an example of the way records may be used in problem identification. The discussion concerns the General Motors Tarrytown plant and the impact of a quality of work life program. The interest for us lies in the use of records and reports documenting the move from Tarrytown as it used to be in the "old days" to Tarrytown as it is in the "new days." In the old days, there were more than 2,000 labor grievances on the docket: it was not unusual to have more than 300 disciplinary cases waiting to be dealt with. There were complaints about the high-speed lines; labor turnover was high; absenteeism was high (7 percent). The records and reports indicated a need for change.

The result was a management decision to make changes. A quality of work life program was instituted. The results disclosed by the records and reports are startling. Absenteeism dropped from 7 percent to 2 percent over a seven-year period. During that same time span, labor grievances dropped from 2,000 to 32 on the docket. The use of records and reports reflects the initial problems and the results effected by the intervention.

Some of the strengths of reports and records are (1) They create little disruption. In spite of performance appraisals and career development material, training needs are identified as part of another process. Performance appraisals are not done solely to identify training needs, but training needs become one of their by-products. (2) Records may be easily collected. Since many of the records have already been collected for other purposes, one may have ready access to them. The trainer makes use of an existing resource.

(3) They provide more quantitative/qualitative evidence. Again, when used in conjunction with other methods, they provide added support.

Major weaknesses are (1) The records may not accurately reflect the current situations. Records document the past, rather than current development. Material given in a career development questionnaire may represent where the person was last month, but not now. (2) Since some of the material is highly inferential, it may be misinterpreted and inappropriately used. In other words, a fair amount of guesswork may have been involved. (3) Finally, the records being kept may not have the information you are looking for. They become useless for your purposes.

WORK SAMPLES

Work samples are a front-line source of training information. If certain products that an individual or department produces are consistently rejected, this identifies a problem area that may benefit from a needs assessment. It is a sign that some type of intervention is needed.

Again, this may be a relatively unobtrusive process. The supervisor simply makes note of the work being done. If there are problems with it, they are taken as a sign that some intervention may be needed.

Assume that the work is secretarial. The supervisor may check the typing of reports and letters for neatness, the number of errors, etc. As a result, certain persons may be recommended for training programs.

The important aspect of this method is that the actual work being done is seen as a source for discovering training needs. As in observation, actual work is being assessed.

The sampling process involves identifying specific units of work to be sampled, an appropriate sampling rate, and an appropriate labor rate. The type of plan will vary from organization to organization depending on the nature of the work.

The work sample concept can be applied to most any kind of work. Inspecting a manager's effectiveness in running a meeting is a work sample. Observing a teacher presenting a lesson is a form of work sample.

Example: Office Forms

An organization with a rigorous office management training program decided to assess the manager's effectiveness. A key element of this organization was filling out forms. Managers needed to be knowledgeable and accurate in filling out ten different forms. The forms consisted of such factors as work orders, man hours, material usage, and material requisitions. Upon examining the forms, it was apparent that they used four basic formats. By selecting a form representing each format, an adequate sample of the work could be identified. Four forms were selected—A, B, C, and D.

Since there were under 20 persons involved, it was decided to sample each person's error rate in filling out the forms. As supervisors visited various offices, they pulled a random sample of the forms on file and checked the error rate. A standard was set for an acceptable number of errors, and any form exceeding that number was pulled.

Essentially, this was a quality control procedure. However, it was found that a certain Form C had a significant number of errors in it. This became identified as an assessment priority. After exploration of the need, a training program was designed to train the managers in filling out the form more accurately.

Example: Staff Development

In addressing a staff development need, a training department instituted an "internal quality control program" by encouraging staff members to observe each other's training style, critique handout materials, etc. One of the consequences was a recognition that audio-visual materials were not being effectively used. Overhead transparencies were of marginal quality, films were not sufficiently introduced or discussed, etc.

By sampling a colleague's work, a specific training need was identified. Further exploration showed that people knew how to use the audio-visual aids, but they did not like the additional work involved—especially with the making of transparencies. The result was finding an outside vendor who would develop transparencies, as well as time sharing an "audio-visual" person.

The major strengths of the work sample, as with observation, are (1) The actual work is being investigated; the immediate performance is being critiqued. (2) Again, there is minimal interruption in the work actually performed. (3) It may provide clues to trouble areas where training might be useful, and may result in very specific corrections being made.

Some weaknesses are (1) It may take excessive time, and if the wrong work sample is selected, produce minimal information. (2) It may be costly and time consuming. If one person is reviewing a predecessor's work, the result is duplication. (3) As with observation, if the workers are aware that sampling is going on, their behavior may shift accordingly. (4) The expertise needed for a sophisticated job sample may not be part of the trainer's skills.

The previous four methods are classified as "unobtrusive." Most of them involve inferring training needs in ways that have a minimal impact on the work of the organization. The next set of methods are "obtrusive." They involve direct intervention in the organization.

QUESTIONNAIRES

One of the first two most widely used assessment methods is the questionnaire. There is probably not one of us who has not been asked to respond to a questionnaire. Questionnaires may be in the form of a needs assessment, attitude survey, opinion survey, problem survey, etc. They may be simple or highly complex. Whichever, their intent remains the same—to get written data needed to make decisions.

An attitude survey focuses on the participant's attitude toward some aspect of the organization. Perhaps the organization is about to make changes and there is concern over what the workers think about the proposed changes. Or maybe an organization has gone through a change and is attempting to determine its workers' attitudes toward it (Carnarius, "The What If Approach to Attitude Surveys," Goldberg and Gordon, "Designing Attitude Surveys for Management Action," and Loffreda, "Employee Attitude Surveys: A Valuable Motivating Tool").

Opinion surveys are quite similar to the attitude survey. The focus is on opinions rather than attitudes. Perhaps it may be an opinion poll on the usefulness of the present performance appraisal system or on a policy toward training. The attempt is to solicit opinions from persons on specific areas of their work life. (See Howe, "Opinion Surveys: Taking the Task Force Approach," Morano, "Opinion Surveys: The How to Design and Applications," and Sirota, "Opinion Surveys: The Results Are In—What Do We Do With Them?")

Problem surveys are yet another approach to the questionnaire. Participants are asked to identify problems in the organization. In most settings the participants will also be asked to weigh the problems against one another. The result—an identification of which problems are perceived by the participants as important.

Some of the previously mentioned questionnaires may provide a trainer with needs assessment material. A specific needs assessment questionnaire is similar to the above questionnaire, except its primary purpose is that of identifying training needs. The questions it contains may be very direct—"What are your training needs?" or they may be subtle—"What is a current problem you are facing as a manager?" The type of question discussed will be the topics of a later chapter.

The questionnaire is probably the most widely used formal method of assessing needs. It may be extremely simple, e.g., "What would be useful training for you as you think of your job," or highly complex involving delicate statistical operations.

The appendix to this book contains a variety of case studies that demonstrate the use of the questionnaire.

Example: Sample Questionnaires

The following questionnaires provide samples of needs assessment questionnaires (see Figures 4-2, 4-3, and 4-4). The samples were selected because of their diversity.

Questionnaires have definite strengths. (1) They readily obtain the necessary information. The same questions can be asked quickly of many persons. The result—tremendous outreach to a great number of persons. (2) Because of the potentially large audience, they can be relatively inexpensive. (3) The data can be readily summarized and put into quantitative form. (4) Questionnaires may provide a significant level of confidentiality. (5) The questionnaire invites the trainer very carefully and intentionally to think through what is being asked and why. The assessment becomes more vigorous since the trainer is consistently asking "Will this question give me the information I need?"

The major weakness (1) derives from the way that the information from the questionnaires is interpreted. If the participant does not understand the question, there will be problems. (2) If the wrong questions are asked, the information will be correct but not useful. (3) It may also be very costly to develop a questionnaire that is highly valid and reliable. (4) Another major weakness is the fact that a questionnaire is a one-way communication, i.e., there is no dialogue to clarify the meaning of a question or word. The result may be a decreased amount of reliable information. (5) Finally, the return rate on the questionnaire may be low. Consequently, the usefulness of the information may diminish.

KEY CONSULTATIONS

The key consultation approach involves the use of key persons or committees to determine training needs. Perhaps management requests a certain type of training. Top managers may have gone through a training program in performance appraisal and sent back a request that supervisors be trained in this area. This is one type of a key consultation.

In this day of federal regulations, the personnel manager may be consulted about those training needs that are about to be mandated. Training may be required to deal with certain regulations. There may be a change in a current safety requirement. Or maybe an EEO

Department ____________________

Directions: Listed below are 37 possible training needs that supervisors have. Each need is followed by two scales: The first identifies how important that function is to your job. The second identifies how important that is to you as a training need.

Example

Ex.	This is important to my job: (Circle a number) Not Important … Very Important					This is something I need training in: (Circle a Number) Low Need … High Need				
Ability to deal with work stress.	1	2	3	(4)	5	1	(2)	3	4	5

This would indicate that this ability is important for the job and that the person does not feel that it is in an important training need.

Figure 4–2. Needs Assessment Instrument. The basic model for this instrument comes from "Assessing Supervisory Training Needs" by A. Braun, *Training and Development Journal*, February 1979.

	This is very important to my job: (Circle a Number)					This is something I need training in: (Circle a Number)				
	Not Important				Very Important	Low Need				High Need
Planning										
1. Ability to set objectives or develop projects	1	2	3	4	5	1	2	3	4	5
2. Ability to develop plans.	1	2	3	4	5	1	2	3	4	5
3. Ability to set priorities on work.	1	2	3	4	5	1	2	3	4	5
4. Ability to budget.	1	2	3	4	5	1	2	3	4	5
5. Ability to use time effectively, i.e., time management.	1	2	3	4	5	1	2	3	4	5
Directing										
6. Ability to assign work to people.	1	2	3	4	5	1	2	3	4	5
7. Ability to use different leadership styles to fit situation.	1	2	3	4	5	1	2	3	4	5
8. Ability to delegate.	1	2	3	4	5	1	2	3	4	5
9. Ability to motivate.	1	2	3	4	5	1	2	3	4	5
10. Ability to develop many workers into a team.	1	2	3	4	5	1	2	3	4	5
11. Ability to understand persons of different backgrounds, ages, races, etc.	1	2	3	4	5	1	2	3	4	5
Problem Solving/Decision Making										
12. Ability to recognize and analyze problems.	1	2	3	4	5	1	2	3	4	5
13. Ability to identify solutions.	1	2	3	4	5	1	2	3	4	5
14. Ability to decide what solution is best.	1	2	3	4	5	1	2	3	4	5
15. Ability to decide in crisis.	1	2	3	4	5	1	2	3	4	5
Communications										
16. Ability to inform supervisor.	1	2	3	4	5	1	2	3	4	5
17. Ability to inform subordinates.	1	2	3	4	5	1	2	3	4	5
18. Ability to conduct meetings.	1	2	3	4	5	1	2	3	4	5
19. Ability to conduct formal briefings.	1	2	3	4	5	1	2	3	4	5
20. Ability to listen to others and hear their views.	1	2	3	4	5	1	2	3	4	5
21. Ability to relate negative information.	1	2	3	4	5	1	2	3	4	5
22. Ability to complete forms and reports.	1	2	3	4	5	1	2	3	4	5
23. Ability to write formal letters.	1	2	3	4	5	1	2	3	4	5
24. Ability to manage conflict effectively.	1	2	3	4	5	1	2	3	4	5
Training										
25. Ability to determine what training people should have.	1	2	3	4	5	1	2	3	4	5
26. Ability to conduct on job training.	1	2	3	4	5	1	2	3	4	5
27. Ability to evaluate training	1	2	3	4	5	1	2	3	4	5

Figure 4-2 (continued)

Item										
Hiring										
28. Ability to interview job candidates.	1	2	3	4	5	1	2	3	4	5
29. Ability to select people for job.	1	2	3	4	5	1	2	3	4	5
30. Ability to orient new employees.	1	2	3	4	5	1	2	3	4	5
Performance Review										
31. Ability to develop work standards.	1	2	3	4	5	1	2	3	4	5
32. Ability to measure people.	1	2	3	4	5	1	2	3	4	5
33. Ability to conduct appraisal discussion.	1	2	3	4	5	1	2	3	4	5
34. Ability to develop individual development plans.	1	2	3	4	5	1	2	3	4	5
35. Ability to recommend rewards.	1	2	3	4	5	1	2	3	4	5
36. Ability to recommend discipline.	1	2	3	4	5	1	2	3	4	5
37. Ability to coach/counsel persons with disciplinary problems.	1	2	3	4	5	1	2	3	4	5
Other:										

Pick from the list above the two most important training needs for you. Put the number and item below:

1. ________ ______________________________

2. ________ ______________________________

Figure 4-2 (continued)

Figure 4-3

Figure 4-3. Vice President (Looking at Manager's Job)

1. Describe the major job responsibilities of your managers. Then rank these responsibilities by priority. ______

2. Describe the best manager you have (or have had). Identify the performance. ______

3. What does he or she do that a poor manager does not do? ______

4. What does he or she *not* do that a poor manager does? ______

5. What are the reasons you feel are responsible for the difference between a good performer and a poor performer? ______

6. Could any of these performance problems be reduced or eliminated by training? If so, what are they? ______________________________

____

____

____

____

7. What are the most frequent problems of new managers? ______________

____

____

____

____

____

8. What would be most useful to a new manager in correcting the problems? ______________________________

____

____

____

____

9. How long does it take a new manager to become fully effective?

____

____

____

____

____

Where do they learn the necessary skills? ______________________

____

____

What form does the training come in? ______________________

____

____

Is it effective? ____________________

____

____

Timely? ____________________

____

____

10. What skills do experienced managers need to perform? Where do they get these skills? ____________________

____

____

____

____

____

11. If you were to set up a training/developmental program for one of your newly-appointed managers, what would it include? ____________________

____

____

____

____

12. Are there any questions that you feel are important to ask before we close this interview? ____________________

____

____

____

____

Source: Modeled after questionnaire used by Ohio Bell in their 1976 needs analysis.

Figure 4–4. Business community educational needs survey.

Listed below are many topic areas. Please indicate the important educational training needs your employees have using the following ratings:

A = great importance B = some importance C = no importance

Room has been provided at the end of the list for additional training needs you may have.

ACCOUNTING

____ 1. budgeting
____ 2. basic accounting
____ 3. cost accounting
____ 4. fund accounting
____ 5. tax preparation

FINANCE

____ 6. consumer finance
____ 7. financial statement preparation
____ 8. real estate finance
____ 9. real estate investment
____10. stock market investments

MANAGEMENT

____11. conflict management
____12. controls and rewards
____13. decision making
____14. evaluation
____15. group dynamics
____16. interpersonal communication skills
____17. leadership
____18. management by objectives
____19. management development
____20. motivation
____21. oral communication skills
____22. problem solving
____23. planning, long range
____24. planning, short range
____25. stress management
____26. supervisory skills
____27. understanding

MARKETING

____28. effective use of advertising
____29. consumer behavior
____30. market research
____31. new product development
____32. salesmanship

PERSONNEL MANAGEMENT

____33. career planning
____34. designing orientation programs

PERSONNEL MANAGEMENT

____35. desciplining the employee
____36. employee recruitment/selection
____37. employee morale (satisfaction)
____38. federal legislation and personnel
____39. grievance proceedures
____40. performance appraisals
____41. personnel development
____42. personnel manual preparation
____43. retirement planning
____44. safety compliance
____45. wage and benefit plans
____46. women and minorities
____47. union management relations
____48. writing job descriptions
____49. office management
____50. office skills

OTHER

____51. assertiveness training
____52. business law
____53. economics
____54. grant writing
____55. how to start a small business
____56. the small business and computer
____57. business ethics
____58. time management
____59. business statistics
____60. general psychology
____61. personality theory
____62. developing organizational structures
____63. alcohol and drug abuse
____64. personal health management

ADDITIONAL ITEMS

____65. ______________________________
____66. ______________________________
____67. ______________________________
____68. ______________________________
____69. ______________________________
____70. ______________________________

Listed below are a number of training possibilities. First, go through the items in each of the major categories and check the boxes in front of the items which you sense to be important training needs for your department. If there are training needs not listed which you see as important, write them in the blank spaces provided in each major category. Second, rank order the three major categories of training from 1 to 3 with 1 being the category of greatest need and 3 being the category of least need.

_______ ORGANIZATIONAL TRAINING NEEDS

- [ ] management by objectives
- [ ] time management
- [ ] managerial grid
- [ ] organizational communication
- [ ] interdepartment conflict management
- [ ] _______________
- [ ] _______________

_______ TECHNICAL TRAINING NEEDS

- [ ] decision making
- [ ] goal setting
- [ ] contracting
- [ ] systems analysis
- [ ] problem solving
- [ ] long-range planning
- [ ] defining measurable objectives
- [ ] _______________
- [ ] _______________

_______ INTER/INTRA-PERSONAL TRAINING NEEDS

- [ ] supervisory skills
- [ ] team building
- [ ] interpersonal conflict management
- [ ] interpersonal communications
- [ ] coping with organizational stress
- [ ] assertiveness training
- [ ] transactional analysis
- [ ] leadership styles
- [ ] motivation
- [ ] _______________
- [ ] _______________

Other comments on training needs . . .

consideration or a labor concern is changing and some type of training is required.

Key consultations involve going to key persons and groups and talking with them about the training needs they perceive. For example, in a current project we are working with, the personnel manager is the one who identifies the needs. He determines what the training will be. We talk with him about supervisory needs and develop a training program from the interviews. This is a key consultation. He is the decision-maker. Training decisions are made by him and must include him.

Key consultation is implied in Section I of the discussion about political considerations. Not only is it important to consult with a particular individual because he or she has important training information, but because he or she may also be an important power person to be reckoned with.

Another aspect of key consultation is the formation of a training advisory committee. An organization may have a special group to coordinate the training program. The group may be composed of management, supervisors, and line persons. Their function is to assess proposed training programs and monitor the effectiveness of training. Such groups can be a tremendous asset for the training program.

To summarize, key consultation may be with

- Supervisors
- "Bosses"
- Trainees
- Advisory Committee
- Professional Groups
- Significant Others

Example

A group of small manufacturers decided to cooperate in order to establish a training program for their foremen and supervisors. They contracted with a consulting firm to secure the services needed. Since the program was to be continuous, an advisory group composed of the personnel managers from the various participating companies was established.

This group became the key consulting group for the consulting firms. It monitored the training as it occurred, evaluated the results, and proposed new training ventures to be accomplished.

Some advantages of key consultation include (1) broadening the information base. The trainer, in effect, has a large number of people working for him. There is simply more input within the process. (2) By getting more input, the trainer may also be developing a broader support base from which to work. More persons will have an investment in and commitment to the training. (3) Once established, a key consultation may be relatively easy to maintain.

The major disadvantage (1) relates to getting the wrong persons involved. (2) Key consultation may deal with a secondary source of information which may not be valid. The consequence may be the development of an inaccurate or distorted picture of training. (3) A consultation group also may retard the decision process. With more persons involved, there may be more vested interests trying to get their programs into the agenda. This is a natural consequence of asking others for input.

INTERVIEWS

Another widely used method of assessing training needs is through the individual or group interview. Again, this may be structured or unstructured. This section will look at individual interviews and the next section will focus on group interviews.

In the structured interview, the trainer has a specific line of questioning that she follows. The questions are constructed in advance and there is little deviation from them. The general format begins with the establishment of rapport followed by the gathering of content, and concludes with a follow-up to the interview process. More will be said about the interview process in a later chapter.

The unstructured interview may begin with a probing question, but flows on freely from that point. It is an open-ended process, and the trainer simply follows the rhythms of the interview, going wherever it takes him. There are few (if any) specific questions that the interviewer has for the interviewee. Interviewing becomes the art of listening, probing, and reflecting.

Interviews may be as simple as asking persons for their ideas or as complex as a highly structured questioning process which is carefully recorded and analyzed. Whether the interview is simple or complex is determined by the nature of the assessment. As the degree of validity/reliability increases, so does the need for complexity in the interview process.

The interview process is a standard, significant tool for performing needs assessment. Chapter 13 provides guidelines for interviewing and also provides ideas on the type of questions that may be asked. Through establishing face-to-face contact, the interview provides information that many other methods do not.

Example

A university department has decided that it wants to establish a set of criteria by which to evaluate the teaching faculty, and eventually, develop training. The decision was made to use an outside consultant to interview the 22 faculty members currently on staff in order to determine their views on the subject.

The consultant decides to use a competency approach based on McClelland's model (Coleman, "The New Competency Tests"). The interviewing process consists of using unstructured questions to explore competencies the faculty members recognize in outstanding faculty.

Questions such as "Think of an effective teacher you have had. What were the characteristics that made that person outstanding?" and "Think of an ineffective teacher you have had. What were the characteristics that made that person ineffective?" were asked of the faculty in the interview process.

The outcome of the interviews generated a list of effective and ineffective behaviors which were later refined and used as an assessment tool.

Further examples of the use of interviewing are found in the case studies given in the appendices.

The major strength of the interview (1) is the face-to-face contact. A two-way communication takes place and there is time for dialogue. (2) The interviewer can probe—"Do you really mean that?"—and elicit feelings—"Sounds like you might be angry with that." There is time to attain in-depth information. Instead of accepting surface answers, the interviewer is able to search more deeply. (3) It is also a way of building rapport between individuals.

The major weakness is that (1) the interviewer may need to be trained to provide consistent interviewing. (2) The process may also prove to be costly. One-on-one interviewing may result in lots of time being used. (3) Also, since the interview is a social exchange, the interviewee and the interviewer may be overly influenced by one another. If the interviewer is a trainer, and the interviewee, the chairman of the board, the interviewer may be swayed. (4) If the interview is unstructured, it may be hard to quantify the results.

GROUP DISCUSSION

The group discussion is a special type of interview. Instead of exploring a single person, several persons are interviewed at the same time. A major advantage of the group interview is the use of group dynamics. As group members begin to share ideas and thoughts, a natural generation of ideas begins to take shape. A key outcome is that the number and the quality of ideas is substantially increased.

There are a number of group processes available for use in determining needs assessments. Ulschak, Nathanson, and Gillan (*Small Group Problem Solving: An Aid to Organizational Effectiveness*) provide a number of group tools that may be used by trainers to work effectively with groups. Chapter 5 details one group process method, the nominal group theory.

Example: Use of a Group Interview in a Hospital Setting

A medium-sized hospital decided to formalize its supervisory training program. The initial step was a series of group interviews with the supervisors. Group interviews was the method chosen because it would involve the participation of all supervisors. Involving all supervisors in the needs analysis was also an attempt to gain their support and backing for the resulting training. It was hoped that group interviews would stimulate ideas.

Each group met for a period of 40 mintues. The trainer began the session by stating its purpose and citing how the information would be used. The supervisors were given a brief questionnaire to fill out which was then used as the basis for the discussion. Each participant had individual time to develop ideas prior to the total group sharing. This was an important step.

Once the participants had an opportunity to respond to the questionnaire, the next step was to use the questionnaire as an interview format. Participants could comment on one another's ideas and "build on them" or critique them. The end result was lots of information on perceived needs.

Another result was that the group provided the trainer with an additional check on the assessment process. One of the last items discussed was the group's reactions to the questionnaire—did they understand it? Did they disagree with questions?

Perhaps the major strengths of the group interview are two-fold. (1) Numerous ideas are generated. People build on one another's thoughts. Ideas are questioned and expanded upon. (2) Group interviews also may build commitment to the training program. By becoming part of the sharing and development process, participants may also grow in commitment. The group interview has other pluses: (3) It may build teamwork and develop group problem-solving skills. (4) By involving a greater number of persons, it is more cost effective.

The major weakness in this system is (1) the group dynamics that may counteract the task. A "group think" may prevail in which group members automatically agree about everything. (2) Or, there may be no discussion at all—everyone drops into silence. (3) It may also be hard to arrive at conclusions—someone said one thing, someone else said something else. The result is a difficulty in quantifying results. (4) The process may be time consuming and require that the trainer have group process skills.

SKILLS TESTS

Skills tests are tests for specific skills. A driver's test is a good example. A person drives an auto in the presence of an examiner who then provides feedback on the performance. If the level of skills was sufficient, a license is issued. If not, it is withheld.

Skills tests are an excellent source of training information. They are useful in a setting where specific, readily identifiable skills are used. Let's return to the driver's test. Specific skills are required to be able to drive. The test can provide feedback on which skills are lacking, e.g., acceleration/clutch coordination (the car jumps down the road). After the skills test, the person is left with reliable information about how well she performed. She now has identified training needs that are necessary to reach the minimum level of competency needed for acquiring a license.

The flow is straighforward:

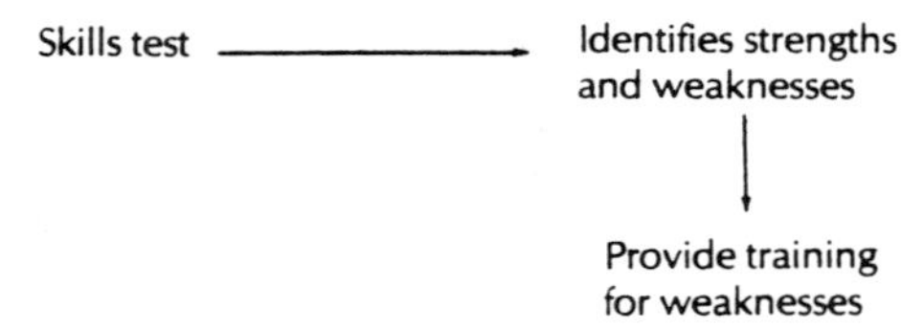

A key part of the process of developing skills tests is validating that the tests do what they are supposed to do. A major field of study is the design and validation of such tests. Denova's *Test Construction for Training Evaluation* (1979) is an example of a text in that area.

Example

A concern among law enforcement persons is skill with a weapon. For long periods of time, an officer may not be required to draw and fire his/her weapon on the job. However, in a crisis, he needs to draw and fire with accuracy. The problem, then, is one of maintaining an infrequently used skill which requires a high level of accuracy.

Skills tests may be required of police officers to check their accuracy. On a shooting range, the officer is required to score at a certain level or face some type of action against him/her. The skills test is straightforward—did the officer score the predetermined score or not? If he/she did not, the next step is to identify the problem—

what is not being done that should be done? Or, what is being done that should not be done?

The major strength of skills tests is (1) that generally they use established skill criteria which are easily verifiable. The results are easily quantified. If the skills test involves typing 50 words per minute with an error rate of five words, we can readily verify if the skill has been accomplished. (2) Also, the problem areas where there are skill deficiences may be readily identified. This may also result in (3) early identification of skill deficiency. (4) Perhaps most important, if the skill training is highly correlated with the job activities, the tests will provide accurate information about whether the person can do the job or not.

The major problem is that (1) skills tests do not necessarily lead to competencies within the employment context. A person may do well on the skills test and poorly on the job. (2) Another problem is the validation; tests need to be validated for each particular situation. This may be time consuming and costly.

MULTIPLE METHODS

In reviewing the strengths and weaknesses of the various methods, an obvious conclusion is that by using multiple methods strengths may be built upon and weaknesses corrected. Instead of using only a questionnaire, for example, a questionnaire may be combined with an interview process. The result: a strengthened assessment method. If two or three methods have been used and the results show similar trends, the trainer has greater certainty that she is on the right track. *A major emphasis of this book is that, whenever possible, more than one method should be used.*

The case studies in the appendices illustrate this point. In almost all cases, interviews are combined with questionnaires.

SUMMARY

This chapter has discussed traditional needs assessment methods, i.e., generic methods. Once we know our goal and have our criteria firmly established, selecting a method(s) becomes substantially easier. We can now discriminate among the options.

In this chapter we have discussed methods, provided examples of their uses, and speculated about the strengths and weaknesses of those methods. Newstrom and Lillyquist provide a further category for evaluating methods of assessment (see following table).

	Trainees Involve	Management Involve	Time Require	Cost	Quantifiable Data Require
Observations	moderate	low	high	high	moderate
Questionnaires	high	high	moderate	moderate	high
Key Consultations	low	high	low	low	low
Print Media	low	low	low	low	low
Interviews	high	low	high	high	moderate
Group Discussions	high	moderate	moderate	moderate	moderate
Skills Tests	high	low	high	high	high
Reports/ Records	low	moderate	low	low	high
Work Samples	low	low	moderate	moderate	high

Source: *Training and Development Journal*, American Society for Training and Development, © 1978; by permission.

As you look over the various evaluations, think in terms of your own organization. What might be some methods or combination of methods that would be useful in your context? The appendix to this chapter has exercises that should help to focus your thinking.

WORKBOOK: METHODOLOGIES

1. As you look over the list of methods below, put an (X) in the box next to the ones you have used most frequently in the past. Then, put a (Y) in the box next to the ones you would like to experiment with in the future.

Methods	Have Worked With	Would Like To Work With
Observation		
Print Media		
Records, Etc.		
Work Samples		
Questionnaire		
Key Consultations		
Interviews		
Group Discussion		
Skills Tests		

A. Reflect on those you have worked with. Which have been most effective? Least effective?

B. Reflect on the ones you would like to experiment with. How might you begin the experiment?

2. Go back to the previous chapter. Take the criteria you developed in the workbook and transfer them below, under the heading called *Criteria*. Then, simply check those methods that will satisfy each criterion. When you are finished, count up the checks for each method.

CRITERIA METHODS	1.	2.	3.	4.	5.	6.	7.	8.	9.
1.									
2.									
3.									
4.									
5.									
6.									
7.									
8.									
9.									
10.									

A. Which methods received the highest totals?

B. As you reflect on the methods with the highest totals, which ones are the best candidates for you?

SUMMARY: STRENGTHS AND WEAKNESSES OF GENERIC METHODS

Observations	
(+)	(−)
—May be relatively unobstrusive, i.e., may not interrupt the continuous work. —Identifies on-the-job priorities, not secondhand reports. —Minimal management involvement. —If casual, costs are low. —May be readily used.	—Trained observer may be necessary. —May involve significant time. —May be highly subjective. —Depends on accurate interpretation of events by observer. —Act of observation may affect work being done (Hawthorne Effect). —Since observation is restricted to work setting, the information may be limited.

Print Media	
(+)	(−)
—Provides picture of what is happening in other firms, and potential future directions. —Inexpensive since there is a constant source of mail. —Readily done on one's own time. —Does not intrude on organization.	—May not be applicable to your firm. —Information simply not useful for your needs. —May invite fads, i.e., since others appear to be doing it you do, too. —Invites selecting solutions before proper problem identification.

Records and Reports	
(+)	(−)
—Unobtrusive and provides clues to trouble spots. —May be easily collected. —Provide additional quantitative/qualitative evidence for training needs.	—May be readily misinterpreted, since patterns may be unclear. —Reflect past situation, not what is currently happening. —Access to the information sources may be restricted.

Work Samples	
(+)	(−)
—Direct data on the actual work. —May be unobtrusive to the work flow. —Provides clues to trouble areas.	—Requires careful analysis of what work to look for. —May be costly and time consuming. —Trainer may not have expertise to do it. —Workers may alter behavior during time being checked.

Questionnaire	
(+)	(−)
—Lots of people may be contacted in short time. —May be relatively inexpensive (per person) and easily put together. —Data may be readily summarized. —May be confidential with information being given without fear of reprisal. —By developing a questionnaire, a trainer may clarify goals of training.	—Since communication is one-way, results may be misinterpreted. —The wrong question may be asked. —There may be bias in the return of the questionnaires, e.g., people with a certain bias may choose not to return or to return the questionnaire with the result being a biased return. —If highly valid/reliable instruments are needed, the development process may be costly. —The return rate may be low.

Key Consultation	
(+)	(−)
—Easy to maintain once established. —Since more persons involved, may establish additional support for training. —Provides for many inputs, different perceptions. —Broadens the information base.	—Bias of individuals selected may impact training's direction. —Improper selection may lead to invalid information. —With more people involved, bringing with them their vested interests, the process may be slowed down. —Interpersonal conflicts and struggles may get in the way of the task to be done.

Interviews	
(+)	(−)
—Provides time to probe; the interviewer can pursue answers given by the interviewee. —In-depth information may be obtained by an interviewer. —Provides an opportunity to build rapport between trainer and others. —Allows interviewer additional information in the form of nonverbal communications.	—The interviewer/interviewee may be influenced by the other person's charisma, etc. —Process may be costly in terms of time and financial resources. —The results may be hard to quantify. —Interviewer needs to be skilled in the interview process.

Group Discussion (Interview)	
(+)	(−)
—Many ideas may be generated. —Commitment to decisions made will probably be increased. —Additional problem analysis will be developed in the participants. —Because a greater number of people are involved in the process, it is more cost-effective.	—The results may be hard to quantify. —"Group think," i.e., members will quickly focus on one idea and not explore others. —Requires skills in group process for the leader. —Group dynamics may counteract the task.

Skills Tests	
(+)	(−)
—Results are easily quantified. —Deficiencies are readily identified. —Early identification of important skill deficiencies may lead to early correction. —Close to "real life" constraints.	—Does not measure on-the-job competencies; a person may be good on tests but not at work. —Tests may not have been validated for that particular setting. —Costs may be high for validation of tests. —Time requirements may be high for test validation.

REFERENCES

Braun, A. "Assessing Supervisory Training Needs and Evaluating Effectiveness." *Training and Development Journal,* February 1974, p. 3.

Carnarius, S. "The What If Approach to Attitude Surveys." *Personnel Journal,* February 1978, p. 93ff.

Coleman, D. "The New Competency Tests." *Psychology Today,* January 1981, p. 35.

Chapanis, A. *Research Techniques in Human Engineering.* Baltimore: Hopkins, 1959.

Denova, C. *Test Construction for Training Evaluation.* New York: Van Nostrand, 1979.

DiLauro, T. "Training Needs Assessment." *Public Personnel Management,* November/December 1979, p. 350–359.

Goldberg, B., and Gordon, G. "Designing Attitude Surveys for Management Action." *Personnel Journal,* October 1978, p. 546ff.

Guest, R. "Quality of Work Life—Learning from Tarrytown." *Harvard Business Review,* July/August 1979, p. 76.

Howe, E. "Opinion Surveys: Taking the Task Force Approach." *Personnel,* September/October 1974, p. 16ff.

Jones, R. "A Caution Signal for HRD." *Training and Development Journal,* April 1981, p. 44.

Kirkpatrick, D. "Determining Supervisory Training Needs and Setting Objectives." *Training and Development Journal,* May 1978, p. 16ff.

Leach, J. "Organization Need Assessment." *Training and Development Journal,* September 1979, p. 66.

Levinson, H. *Organizational Diagnosis.* Cambridge, Mass.: Harvard Press, 1972.

Loffreda, R. "Employee Attiude Surveys: A Valuable Motivating Tool." *Personnel Administrator,* July 1979, p. 41ff.

Moore, M., and Dutton, P. "Training Need Analysis: Review and Critique. *Academy of Management Review,* July 1978, p. 532ff.

Morano, R. "Opinion Surveys: The How to Design and Applications." *Personnel,* September/October 1974, p. 8ff.

Nadler, D. *Feedback and Organizational Development.* Reading, Mass.: Addison-Wesley, 1977.

Newstrom, J., and Lillyquist, J. "Selecting Need Analysis Methods." *Training and Development Journal,* October 1979, p. 52ff.

Schien, E. *Process Consultation: Its Role in Organizational Development.* Reading, Mass.: Addison-Wesley, 1969.

Sirota, D. "Opinion Surveys: The Results Are In—What Do We Do with Them?" *Personnel,* September/October 1974, p. 24ff.

Steadham, S. "Learning to Select a Need Assessment Strategy." *Training and Development Journal,* January 1980, p. 56.

Ulschak, F.; Nathanson, L.; and Gillan, P. *Small Group Problem Solving: An Aid to Organizational Effectiveness.* Reading, Mass.: Addison-Wesley, 1981.

Webb, E; Campbell, D.; Schwartz, R.; and Sechrest, L. *Unobtrusive Measures: Non-Reactive Research in Social Sciences.* Chicago: Rand McNally, 1973.

Weisbord, M. *Organizational Diagnosis.* Reading, Mass.: Addison-Wesley, 1978.

Zemke, R., and Kramlinger, R. *Figuring Things Out.* Reading, Mass.: Addison-Wesley, 1982.

Zemke, R.; and Gunkler, J., in "Needs Analysis: A Concept in Search of Content." *Training,* July 1981, p. 57.

5

Nominal Grouping and Needs Analysis

INTRODUCTION

The nominal group technique (NGT) is a group process which incorporates the creative features of brainstorming into a controlled framework for needs analysis, problem-solving, and decision-making. Often, using groups for needs analysis is both frustrating and unrewarding. Staff meetings, for example, often drag on endlessly, develop into show and tell sessions, and degenerate into classical demonstrations

---

Dr. Mark J. Martinko, the author of this chapter, is an associate professor of management at Florida State University. He has worked and consulted with a variety of organizations including Western Electric Corporation, Omaha Public Power District, Florida Department of Law Enforcement, and Guinness Group Sales, Ireland. He is the co-author of *The Principles of Supervision and Management* and his work in the area of education and training has been published in a variety of journals including *The Academy of Management Review, American Educational Research Journal, Group and Organization Studies, Human Resource Management, Training,* and *Training and Development Journal.*

Jim Gepson, co-author of this chapter, holds an M.A. from the University of Nebraska at Omaha, and has 20 years of experience as a supervisor and manager. He is a private consultant who teaches management courses at

of the games described in the transactional analysis literature. These behaviors, while occasionally entertaining, therapeutic, and even informative, hinder groups in identifying and solving problems and sharing information. Even when meetings are effective, valuable data is often not recorded for future reference and follow-up. Minutes or recordings, especially in political environments, often encourage showmanship and other counterproductive games. As a result, problem-solving and training needs analysis often do badly in these "group encounters." It is tempting to simply give up on groups as a useful source of data and adopt surveys as a more efficient means of gathering data. By using surveys, the group hassle is no longer a factor. Unfortunately, however, survey results are often sterile, failing to accurately depict or describe real world needs related to job performance. NGT is a solution which copes with the dysfunctional characteristics of both groups and surveys, combining their positive features to result in a powerful diagnostic tool for training needs analysis.

The early work focused on NGT as a methodology to help involve clients and resource persons in long-term planning processes without the dysfunctional behaviors often associated with groups (Delbecq and Van de Ven, "Nominal Group Techniques for Involving Clients and Resource Experts in Program Planning," and "A Group Process Model for Problem Identification and Program Planning"). Since then, NGT has been used for a variety of related purposes including identifying communications problems (Huseman, "Communication Thermoclines—Toward a Process of Identification"), goal setting (Hopkins, "Improving MBO Through Synergistics"), generating performance measures (Steward, "A Yardstick for Measuring Productivity"), and training needs analyses (Gepson, Martinko, and Belina, "Nominal Group Techniques: A Diagnostic Strategy for Training Needs Analysis"). The purpose of this chapter is to explain the NGT process and how it is used for training needs analysis.

PREPARATORY CONSIDERATIONS

Before describing the process of conducting an NGT diagnostic session, decisions need to be made regarding the size of the workshop, the length of the sessions, and the make-up of the group.

Size

Size may vary considerably. As a rule of thumb, five to fifteen members are optimal. Smaller groups, while effective, create time/

---

the College of Saint Mary. Over the years, he has conducted a wide variety of seminars for supervisors and managers on the east and west coasts as well as in Alaska and Latin America. He is currently working on a training textbook and has written several management articles for national training magazines.

cost problems in large organizations. The authors have used NGT successfully with groups of 20 to 30, but larger groups are less effective over long periods.

Time Considerations

A second important variable is the length of NGT sessions. Attention spans, problem urgency, topic interest, and process familiarity may not be as important as participants' perception of whether or not their efforts will result in organizational action. Repeated use of NGT as a form of data gathering can lead to less participation if no feedback occurs or if problems identified are ignored. In short, populations that frequently participate in NGT may react the same as populations frequently asked to participate in "no feedback" or "dead end" surveys. In general, we have found that, provided feedback does occur, sessions of 45 minutes to one and one-half hours are optimal.

Participant Selection

There are at least four different types of persons who should attend an NGT meeting for training needs analyses. They are (1) the job incumbents; (2) line management; (3) known experts; and (4) the facilitator(s). The job incumbents obviously must be included because they are closest to the job, its problems, and related needs. Therefore, they are probably the best source of data about the job. Since it is preferable to keep the group participation level at 25 or less, several NGTs may be conducted concurrently or successively if there are more than 25 employees. Random selection can be used if work groups are particularly large.

The line manager is another important participant. The presence of the line manager confirms the importance of the process and demonstrates that follow-through is intended. Also, because the line manager has a daily responsibility for analyzing and diagnosing performance problems, he or she has a unique perspective on training needs.

The third type of participant is the expert. This may be a person or persons who have developed unusual proficiencies regarding the job. It may also be a person who has developed some particular competency in one aspect of the job. Thus, for example, a statistician may be a helpful member of a group diagnosing training needs for baseball managers.

The fourth and final type of person required is the facilitator. Before describing the selection of the facilitator, it is necessary to describe the role of the facilitator. In general, the facilitator explains the process, records concepts, and guides the discussion. The facilitator begins the meeting by briefly explaining the subject matter for analysis without attempting to bias participant output. The facilitator's explanation of NGT should be straightforward and neutral on subject matter. It is important that the facilitator avoids expressing value judgments via verbal or nonverbal behavior.

Supervisors, managers, or group members can serve as facilitators, but several possible negative consequences favor the use of "outside facilitators." Supervisors may intimidate participants or bias the creative process. This is especially true when NGT is used to identify performance discrepancies or training needs. A group member as facilitator may be hard pressed to stay out of discussions, may influence the use of terminology, and could become so interested in content that the NGT process is forgotten. In short, job incumbents and managers generally are poor facilitators because of their preconceived notions and biases regarding the job. Whenever possible, outside facilitators should be used.

THE NGT PROCESS

Delbecq and Van de Ven (*Group Techniques for Program Planning*) describe four steps in the NGT process:

1. Silent, written generation of ideas.

2. Round-robin feedback from each member recorded on a flip chart.

3. Discussion and clarification of each recorded idea or problem of 3.

4. Numerical weighting of each idea or problem.

Each of the next four sections will carefully describe one of these steps, focusing on the rationale for the step and possible pitfalls in implementation.

Written Idea Generation

After the facilitator has described the general nature and purpose of the NGT needs diagnosis section, the process begins with the facilitator asking the participants to write on paper, without discussion, a list of the training needs that they perceive to be most important. The specific request may be stated as follows:

> Using your experience of the past year, please identify the performance problems that you believe to be most detrimental to our organization.

Using a similar statement and process, the present authors were able to generate almost 400 different problem statements from an organization of approximately 20 employees (Martinko, Gepson, and Belina, "An Evaluation of the Nominal Group Techniques as a Primary Diagnostic Strategy for Organization Development").

The basic purpose of this first step is to bring to the surface the expertise of the group members without having to deal with the complex and negative aspects of interacting groups. At this point, the nominal group is, in a sense, not really a group although proximity and purpose appear to make it so. By carefully structuring the group at this stage, a major characteristic of groups, interaction, is missing along with its negative side effects.

The major reason for inhibiting group processes at this stage is complexity. For example, Graicuna's analysis of subordinate-supervisor relationships indicates that one supervisor or group leader with seven subordinates faces up to 490 possible relationships. As the number of subordinates increases to 12, the frequency of relationships soars to 24,708 (Galick and Urwick, "Papers on the Science of Administration"). In addition, the rate at which we speak is significantly slower than the rate at which we can listen. Thus, participants' minds drift while "listening," thereby compounding difficulties faced by groups attempting to cope with relationships that are already extremely complex. It is not surprising, then, that groups have difficulty focusing attention on specific organizational problems.

Silent generation of ideas, written in terse phrases, slices through the distractions and annoyances characteristic of interactive groups. For a brief time, perhaps five to ten minutes, group members can concentrate their efforts on conceptualizing and recording. During the silent idea generation phase, more vocal and perhaps influential individuals will be restrained, allowing other individuals to think and write. At this point, the group is a group in name only. All concepts are equally important and unweighted at this time. The participants are unaware of what the others are thinking and writing. The influence of leaders, subgroups, and cliques has less impact on the creative process.

For the most part, this phase of the process usually goes smoothly as long as the participants understand that they are not to interact at this point. The only difficulty that the authors have experienced in this step has occurred when the participants' actual or perceived writing skills created embarrassment and reluctance to commit their ideas to paper. The situation was partially erased by telling them that they would not be required to "hand-in" their notes.

Round-Robin Feedback

After the idea generation phase, the facilitator asks one individual at a time to verbalize the first concept or problem on his/her list. In a terse phrase, the concept or problem is recorded on the flip chart. The frequency with which others have the same concept is recorded next to the concept. All participants are asked to cross out that idea and not to repeat it if it appears on their lists to save time and avoid redundancy.

The round-robin process continues until all the ideas are recorded, and numerical frequencies are written next to the appropriate ideas. The frequencies, obtained by a simple show of hands, are useful in reflecting the relative importance with which a given group views a specific problem. Comparison of group frequencies may reveal differing perceptions at various organizational levels. A maintenance operation may perceive similar concepts differently than a maintenance unit.

While most ideas result from the idea generation phase, the round-robin exercise stimulates concepts which participants often add to their lists. It should be noted that the size of the group is related to the number of ideas produced. When the goal of the NGT session is exclusively sampling or generating ideas, large groups can be managed providing discussion is sharply curtailed.

There are few problems in this phase if the facilitator manages the group and makes sure that people participate in order. Occasionally, the concept or problem will be so ambiguous or general as to have little value. In one NGT session, one of the authors, serving as facilitator, was obliged to seek a more specific description than "the whole g—d—— place needs training." This situation would have been less likely to occur had the facilitator placed sufficient emphasis on specificity while explaining the process.

Discussion and Clarification

The facilitator begins this phase by stressing that the objective of the discussion is the clarification of the ideas already listed on the flip chart. The originator of each concept is given the opportunity to explain the concept and answer questions related to clarification. The facilitator adds to the flip chart words or brief phrases next to the appropriate concept. Silent written generation of ideas related to an existing concept may serve to re-establish the nominal group and provide clarification. The timing and control of the discussion is affected by factors such as individual characteristics, group behaviors, number of concepts, complexity of concepts, and facilitator skills. Throughout the discussion, the facilitator guides the participants through the lists of ideas which, in effect, become the ad hoc agenda for the meeting.

Ideally, the interaction should be with concepts rather than with groups or individuals. Thus, "air time" is concept-related, rather than people-related. One problem that often occurs is that nominal groups tend to drift into interaction during the discussion phase. In these cases, maintenance of the round-robin sequence and concentrating on the concepts or problems visually displayed on the flip charts minimizes interaction. The initial explanation of the NGT process also has a great impact on behaviors during the discussion and may have to be repeated by the facilitator if interaction becomes disruptive.

A second problem that sometimes occurs is the tendency of individuals to leap into problem-solving, thus impeding the clarification of ideas. In these cases, it may be necessary to refer to later sessions which are scheduled for action planning and problem-solving.

Numerical Weighting

The major purpose of this step is to allow the participants to establish the relative importance of each item. During this numerical weighting process, the concepts are listed and individuals vote, ranking each item on a scale of one to ten or using some other appropriate interval scale. Rank-ordering the items on the list can also be done. Rating or rank ordering may be sought for the following types of factors:

1. Importance, as defined in terms of organizational and performance impact.
2. Safety in terms of whether or not the item affects the safety of employees.
3. Mechanical or technical in origin, indicating whether or not the problem is solvable by mechanical or technical means.
4. Knowledge or training, indicating whether or not the problem is caused by a skill or knowledge deficiency.
5. Probability of solution, indicating the likelihood of being able to solve the problem.
6. Motivation or execution, indicating the extent to which employees may know how to perform but are not because of environmental deficiencies.

These factors closely parallel those suggested by Mager and Pipe's training needs analysis model (*Analyzing Performance Problems, or 'You Really Oughta Wanna'*). If these same factors are used, a short lecture clarifying the factors should be provided before the rating process begins. If a survey process is used for rating the items, more thorough explanations of these categories should accompany the survey.

Whether or not rank-ordering or scaling processes are used is another important consideration. Rank-ordering of items is often preferable because it generates a wider range of scores, making priorities more easily identifiable. The results from scaling processes, on the other hand, are often so similar that they do not adequately differentiate the priorities of the various items. Rank-ordering, however, is very time consuming and can cause problems of comparison if several groups of differing sizes participate in different sessions. One solution to this problem is to conclude the NGT session after the discussion phase, collate all of the data, and re-assemble the groups for rating after the data has been combined. Another solution is to employ a survey method as the last step which allows the NGT participants to rate or rank-order all items developed in all groups.

Once the priority of the items has been established, they become the basis for further analyses. Using surveys or follow-up NGT sessions, participants may be asked for further analyses of the concepts developed in order to more clearly describe and rate the importance of priority items. Action planning and developing solutions for priority items is, of course, the next step in training needs analyses. However, it is not a part of the NGT process and thus is not described in this chapter. The NGT process, as described here, provides a priority listing of major training issues and needs. The action planning process described in Chapter 14 should then be applied to complete the program design process.

During this final step, there are a variety of possible pitfalls. First, participants often become frustrated when they are asked to rate and rank-order items. Rank-ordering is generally more frustrating than rating. While the frustrating aspects of these processes cannot be totally eliminated, they can be minimized by making sure that (1) the categories are well defined and understood and (2) the problems and/or needs are clearly described. Although frustration will probably occur, it is worth both the effort and the waiting if a clear statement of priorities can be generated.

If a survey is used for this last step, follow-up is often a problem. Be prepared to log survey returns and provide feedback to delinquent participants. Although anonymous returns are sometimes preferable, they make it almost impossible to identify persons not participating.

A third consideration is data processing. Since this is often a time-consuming process, it frequently cannot and is not carried out during the session. Care in planning and designing rating forms can greatly facilitate collating the results. Where larger organizations are involved, computerized data processing systems may be warranted.

The final concern is feedback and follow-up for the participants. Most will have cooperated voluntarily and will be interested in the results. After the results are compiled, they should be summarized and given back to the participants with a brief description of how the data will be used in the identification and establishment of relevant training programs. If carried out well, this last step will reinforce the participants' interest and create realistic pressure for both the management and training organizations to respond to the priority needs.

SUMMARY

The data generated in NGT sessions is rooted in the day to day reality of specific organizational problems. Problems identified are operational providing training organizations with "real world" or "bottomline" needs analysis. Other more traditional needs analysis processes such as surveys often miss the nitty-gritty of organizational problems, especially if academic institutions, training divisions, or consultants prepare the process based on the language and perceptions of trainers. Other trainers may understand what is intended, but line managers and employees may be guessing when they see survey results that suggest courses in communication, supervision, or what not. When the concepts, problems, and priorities are produced from the heart of the organization, in the language of the organization, trainers may more realistically begin planning, developing, purchasing, and/or eliminating programs to suit organizational needs.

REFERENCES

Delbecq, A.L.; Van de Ven, H.H.; and Gustafson, D.H. *Group Techniques for Program Planning*. Glenview, Ill.: Scott, Foresman and Company, 1975, pp. 10–11.

Delbecq, A.L., and Van de Ven, A. "Nominal Group Techniques for Involving Clients and Resource Experts in Program Planning." *Academy of Management Proceedings,* 1970, pp. 208–227.

Delbecq, A. and Van de Ven, A. "A Group Process Model for Problem Identification and Program Planning." *Journal of Applied Behavioral Science,* 7(4), 1971, pp. 466–492.

Gepson, J.; Martinko, M.; and Belina, J. "Nominal Group Techniques: A Diagnostic Strategy for Training Needs Analysis." *Training and Development Journal,* 35(4), 1982, pp. 78–83.

Galick, L., and Urwick, L. (eds.). *Papers on the Science of Administration.* New York: Institute of Public Administration, 1937. pp. 181–187.

Hopkins, D. "Improving MBO Through Synergistics." *Public Personnel Management.* Vol. 8, No. 3 (May/June 1979). pp. 163–169.

Huseman, R. "Communication Thermoclines—Toward a Process of Identification." *Personnel Journal,* Vol. 53, No. 2 (February 1974), pp. 124–130.

Mager, R.F., and Pipe, P. *Analyzing Performance Problems, or 'You Really Oughta Wanna.'* Belmont, CA: Lear Seagler, Inc./Feron Publishing, 1970.

Martinko, M.; Gepson, J.; and Belina, J. "An Evaluation of the Nominal Group Technique as a Primary Diagnostic Strategy for Organization Development." Proceedings of the Southeast American Institute of Decision Science, Orlando, 1980.

Steward, W.T. "A Yardstick for Measuring Productivity." *Industrial Engineering,* Vol. 10, No. 2 (February 1978), pp. 34–37.

6

The Delphi Technique

INTRODUCTION

Frequently, businesses and organizations are faced with the problem of predicting or forecasting future events and relationships in order to make appropriate and reasonable plans or changes. Several methods exist for forecasting, one of which is called the Delphi technique. Named after the Greek oracle, who was known for predicting events, the Delphi technique is a methodology that was developed to utilize the subjective judgments of experts. ("Experts" will be referred to as "respondents" in this chapter.)

The Delphi technique had its beginnings in the 1950s, when a group of Rand Corporation scientists discovered a method of combining individuals' estimates of how to bet at the horse races to the advantage of all. Gordon and Helmer ("Report on a Long-Range

Gustave Rath, Ph.D., the co-author of this chapter, is a professor at Northwestern University, Evanston, Illinois. He is also a partner in Cassell, Rath, and Stoyanoff consulting firm, Evanston, Ill.

Karen Stoyanoff, Ph.D., the co-author of this chapter, is a private consultant and a partner in Cassell, Rath, and Stoyanoff consulting firm, Evanston, Ill.

Forecasting Study") made the first official use of the method in a long-range forecasting study to predict the dates of breakthroughs in scientific areas, particularly space technology. Because the technique was given security classification, it was not publicized for nearly a decade. These original studies included Dalkey and Helmer's work ("An Experimental Application of the Delphi Method to the Use of Experts," pp. 458–467) on the prediction of defense needs with reference to optimal planning of an industrial target system by estimation of the number of nuclear bombs needed to reduce munitions production by half. However, since that date the Delphi method has become increasingly popular in many business organizations as a forecasting and planning tool. In fact, such has been the impact of the Delphi method that at least 150 companies reported using it in 1969, and since then the number has increased considerably. Government agencies, universities, and other organizations have also begun to experiment with the possibilities it offers. Dalkey and Helmer and Pill ("The Delphi Method: Substance, Context: A Critique and Annotated Bibliography") have all stressed that one of the greatest assets of the Delphi technique is its stimulating approach, for there is no doubt that it motivates innovative thinking. There are three traditional uses of the Delphi technique: forecasting, policy investigations, and goal setting. Trainers will find it useful in needs assessment, setting training department goals, identifying future areas that need to be considered in the training function, etc.

The vast majority of reported Delphi studies have been involved with forecasting, and most of these have been carried out by companies interested in long-range estimates for planning purposes. The reason for the concentration of Delphi applications in this field is probably the result of the extraordinary suitability of Delphi to this sort of decision-making and of its first having been used as a forecasting tool.

Use of the Delphi technique in other fields began with an education innovation study which attempted to sort many of the possible future developments in education into some sort of priority order (Adelson, "The Education Innovation Study"). Of more interest to planners is the so-called policy Delphi, which was developed by Turoff ("Delphi Conferencing") to formulate policies for urban development. Reisman ("Measurement of Output in a System of Social Agencies") carried out another interesting Delphi study to evaluate the social services offered by a number of agencies. He designed the study in such a way that the agencies could be evaluated on seven different "quality scales," these qualities first having been rated for their relative importance. Dalkey and Rourke ("Experimental Assessment of Delphi Procedures with Group Value Judgment") have concluded the Delphi technique to be quite suited to issues involving strictly value judgments; they used it to develop goal statements concerning the quality of life. The main difference between these and the earlier studies in forecasting is that they deal with issues in which values and sometimes emotions are the input rather than hard facts. This use puts a rather different light on the possibilities of Delphi, indicating that it might be used not only in problem-solving situations as before but perhaps as a political decision-making tool.

Some more recent Delphis have included

1. A study of the future of affirmative action programs and regulation. Reported by Fred L. Fry ("The End of Affirmative Action"), the study pinpoints issues on which consensus can be reached and areas where attitudes are so highly polarized that no single prediction can be made. The study concerned equal opportunity for minority races and women.

2. Another is the 1974 National Coordinating Council on Drug Education study conducted with 38 respondents on drug abuse policy (Linstone, "The Delphi Technique").

3. In 1979, the Center for Future Research at the University of Southern California conducted a Delphi with 20 professors in business to predict changes in government-corporate relations (Fleming, "A Possible Future of Government–Corporate Relations").

4. Finally, in 1980 in Great Britain a Delphi was conducted to determine the point at which the benefits of production outweigh the cost (pollution) to society.

Overall, it seems likely that the published and available literature on Delphi represents only a fraction of the studies actually carried out. From more distant sources it has been reported that Delphis have been carried out in many European countries, the U.S.S.R., and Japan.

The purpose of this chapter is to discuss the process by which a Delphi is carried out, to identify and discuss important considerations in the use of a Delphi, and finally to present a case study of a Delphi. While the traditional Delphi is focused on forecasting and long-range planning, we are offering it as a tool a trainer may use in needs assessments. Delphi may productively be used in need identification and setting training priorities. As Delbecq, Van de Ven, and Gustafson (*Group Techniques for Program Planning*) indicate, Delphi has become a multiple-use planning tool.

THE METHODOLOGY: AN OVERVIEW

The Delphi technique is described here as a general methodology rather than a hard and fast method, because the exact procedure has never been fixed. Indeed, one of the great advantages of Delphi is its flexibility to circumstance and degree. The underlying principles, though simple, are important. The chief characteristic of the technique is its iterative structure, i.e., the respondents are constantly interacting with the material being generated. Essentially, Delphi is a series of questionnaires which are circulated among a group of respondents.

A second characteristic is anonymity to the respondents. The participants do not know who is saying what. The result is that people are not swayed by the persona of other participants. The result is greater generation of ideas.

A "typical" overview of the Delphi process is shown in the following flow chart:

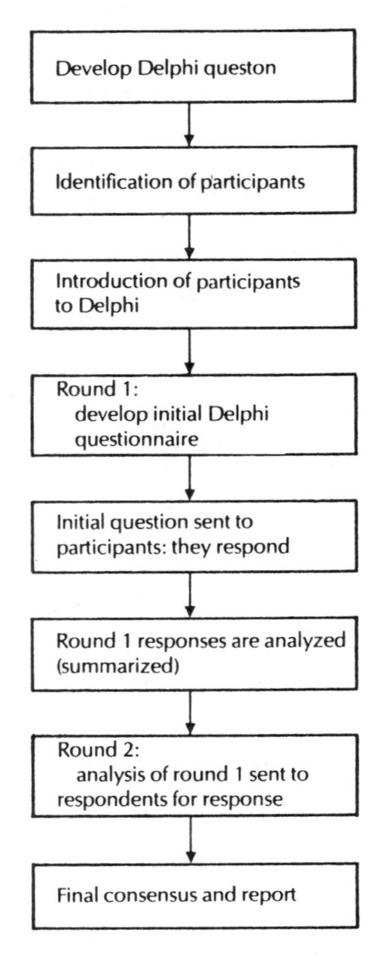

The first step of any Delphi is the establishment of the Delphi question. What question is to be asked of the participants? This is obviously tied to the objectives of the Delphi—what are the outcomes desired? The case study at the end of this chapter provides an example of the objectives behind a Delphi.

Another question becomes "Who should be included as participants in the study?" This will be discussed later in this chapter.

The Delphi question has been stated and the participants have been selected. One more step remains before getting into Delphi proper, i.e., introducing participants to the Delphi process. This step is key: If participants are not properly introduced, significant dropoff may occur. This is also touched on later in the chapter.

The Delphi process is now ready to begin. It begins with the Delphi question presented to respondents. Their responses are summarized and, along with the questions, are re-presented to the respondents. The new set of responses is again summarized and re-presented until a consensus is achieved or a polarity identified. The process can be viewed as a series of rounds; in each round every participant works through a questionnaire, which is returned to the organizer, who collects, edits, and returns to every participant a statement of the position of the whole group.

This position statement shows what the group as a whole was thinking during that particular round. It usually has two parts: (1) a mean or median and some measure of dispersion of opinion on each item, and (2) a summation of the comments from the group. Thus, before the next round commences, each participant is made aware of the range of opinions throughout the group. Since in every round each participant is required to support his opinion with some rationale, he is also made aware, via the summing-up, of the reasons that underlie the spread of opinion. He is therefore in a position to assess his own responses against the responses of the group as a whole, and to consider the rationalizations that other people in the group have made for their responses.

At no time, however, is he aware of the specific response of any individual member of the group—this is where the anonymity of the process comes in. While the intention is for the feedback to impact each participant, anonymity of participants is protected. This allows for a freer expression of ideas, values, and judgments than frequently occurs in face-to-face discussions.

The feedback mechanism is central to the operation of the Delphi. This is the means by which ideas and opinions are exchanged from round to round. Each participant may change or reformulate his opinion as he comes into contact with new facts, ideas, or understandings that are different from his own. Since no individual knows who puts forward which ideas, ideas cannot be rejected or accepted for purely personal reasons of trust or mistrust of another respondent. Each idea must be examined on its own merits.

Typically, the onus is on "extremists" to justify themselves; that is, it is usually demanded that people who persist in holding an opinion that lies outside the norm justify their position. As background information on the subject is accumulated, there is a tendency for people to move closer to the center of the distribution of opinion.

At each round, therefore, a change in position is entirely voluntary and, of course, anonymous. When there are a number of issues to be agreed upon, consensus is reached rapidly (in two to three rounds) on a few of the issues, and more slowly (five or six rounds) on the more controversial issues. The tendency in almost every case is for the opinions of the individuals in the group to move closer and closer together as key facts are elucidated and as misunderstandings and misinterpretations are resolved.

The overriding motivating force in Delphi is undoubtedly that of anonymity of opinion. Anonymity of opinion acts to break down many of the traditional barriers to forthrightness and honesty. As Turoff ("The Design of a Policy Delphi") acidly remarked, ". . . Only two types of individuals are likely to exercise this option (signing their responses)—experts and fools." By the use of anonymity, the respondents are put in a position to share what they really think and feel.

Many studies confirm the prevailing claim of Delphi proponents that the more people are actively encouraged to put forth their ideas, the better the final answer produced by the group. A multitude of studies show that in an open group situation the individual is under considerable pressure to conform to the dominant view, not by intellectual reasons or the rational superiority of this dominant view, but by reasons of self-confidence (or lack), status, and other similar personal variables. These interpersonal factors are minimized by the operation of the Delphi in decision-making. Consensus may be reached by reason of the content of the communications and the subject matter rather than the interpersonal factors.

To quickly summarize this section, the Delphi process involves (1) identifying a group of respondents, (2) developing a Delphi question(s), (3) introducing the Delphi to the participants, (4) circulating the Delphi among the respondents, (5) analyzing the responses of the respondents, and (6) circulating the analysis from round 1 back to the respondents, etc. Depending on the Delphi, the process may take four rounds or it may take six or more. The case study at the end of this chapter provides an example of a startup of a Delphi.

Key to the process is the anonymity of respondents. The next section of this chapter will explore a number of important considerations in doing a Delphi.

DELPHI CONSIDERATIONS

A number of important considerations are involved with a Delphi project. This section will look at some of these considerations.

Setting up the Delphi

Frequently, the Delphi is proposed by a decision-maker in an organization (private or public) even though it is designed and run either by an outside consultant or by a subordinate. The reasons why a decision-maker proposes and someone else runs the Delphi are (1) running the design requires considerable time, (2) running the design may require specialized knowledge, and (3) the anonymity principle means a neutral person must run the Delphi. This "neutral" person will be referred to as the "consultant."

In general, the consultant and the client together must be responsible for many of the nontechnical elements of the design, e.g., scheduling, determining who will be respondents, technical support. How the results of the Delphi will be used is the responsibility of the decision-maker.

One issue in particular that may arise in this respect is that of the identity of the participant (respondent). The equation of the terms "expert" and "participant" in the Delphi literature is misleading. Although most Delphis have been concerned with technical matters and have therefore involved experts in the sense of scientifically knowledgeable persons, there is no reason why the term should not be extended as the subject matter of the Delphi changes. Users of a public library, for example, are "experts" as to the needs of users. Supervisors or managers are the "experts" to be looked to when the trainer is identifying training and development needs. The choice of respondent is generally one that must be made by the client, and particularly so in the case of value Delphis which are to be used to develop policies or goals. If the client is in need of information of the type that may be generated by a Delphi, it is safe to assume that he is in need of information in which he has some measure of confidence; it is therefore his prerogative to choose participants.

Example. XYZ Corporation has a management development task force to guide the management development efforts. The task force has the responsibility, along with the training director, of setting objectives for the coming year. The task force is geographically spread out.

The training director decides that prior to the projective setting meeting, a Delphi will be run. The meeting will then provide an opportunity to discuss the objectives further and to look at other issues as needs.

Initiating the Delphi

Since the cooperation of the participants is essential to the success of the Delphi, it is prudent for either the client or the consultant or both to provide explanation of and rationale for the Delphi process before it begins. (Note the case in the appendix.) In fact, the need to establish rapport between the Delphi organizers and the participants seems unavoidable to clear up any misapprehensions about the purpose and operational mechanism of the Delphi. A lengthy briefing of the participants is not time wasted; this may contribute greatly to the ability of the Delphi to explore the subject matter in depth. The introductory session, however, need not necessarily be a one-way process. A Delphi designer with little expert knowledge of the subject matter of the Delphi may gain considerable insight by discussion with participants at this stage. A mutual understanding between Delphi organizers and participants is essential.

Frequently, a cover letter of the type illustrated in the examples at the end of this chapter is one part of the initiation process. It not only provides an overview of the process once again but provides the rationale for it as well.

Example. The task force has a membership of 18. The training director decides to use the total task force for the project. The time objective is to have a minimum of four rounds (if needed) and to complete it within six weeks.

The training director calls each respondent to

1. Explain the Delphi process.
2. Explain the rationale for using it in this setting.
3. Obtain their commitment to responding to the various rounds.

Methods of Communication and Scheduling of a Delphi

The method by which feedback is communicated, the size of the Delphi, and the schedule on which it is organized may in some cases also be the concern of the client rather than of the consultant. The majority of studies have used operating units of between 15 and 20 people. Larger numbers of participants are often divided into panels on the basis of common fields of interest. Experiments have shown that Delphis with up to 100 people in one group are quite feasible. The limits on size seem to be dictated by the constraints on the processing of large numbers of responses between rounds.

The method by which feedback is maintained will be dependent on both the size of the group and the time schedule required. From the organizational viewpoint, the timing and schedule of a Delphi may be one of the most important elements of its design. Most Delphis have been run over periods of several weeks, with a week or two between rounds. However, in some situations Delphis have been done in a session. Delbecq, Van de Ven, and Gustafson suggest a minimum time of 44.5 days.

The greatest bulk of time invested in a Delphi session is in the planning and editing of responses between rounds. Perhaps because of the experts that have been used in Delphis to date (mainly top-ranking executives and scientific notables), the trend has been to minimize the time-effort on the part of the participants. Turoff's (1970) study using a computerized system is one of the most advanced Delphis using this principle. With access to a number of terminals, the participants were able to tune in at any time to the course of the Delphi to keep up with events and were able via the terminal to vote on issues and/or add comments at any time. It was even possible for a participant to leave instructions with his secretary to type in his responses. Less complicated automated systems dealing only with the quantitative side of the Delphi are much more readily available to Delphi designers. If Delphis are to continue using valuable respondent time, then this seems to be a development well worth following.

Three concerns are the method by which feedback is communicated, the size of the Delphi, and its schedule.

Example. The participants to the Delphi have all agreed to proceed with it.

The training director now sends out the following materials via the mail:

1. A letter thanking the respondents for their cooperation.
2. A schedule of the Delphi (tentative).
3. Questionnaire 1.

Questionnaire 1 is an open-ended question: "What are the objectives you see as important for management?"

Formats and Rating Scales

Another topic that is not usually given much emphasis in the analysis of Delphis is the way in which questions are presented or comments solicited. The majority of studies, concerned with forecasting dates of events in the future, have used simple probability format of the type:

- What is the probability of X occurring in or before 1985?

or

• In what year would you be 75 percent certain that X would occur?

These formats have the advantage of allocating simple but definite quantification to events in time. The chief requirements on a quantification scheme are that it be consistent and that it give output in a useful form. It must be simple enough to be comprehended and handled by the participants. In Delphis concerned with complex issues rather than with one-dimensional forecasts in time, for example, those concerned with producing goal sets, problem identifications, needs assessments, etc., the question of measurement is crucial. Scales to measure such qualities are not easy to develop. In general, Delphi designs tend toward simplicity rather than sophisticated quantification, and lateral scales are usually used. The following is an example:

_______ 5 4 3 2 1 _______

Very Important.............................. Not At All Important

Scaling of phenomena becomes difficult where the events concerned are not independent of one another and are therefore not ordered measurably in the minds of the participants. This has prompted a number of studies using scenarios of possible combinations of events, for example in descriptions of the future as might be given in a newspaper article. This grouping of events creates a picture for participants that may be more meaningful to them than the individual events alone. Similarly, in using Delphi to create and rate sets of goals, overlapping objectives may be grouped into what are essentially higher level goals so that the participants may relate more easily to the subject material. A number of cluster techniques are available for the analysis of such groupings (Rutherford, "Case Study in the Use of the Delphi Technique in Goal Setting: The Morton Arboretum" and Dalkey and Rourke, "Experimental Assessment of Delphi Procedures with Group Value Judgment").

Example. The return of round 1 results in about 40 objectives for the management development program. The training director lists all of the objectives from round 1 and uses them for the basis of round 2.

Respondents have several options in round 2. They may

1. Add other objectives.
2. Rewrite the present objectives.
3. Comment on present objectives.
4. Vote to delete an objective.

Round 2 is returned and the process above is repeated. By round 3, it appears that the list of objectives has pretty well stabilized.

Presentation of Feedback

Presentation problems occur both at the beginning of each round and at the conclusion when the information created by the Delphi must be summarized and interpreted. It is general practice to present a statistic such as the mean or median as the "score" and sometimes to give the interquartile range as an indication of the dispersion of the distribution, as well as the verbal feedback on "reasons." This procedure, however, is not without risk. First, the implications of the mean and the median are not the same and should not be treated as such. A second point is more serious. The Delphi process has a tendency to create convergence, and though this is usually to a single point, there is always the possibility that polarization will occur. When this happens both the mean and the median will be misleading as descriptive parameters. Sometimes the results may cluster around two or more points (e.g., 60 percent believe that supervisory training is most important while 40 percent say training in small group problem-solving is most important). It is important that the effects of all the different central tendency statistics are examined before making a choice. The possibility of using the mode as the feedback parameter has been largely ignored in Delphi work. However, given a visual feedback system in which a histogram is displayed, it would seem more plausible that the mode, which is after all more visible than either the mean or the median, has the greater influence in inducing change toward the center.

In any event, one possible result of a Delphi is the identification of polarized issues on which agreement of respondents is unlikely, no matter how many rounds of voting may be offered. In a Delphi conducted in 1980 to predict when the need for affirmative action programs and laws would end (due to assimilation of currently disparate groups and significant changes in discriminatory employment practices), it was determined that consensus was not possible on when full integration of races would be achieved (Fry, 1980). This knowledge is indeed valuable as a planning guide and the interpretation of Delphi data should render it presentable to both participants and those commissioning the study.

Dalkey and Helmer studied the effects of verbal feedback alone against those of statistical feedback alone and found that the presentation of verbal feedback by itself was not satisfactory in terms of reaching a consensus in the Delphi. Statistical feedback without any verbal explanations was very much superior in this respect. They showed, however, that given statistical feedback, groups that were also provided with a "relevant fact" produced better results than groups that were not so provided. We favor the use in Delphi of a combination of visual statistical feedback, together with a carefully edited summary of the "reasons" given.

The method of presentation of the verbal part of the feedback will depend largely on the general format of the Delphi. If weeks or days elapse between rounds, then clearly a written summary is the simplest manner in which feedback may be achieved. In a single-session Delphi, however, the time required for careful editing may not be available, and the Delphi organizer may have to ad lib somewhat in reading selections from the "reasons" to the group as a whole. Clearly, the advantages of an extended Delphi are great if the feedback is voluminous.

Example. With the management development objectives fairly well stabilized, the training director now divides the remaining objectives into goals for the weighing round.

The 45 objectives fit nicely into five goal categories, e.g., in-house training classes, individual training needs, etc.

Round 4 questionnaire asks the participants to divide 100 points among the five goal categories. Each respondent also rates each objective within the goal categories for its appropriateness in being in that goal set.

Round 4 is now sent out.

Measurement of Consensus

It is common practice in running Delphi sessions to drop from the Delphi those items that at any round reach a point of consensus. In general, the process is continued until amost all the items are so characterized. The definition of consensus has usually been relatively ad hoc, taking such arbitrary levels as

- Consensus is reached when 80 percent of the votes fall within two categories on a seven-point scale.

Such measures have a rule-of-thumb usefulness, but they do not contain much information on the nature of consensus, nor do they allow for cases in which bimodal consensus appears. In addition, there is a strong tendency in reporting the results after the Delphi to push into the background the items on which such a consensus was not achieved. This emphasis on successful consensus represents only one side of the Delphi process. The founding fathers of the Delphi school included in the objectives of the Delphi technique the exploration of divergence as well as of convergence of opinion (Turoff, 1970).

An alternative approach is that of using the entire distribution curve rather than a single statistic in the measurement of consensus. Since each round supposedly brings the distribution to a more peaked and balanced form, it is possible to measure the change in shape of the histogram from round to round, and over time the variance would be expected to decrease steadily. Consensus may then be measured as the point at which the histogram stabilizes such that further rounds do not induce significant changes in the shape of the histogram, as measured by the variance.

Example. By round 5, it appears as if four of the goals have an acceptable level of consensus. The fifth goal, relating to management development marketing services outside of the organization, has divergent opinions.

However, the training director decides to stop the Delphi at this point. The process outcomes now become the agenda at the task force's next meeting.

ADVANTAGES/DISADVANTAGES OF DELPHI

Ulschak ("A Delphi Study: Prioritizing Programs for Conference Ministry") identifies some of the advantages and disadvantages of the Delphi process. Some of the advantages include

1. Because there is no face-to-face contact, the Delphi encourages greater participation than other group problem-solving methods. Participants do not know who is responding, therefore they are not influenced by the person but only respond to ideas.

2. With group pressure removed, creative thinking increases because threat of judgment or "group think" is eliminated.

3. Interpersonal problems are eliminated. Power "struggles," issues of leadership, "group think," etc., are avoided.

4. Equal time is provided for all participants.

An additional advantage that might be added to this list is

5. Delphi can be readily used when a group of persons are not in close proximity. It eliminates the need to have face-to-face meetings.

Disadvantages include

1. Delphi is extremely task oriented. Once underway, it presses to grind out a product. Participants may end up feeling alienated.

2. The questionnaire method may slow down the process greatly. There may be several days or weeks between rounds. This may mean participant motivation and interest will drop off.

An additional disadvantage that might be added is

3. Large numbers of persons may generate a multitude of items, creating problems of categorizing.

SUMMARY

Delphi technique may be a useful tool for the trainer in identifying training needs. Its steps include

1. Establishing the Delphi question.
2. Identifying the participants who will respond to the questionnaires.
3. Developing a questionnaire, distributing it, and analyzing it.
4. Developing questionnaire 2, etc.
5. Writing the final summary.

The case studies presented in the appendix provide an example of the use of the Delphi.

CASE STUDY: THE SCHOOL DISTRICT ADMINISTRATION DELPHI

A Delphi goal-setting project was carried out at Northwestern University in 1972. It was designed in conjunction with the superintendent of a school district, who for some time had been interested in (1) developing a structure of goals on which to base evaluation studies within the school district and (2) encouraging communication and participation in the school decision-making from all areas of the community. He had, in fact, been actively involved in several projects concerned with the organizational development of the school district and felt that a Delphi goal-setting exercise might further this policy. The direct output of the Delphi, however, was planned to be incorporated in the planning, programming, and budgeting (PPB) system that the district was developing. The importance of producing a comprehensive goal set was therefore paramount. The Delphi evolved with the administrators' needs and their understanding of the problems as well as with those of the researchers.

The school district itself is located in a northwestern suburb of Chicago, and has three junior high schools and nine grade schools. It serves a fairly homogeneous white middle-class society, has not been the scene of any major racial strifes, and busing has not been an issue of contention in the area. Thus, the study approached a community that was genuinely concerned with the direct educational needs of the school district. It was designed to include in the goal-setting process representatives from throughout the community so that a diversity of opinions might be accommodated. (Note: How was the Delphi communicated to them?)

Step 1: Generation of the Initial Objectives

The participants in the Delphi were selected by the superintendent and represented the community as follows:

Principals	15
Curriculum Coordinators	5
Teachers	26
Central Administrators	5
Parents and other Lay People	15
Board Members	7
Students (from the junior high)	9
Total	82

Since this large number presented problems in terms of editorial work on the part of the Delphi organizers, a "seed" round was the initial step. It was decided a sample of 30 people selected from the total participant list would generate an initial list of objectives for the school system. With the cooperation of the superintendent, the 30 people were invited to attend a preliminary Delphi session. At the session each person was scheduled for a 15-minute interview with the two Delphi organizers. It was planned that this time would be sufficient for a brief explanation of the Delphi process, and for each participant to write on paper the objectives for the school system that seemed to him to be the most crucial. (In other words, the participants were asked for the ideal objectives, not the ones currently operating.) In general, the participants seemed open and trustful of the Delphi and were enthusiastic about participating. As it turned out, however, 15 minutes was not sufficient to fulfill the task. Fortunately, it was possible to allow the participants to overlap. At one point, there were as many as ten persons working in the same room with each new arrival being greeted and briefed on the nature of the task as he arrived. The participants were exceedingly cooperative in maintaining the "individual response" character of the Delphi, and did not confer much while developing their objective lists.

Step 2: Feedback on the Initial Objective Lists, I

Editing reduced the numerous objectives produced by the seed round to a manageable list of 58 by eliminating overlapping objectives and by dismissing statements that were not truly objectives. This task required considerable discretion on the part of the Delphi organizers since only some of the participants were familiar with the concept of goals and objectives. Despite initial briefing procedures, many responses were essentially gripes and comments. These were rewritten by the organizers to reflect the probable underlying objective. For example, the comment "Who checks up on the teachers, then?" was paraphrased with some license as "Teachers should be evaluated throughout."

In many cases, objectives that were highly related were combined into a single double-barreled objective. For example: "Children have developed the ability to interact and make friends with others, to understand problems of other people; children are emotionally stable." The purpose of this simplification was to reduce the number of objectives with which the participants would have to deal. One of the difficulties that derived from the very large number of participants was that of maintaining organizer objectivity. To some extent, this was sacrificed in order to make the exercise feasible. However, at each new round participants were free to announce any bias they detected, and in fact, it was felt that with feedback the level of distortion was minimized.

All the objectives were stated in the present tense as states which the *ideal* school system attains. This presentation style apparently caused little difficulty except in the case of one or two of the students, who seemed to misinterpret this meaning. The list of 58 objectives was returned to all 90 participants as round 1 of the Delphi.

Participants were then asked to work with this list to create a more comprehensive list and to alter any of the existing objectives. An abbreviated form of this list is attached to this chapter. Blank sheets were distributed at a meeting at which all participants were present, and some discussion of the Delphi and its purposes was held. The organizers at this point were very anxious not to alienate any of the participants through misunderstandings. Despite the large number present, the meeting closed with an air of great interest and friendliness.

Step 3: Feedback on Objectives, II

From the comments, suggestions, and additions generated through round 1 of the Delphi, a second and augmented list was prepared. As in the first round, this was done by comparing the similarity of suggested objectives and altering the original objectives as well as adding new ones. Objectives were written on cards to simplify the process. Similar and overlapping objectives were physically placed together during the editing process. This new list contained 82 objectives and it was circulated to all the participants with instructions to add and to alter the objective statements. This time, however, the lists were mailed with return envelopes to all participants.

Step 4: Feedback on Objectives, III

The returns to this round 2 resulted in the expansion of the list of objectives to 115. Comments sent in by participants, along with their responses, indicated that they, as well as the organizers, felt it was time to reorganize the list into some more meaningful groupings.

Step 5: Feedback on Objectives, IV

The presence of so many participants made the problem of grouping the objectives difficult. However, grouping clearly was an essential next step since the 115 objectives were in no way organized. Therefore, for round 3 a strategy was proposed in which members of the research team were to do the grouping on behalf of the participants. Tests made during an earlier Delphi had indicated that this could be done without undue bias. The six researchers proceeded to group the objectives.

The result of the grouping round was a list of 12 goals representing the 115 objectives.

Step 6: Developing Goal Weights

Round 4 of the Delphi involved weighing both the goals and the objectives. Because of the number of objectives present, a rating scheme for the objectives was employed. Participants were asked to assign a number between 1 and 10 to each objective to represent its relative importance. For weighing the goals, a fractionation approach was employed. Participants were asked to divide 100 points between the 12 goals. As in the previous round, participants were contacted by mail, so that several weeks elapsed.

Step 7: Adjustment of Design

After most of the responses from round 4 had been collected, some changes were made in the Delphi design in response to feedback on the way the Delphi was going. There was some anxiety among the administrators of the school district, who would be responsible for the incorporation of the goals produced in the Delphi into the PPB system, that the "options were being closed" before the full range of goals had been explored. It was true that at each round the number of objectives had swelled considerably, and that the expected drop-off in additions had not occurred. In order to remedy the situation, round 5 was designed specifically to fulfill two functions: first, to continue the weighing scheme begun the previous round, and second, to add more objectives, alter the hierarchy, and comment on the process.

The form used in round 5 contained the statistical feedback from the previous round as feedback.

Step 8: Termination of the Delphi

The distribution of weights on the goals and objectives had been simplified to a three-category scale to make the task easier and more meaningful for the participants. There was a marked increase in consensus on almost all the goals and objectives in this round. There was strong agreement on many issues. In general, the more specific and measurable objectives had less solid consensus than the vaguer ones.

The returns in terms of added objectives and changed goals and hierarchy were, however, exceedingly disappointing. Despite the obvious concern on this issue by a number of the administrative staff, who were also participating members of the Delphi, only three new objectives were added while no changes were made at all at the goal level. Because of this outcome, the researchers felt that the Delphi should terminate and expressed this feeling to the administrative staff, who had asked for the adjustments to be made after the previous round.

Step 9: Feedback on the Process

At a meeting with these administrators, it became clear that at least part of the reason for the poor response had been a gradually increasing feeling of alienation by participants from the beginning of the Delphi. A number of individuals mentioned that they felt that their contributions had been ignored by the Delphi. This was partly due to the "all-inclusive" policy with which this Delphi was run—that is, objectives might be added to the list but not deleted except at the wish of a fair majority. Many of the comments made by the participants on their returns were: "Delete objective number X," and "Objective number Y repeats number Z." Since these offered no constructive alternatives, they had been systematically ignored by the researchers. In general, the researchers did try to incorporate both constructive comments and certainly added objectives; but in all honesty, it must be admitted that some fell by the wayside during the mammoth task of editing.

The feeling of alienation seems very regrettable, since one of the aims of the Delphi is to combat alienation. All communication with the majority of the participants had been by mail, which may have contributed to the effect. A better design would have included more general meetings, as at the beginning of the Delphi.

The administrators in the school district felt that the weighing of objectives had been useful and the information contained therein would be employed in policy-making decisions. It was clear, however, that the list of goals and objectives was not at all complete and would require some major reworking—not just at the lower level (classroom-behavioral objectives), but also at the goal level.

SAMPLE ROUND 1

GOALS DELPHI—SCHOOL DISTRICT 21

Following is a list of objectives that have been compiled as an *initial, tentative* statement of the objectives of the school system.

Some are contradictory, some overlap; this does not matter for the time being.

Some you will agree with, some you won't—this is more important.

Put an X in the margin beside each objective you *disagree* with; that is, mark any objective you think should be deleted from the list.

If you wish to rephrase any objective, there is a space to rewrite the objective at the end of the list. Please put the number of the objective you have rephrased beside the rewritten objective, for our reference.

If you want to add any new objectives, there is a special page to do so.

Objectives for the School District

1. Children learn enough math in K-8 to manage everyday computational tasks such as bank-book balancing and income tax calculations.

2. Children reach their fullest potential at each grade level before progressing.

3. Children are primarily encouraged to find pleasure in learning.

4. Children are taught in such a way that each can progress at his own pace.

5. Children are taught how to learn, not what to learn.

6. Children progress at the standard grade rates in reading.

7. Children progress one-year grade level in reading in nine months.

8. Children read well enough in Grade 8 to master high school texts and newspapers.

9. Children are taught to read in the most efficient available way.

10. Children can communicate effectively in writing.

11. Children have knowledge of local government and community services.

12. Children have understanding of the nature of society in the United States and of their cultural heritage.

I would rephrase the following objectives:

NUMBER	REWRITTEN OBJECTIVE

New objectives I want to add to the list:

REFERENCES

Adelson, M.; Alkin, A.; Carey, C., and Helmer, O. "The Education Innovation Study." *American Behavioral Scientist* (1967), Volume 10, No. 7.

Dalkey, N.C., and Helmer, O. "An Experimental Application of the Delphi Method to the Use of Experts." *Management Science* (1963), Volume 9, pp. 458–467.

Dalkey, N.C., and Rourke, D.L. "Experimental Assessment of Delphi Procedures with Group Value Judgment." Rand Corporation, 1971, R-612-ARPA.

Delbecq, A.; Van de Ven, A.; and Gustafson, D. *Group Techniques for Program Planning.* Coleview, Ill.: Scott, Foresman and Company, 1975.

Eilon, Samuel. "An Editorial." *Omega* (1978), Volume 6, No. 2, p. 103.

Flemming, John E. "A Possible Future of Government-Corporate Relations." *Business Horizons* (1979), December, pp. 43–48.

Fry, Fred L. "The End of Affirmative Action." *Business Horizons* (1980), February, pp. 34–40.

Gordon, T.J., and Helmer, O. "Report on a Long-Range Forecasting Study." Rand Corporation, 1964, p-2982.

Linstone, Harold A. "The Delphi Technique." *Handbook of Futures Research,* J. Fowles, ed. Westport, Conn.: Greenwood Press, 1978.

Pill, J. "The Delphi Method: Substance, Context: A Critique and Annotated Bibliography." Tech. Memo #183, Department of Operations Research, Case Western Reserve University, 1970.

Reisman, A.; Mantel, A.J.; Dean, D.V.; Eisenberg, N.C.; Markus, E.; and Senis, A.L. "Measurement of Output in a System of Social Agencies." Tech. Memo #188, Department of Operations Research, Case Western Reserve University, 1970.

Rutherford, G.S. "Case Study in the Use of the Delphi Technique in Goal Setting: The Morton Arboretum." Mineo Paper, Urban Systems Engineering Center, Northwestern University, 1971.

Turoff, M. "The Design of a Policy Delphi." *Technology Forecasting and Social Change* (1970), Volume 2, No. 2.

Turoff, M. "Delphi Conferencing." Tech Memo TM-125, Washington, D.C., Executive Office of the President, Office of Emergency Preparedness, 1971.

Ulschak, G. "A Delphi Study: Prioritizing Programs for Conference Ministry." Unpublished Doctor of Ministry Thesis, McCormick Theological Seminary, Chicago, Ill., 1981.

7

Critical Incident

INTRODUCTION

Just as the result of training should represent behavioral impact, effective needs assessment should formulate a structure upon which "training programs" may effect a behavioral impact. The critical incident technique has perhaps the most direct behavioral link of any method of needs assessment. As stated by the originators of this method, "the critical incident technique consists of a set of procedures for collecting direct observations of human behavior in such a way as to facilitate their potential usefulness in solving practical problems and developing broad psychological principles. The critical incident technique outlines procedures for collecting observed incidents having special significance and meeting systematically defined criteria" (Flanagan, "The Critical Incident Technique," p. 327).

The critical incident technique was a result of a charge placed to

Steven L. Johnson—B.S. in Psychology from the University of North Dakota, M.S. in industrial/organizational psychology from Georgia Institute of Technology. He has held positions with Northwest Bancorporation, including corporate office human resource and generalist experience in affiliate bank. Northwestern National Bank of Sioux Falls, South Dakota.

John C. Flanagan during World War II to reduce the rate of pilot error. Incidents or stories of behaviors that led to success or failure were collected and categorized into behavioral dimensions. These dimensions were critical to the performance of the job of a pilot. The dimensions that were developed proved to be capable criteria for the construction of selection instruments, as well as the basis for development of training programs to improve pilot success. The term "critical" was very appropriate in this case, because failure frequently meant fatality.

The critical incident technique has been used towards numerous ends: criteria development, measures of proficiency, selection, job design and purification, establishing operating procedures, equipment design, motivation and leadership, as well as training. One of the most important features of this method is its flexibility. The method is a flexible set of principles which allows for modification to adapt to the specific needs of a particular situation. The ultimate outcome is a description of observable behaviors that are "critical" to effective performance in a defined activity.

Specifically, an incident is an observed human activity which is itself a completed action. Essentially, this is necessary so that inferences and predictions can be made about the person performing the act. The incident must occur in a situation where the action and its consequences are determined to be critical to performance, either negatively or positively. Psychologically, extreme incidents can most accurately be remembered or described; hence, these incidents are more valid and reliable.

Two examples of positive critical incidents of behavior follow:

A. Professor X brought in real life examples to illustrate his lectures. When he was discussing harmonic distortion, he brought in his guitar and gave us an example of harmonic distortion. When tested over the material, very few people in our class didn't understand harmonic distortion.

B. About three months ago, Sally came to me and recommended a method of work assignment and job standards for the work unit which I supervise. Sally pointed out that there were basically three levels of difficulty regarding routine jobs assigned to our unit, and people did not seem to assign themselves work in a fair manner. She proposed that we label three "in boxes" and set a standard for all employees that work must be taken from all three boxes before the employee could come back to the original box. We implemented Sally's recommendation, and both quantity and quality of work for our unit has improved. I also feel morale has improved because of Sally's recommendation.

Two examples of negative critical incidents of behavior are

C. Last week, Professor Y presented a rather complex topic in a manner that left most students rather confused. When a student asked Professor Y to summarize the procedure for the class, he responded angrily, "You should stay awake and not ask stupid questions which slow down the rest of the class." The student who asked the question is nearly a straight "A" student. We need the class to graduate in our major and cannot drop the class. We are considering going to the Dean about this guy.

D. Tom can be counted on to take my directions and screw them around to suit him. Last week the section head called me to his office with the directions that we had a problem that would create overtime for my unit. I supervise four people. Two were out of the work area, leaving only Tom and my lead operator. Being fairly new to the job, I asked the lead operator to come with me and told Tom that I would need the rest of the unit for a project. When we got back, the rest of the unit was gone. It took the lead operator and me four hours of overtime apiece to complete a project the entire unit could have done in about an hour. Tom had told the unit we had a big project "tomorrow" and pleaded ignorance about the actual request. I later found out that the project came up on Tom's bowling night.

These are actual examples taken from critical incident studies ("An Attempt to Predict Critical Incident Categories from Three Personality Variables," Carroll, and "Exploratory Study of Bias in Job Performance Evaluation," Johnson and Ronan). These examples will be used throughout this section to emphasize elements of a critical incident.

Throughout this section on the critical incident technique, we will discuss the principles of the technique, required conditions, methods of collection, advantages versus disadvantages, and also the procedure of conducting this form of needs analysis. We will discuss general philosophical issues behind the critical incident technique. Further, the translation of behavioral incidents and dimensions into behaviorally anchored rating scales will be presented.

PRINCIPLES OF THE TECHNIQUE

Several principles are vital for a critical incident approach to be successful. The four principles are

A. Only simple judgments (success or failure) are required of the observers. In example "A," the professor's demonstration created success—the understanding of harmonic distortion by the students.

B. Only qualified observers—supervisors, peers, or incumbents of the job—should be used. Notice that all the examples used individuals who had the opportunity to observe actual behavior.

C. Incidents must represent behaviors that have consequences directly attributable to them. The behavior can be identified as causal to the outcome. In example "B," the employee's recommendation led to increased quantity and quality of the unit's output.

D. Specified requirements or standards for the incidents are established. These standards will vary depending upon the use of the material. Typical standards will include requirements such as: The incident *must* be observed firsthand; the incident reflects attributes of the behavior, not the individual or his or her personality; and the incident has occurred within a specified recency, such as the last six months.

This technique's basis in observable behaviors is believed to maximize objectivity while minimizing subjective components of inference and interpretation. Deficiencies in objectivity evolve from the use of the basic incidents, not from the actual incidents of behavior.

Subjective judgments are introduced primarily in the development of a classification system to dimensionalize the information. This step is the category formation stage where the individual incidents are grouped into similar categories. Due to the subjective nature of this task, the need for multiple independent raters and a preliminary strategy is emphasized.

The critical incident process involves a number of decisions and steps. The following flow chart represents those to be discussed in this section:

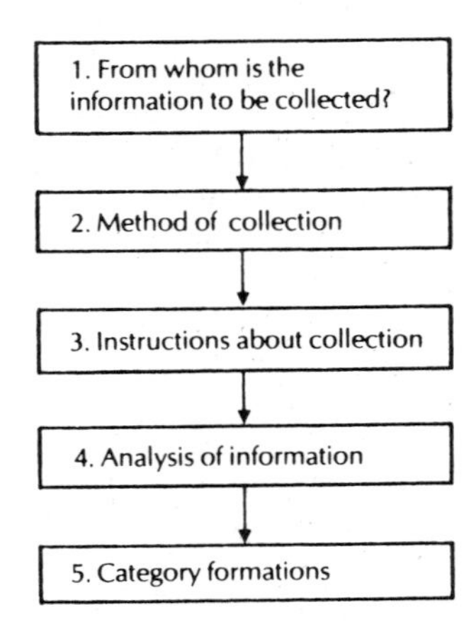

THE CRITICAL INCIDENT PROCESS

From *whom do we collect initial incidents?* Incidents are actual behaviors that have been observed. Any group having the opportunity to directly observe the incumbent's performance may be used, i.e., supervisors, incumbents, peers. The specific function and parameters of the situation will dictate who should be used.

Methods of collection is a decision that is based upon the group selected and the parameters involved. Are the observers immediately accessible or are they spread throughout the country? Care should be exercised to insure cooperation of this group. Cooperation can best be gained by three steps: involvement, facilitating, and expediting the process. Involvement of the group cannot be stressed enough. Ask the observers what method would be easiest for them. Involvement also denotes a sense of ownership. Facilitating the observer's job of recording incidents will also increase their cooperation. Even dedicated observers can become uncooperative or bored when a project is unduly delayed or plodding. This point argues against the use of the diary method of incident collection. Regardless of the method selected, some means of clarifying the incidents must exist. Manageable numbers with the group technique would allow the opportunity to question observers about the incidents (Johnson and Ronan).

There are various forms of collecting critical incidents. A primary distinction is generally made between the reports that are recalled and those that are made at the time of the observation. Campion et al. ("Work Observation Versus Recall in Developing Behavioral Examples for Rating Scale") found that both methods were equally effective in providing reliable behavioral incidents. Recall methods are more immediate involving less time delay. Should one decide to record behavioral incidents at the time of observation, concern for facilitating the observers becomes paramount, i.e., simplified recordkeeping, reminders, checklist, etc.

Interviews. Trained personnel explain to observers the procedure and probe for behavioral incidents. Following completion of the interview, some form of follow-up is required to ensure accuracy of interpretation of the incidents. This method is extremely time-consuming, and for most purposes, limited interviews can accompany another method to increase efficiency of collection and still provide some firsthand incidents that increase participant involvement and help the trainer to form a sense of direction and job framework. Figure 7-1 is an example of an interview format.

Figure 7-1
Sample Interview Format

Think of the best worker you supervise. Tell me about something this person did that made you think of this person as your best worker. We are looking for a specific behavior, something that was actually done, including the result of that behavior.

What was the specific behavior? ____________________

____

____

____

When did this occur? ____________________

____

____

Why was this an example of effective performance? ____________________

____

____

What was the outcome of the behavior? ____________________

____

____

What is the job title of this person? ____________________

____

Did you observe this behavior? ____________________

____

Did you see the outcome of the behavior? ____________________

Group Interviews. Incidents are recorded by the observers on forms submitted to them. This method seems to maximize efficiency with no noticeable reduction in the reliability or accuracy of the incidents (Ronan, "Training for Emergency Procedures in Multiengine Aircraft"). Keeping groups to a manageable number of people will allow questions and clarifications of the incidents as the observer finishes the questionnaire. One would be advised to build this post-report review process into the procedural design. Example C of the critical incidents is an example where the initial response of the supervisor was virtually unusable until it was clarified by probing the topic. The initial response was something to the effect, "Tom would rather bowl than work." Interesting, but not behaviorally specific. A sample sheet for a group interview is shown in Figure 7-2.

Figure 7-2

Think of the best worker you supervise. Will you please write an incident describing something done in the job that makes you think this. Remember, this is a story describing something that was done.

Questionnaires. This procedure has a wide number of derivations, including the mailed questionnaire. It has been used in situations where the group is particularly large. Where the observer is motivated to read the instructions carefully and answer conscientiously, the results seem not to differ essentially from results using the interview method. Figure 7-3 is an example of a critical incident questionnaire.

Figure 7-3
Sample Critical Incident Questionnaire

The veterinary profession requires that appropriate standards be maintained in the profession, both from training in veterinary school and through examination board standards. Please take the time to fill out this questionnaire and give us your input for this important issue. We would like the results returned by _________, 1978 to:

D. B. Smith, D.V.M.
Horse Hill
Trotsville, Kentucky

A. Think of the most difficult situation that you have handled successfully because of your training as a veterinarian.

Briefly describe the situation.

What training (specific class or seminar) helped you to appropriately respond?

How recent to the incident did the training occur?

What was the outcome of your action?

Why do you feel this was the most difficult situation you have faced?

B. Think of the most difficult situation you have handled which was unsuccessful because of a lack of (or poor) training.

Briefly describe the situation.

Have you faced the situation since?

Do you now know the appropriate way of handling the situation?

How did you learn the appropriate treatment?

What was the specific outcome of the unsuccessful handling of the situation?

How would you recommend training other veterinarians to handle the situation?

Record Forms. The observer is given introductory statements and may ask questions. Incidents are then reported as they occur. The recording form may use a tally type of recording, so as the incident occurs, it is checked with the date, and situation information is appended. This method seems most appropriate when there is a relatively limited pool of behaviors involved in the performance of the position. This method generally uses a diary format for collection of incidents. Care should be exercised to remind and prompt observers to continue recording incidents.

Instructions given to the observer will vary depending upon the method of collection. The standards or rules are described in the instructions and are a very important element of the critical incident technique. These precise instructions focus observers' attention on behaviors crucial to the definition of the position. The instructions should include seven specific items:

1. Explain the general purpose for which you are collecting incidents. Specific information is unnecessary, but a general orientation is helpful.

2. Assure anonymity of the observers, as well as those reported in the incidents.

3. Explain that an incident is an observed specific behavior which led to a specific outcome which was either a success or a failure.

4. An effective optional step is to give the observers an example of a critical incident. *Caution:* Should you use this step, the example should be obviously positive or negative. Further, if the critical incident is close to something the observers have seen, there may be a "parrot" phenomenon.

5. Define precisely what you want the observers to report, e.g., think of the situation that an employee you supervised handled ineffectively because of a lack of training. Describe the incident, as well as the type of training required for the employee to be successful.

6. Specify rules of the technique.

A. Time limits.

B. Specify job or situation observed.

C. Necessity of actual observations of behavior.

D. Completed action with a result.

7. Lay out the mechanics of the collection phase, i.e., when, where, and how incidents will be collected.

A sample set of instructions are found in Figure 7-4.

Figure 7-4
Instructions Given Supervisors

I would like to thank all of you for being here and say that we really appreciate your cooperation. If you have any questions while filling out these forms, please feel free to bring them to me. When you are finished, I would like to briefly check them before you leave.

We are asking you to give us "incidents" concerning the work behavior of your subordinates. Incidents are "stories" concerning your better and poorer workers. For example, in a recent study, college students were asked to think of the "best professor" they had during the present school year. Many of them indicated that the professor was "interesting." People can be interesting in many ways, so the students were directed to describe what the professor *did* that made him interesting. An example of one of these incidents is: "Professor X brought in real life examples to illustrate his lectures, like when he was discussing harmonic distortion, he brought in his guitar and gave us an example of harmonic distortion."

This is what we are asking you for, a specific behavioral incident, something that was actually done. So think of the best employee that you supervise and write an incident describing something done by this employee that made you think of this subordinate as your best.

I will give you two sheets. At the top of the first, it says "Think of the best worker you supervise." Write an incident about your best employee. The next sheet says "Think of the worst worker you supervise." Write an incident about your worst employee. Remember, what we need is a story about something that was done.

All parties involved in this research shall remain anonymous. For clarity of incident, please try to think of a recent incident, something that has occurred in the last six months.

The *analysis of the data* is primarily intended to increase the usefulness of the data while sacrificing as little comprehensiveness, specificity, and validity as possible. The main considerations involving this step are the frame of reference, category formulation and generality versus specificity of the behavioral headings or dimensions.

The frame of reference delineates the ways in which a given set of incidents can be classified. The principle consideration is how the data is to be used. For training and development purposes, broad training goals or courses would be the most relevant system.

Behavioral incidents would then be grouped together in such a way as to isolate an area that could be affected by a specific type of training. Particular proficiency or skill incidents could be one grouping or a general lack of mathematical knowledge may be another.

Category formulation is the process of developing critical behavior dimensions. Similar behaviors are grouped together, and descriptive statements in terms of behaviors are formulated to represent the group. This is a task that requires experience, insight, and judgment. Unfortunately, this stage is primarily subjective, rather than objective. The process is divided into five stages.

Stage One: The evaluation of incidents to determine whether they meet previously established standards. Generally, a separation of behavioral incidents from vague, general descriptors.

Stage Two: The development of a classification system. This step may be accomplished by an initial general sorting of incidents into categories or by other "consensus" methods. The system must yield orthogonal (non-overlapping) categories.

Stage Three: The incidents are studied and classified into one of the previously developed categories. A measure of validity of the dimensions and sorting can be determined in this stage by independent intra-rater agreement.

Stage Four: The behaviors in each group are studied and classified into subgroups. These subgroups are so closely related that the behaviors are virtually identical. Statements describing the behavior of the groups are written, which sufficiently describe the behavior involved.

Stage Five: The objective of this step is to reduce the number of descriptive statements that represent the incidents. Incidents of similar behaviors are grouped together, and new statements describing them are written. This process may be repeated until the results are appropriate in nature for the purpose of the study.

It is necessary that following the derivation of the classification system the system is tested by trial classification. This trial assesses the functionality of the system and can provide a substantial number of recommendations to improve the system.

Another set of independent analysts are used in this trial classification. The purpose of these analysts is to classify the incidents into the categories provided by the initial analysis. The result of this trial can indicate categories where the group behavior may be inconsistent or the category may be inappropriately defined. You are looking for the percentage of agreement between the analysts to insure validity.

ADVANTAGES/DISADVANTAGES

As with any needs assessment methodology, there are advantages and disadvantages to be weighed. Some of the advantages of the critical incident method are

1. Develops behaviorally-based criteria. Each incident provides objective evidence of job behaviors. This evidence can be used for criterion development, development of training dimensions, and as raw material to develop training instruments.

2. A more objective procedure than other methods. Observers are asked to report objective incidents that define the behavior and the result of that behavior (see the critical incident examples).

3. Takes into account the multi-dimensionality of performance. Incidents are categorized into a structure that should represent the natural job dimensions. The dimensions of the job are not established artificially, but are based on reports from those working close to the position.

4. Provides reliable, relevant, and valid criteria. Studies using the technique have substantiated these claims, as well as shown content validity (Anderson and Nilsson, "Studies in the Reliability

and Validity of the Critical Incident Techniques"). These results have been corroborated, and criteria developed from this technique exhibited concurrent validity as reported by Ronan and Lathan ("The Reliability and Validity of the Critical Incident Technique: A Closer Look").

5. Provides comprehensive information. Observers report these behaviors in their own language, generally expanding the amount and nature of reported incidents commensurately to the complexity of the position. This factor leads to the conclusion that the observations are representative and fairly comprehensive.

6. Incidents are naturally translated into behaviorally based performance appraisal instruments. The development of Behaviorally Anchored Rating Scales (BARS) requires the use of behaviorally based information about the position. This information is naturally developed from a critical incident study.

Some of the disadvantages of the method that need to be weighed against the advantages are

1. Reliance on observers. One of the required conditions is the opportunity to observe performance of the positions. Should you include inappropriate observers, you will distort or dilute the impact of appropriate observers. Unmotivated observers can present validity and credibility problems.

2. Impact on reported incidents of slight changes in the question asked observers. The directions and instructions given observers have considerable impact on quantity, quality, and content of incidents. Hints regarding type of incidents suspected may lead to a "parroting" response.

3. The subjectivity of category formulation. As Flanagan ("Measuring Human Performance") notes, the largest psychological deficit of the technique lies in the structuring of incidents into a dimensional framework representing the dimensions of the job.

4. Cost and time. The critical incident technique requires considerable time to be used effectively. The project will require substantial planning and implementation time.

5. Does not cover routine job aspects. The technique defines critical elements of the job. Frequently, with this technique, supplemental analysis is needed to gather behavioral information about average and routine job dimensions for appraisal or job analysis purposes.

The result of the critical incident study is a structural system of behavioral statements (see example). This is a framework for the development of training programs which should have a significant impact on job behaviors and performance. A critical incident technique approach to assessing training needs begins with behavior and should conclude with behavioral impact.

EVOLUTION OF BEHAVIORALLY ANCHORED RATING SCALE

One spinoff of the discussion of critical incidents is the topic of Behaviorally Anchored Rating Scales (BARS). While BARS discussions are generally performance appraisal instruments, a frequently overlooked prospect is the use of BARS in specifying behavioral training objectives. BARS were a direct offspring of Flanagan's work with the critical incident technique. Performance appraisal instruments developed by Flanagan were largely behavioral checklists (see Figure 7-5) or performance record forms which "captured" behavioral incidents (Flanagan, 1949, 1954, 1974; Flanagan and Burns, 1955).

Figure 7-5

Categories of Positive Critical Incidents of Job Performance

I. Unit-oriented behavior.

A. Will do other work not specifically assigned to them.
Frequency = 11.

B. Willing to do any type of job (not picky about assignment).
Frequency = 7

C. Accepted or selected for special assignment (completed accurately and efficiently).
Frequency = 12

II. Work-oriented behavior.

A. Willing to work overtime (or simply works overtime).
Frequency = 5

B. Schedules leave in advance and around work schedule.
Frequency = 6

C. Never tardy.
Frequency = 4

D. Never absent.
Frequency = 2

E. Makes personal sacrifices for work.
Frequency = 7

F. Volunteers for special assignments (or does).
Frequency = 15.

III. Has learned, or attempted to learn, all job skills.

A. Studies or does extra work to improve oneself (own training).
Frequency = 11

B. Competence—exhibits greater ability to do job than most.
Frequency = 11

IV. Production (quantity and quality).

A. Quantity of work produced.
Frequency = 19

B. Quality of work produced.
Frequency = 20

V. Interpersonal relationships (with peers and superior).

A. Helps other employees.
Frequency = 21

B. Always keeps composure and retains authority.
Frequency = 2

C. Accepted or took upon themselves a leadership role or extra responsibilities, effectively accomplished task.
Frequency = 4

D. Acts as a communication link for the supervisor; acts as a confidant or to give feedback on work performance.
Frequency = 4

E. Diplomatic and tactful in relations with other people.
Frequency = 1

VI. Concern for job improvements and work flow.

A. Improves upon assignment—does more than required; tries to do things in a "better" way.
Frequency = 11

B. Does things to keep work unit producing and timely.
Frequency = 3

C. Willingness to try new methods and to expend the effort to make them work.
Frequency = 2

The general movement toward BARS began with the behavioral retranslation method developed by Smith and Kendall ("Retranslation of Expectations"). Research had shown (Barrett, Taylor, Parker, and Martens ("Rating Scale Content: Scale Information and Supervisory Ratings") that the use of a "behavioral anchor" method rating scale resulted in greater reliability than did strictly numerical rating scales. Smith and Kendall felt that raters should be asked to relate behaviors the rater could actually observe. Furthermore, an objective performance measure would occur "only if the persons who will be rating indicate, in their own terms, what kind of behavior represents each level of each discriminately different characteristic, and which trait is illustrated by each kind of behavior" (Smith and Kendall, "Retranslation of Expectations," p. 149). The initial step was to collect critical incidents of behavior from qualified observers, and then following methods listed in the critical incident section, behavioral dimensions were developed. Within each behavioral dimension would be logically sorted incidents representing varying degrees of the behavioral trait. These behavioral statements were ordered into a five- or seven-point scale with the behavioral statements arrayed from extremely ineffective behavior to extremely effective behavior. The use of the behavioral statements then described to the raters what behavior they were to observe in order for the individuals to deserve a specific rating.

A classic example of the development of BARS is a study by Dunnette ("Personal Selection and Placement") to develop BARS for nurses. A summary of the steps follows:

A. General nursing groups were solicited for critical incidents of behavior that led to either successful nursing or to an unsuccessful situation. The major qualities were listed by the nurses with supporting critical incidents of behavior. The nursing terminology and the nurses' own language was retained throughout the study.

B. The groups formulated general behavioral statements defining high, low, and acceptable performance for each of the general qualities listed originally. Additional behavioral incidents were also solicited to "fill in" these gaps.

C. Nurses then indicated independently what quality was being exhibited in each incident. Those incidents where clear agreeement was not found were eliminated. Qualities or dimensions were also eliminated when the incidents could not reliably be reassigned to the qualities in which they were originally attributed.

D. The incidents were then judged by another group of nurses who rated the behaviors as to their appropriateness as illustrations of nursing behavior. Incidents were eliminated if the judgments of appropriateness showed a significant dispersement. This procedure provided another safeguard assuring absolute agreement and lack of ambiguity.

Dunnette points out that Step C was a "crucial innovation" in the Smith and Kendall approach. This step basically translates the retranslation into its original form. An example of a BARS developed by Dunnette is shown in Figure 7-6.

The utility of BARS as an evaluation of the behavioral impact of training carries an interesting concept. From the use of the critical incident technique for needs analysis evolves critical behavioral dimensions for the development of training programs. These dimensions and, in fact, the raw data developed can be utilized to assess the behavioral consequence of the training.

Figure 7-6

Skill in Human Relations (with patients, families, and co-workers) behaves in a manner appropriate to the situation and individuals involved. (NY: National League of Nursing, 1964, p. 19; by permission.)

Scale	Description
2.00	Even when there is considerable emotional self-involvement, behavior with others is so skillful and insightful that it not only smoothes but often prevents difficult emotional and social situations; this implies the ability to recognize the subtle as well as the more obvious components of basic emotional reactions in self and others (e.g., anxiety, fear, frustration, anger, etc.).
1.75	This nurse could be expected, whenever possible, to sit down and talk with a terminal-cancer patient who is considered to be "demanding."
1.50	If two aides asked this nurse, acting as team leader, if they could exchange assignments because of rapport problems with the patients assigned, would expect this nurse to discuss the problem with the aides and make certain changes which would be satisfying to them.
	If this nurse were admitting a patient who talks rapidly and continuously of her symptoms and past medical history, could be expected to look interested and listen.
1.25	If this nurse were assigned for the first time to a patient who insists upon having her treatment done in a certain order, could be expected to do as the patient wishes without making an issue about it.

Anchor description	Scale	Critical incident
If emotional self-involvement is minimal, behavior with others is such that it does not complicate difficult emotional and social situations; this implies the ability to recognize the more obvious components of basic emotional reactions in self and others.	→1.00	If the husband of a woman, who is post-operative and in good condition, asks about his wife, this nurse could be expected to reply as follows: "Her condition is good."
	0.75	If a convalescent patient complained about the service in the hospital, this nurse would be likely to tell the patient that the hospital is short of nurses and the needs of the sickest patients have to be met first.
	0.50	If this nurse were assigned to care for a terminal-cancer patient, in a 2-bed room, who is depressed and uncommunicative, could be expected to carry on a conversation with the other patient while giving care to the terminal-cancer patient.
		In the presence of a woman who is crying because her husband is dangerously ill, this nurse would be expected to tell the woman not to cry.
	0.25	If this nurse were told by an ambulatory patient that a patient in the ward was having difficulty in breathing, could be expected to tell the ambulatory patient that his help in caring for the patients was not needed.
Behavior with others is such that it tends to complicate or create difficult emotional or social situations; this implies an inability to recognize even the obvious basic emotional reactions of self and others.	→0.00	

SUMMARY

The critical incident technique is a flexible set of principles with multiple-purpose capabilities. Each incident is a behavioral outcome or story. The technique has four principles:

A. Only simple judgments are required of observers.

B. Only qualified observers are used.

C. Incidents must represent behaviors that have consequences directly attributable to them.

D. Specific requirements or standards for the incidents are established.

Various methods of data collection exist for this flexible technique. Methods that are described are interviews, group interviews, questionnaires, and record forms (diary).

Once gathered, the incidents are categorized into a functional system of behavioral dimensions. The steps of category formation are

1. Determine if the incidents meet the rules and are actually incidents of behavior.

2. Develop a basic structure or classification system; entails sorting of incidents into like categories.

3. Study incidents and reclassify into the previously established categories as a test of those categories.

4. Study behavioral incidents in each category and condense so that behavioral statements can be developed to describe each subgrouping.

5. Purify the incidents to focus the content towards the purpose of the study, i.e., training, performance appraisal, or criterion development.

This category formation task is the most subjective element of the technique. For this reason, care must be exercised to ensure that independent raters and category formulators are used; measures of inter-rater agreement should be taken to establish a level of validity of the categories.

Not only is the critical incident technique useful for identifying training needs, but it also produces raw data that can be used for development of training vehicles. The incidents are readily translated into behaviorally based evaluation instruments as well.

REFERENCES

Barrett, R., Taylor, E., Parker, J., Martens, L. "Rating Scale Content: Scale Information and Supervisory Ratings." *Personnel Psychology*, 1958, *11*, pp. 333–346.

Campion, J., Greenor, J., Wernli, S. "Work Observation Versus Recall in Developing Behavioral Examples for Rating Scales." *Journal of Applied Psychology*, 1973, 58, pp. 286–288.

Carroll, K. *An Attempt to Predict Critical Incident Categories From Three Personality Variables.* Unpublished thesis manuscript, Georgia Institute of Technology, 1974.

Dunnette, M. *Personnel Selection and Placement.* Belmont, CA: Brooks/Cole, 1966.

Flanagan, J. "Critical Requirements: A New Approach to Employee Evaluation." *Personnel Psychology*, 1949, 2, pp. 419–425.

Flanagan, J. *Measuring Human Performance*. Pittsburgh, Pennsylvania: American Institute of Research, 1974.

Flanagan, J. "The Critical Incident Technique." *Psychological Bulletin*, 1954, 51, pp. 327–358.

Flanagan, J., and Burns, R. "The Employee Performance Record: A New Appraisal and Development Tool." *Harvard Business Review*, 1955, *5*, pp. 95–102.

Johnson, S. and Ronan, W. "Exploratory Study of Bias in Job Performance Evaluation." *Public Personnel Management*, Sept–Oct, 1979, Vol. 8, No. 5, pp. 315–323.

Smith, P., and Kendall, L. "Retranslation of Expectations: An Approach to the Construction of Unambiguous Anchors for Rating Scales." *Journal of Applied Psychology*, 1963, *47*, pp. 149–155.

Andersson, B.E. and Nilsson, S.G. "Studies in the Reliability and Validity of the Critical Incident Technique." *Journal of Applied Psychology*, 1964, Vol. 48, pp. 398–403.

Ronan, W. W. "Training for Emergency Procedures in Multiengine Aircraft" Pittsburgh, Penn.: American Institute for Research, 1953.

Ronan, W. W. and Lotharn, G.P. "The Reliability and Validity of the Critical Incident Technique: A Closer Look," *Studies in Personnel Psychology*, 1974, Vol. 6, pp. 53–64.

8

Competency-Based Management

INTRODUCTION

To develop effective human resource management systems, organizations need to develop models of managerial effectiveness for use in recruitment and assessment, training and development, and performance appraisal. The development of these models requires both an assessment of the status quo as well as a look at problems to be faced by managers of the 80's and 90's, so competency models can be built that reflect both present and future needs. Reward systems in organizations then need to be brought in line to support these models.

Business and the nation face vast problems in the 80's. These include the transition from an industrial age to an age of communication, the transition from hierarchical organizations to more horizontal models. The transition in values also includes, according to Daniel Yankelovich (professor of psychology at New York University and

---

Alice Sargent, Ed.D., is the author of this chapter. Dr. Sargent is a consultant, professor, trainer, and author. She has worked with business, government, and educational institutions with a variety of training programs. She is currently based in Washington, D.C.

head of a research firm bearing his name) moving from an ethic of self-centeredness to one of commitment. Those of us who grew up in the 50's were taught guilt and responsibility. The next generation became the "me generation." Now, the 80's call for commitment that is a blend of concern for ourselves, our community and others.

Surprisingly few organizations attempt to develop managers systematically for entry, mid-level, and executive management positions. Many rely on an apprenticeship model or a random learn-as-you-go process, neither of which are systematic or cost-effective. Among the better-known firms that do have programs are IBM at Armonk, General Electric at Croton, Xerox at Leesburg, INA in Philadelphia, the Federal Executive Institute (FET) in Charlottesville, and Texas Instruments in Houston. There are not many executive development programs except for FET, and now several major oil companies are looking at the problems of how to develop their managers to manage the companies' vast resources. The major training firms in the management education field are the American Management Association, particularly their new competency-based Masters in Management Program; the National Training Laboratories; and some of the major universities who operate education centers and certificate programs. These include Harvard Business School, Sloan School at MIT, University of Michigan, Wharton, University of Southern California, and UCLA.

The education of managers is a critical issue. In an article in *The Washington Post,* Walter Mondale was quoted as saying that managers don't know how to manage because business schools have not figured out what skills managers need. The American Association of Collegiate Schools of Business arrived at the same conclusion—MBA programs lack an effective model for developing practitioner managers, partly because they have relied too heavily on the case study method. A number of firms are seeking to grant degrees—major businesses such as Arthur D. Little, Wang, and Massachusetts General Hospital have moved or are moving toward degree granting. While business currently spends $30 billion a year for training, it would seem that business believes schools and colleges have not done, nor are ready to do, the job of "growing" managers effectively.

William Ouchi, in *Theory Z,* concludes that the key issues facing American business today are not technology, investment, regulation or inflation, but that the Japanese know how to manage better than we do. The Japanese emphasis on intimacy, trust, subtlety in the workplace is more effective and enlightened than our own heavy focus on task and technology. Whether or not we put it as boldly as Ouchi, the task confronting us is to define a curriculum for practitioners in management.

This chapter focuses on competency-based management training as an assessment tool. Competency-based programs identify the key training and development targets for present and future managers.

THE NEED FOR A COMPETENCY MODEL

We have grown up without much education in psychology. What we learned in that area, we tended to learn at home or from our peer group, without the opportunity to select from options. Hence, our society is basically emotionally illiterate. Many people do not express feelings easily, are uncomfortable with conflict, and/or don't work effectively in teams. Instead they try to "problem-solve" feelings rather than be empathetic. Many of these same people become managers without a lot of training in people management skills. They have been promoted on the basis of technical competence. Yet, we know that other competencies—interpersonal, entrepreneurial, self-awareness, analytical—are critical to effective management. What we need are competency models which encompass all those elements which make for effective management.

Engineers, particularly those who have moved into project manager positions, have understood the need for management education. Now politicians and doctors recognize that they never have had applied behavioral science courses, either. In fact, lawyers have been taught exactly the opposite of interpersonal competence; they have learned adversarial skills and mistrust. As lawyers and accountants are being organized in teams of organizations, they are found to lack the skills to work effectively in that mode.

The prevailing theory of management today is situational management or contingency management, which means selecting the appropriate behavior to get the desired results in any given situation. Therefore, the critical skills managers need are to be effective participant observers to diagnose the impact of their behavior.

Buried inside managers is a management curriculum which enables them to be valuable resources in building a model for managerial effectiveness and in developing a common language for organizational management. In developing the new competency-based model of management, it is critical to capture the language of each organizational culture, rather than impose language from outside.

DEVELOPING A COMPETENCY-BASED MODEL

There are a number of approaches to competency-based management. One approach is the "generic" approach. In this approach, general management competencies are overlaid on an organization. It is assumed that the general competencies will be applicable.

A second approach is based on a research model. Using a

research approach, external or internal consultants identify the management competencies within the organization and then present them to the organization.

A third approach is based on organizational development. This chapter is built on this approach. The starting point with the organizational development approach is using the language of the organization.

If the language of the particular organizational culture is not used to build the competency model, there may not be validation and ownership. The model may be treated as another instance of social science jargon. It is essential to develop different competency models for executives, for middle managers and for supervisors, and to involve those managers in the development of the model.

Many line managers feel apprehensive about embarking upon the task of building competencies. They may not recognize that they are capable of defining the needs of managers, particularly if they come from a technical specialty such as engineering or law. A half-day to a day should be set aside to work in small groups to build the first iteration of the model. It may be necessary to invite the response to the question, "What words would you use to describe effectiveness?" The intent of this discussion is to begin the process of defining what effectiveness means in the organization.

Subsequently, a refinement of terms can be attempted. The goal is to generate behavioral descriptors that are objectively verifiable but not necessarily quantifiable. Neither are we trying to return to the old-style traits, nor are we trying to come up with only characteristics that can be counted. We are trying to capture the language people use to describe effectiveness.

It is necessary to identify competencies for at least three levels of management: the first-line supervisors, mid-level managers, and executives. Robert Katz (in "Skills of an Effective Administrator") described the degree of competence required at each of these three levels for three competencies he labeled conceptual, human and technical. As we can see from the chart, technical competence diminishes in importance as one moves up the corporate ladder. The executive has really left behind his/her technical specialty, utilizing at best technical judgment, whereas the human or interpersonal competencies remain stable at each level of management.

	Executive	Mid-level	First-line supervisor
Conceptual	47%	31%	18%
Human	35%	42%	35%
Technical	18%	27%	47%

The Department of the Army has conducted one of the only studies available that differentiates competencies at different levels: those between the colonel (middle manager) and the brigadier general (executive) (see Figure 8-1). The colonel influences others with a personal style that is charismatic and highly visible. The brigadier general influences others with an interpersonal style that is confidently assertive, but not so dramatic and spectacular. With that much power at the top, one need only say, "I want it this way."

For the colonel as middle manager, however, the concern with subordinates focuses on their supervision and performance evaluations. The executive is more concerned with support and development of employees. The mid-level manager looks after short-term issues, while the view from the top is longer range.

Richard Boyatzis, author of *The Competent Manager* and president of McBer & Company, has compiled an excellent competency list through research on critical incidents involving high performing managers (see Figure 8-2). The McBer model is useful to hold up to other models compiled in the language of the organization to see what might have been omitted.

The high-performing manager's number one characteristic is holding high standards for self and others. This manager produces compliance by being a role model, not via threats or punishment. Coaches often are held up as models of effective managers. People say, "He/she wouldn't ask the team to do anything that he/she wouldn't do." In the same way, the high performer gets compliance by doing a good job, which others imitate. Old-style management used to be, "Don't do as I do, do as I say." Now we demand congruence in our role models, so they need to know that we will "do as they do, not as they say." Without alliances, cohesiveness and a focus on morale, employees are likely to burn out, to lose motivation.

The major part of the process of developing a competency-based model, then, is spending time building the competencies in the language of the organization. This happens in sessions where various levels of managers talk about what effective management means and what it may mean in the future.

THE ADROGYNOUS MANAGER

From the beginning, management has been concerned with people and tasks, productivity and morale. The link between the two is becoming obvious. Morale and people are no longer simply frosting for task and productivity. We almost encourage alienation and isolation at work by thinking that business and personal lives should be kept separate. Yet, the critical interface at work is the manager/subordinate relationship and then the work team. These relationships

Figure 8-1 U.S. Department of the Army Leadership Profiles*

Profile Of The Successful Military Leader (COL) At Senior Management Levels		Profile Of The Successful Military Leader (GO) At Senior Executive Levels
Strong self-image		Strong self-image
Self-starter		Self-starter
Strong success orientation		Strong success orientation
Deals with complex problems by conceptualizing in terms of problem elements, functions, and tasks	→	Deals with complex problems by conceptualizing in terms of total systems, subsystems, and processes
Aggressive with peers and subordinates	→	Aggressive in dealings outside the organization
Takes initiative in determining strategies for accomplishing goals and implementing policy	→	Takes initiative in determining strategies for formulating goals and articulating policy
Influences others with an interpersonal style that is charismatic and highly visible	→	Influences others with an interpersonal style that is confidently assertive but less dramatic and spectacular
Highly active and directive with subordinates; delegates hesitantly	→	Highly situational and less coercive with subordinates, delegates real responsibility and accountability
Tends to focus activity in areas of proven expertise and high confidence	→	Activity not limited to areas of proven expertise and high confidence
Concern with subordinates is concentrated primarily on their supervision and performance evaluation	→	Concern with subordinates is concentrated primarily on their support and development
Sees own self-development as a product of past experiences and opportunities provided by the institution	→	Sees own self-development as an on-going process of self-assessment and self-management; seeks developmental opportunities outside as well as within the institution.

TRANSITION INVOLVES CHANGES IN (1) interpersonal relationships, (2) group and organizational dynamics, (3) information processing and decision making, and (4) self-management

*From Bradford F. Spencer and Jerald R. Gregg, "Successful Behaviors Which Breed Failure," *University of Michigan Business Review* (1979). Developed by John Hallen, consultant, Washington, D.C., and Lt. Col. Frank L. Burns, U.S. Army.

COMPETENCY: Some characteristic of a person which underlies or results in effective performance.

I. Knowledge competencies
specific knowledge base

II. Emotional maturity
self control
spontaneity
perceptual objectivity
accurate self-perception
stamina and physical energy
adaptability

III. Entrepreneurial abilities
efficiency orientation
productivity—goal setting and planning
proactivity—problem-solving and information-seeking skills
concern for unique achievement
task efficiency

IV. Intellectual abilities
logical thought—perceive cause/effect relationships—inductive thinking
diagnostic use of concepts—deductive thinking
memory
conceptual ability
political judgment

V. Interpersonal abilities
social sensitivity
self-presentation
counseling skills
expressed concern with impact
compliance producing skills
alliance building skills
language skills
non-verbal sensitivity
respect for others
effective as team member

VI. Leadership skills
presence
persuasive speaking
positive bias
negotiating skills
takes initiative
management of groups—team building skills

Figure 8-2 Managerial competencies

Source: Richard Boyatzis, President, McBer & Co., Boston.

must be characterized by trust if effective performance management, career development, team effectiveness, even strategic planning—which requires risk and creativity—are to result.

Amid rapid technological changes, people almost have been overlooked as the critical resource. We cannot be effective unless we pay attention to the management of people. If we rely on our current management model, we will end up with the status quo. What is wrong with that model? It does not respond to people's affiliation needs nor does it build the necessary teamwork to get the job done, particularly in a communication society. It may have worked at times to support a hierarchical, competitive model, but with shifts in forms of management, it is insufficient. We need to focus on self-awareness, competence, interpersonal competence, effectiveness as a team leader and member, and ability as a participant observer.

One model that offers some possibilities in the 80's is the androgynous manager, a blend of masculine and feminine skills and behaviors, of toughness and tenderness, of instrumental and expressive behaviors, of concern for both people and task, of caring for both productivity and morale, of analytical and intuitive thinking (see Figure 8–3).

Figure 8-3 Androgynous management competencies

Masculine	Neutral	Feminine
Instrumental behavior	Command of basic facts	Expressive behavior
Direct achievement style	Balanced learning habits	Vicarious achievement style
Compliance producing skills	Continuing sensitivity to political events	Alliance-producing skills
Negotiating/competing	Quick thinking	Accommodating/ mediating
Proactive style	Creativity	Reactive style
Analytical/problem-solving, and decision-making skills	Social skills	Self knowledge
Visible impact on others		Non-verbal sensitivity

The Androgynous Manager, A. Sargent, AMACOM © 1981; by permission.

The competencies labeled as masculine describe the way organizations have done business and managers have been rewarded. To date, the dominant style has been that of a rational, analytical problem-solver, an instrumental, direct, visible, results-oriented style. It emphasizes having a direct visible impact on people and producing compliance. Such a manager is effective through negotiation, competition, assertiveness, proactivity and thinking in a logical, linear fashion.

To date, however, the behaviors labeled feminine have not been as highly valued and rewarded in organizations. Nonetheless, a number of managerial functions require the full range of androgynous behavior—long-range planning, creative problem-solving, career development, performance management, and team-member effectiveness. These and other management functions require expressive behavior, self-disclosure, a vicarious achievement style in order to enjoy the development of others, mentoring, and skills in producing alliances.

Peter Block and Neil Clapp, consultants at Block Petrella Associates, presented good definitions for instrumental and expressive behavior (see Figure 8–4). Instrumental behavior is data based, rational and problem solving. It is planned, predictable, and certain. Instrumental behavior avoids surprises, where expressive behavior encourages spontaneity, strives to avoid boredom and welcomes self-disclosure.

Figure 8-4 Managerial behavior

Description	*Instrumental Behavior*	*Expressive Behavior*
Purpose	Problem solving: to avoid failure, to achieve success	Self-expression: to get acknowledged, to get connected
Exchange	Services; information	Empathy
Basis	Data	Feelings
Needs served	Control; power	Spontaneity
Time orientation	Future-oriented; planned	Spontaneous
Structure	Predictable, certain, clear, agreed-upon, negotiated, contracted	Flexible, ambiguous
Avoid at all costs	Surprise	Boredom

Neale Clapp & Peter Block, Block Petrella Associates. Source: see Fig. 8–3.

Expressive behavior is critical to an intimate relationship at home. "Did you get the car fixed? Did you pay the insurance? Where should we go Saturday night?" all focus on instrumental behavior. It is the same when the parent/child relationship involves only, "Is your room cleaned up? Is your homework done? Did you brush your teeth?" But "How do you feel?" or "What is new?" is expressive behavior that is accepted as important at home. So, too, expressive behavior is needed at work to communicate between boss and subordinate, within work groups, and among work groups. Boss/subordinate communication needs to be characterized by conversations that involve "How are things?" "Where do you want to be two years from now?" "What new skills would you like to learn?"

The androgynous blend offers effective behaviors to both sexes to improve communications between male/male, female/female, and male/female, plus cross-cultural relationships: old/young, black/white, Hispanic/white, north/south, east coast/west coast.

NEXT STEPS

We are in the early stages of building competency-based management models. It may take several years to go through various iterations of building the competency model. The model needs to be tested by putting it on the performance appraisal form, to see if the organization will put its rewards behind it as well as to institutionalize the model as part of the management system. It also needs to be institutionalized in the assessment process and in training and development modules.

THE COMPETENCY MODEL: ITS USE IN TRAINING

While the ultimate use of competency models relates to performance appraisals and effectiveness, it is very useful in training and development. The outcome of the competency process is a profile of an effective manager. This provides an excellent basis for assessment of managers for training and development needs.

The first step is to ask managers at different levels to do a self-assessment based on the competencies in order to select training modules that develop their flat sides. A number of already developed instruments can be used to assess a baseline competence level in interpersonal competence: Kilman Thomas, the Lead Self, the New FIRO, the Strength Deployment Inventory, Myers Briggs, the Androgyny Scale—all offer data in interpersonal competence.

Once competencies have been identified, the assessment process is readily completed by simply assessing the managers in light of those competencies. Then the individual manager's specific training needs can be targeted.

CONCLUSION

Competency-based management programs provide unique assessment possibilities. Since competencies have been identified, the process of assessment is readily done. By using a competency-based approach, training can be readily directed to the needs most vital to individual managers.

It is time for the human resource development professionals to involve line managers in building a competency model. In order for this model to be effective it must be institutionalized in the other HRD management systems (assessment, career development training and development, and performance appraisal); and it must be responsive to management issues of the future, not just the status quo.

One such model for the future is the androgynous manager. In effect, androgyny synthesizes the best of the feminine and masculine styles to develop a more complete manager and individual who can handle both technical and interpersonal issues. The androgynous manager is able to express emotions as well as to handle intellectual, analytical tasks. These are the values and behaviors necessary to carry us in the age of communication which requires interaction and understanding.

REFERENCES

Boyatzis, Richard. *The Competent Manager.* New York: John Wiley and Sons, 1982.

Katz, Robert. "Skills of an Effective Administrator." *Harvard Business Review,* Vol. 52 (September 1974).

Ouchi, William. *Theory Z.* Reading, Mass.: Addision-Wesley, 1981.

9

Assessment Centers

INTRODUCTION

Assessment centers in the United States had their first extensive use in the cloak and dagger world of the OSS, the Office of Strategic Services. Assessment centers were used to select spies and operatives for clandestine assignments in World War II. American Telephone & Telegraph and other major corporations began their association with the assessment center method in the early 1950s. Many who began using centers in those days still are advocates and practitioners of the method today. Major corporations such as AT&T, IBM, Sears, and General Electric have had extensive experience with the technique. Many government agencies and corporations use assessment centers today. Assessment center practitioners claim that over 30,000 individuals will be assessed in any given year and that over 1,000 organizations currently use the technique. The

*Larry Beck, the author of this chapter, is in charge of training and development and test research and validation for the state of South Dakota. He has been involved in skills and management training since 1967. His experience with assessment centers involves both training and selection uses.

assessment center has a healthy research base and a history of successful application. The method has much to recommend itself to the training practitioner as a means of assessing training needs. For more about the basics of assessment centers, you should refer to the references at the end of this chapter. *The Assessment of Men* is highly recommended. This book details the original OSS assessment centers used in World War II.

The purpose of this chapter is to provide an overview of an assessment center process, discuss the training and role of assessors, provide examples of exercises used, discuss advantages and disadvantages, and finally, look at resources needed. Lastly, the appendix provides a personal look at one day in the assessment center.

Of the many methods that are available to us as trainers for needs assessment, the method that comes closest to approximating the behaviors needed for management and supervisory positions is the assessment center. In a training session, the best chance for transfer of learning occurs when training is as close as possible to the real world. This strategy is at the core of the assessment center.

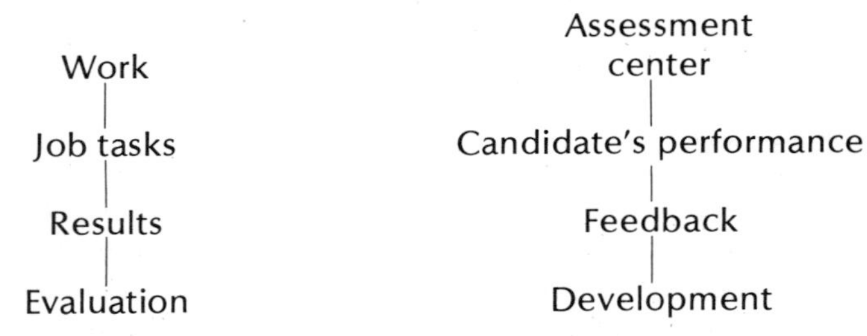

Assessment centers are most widely used in the area of selection and promotion. The next most frequent use of assessment centers is for assessing training and career development needs. Because assessment centers are one of the most expensive techniques available, they are frequently multiple use events i.e., an assessment center may be held for promotional purposes with the offshoot being a base for designing training and career development programs.

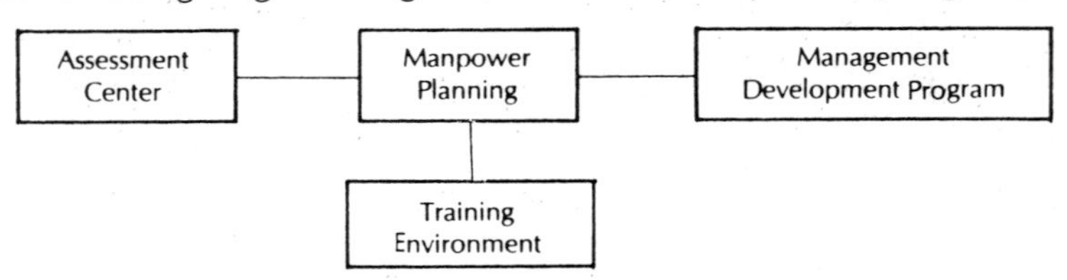

Because of this association with selection processes, the EEOC and related regulatory agencies take a strong interest in assessment centers. To the practitioner, this means that job relatedness is the key to survival. Fairness in the selection of candidates for the assessment center is a critical issue. If the results of an assessment center figure in any way in the promotion process, then the center is a test in the eyes of the EEOC and must comply with the rigorous demands of the uniform selection guidelines. These requirements for documentation of validity and reliability can make the process even more expensive. However, a validated needs assessment tool is well worth the time, effort, and resources required to create it. It is much more efficient to train a manager in the skills he or she needs and not waste valuable executive time telling managers what they already know. People trained in the skills they need can increase the effectiveness of an organization's management measurably.

The research base for assessment centers probably contains more validation studies than any other needs assessment techniques. Additionally, the assessment center method has a high degree of face validity. Most candidates who have participated in assessment centers feel that they have had a chance to thoroughly demonstrate their existing skills and competencies.

As a trainer, you should be aware that any information can be used for a variety of purposes. There have been occasions when management personnel, who have previously been on a fast track in terms of career advancement, suddenly slow to a snail's pace in their career after performing poorly in an assessment center. If the information is not used wisely, a poor showing in an assessment center can be the "kiss of death" for an executive's career. There are horror stories about unfortunate trainers who convinced their bosses to participate in assessment centers that pointed out areas for development to which the supervisor took strong exception. This can be a blow to the trainer's career development.

Because assessment centers tend to focus on specific behaviors, the output from these centers may be very specific and frank. Many executives and management and supervisory personnel are not used to being evaluated in highly specific terms. Problems may result. It is important that a trainer contemplating using an assessment center be sensitive to the implications the feedback process may have.

PROCESS

An assessment center is not a physical setting. It is a process whereby a standardized evaluation of the subject's capabilities and behavior is compiled based on an experience involving a number of assessors and a number of exercises. Candidates are evaluated by a team of trained observers. The exercises that the candidates participate in are typically simulations of behaviors and tasks found on the job.

The general scenario for an assessment center proceeds as follows:

1. Participants in the center will be there from half a day to two weeks. The mode is one day. Time varies according to the objectives of the particular organization sponsoring the center.

2. During the center, participants will engage in a number of exercises. Typically, four to seven exercises will be used. (A later section will discuss the exercises in greater detail.)

3. As participants do the various exercises, trained evaluators observe their performance. At the conclusion of the process, the evaluators pool their observations of a candidate's performance. The result is a consensus as to the management or supervisory potential of the candidate.

Specific steps in the assessment center process include

Step 1: Conduct job analysis

1. Identify tasks.
2. Develop KSA—knowledge, skills, attitudes.
3. Select critical performance dimensions.

Step 2: Develop exercises

4. Select exercises that tap key performance dimensions.
5. Keep exercises job-related.

Step 3: Behavioral anchors

6. All rated dimensions must have behavioral anchors.

Step 4: Train assessors

7. Train assessors in observing and reporting behavior.
8. Train with the specific exercises used in the center.

Step 5: Schedule and run the center

9. Write a detailed time schedule for the center.
10. Have time schedules for assessors and participants.
11. Get initial feedback on your performance from assessors and participants at the end of the center.

Step 6: Final feedback

12. Summarize assessors' comments, ratings, etc., and review with participant.
13. Develop goals and plans with participants.
14. Set timetable to review those goals and plans.

In May 1975, a task force of the 3rd International Congress on the Assessment Center Method presented a report entitled "Standards and Ethical Considerations for Assessment Center Operation." A few of the highlights from their definition of a true assessment center are

1. Multiple assessment techniques must be used.

2. Multiple assessors must be used.

3. Judgments resulting in an outcome must be based on pooling information from assessors and techniques.

4. An overall evaluation of behavior must be made by the assessors at a separate time from observation of the behavior.

5. Simulation exercises are used.

6. The dimensions, attributes, characteristics, or qualities evaluated by the assessment center are determined by an analysis of relevant job behaviors.

7. The techniques used in the assessment center are designed to provide information that is used in evaluating the dimensions, attributes, or qualities previously determined.

As may be inferred from the preceding list, the key to an assessment center or any selection/assessment technique is a *thorough* job analysis. The job analysis is the prerequisite to the writing of the very first exercise.

Typically, the job analysis will identify a number of critical behavioral dimensions such as the ability to cope with stress, the ability to effectively manage time, personal self-confidence, mental alertness, analytical ability, leadership, self-control, and oral and written communications. Not all of the dimensions discovered in the job analysis will be used in the assessment center. A good job analysis will identify the dimensions that are critical to the job; only those dimensions should be assessed.

A Process Option

Many assessment center practitioners rely on the traditional assessment method which has assessors defer rating dimensions until all exercises are completed and a consensus can be achieved among the assessors. Another option is to rate dimensions (according to behavioral anchors) after each exercise. This does not require a consensus by the assessors. All observations are totaled by dimensions. The comments and observations of the assessors are compiled and edited for feedback to the participants.

Our rationale for this procedure is part philosophy and part pragmatism. Being an assessor is hard work and requires long hours. By the end of all the exercises, assessors are fatigued. The process of arriving at a true and reasoned consensus takes time, time that tired assessors are reluctant to take.

By waiting until the end of the assessment center, the assessors' memory for behavioral detail fades. Thus, they must rely on their notes. Exceptional performance (good or bad) will stand out in the assessor's memory. And, at this point, halo effect can easily set in, i.e., participants being rated because of some outstanding characteristic.

Group consensus on behavioral dimensions is also subject to the aberrations of all small group decision-making. As we are further removed in time from the actual behavior, we must rely more and more on overall impressions and prejudices.

Highly verbal and competitive assessors tend to "win" for their candidates more frequently. If there is any deference (status or otherwise) to any of the group members, this can affect the outcomes. Assessors with good information may withdraw from the consensus discussion. The more stringent or lenient assessors may dominate the discourse. (On this point it should be noted that assessors should be watched for inter-rater reliability—stringency or leniency can be handled with standardized scores.)

Our preference is clearly for multiple, rated observations of behavioral dimensions. There is evidence that a statistical combining of the assessors' scores on dimensions and exercises is considerably more predictive than scores arrived at in traditional integrative discussions with staff and assessors (Wollowick and McNamara, "Relationships of the Components of an Assessment Center to Management Success").

With appropriate training to insure inter-rater reliability, this technique can be very effective. The caveat associated with this technique is "*Beware the tyranny of numbers.*" The potential exists for a great deal of artificial precision. This is the "sin of confusing scalpels with chain saws." While both are cutting instruments, there is considerable difference in the precision of their work.

A small difference in numbers may not be a real difference in performance or training needs.

THE ASSESSORS

One of the keys to the success of an assessment center is the selection and training of the assessors. The participants' confidence in the competence of the assessors, and the assessor's ability to identify with the participants' problems and work situations are critical elements in the perceived fairness of the assessment process.

Assessors need to be selected from successful people. People who have themselves achieved some success in the same field as those being assessed, or persons who are highly successful in other areas, are good prospects. If you are working for a large corporation, you may have access to people who are intensively trained in assessment centers. However, that may be a luxury for people who run assessment centers on an occasional basis. They will need other methods for obtaining assessors.

The personal competence and charisma of the assessors can also assist in alleviating some of the tension that generally occurs in participants in an assessment center. (In short, if your assessors are impressive and competent, the entire process will be seen as impressive and competent by the participants.)

Once assessors are obtained, the next step is training the assessors. While most assessors are readily willing to evaluate and make judgments concerning the participants, the key is getting them to make evaluations and judgments about specific behavioral dimensions. The assessors are expected to observe and document behavior and later to document their judgments in specific behavioral terms. Training assessors, then, means training them in how to make specific behavioral observations. These behavioral observations are vital for later discussions with other assessors regarding participants.

In the training process, the assessors should first go through the exercises themselves. For example, if an in-basket is used, the assessors should go through it and be very familiar with the contents. If role plays are to be used, the assessors should practice the role plays. Specific examples of behaviors being looked for might be modeled so the assessors have a clear sense of what to look for.

The important result is that trainers understand the process, materials, and what behaviors mean.

Selecting Assessors

Good assessors are critical to your success. Some places to look are

1. The business school of your local college or university. The public administration area has prospects.

2. Successful managers—particularly those who have hired and trained top-notch staffs.

3. Subject matter experts. If you are running an assessment center for engineers or other special groups, it is nice to have an interpreter who speaks the language.

4. Experienced assessors. I won't say these folks are rare—but if you find one, latch on.

5. Fellow trainers and personnel types. If you need volunteers, these folks will be very interested professionally and will work their tails off. Be prepared to reciprocate at a later date.

EXERCISES

There are a wide variety of exercises that have been used in assessment centers. Some of the most frequently used techniques are

- In-basket exercises
- Written exercises
- A group discussion with a designated leader
- Group discussions without a designated leader
- Role plays
- Business games
- Presentations
- Interviews

Occasionally, management simulation games are used. Paper and pencil tests ranging from the MMPI to FIRO-B have been used.

Role playing occurs frequently in assessment centers. An example is a candidate being asked to role-play a supervisor interviewing a problem employee in order to observe the candidate's counseling skills and interpersonal sensitivity.

Assessment centers may even include the more traditional oral interview with the panel of evaluators. Structured questions are devised so that specific dimensions can be assessed in the oral interview. Standardization of exercises is needed to ensure equal treatment of all participants.

Occasionally, peer evaluations are used in assessment centers. Participants are asked to rate the others according to their leadership qualities. This information then becomes part of the feedback to participants.

In-basket exercises are used to assess a participant's ability to set priorities, to identify critical problems, and to effectively communicate in writing. A packet of memos, letters, and other material is given to the participant. The papers represent organizational and personal problems that the participant must respond to in a given time period. At the end of that time period the participant's written material will be evaluated and the participant may also have to discuss and defend the material and his/her reasoning.

ADVANTAGES—DISADVANTAGES

The advantages of assessment centers are many. First, the assessment method is probably the closest approximation of real life behaviors of any needs assessment technique. It provides a depth and precision of behavioral observations about individuals which we cannot obtain by any other common assessment methods. There is a high degree of reliability and validity associated with the assessment centers. Bray ("The Assessment Center and the Study of Lives," p. 183) in reporting on a 20-year management progress study at AT&T states: "... Perhaps the most significant single finding from the management progress study is that success as a manager is highly predictable." The assessment center process has validity and reliability.

Second, the results are easily translated into training needs. The dimensions rated and commented on by the assessors can be easily identified in most management and supervisory courses. Bibliographies can be prepared based around the dimensions involved in the assessment center as part of the feedback process. The assessment center can frequently be used for multiple purposes: (1) promotion, (2) career development, (3) training needs, and (4) selection.

Third, assessment centers are perceived as extremely fair and accurate representations of behavior by the participants. Participants feel they learn a great deal by participating in the centers. As trainers, we know that the first condition for success in training is that the managers must realize there is a need for the training. The believability of the results in an assessment center can be a great plus to a trainer as well as a motivator for the trainees.

The technique is not without disadvantages, however. First and foremost is the high cost of the assessment center technique. An assessment center designed by a consultant can be very expensive. The process will involve the consultant in designing the center, training assessors, etc. If the need for the center is infrequent, the cost/benefit ratio may heavily favor cost over benefits. If the decision is made to design the center "internally," there will be significant costs in staff time. There simply is not a "quick and dirty" way to design a valid assessment center. Assessment centers are costly in time and money.

Second, there are risks concerned with assessment centers. The misuse of the information could result in a labeling of participants, resulting in a self-fulfilling prophecy for the participants' careers. This was alluded to earlier in this chapter.

Third, the training and ability of the assessors can strongly influence the results of the assessment center. If there is not an available supply of trained assessors, or if the training of the assessors is ineffective, problems can result.

EXERCISE EXAMPLE

Following are some examples of exercises taken from an assessment center conducted for a state police organization. The results of the assessment were used for training and promotional purposes.

The assessment center consisted of the following exercises.

1. An in-basket exercise consisting of 40 items. Participants had two hours to complete the in-basket, and they were then evaluated on their written work as well as an oral defense.

2. Personnel interview role play. Essentially, participants conducted a personnel interview and were rated by two assessors on how they handled it.

3. Written memo. Participants had to write a memo that was evaluated by four assessors for clarity, usage, and effectiveness.

4. Oral presentation. Participants gave a 10-minute talk to two assessors and were then evaluated on their presentation skills.

5. Leaderless group. Lastly, participants engaged in a leaderless group observed by several assessors.

Exercise 2 above was a personnel interview with a trooper who had a performance problem. The trooper's role was played by one of the assessors. A second assessor observed the interview. Prior to the interview, each participant was given a file folder with appropriate information about the employee's previous excellent performance and commendations and then subsequent documentation of performance problems and diminishing work output.

The exercise was rated on four dimensions.

1. Interpersonal sensitivity, defined as the ability to consistently identify and respond to the needs of subordinates.

2. Fact finding. The ability to seek information relevant and necessary to accomplish the task.

3. Problem analysis. The ability of the candidate to consider all relevant information describing the problem and solution.

4. Career development. The ability of the candidate to take action designed to improve the professional competence of the subordinate.

The candidate was given 25 minutes to hold a mock counseling interview with the role-playing assessor. A complete role was written out for the assessor which included a series of personal problems which occurred about the same time that the trooper's performance started to deteriorate. The assessors observing were given behavioral anchors for each of the dimensions assessed in this exercise. The following is an illustration of problem analysis:

- Complete comprehension
- Identifies problem with little effort
- Solution is adequate in long and short term
- Adequate comprehension
- Identifies problem after moderate effort
- Solution is adequate in short term only

- No comprehension of problem
- Does not identify cause of poor performance
- Inadequate solution

Another example of an exercise from the assessment center was an in-basket exercise. Each participant was given two hours to respond to 40 items in the in-basket. During that time they needed to prioritize the items and write instructions to a secretary on what to do with various items. Some of the incidents included

- Work scheduling problems, i.e., several troopers requesting the same day off.
- Complaint against a trooper for sexual harassment.
- Conflicting requests to speak to various organizations.
- Organizational requests for immediate information.
- Personnel problems within the district office.

The participant was then rated by two assessors on his written work and by two observers on his oral defense of the priorities.

RESOURCES NEEDED

The most critical resource needed for an assessment center is time. The next need is money. It is very expensive to bring a group of people together for the time it takes to present an assessment center. Assessment centers may run 8 to 12 people per day for 1 to 14 days. Several assessors will be needed, depending upon the number of candidates in the assessment center.

Typical ratios of assessors to candidates run from one assessor to every two candidates up to one assessor to every six candidates. To have a higher ratio would require superhuman skills from your assessors.

One of the resource people for an assessment center needs to be a person with organizational and detail skills. With a multitude of exercises, several assessors, and participants needing to be in the right place at the right time, coordination is vital. Total confusion on the part of the assessment center staff does not contribute to the perceived effectiveness of the center.

Several breakout rooms will be needed to run an assessment center. Separate areas will be needed for the assessors, for staff to handle the paperwork associated with the center, and of course, for the candidates to participate in the exercises (multiple rooms if multiple exercises are scheduled simultaneously). Lastly, while most trainers will be familiar with the various exercises, if it is the first time through for the assessment center, having access to a person experienced with the method is invaluable. That resource may be a consultant or another trainer.

HINTS ON SETTING UP CENTERS

The image you project to the assessors and to the participants in the center cannot be stressed too greatly. Your schedules should be accurate, and the written materials should look as clean and professional as your budget will allow. Use a printing professional if you have access to one. Your attitude should be one of concern for the participants and also of professional competence. Keep the little problems and glitches that show up out of sight of the participants and the assessors. After all, the participants are there to explore their personal competence. They have the right to expect competence and professionalism from you.

Have contingency plans. If your center runs on a tight time schedule, know what you are going to do if one of your assessors becomes ill or a participant is late or missing.

Keep extra sets of assessment materials on hand to take care of the materials that get lost, ruined or miscollated by the printer.

The participants and the assessors will probably work harder at the center than they ever would in their normal jobs. Maintain coffee and other essentials or you will have a surly group on your hands. In short—meticulous planning, professional appearance, and a good sense of humor are the best hints for a successful assessment center.

SUMMARY

Assessment centers are a very high-powered tool. They produce specific, reliable, and valid information about a manager's strong and weak points. The quality and quantity of the information assessment centers provide does not come easily, nor does it come cheaply. The trainer who embarks on an assessment center will in all likelihood learn more about management styles and techniques than he or she has ever experienced in one place before.

APPENDIX: A DAY AT THE CENTER

Your first day at an assessment center as a participant begins early in the morning. There is some briefing held by the staff in which you will be given some idea of what is to happen during the day. It is almost impossible to keep from sizing up the competition.

During the briefing the staff tries to cut the tension and bring about a relaxed atmosphere. They are only partially successful. The briefing finishes and you check the schedule. Your first exercise is an in-basket. You pick up your in-basket materials and find a table to work on. The instructions tell you that you are a newly-promoted executive who has come in to the office on Saturday and you have two hours to complete the work in your in-basket before you leave town for a week. There is no telephone and no one else can help you or give you additional information. At first glance, the in-basket looks like a stack of policy memos, letters, and other unrelated trivia. There is more work there than you can possibly get done in the time allowed. Your first job is to set priorities: What items are important. What items are unimportant but urgent, and what is "administrivia." By the time the two hours are up, you have had three attacks of writer's cramp, two broken pencils, and about four bouts of nausea. You have also come to some tentative conclusions about this mythical agency. You have spotted bypasses, the potential grievance, and the coworker who may give you problems.

When your interview with the assessors arrives, the issues from the in-basket come back to you quickly. As you explain what your priorities were and why you answered certain letters the way you did, the assessors' questions reveal some flaws in your logic. Panic sets in. You should have seen that problem area. However, the rest of the interview goes well and you leave the assessors with somewhat mixed feelings about how well you did.

The next exercise is the oral presentation. A lot of people dread this one. Didn't one of those national polls put public speaking as Americans' #1 fear . . . even above snakes or flying? Your choice of topics for the presentation looks familiar though, and you could almost ad lib a half day on any of them so the preparation time goes quickly. One of the staff introduces you to the assessors again and you step in front of the room. It is there that you notice the video tape camera and the monitor turned so you can see yourself in nearly living color. Your mouth goes dry. Your tongue seems improperly installed. Simple words like "chair" and "table" escape your conscious memory. Ten minutes later it's over. After the first few minutes, your confidence returned and you presented a smooth, polished talk.

There were other exercises during the course of the center but the one that stands out was the final one—the leaderless group discussion, as the staff called it. The participants sat in a semi-circle and read the instructions. We were given a problem to solve and a time frame to solve it. No one wanted to speak first and the silence became oppressive. Finally, someone was brave enough to offer a first tentative comment. As soon as the ice was broken, the discussion really took off. Some of the participants were very helpful in working on the problem; others seemed to defend their solutions and attack anyone else's. One person totally withdrew and didn't speak after his idea was rejected.

After the discussion there was a general debriefing by the staff and you were told when you could expect feedback on your performance.

You leave with a mixture of relief, exhaustion, and excitement.

REFERENCES

Bray, D. "The Assessment Center and the Study of Lives." *American Psychologist*, February 1982, p. 180ff.

Kraut, A.I., and Scott, G.J. "Validity of an Operational Management Assessment Program." *Journal of Applied Psychology* 56: 124–129.

MacKinnon, D.W. An Overview of Assessment Centers. Center For Creative Leadership, Greensboro, N.C., 1975.

Moses, J.L., and Byham, W.C. *Applying the Assessment Center Method.* New York: Pergamon Press, 1977.

OSS Assessment Staff. *The Assessment of Men.* New York: Reinhart, 1948.

Standards for Ethical Considerations for Assessment Center Operations. Endorsed by the Third International Congress on the Assessment Center Method, Quebec, May 1975.

Wollowick, H.B., and McNamara, W.J. "Relationships of the Components of an Assessment Center to Management Success." *Journal of Applied Psychology* 53: 348–352.

10

Performance Appraisal

INTRODUCTION

The purpose of this chapter is to discuss the use of performance appraisal material for training and development needs assessment. Most companies have some formal process of performance appraisal or evaluation. Locher and Teel ("Performance Appraisal: A Survey of Current Practices") report in their survey of South California companies that 89 percent had formal performance appraisal processes. The implication for the trainer is performance appraisal may be a useful information source.

Generally, within the performance appraisal process there will be questions to the appraiser about strengths, weaknesses, and areas to be developed. This becomes a "treasure chest" of data for the needs assessor.

This chapter will review some basic concepts of performance appraisal. The intent is not to go into these areas in detail but simply to refresh the reader's memory about the performance appraisal

Charles L. Roegiers, Ph.D., the author of this chapter, is an associate professor of communication management in the School of Business at the University of South Dakota, Vermillion, S.D.

process. Second, the chapter will focus on how a trainer may use the performance appraisal process as a source of needs assessment material.

PERFORMANCE APPRAISAL

A starting place is the question "What is performance appraisal?" Beach (*The Management of People at Work*, p. 290) provides the following definition: "Performance appraisal is the systematic evaluation of an individual with respect to his (her) performance on the job and his (her) potential for development."

Beach's definition is representative of most performance appraisal definitions. Beyond this definition the appraisal is, first, "systematic evaluation." Unlike other evaluations that may take place informally, the performance appraisal is structured and planned. They are planned to happen at various times, e.g., this author, in research in South Dakota, found 54 percent of the respondents do an annual evaluation, 35 percent do a semi-annual evaluation, 14 percent do evaluations three or four times per year, and 5 percent list sporadic evaluations over the year. Probably the most common appraisal happens annually. The appraisal takes place at specific times and in a specific manner.

Second, the performance appraisal focuses on an "individual's performance with respect to a job." Performance appraisals are focused on job-related behaviors. This is important not only in preventing extraneous factors from entering into the appraisal but also for the legality of the performance appraisal process (Lubben, Thompson, and Klasson, "Performance Appraisal: The Legal Implications of Title VII," and Crane, *Personnel: The Management of Human Resources*). Holley and Field ("Will Your Performance Appraisal Hold Up in Court?") identify lack of adequate job analysis during the development of the appraisal system as one of the factors which leads to unfavorable court decisions. The performance base of appraisal is a critical aspect of the definition.

Third, performance appraisal also focuses on the "development" of individuals. The appraisal does not simply look at what is past but it also looks forward at what might be areas of improvement. This becomes an area of special interest to us. Within the appraisal process is a gold mine of potential training and development needs. More will be said about this later.

THE APPRAISAL SYSTEM

The majority of the books on performance appraisal will have an appraisal system identified. The key characteristics that extend across most all of these systems are

A. Identification of performance standards. This is the first question of assessment—what is to be measured? A key ingredient for the performance appraisal is the job analysis. An accurate (and this is an important assumption) job analysis will provide the basis for determining what specific behaviors (performances) are desired. If the job analysis no longer accurately reflects the desired performance on the job, it needs to be updated. Step 1, then, is using the job analysis as a basis for determining the desired performances.

B. Once the desired performances are identified, the next step is deciding how to measure the performances. Typically, with performance appraisal, some type of instrument is developed that indicates where an employee is performing with respect to the desired levels of performance. These instruments vary somewhat from place to place but do so out of necessity.

An important ingredient is developing a valid instrument that is job related. Any factor not significant for the job an individual is doing should not be included. And, each factor on the instrument needs to be tied to job specific behavior.

The instrument will generally identify performance goals expected, how the employee is doing with respect to those performance goals, and a plan for development, i.e., future performance goals. The plan becomes especially valuable for the trainer. The appendix at the end of this chapter has a sample performance appraisal form. Note the various sections it contains. While most every form is different, they generally have the same type of question, i.e., what are the person's strengths, weaknesses, and what does he or she need to do by way of development.

C. Once the instrument has been developed, the next question is "who" will record the information and how will this be done? Who will do the performance appraisal?

Normally, the answer to this question is that the first-line manager or supervisor is the one who will do the appraisal for his/her subordinates. The immediate supervisor is the person who has the responsibility for the work that is being done.

Other approaches to the performance appraisal include

1. The supervisor and supervisee fill out the form and they compare how each has filled it out. This may be an excellent place for discussion of perceived differences.

2. Peers fill the instruments out for each other. Since peers will be working side by side, they may have excellent observations about one another's work.

3. Self-rating, which is a process where the individual rates himself/herself.

Any combination of the above may be done. The method chosen should be the one that does the most good and provides the best feedback.

Another question that arises with the "who" is the training of the appraisers. Locher and Teel ("Performance Appraisal—A Survey of Current Practices") indicate that in large organizations 56 percent report no training for their evaluators, 17 percent provide initial training, and 27 percent provide refresher training.

In actual practice only a small percentage of appraisers receive training in how to appraise. This can be a significant problem with performance appraisals. More will be said about this later.

Another aspect of the "how" is the formal process by which the appraisal is to be done. This includes such things as activities needing to be done prior to the actual appraisal, e.g., the appraiser preparing the instrument, how the actual appraisal session will be done, and the post-interview session. While the "how" will differ from company to company what is important is that there be a plan.

D. The instrument has been developed, the "how" has been determined and now comes the "when." As mentioned earlier, the when varies considerably from one organization to another. Some will do it annually, some semi-annually, etc. If given too frequently, performance appraisals may be disruptive and lead to short-range thinking; if not given frequently enough, they may become fairly meaningless and obsolete. An organization needs to decide somewhere between these two extremes.

E. Performance interview. This interaction experience is, first and foremost, a social exchange. Even though the purpose of the time is to exchange information, it is primarily a social interaction, i.e., the appraiser and appraisee affect and influence one another significantly. The appraisal interview has two basic content parts. First, the review of past performance. Previous performance goals are discussed and their attainment evaluated. Problems that have arisen are also discussed and evaluated. Second, the development of new performance goals for the coming time period. This provides the basis for future evaluation and also coaching during the coming time. The appraisal interview is a time of feedback to the employee as well as to the organization.

F. Post-performance interview. A fairly standard practice is that performance evaluations are passed to the next higher authority in the chain of command for his/her review. That person then (theoretically) reviews the appraisals made by his/her subordinates and passes judgment on them.

One last comment: Another aspect of the post-interview time may be a coaching and counseling plan by the first-line manager of his/her subordinates. The goal is to provide the subordinate with an obstacle-free pathway to successful completion of the performances desired.

The above, then, are fairly common components of the performance appraisal process. An obvious one that has not been discussed is the relation of the appraisal to compensation. There are two major schools of thought. The first is that the appraisal process needs to be discussed separately from compensation. If the two are discussed together, the issues will cloud one another.

The second is that the two processes cannot be discussed separately. They go hand-in-hand. Performance appraisal needs to happen in a context where good behavior is rewarded directly and poor behavior is not rewarded. "You get what (the performance) you reward." Again, Locher and Teel's study is interesting in this respect. The major use of performance appraisal in the companies they surveyed was compensation; 71 percent indicated this as the major use. This would certainly indicate that the vote was on the side of tying compensation to performance appraisal.

The trainer needs to be sensitive to how his/her organization relates these two areas.

PERFORMANCE APPRAISAL: PROBLEM AREAS

There are four major potential problem areas in doing performance appraisals. They are

1. Problems relating to organizational environment.
2. Problems relating to the instrument and its administration.
3. Problems with the appraiser.
4. Problems with the appraisee.

Problems of the organizational environment. There are many factors in the environment of an organization that may influence the performance appraisal process. For example, an organizational restructuring may result in uncertain positions and may lead to lower performance. Threats of layoffs may also affect the assessment process.

Another obvious factor here is governmental regulation. A particular regulation may require that certain kinds of information be kept and that the assessment process be done in a particular way. The result may be problems with the appraisal.

Problems with the instrument. Another potential problem area with performance appraisals is the instrument. Does the instrument reflect the performances that are truly reflective in the job? An instrument may be reliable but not be representative of the performances truly desired.

Another aspect of this is the administration of the instrument. Is the instrument used in such a way that the information it contains is accurate? One problem may be the lack of use of the instrument other than when it is filled out. Another problem may be not giving sufficient time for the instrument to be accurately filled out, or not training the assessors in the use of the instrument.

Problems with appraiser. What are the expectations, values, beliefs, or prejudices of the appraisers about the performance appraisal process? Do they see it as valid? Do they feel that the information collected is used and valued? Do they vary the standards as they evaluate Joe who has been here 20 years and Martha who has been here five years?

The appraiser brings to the situation his or her values, feelings, attitudes, and prejudices and any or all of these may get in the way of an effective apparaisal. The appraiser may have a certain pattern of rating or rate certain individuals high or low based on a single characteristic. Awareness of these biases is essential.

The appraisee. Many of the same comments about the appraiser come into play here. The appraisee comes into the evaluation with feelings, thoughts, attitudes, prejudices. Again, this is a time of a social exchange as well as content exchange. Human error may enter into the final appraisal with the result being inaccurate information or incorrect impressions.

The above represent problems with appraisals. They are important for the trainer to keep in mind. Any one or a combination of them could readily influence the resulting data. Since the trainer wants to use that data, he/she wants to be aware of potential problems with it. A clear and effective exchange is the goal, and both parties must equally share the concern for achieving it.

NEEDS ASSESSMENT AND PERFORMANCE APPRAISAL

The previous pages discussed some general points about performance appraisal. The intent of this section is to discuss how the trainer may find performance evaluation data useful as a source of training needs. This section looks at four basic questions:

1. Is there a source of information from performance appraisals?
2. Does the trainer have access to that source (if it exists)?
3. What might be problems with the accuracy of the material?
4. How to work with others (first-line managers, etc.) to service needs?

Question 1: Does the information exist?

The first question to be asked by the trainer is "Do we have performance appraisals here?" While this may appear to be a trivial question, it is a vital question to be asked. Obviously, if the answer is "no," this chapter will have little applicability. The result is an "end."

It is not unusual to have an organization that has performance appraisals at one level and something "other" at other levels. By asking the question, the trainer can begin to identify if this information source exists and to what degree it exists.

Question 2: Does the trainer have access to the information?

Question 1 deals with the existence of an information source. Question 2 raises the issue of access to that source.

A trainer may find that the information from the performance appraisal is privileged to a certain few people in the organization. The information exists, but the trainer does not have access to it. Again, this may mean an end to the use of this type of information. However, the trainer may also talk with those possessing the information about ways of obtaining it that do not violate privacy, e.g., they might summarize the results in a way that protects confidences. Nadler (*Designing Training Programs,* p. 91) cites a frustrating example of an organization with which he was working which had an elaborate performance appraisal system but they would not release the information. Finally, the CEO was willing to release it in a summarized form. Later, Nadler suggests that one way upper management may be supportive of the training function is to allow the appropriate use of performance appraisal data.

Another aspect of this is that the information exists but exists in such a form that its usability is questionable. For example, there may be no central filing office and the instruments are scattered in file cabinets all over a building. The end result may be the effort required by the trainer to get the information is greater than the benefits derived from the information.

Question 3: Is the information valid?

The next question focuses on the information itself—how valid is it? In the previous section, we discussed problem areas of performance appraisals. The trainer needs to be aware of possible problems of validity and compensate for them. Questions the trainer might ask himself/herself are

- Were there important organizational changes going on during the time of this evaluation?

- Does this instrument do justice to the job analysis? Are there loopholes with how it was administered?

• Were the appraisers trained in how to do performance appraisals? Are these particular patterns shown in a specific appraiser's appraisals? (i.e., are some appraisers consistently "hard" and others "soft"?) There is some evidence that training of assessors can significantly reduce the bias that is otherwise built into the performance appraisal. Also, having at a minimum written instructions may increase the "defendability" of a performance appraisal system.

• Are there qualifying factors about the appraisee that need to be considered?

Most appraisal forms will identify standards (or performance goals) and have some type of rating system for what the employee is doing correctly and incorrectly. In addition, there will likely be a "development plan"—what needs to be happening to assist the employee in performing more effectively? A valuable source of information for the trainer is this "development plan." It may summarize the conclusions from the instrument itself. Look for this material when evaluating an appraisal instrument.

Question 4: How can the trainer be of service to the first-line manager in meeting training needs?

Ultimately, the trainer's role is that of assisting the line manager with meeting training and development needs. As has been discussed earlier, not all needs will be "training" needs. Not all the developmental needs coming out of a performance appraisal will be training issues. Some will be motivational problems, personal issues, etc.

One of the first steps, then, is beginning to identify which needs will be best serviced by a training and development approach and which will not. The next step is assisting in providing mechanisms for getting the needs met. In some situations, that may mean the trainer sets up a formal training event. In other situations, the trainer may assist the first-line manager in identifying resources for an employee. And in still other situations, the trainer may coach/counsel the first-line manager about how he/she can effectively work as an on-the-job trainer. The needs become acted upon.

SUMMARY

The purpose of this chapter has been to overview and discuss how a performance appraisal may be a source of information on training needs assessment. The trainer will be able to find much valuable information concerning training needs from performance appraisal material. At the same time, the trainer needs to be sensitive to possible trouble areas.

APPENDIX

Figure 10-1 Sample Appraisal Form I

Below Job Requirements	Meets Minimum Job Requirements	Occasionally Exceeds Job Requirements	Consistantly Exceeds Job Requirements
1	2	3	4

	1	2	3	4
1. JOB KNOWLEDGE Possession of information and understanding all types of work which the employee must perform	☐	☐	☐	☐
2. QUALITY OF WORK Thoroughness and accuracy of work	☐	☐	☐	☐
3. QUANTITY OF WORK The volume of passable work regularly produced.	☐	☐	☐	☐
4. RESPONSIBILITY The extent to which the employee can be depended upon to carry a task through to completion (Dependability - Reliability)	☐	☐	☐	☐
5. DECISION MAKING Ability to decide correct course of action when some choice is needed.	☐	☐	☐	☐
6. WORK RELATIONSHIPS Willingness to receive directions and instructions without responding defensively. Cooperates willingly with others with whom employee must work	☐	☐	☐	☐
7. COMMUNICATIONS Ability to convey ideas simply and convincingly.	☐	☐	☐	☐
8. TEMPERAMENT Ability to work under pressure and meet deadlines.	☐	☐	☐	☐
9. ATTITUDE TOWARD JOB Expresses and exhibits positive feeling towards job and company.	☐	☐	☐	☐

AVERAGE OF RATINGS

MAJOR ACHIEVEMENTS FOR PAST PERIOD

FUTURE GOALS FOR NEXT PERIOD

Figure 10-2 Sample Appraisal Form II

PROFESSIONAL KNOWLEDGE (Consider requirements of position)				
Has exceptional knowledge of position. Extremely well informed.	Has excellent knowledge of position. Occasionally demonstrates exceptional knowledge.	Has good knowledge of position. Infrequently demonstrates excellent knowledge.	Has satisfactory knowledge of position.	Serious lack of fundamental knowledge of position.
COOPERATION (Consider ability and willingness to work in harmony with and for others)				
Extremely successful in working with others. Has an ability to create harmony.	Promotes harmony in dealing with others. A very good team worker.	Gets along well with most people. Knows how to take orders. Fits in with team.	Indifferent to others. Cooperates only when it is directly beneficial to him.	Inclined to create friction. Generally not cooperative.
INITIATIVE (Consider drive and amount of direction required to accomplish job)				
Has exceptional initiative beyond that which present position can fully utilize.	Exercises initiative beyond job requirements.	Exercises initiative required to capably perform job. Occasionally needs direction.	Lacks initiative required by position but "gets along." Requires some direction.	Lacks initiative required to make position function. Requires much direction.
JUDGEMENT (Consider ability to grasp a situation, think clearly and develop correct and logical conclusions)				
Outstanding sound & logical thinking with an exceptional grasp of the situation involved.	Exceptionally good judgement based on sound evaluation of all factors involved.	Judgement is usually sound and reasonable.	Is prone to neglect or misinterpret facts. Occasionally commits errors in judgement.	Faulty judgement. Decisions or recommendations are too frequently wrong.
LEADERSHIP (Consider organizing ability, obtaining cooperation from others, direction of efforts of others & smoothness of operation supervised)				
Outstanding skill in directing others. Results in a very effective unit. Inspires confidence.	An excellent leader. Directs others well and maintains good morale. Has excellent cooperation from group.	Capable leader, develops good cooperation and team work. Knows how to give orders & gets the job done.	Generally obtains effective cooperation from group. Usually gets the job done.	Unable to control a group.

Figure 10–2 (continued).

JOB ATTITUDE (Consider interest and enthusiasm shown in work)				
Extraordinary degree of enthusiasm and interest.	High degree of enthusiasm and interest.	Favorable and completely acceptable attitude.	Attitude needs improvement to be acceptable.	Attitude too poor to retain in position without great improvement.
MANAGEMENT EFFECTIVENESS (Consider utilization of people, money and materials)				
Is most effective in utilization of people, money and materials.	Is effective in accomplishing extra savings by implementing & maintaining improved management procedures.	Conserves people, money, & materials by implementing and maintaining routine management procedures.	Utilizes people, money & materials in a satisfactory manner.	Is irresponsible in this regard.
EFFECTIVENESS IN DEALING WITH PEOPLE (Consider contacts with employees and customers)				
Obtains highest respect from all. Extremely capable of selling his ideas.	Is respected. Capable of getting ideas across to others.	Is well liked. Can sell ideas but must be prepared.	Has some difficulty getting along with people, but gets by.	Should not be representing company to customer.
PROMOTION POTENTIAL (Consider capacity to handle jobs of greater responsibility, ability to learn, personality, self-improvement efforts, special ability and training)				
Capable of increased responsibility & rapid advancement.	Very promising. Promotional material.	Demonstrates promise for further growth at moderate rate.	Present job is taxing his capabilities. Requires considerable amount of training.	Definitely limited.

EMPLOYEE STRENGTHS: ______________________________

____

____

____

____

EMPLOYEES WEAKNESSES: ______________________________

____

____

____

____

OBJECTIVES FOR NEXT APPRAISAL PERIOD: ______________________________

____

____

____

____

____

EMPLOYEE COMMENTS ______________________________

____

____

____

____

____

REFERENCES

Beach, D. *Personnel: The Management of People at Work.* New York: Macmillan, 1980.

Crane, D. *Personnel: The Management of Human Resources.* 3rd Ed. Boston: Kent Publishing Co., 1982.

Holley, W., and Field, H. "Will Your Performance Appraisal Hold Up in Court?" *Personnel*, January-February 1982, p. 59ff.

Locher, A., and Teel, K. "Performance Appraisal—A Survey of Current Practices." *Personnel Journal*, May 1977.

Lubben, G., Thompson, D., and Klasson, C. "Performance Appraisal: The Legal Implications of Title VII." *Personnel,* May–June 1980, pp. 11–21.

Nadler, L. *Designing Training Programs.* Reading, Mass.: Addison-Wesley, 1982.

Roegiers, C. Unpublished Report. *Performance Appraisals in the State of South Dakota,* 1981.

11

Assessment of Training Needs for Career Development

INTRODUCTION

Training needs frequently arise from the tensions that exist between organizational needs and the social and psychological needs of an organization's employees. Stress management training is an obvious example. Career development training is another, and one that is rapidly approaching a prominent position in the organizational training repertory. Many organizations are offering these programs and are developing skills that were generally taken for granted a decade ago. Organizations do not automatically provide satisfying careers to their employees. Even the most able employees do not automatically prepare themselves to take advantage of the opportunities the organization does make available.

Career development training includes a variety of programs. Aetna Life and Casualty Company offers two-day "self-awareness" workshops to its employees. Managers and supervisors get a third day designed to help them assist subordinates in developing their careers

---

Dr. Phillip Fisher, the author of this chapter, is a professor in the School of Business at the University of South Dakota, Vermillion, South Dakota. He has a special interest in the area of career development.

(Anderson, "Aetna Workshops in Identity"). Over 1,500 employees who work for a manufacturer of engineering intensive products have attended an off-site three-day workshop which focuses on self-identification of strengths and weaknesses and encourages the employees to take responsibility for their own career development (Anderson, "Corning Glass Work Career Path Review"). CitiCorp is embarked on an effort to include its entire management staff of 10,000 in a five-day workshop of self-evaluation and skill development in management practices, including such developmental areas as coaching, appraisals, and managing for continuity (Anderson, "CitiCorp's 39 Steps"). These are just a few examples of the rapidly growing interest in career development training. A recent survey of corporate training and development professionals found more respondents predicting a growth in career development programs than for any one of 40 types of programs included in the study (Jones, "A Caution Signal for the HRD").

This interest in career development is partially the result of a widespread feeling on the part of managers at all levels that their working life, while not necessarily unpleasant, is not entirely satisfying. A 1973 survey of 3,000 managers found that a majority of managers at mid and lower levels were either searching for a career change or were considering changing their occupational field (Tarnowieski, "The Changing Success Ethic"). The great popularity of books and magazine articles on the mid-life crisis is further evidence that many people are not fulfilled by their careers.

It may be that the current preoccupation with occupational fulfillment is simply a rediscovery of an old problem; one is reminded of Peggy Lee's popular song, "Is That All There Is," or the complaint of *Ecclesiastes*, "Vanity of vanities, all is vanity. . . ." It may also be that the slower economic growth of the seventies has not provided adequate opportunities for a generation of men and women whose expectations were raised by 25 years of economic growth and a prevailing ideology of self-actualization. The manufacturer cited earlier found that employees' frustration with their inability to advance in a company which, in fact, has few opportunities for advancement, was one of the major issues to surface in their workshops (Anderson, 1981). If slower economic growth is a major factor behind the boom in career development training, it may be that interest in this training will last for quite a while.

Two factors appear to have the potential to create more difficulty for the development of satisfying careers. One is demographic. As the last of the post-World War II baby-boom is emptying out of colleges and universities, the rate of new entries into organizational and economic life is beginning to decline. The trailing ranks of that boom will not have the benefit of being pushed up organizational pyramids at the same rate that they pushed their predecessors. The other factor is that a scarcity of natural resources may, in the opinion of many economic experts, put constraints on economic growth which have not existed in the past.

If organizational growth will in fact be slower in the eighties, organizations are likely to devote more time and effort to career development. These efforts will include realistic career planning, the creation of opportunities for self-development that do not require moving up the pyramid, and training employees and their supervisors to take more responsibility for creating a satisfying adjustment to the new realities of organizational life.

THE CAREER PERSPECTIVE

There is a plaque near the entrance of the building where I work which is inscribed as follows: "There is no future in any job, the future is in the man who holds the job." Aside from its sexist language, this platitude overlooks what common sense has always told us and what research has recently come to verify. Advancement often depends on such factors as the visibility of early jobs or the upward mobility of one's supervisor (Schein, *Career Dynamics*). Certain positions can only be reached by preparation in a limited set of subordinate or related jobs. If one wishes to be a sales manager, for instance, it is probably necessary to become a successful sales representative first.

A career perspective recognizes this fact. A career is seen as an occupation that provides a pattern of systematic advancement (Caslio and Elias, *Human Resource Management*). We often speak of a career path or the corporate ladder. Implicit in these terms is the notion that, if people want to reach a given position in an organization or profession, there are certain prerequisite steps that they must take.

Career development, then, prepares people to better manage themselves, to better chart and navigate their occupational development, or to assist others in their development. This would include assessing one's values and potential, identifying promising career goals and career paths, and seeing that the necessary experience and training are provided.

Career development requires the mutual efforts of both organizations and their individual members, and supervisors are potentially the most effective source of assistance in these efforts. Organizations must provide specific developmental opportunities and a climate that fosters personal growth. Individuals must make accommodations to organizational needs while acquiring the training, experience, and exposure necessary for their own growth. Supervisors must teach, evaluate, advise, and promote their subordinates. Training needs are likely to exist at all three levels: system management, supervision, and personal career management.

ORGANIZATIONAL NEEDS—TRAINING AT THE TOP

Most organizations will need to have well-articulated, systematic programs of career planning and development if significant opportunities are to exist for most organizational members. These programs will probably include organizational manpower planning, definition of career paths, employee assessment, counseling, and specific attention to such special issues as minority employee opportunities and accommodation to employees in dual career marriages. The existence of such programs requires a commitment by top management and a knowledge of what is required.

Outright rejection of career development responsibilities by top executives is unlikely. Most are likely to agree that career development activities can benefit both their organization and their employees.

The problems are more likely to be that just what is needed in the way of a program may be unclear, and consequently, responsibilities for activities are not well defined and supervisors are not really rewarded for developmental efforts. Also, executives may have legitimate concerns about raising false expectations on the part of their employees (Zenger, "Career Planning: Coming in From the Cold").

A fairly common place to start with providing executives with some knowledge of what an effective program entails is to provide opportunities to find out about effective programs in other organizations through reading or attending workshops and conferences. Once the commitment to such a program has been made, there will be a continuing need for information about the design of the program, along with the need for combined guidance and commitment.

Successful program design and implementation will require leadership and initiative from the training director and the participation and support of key managers. A practical procedure is to prepare a first-draft proposal and invite comments and suggestions by influential managers who have shown some interest in the concept of career development training. Their recommended alterations can be incorporated into a second draft which would in turn receive a somewhat wider circulation. This process is repeated until (1) there is a consensus that the program design will meet the needs of the organization; (2) key managers understand the goals and operation of the program, and (3) there is widespread support for the program (Otte, "Creating Successful Career Development Programs").

SUPERVISORY TRAINING

Most of the direct assistance received by individuals in their own career planning and development will be provided by their supervisors. Most supervisors will need training in several areas in order to be able to function effectively in this role.

The career path review used by Corning Glass for employees in their seventh or eighth year of employment will serve as an example of the type of supervisory activity typical of a career development program. Employees and their supervisors fill out an extensive questionnaire which details the employee's accomplishments, strengths, and weaknesses. More to the point of career development, it covers the employee's probable next assignment, a five-year projection of assignments, and an estimate of the employee's highest ultimate assignment. It also includes a list of actions to be taken by the employees to shore up their weaknesses and prepare them for future assignments.

The process is completed by an interview between employee and supervisor. Both have committed themselves to an evaluation and, by the conclusion of the process, to a plan of action agreed to be important to continued development. Employees know where they stand and are able to make informed decisions about their future with the company (Anderson, "Corning Glass Works Career Path Review").

Training for this kind of program is likely to encompass training in knowledge and training in skills. Before supervisors can begin to be of real assistance to their subordinates, they must know what assignment opportunities exist in their organizations and what their organizations are seeking in individuals who will be given these opportunities. More time in an organization does not guarantee that supervisors will have this knowledge, and the task of preparing supervisors to accurately advise employees on these matters is probably one of the first areas for training.

Supervisors must also have the skills necessary to give valid feedback on employee performance and capabilities and to counsel them in designing effective career development action plans. Supervisors may need training in performance evaluation, assessment of skills and potential as they pertain to future opportunities, and to be able to assist their subordinates in designing and executing career-enhancing action plans.

Supervisors are also likely to need training on how to assist employees with special problems such as dual career marriages or on the relationship of affirmative action programs to career development activities.

Leibowitz and Schlossberg ("Training Managers for Their Role in a Career Development System") have developed a training model designed to prepare supervisors for the additional roles their participation in career development will require. Their proposed two-and-a-half day program begins by creating an awareness of career planning needs and helping managers assess their own abilities to assist their subordinates in this process. The program then provides managers with career development and planning concepts and helps them develop their own action plans.

Awareness of career planning roles is created through asking supervisors to define career planning and discussing misconceptions. A presentation of the various ways career development can take place can follow. Kaye ("How You Can Help Employees Formulate Career Goals") has described six types of development: vertical mobility, lateral mobility, realignment, exploratory research, job enrichment, and relocation. This approach emphasizes that "up" is not the only direction in which development can occur. The organization's own program should be introduced at this stage.

Supervisors are helped to evaluate their own abilities to assist their subordinates in career activities by responding to a questionnaire which asks them to rate themselves on their ability to engage in specific behavior which will be required by the organization's program.

Leibowitz and Schlossberg recommend introduction of three major concepts to assist supervisors in understanding the career development tasks they will be asked to perform. These are Kantor's ("Quality of Worklife and Work Behavior in Academia") concept of "the moving" and "the stuck," Schein's categories of career anchors, and the idea of career stages advanced by Dalton, Thompson, and Price ("The Four Stages of Professional Careers—A New Look at Performance by Professionals").

The concept of "the moving" and "the stuck" is useful in helping supervisors understand resistance to career development. Being stuck means believing that there are no opportunities available. It lowers aspirations, reduces self-esteem, alienates people from their work, and turns loyalty away from the organization and toward coworkers.

Schein's study of careers led him to categorize managers by their self-identification of talents, motives, attitudes, and values. These act as forces that shape and constrain the direction of career development. Schein's list includes (1) a concern with the ability to perform technical/functional competencies; (2) managerial competence; (3) security, a concern with having trust in the organization; (4) creativity, a concern for creating products or processes; and (5) a concern for autonomy. Schein's conclusion is that people work best when their jobs and organizational climates are supportive of their career anchors. Supervisors who are able to identify the career anchors of their subordinates will be better able to help them in career development.

The identification of career stages aids supervisors in helping employees identify where they are and what they need to do to move to the next stage. Dalton, Thompson, and Price found four stages: (1) apprentice, in which individuals must adapt to the organization and develop some occupational specialty; (2) colleague, in which one is a full contributing member of the organization; (3) mentor, in which the emphasis switches to managing people and helping apprentices develop; and (4) sponsor, in which the full powers of high performers can be applied to initiating activities.

Action plans are based on the belief that supervisors share with employees the responsibility for career development and that effective action is most likely when important preliminary stages have been shared. Initially, the employee explores career concerns and the supervisor listens and supports. As concerns become known, supervisors can help employees understand them by identifying and clarifying. When these processes have been worked through, the employee is in a position to act and the supervisor is able to help. Skill training will be needed to prepare supervisors for this. Role playing, case studies, and presentations on active listening, paraphrasing, and other counseling skills are suggested to build the necessary skills.

TRAINING IN PERSONAL CAREER DEVELOPMENT

Primary responsibility for career planning and development must rest with the individual. Ultimately, each person must be able to make realistic assessments of himself/herself and come to an understanding of what the organization can offer and what it will require. Individuals must also assume prime responsibility for their own growth. Training can be helpful at all these points.

Self-assessment requires a variety of judgments and decisions that can be aided in training. Training can assist people to clarify their values and develop life goals that are appropriate for their value systems. It can assist employees in learning to evaluate themselves with hard-headed accuracy so that they can perceive their own developmental needs and make realistic assessments of their potentials.

An understanding of what opportunities the organization offers can also be achieved through training. Employees can be made aware of the current assessments of future manpower needs, the career paths open to them, and the kind of preparation and performance required to obtain these opportunities.

Training will also be needed to assist individuals to take charge of their own program of development. The tasks here will be different for people at different stages in their careers.

Individuals in the early stage of their career will need to reach accommodation with the organization and to develop skill in one or more occupational specialties. Traditional orientation programs and functional skill training are appropriate here, but emphasis on the skills required to establish mentor-sponsor relationships with their organizational supervisors would also be helpful.

Managers in mid-career must make the frequently difficult transition from managing processes to managing people. The training most needed in this respect is likely to focus on management skills. The type of training offered here is not different in content because of career development programs, but will benefit from a perspective that looks forward to the skills required for future assignments.

Lawrence Livermore Laboratory began career planning programs in 1975. The program was built around a series of workshops of 35 hours delivered over a five-week period. An orientation workshop introduces the importance of career planning. Small groups are used to allow participants to discuss their own knowledge and attitudes about career planning and to set an active learning climate from the beginning.

Orientation is followed by a series of workshops in which participants identify their own career stages, interests, values and skills, set realistic career goals, identify personal developmental needs, and set plans to meet those needs. Participants are encouraged to evaluate their plans, identify obstacles and support, and to understand their own level of commitment.

Those workshops employ small group discussions, assessment instruments such as the Strong-Campbell Interest Inventory, and self-identification of skills through identifying past accomplishments and the skills and satisfactions associated with one's past accomplishments. (See Bolles' popular book, *What Color Is Your Parachute?* for a good example of this approach.)

The program at Lawrence Livermore Natural Laboratory has been a success, as have been similar programs by the Synder Corporation and Crocker National Bank (see Hanson, "Career/Life Planning Workshops as Career Services in Organizations—Are They Working?"). Participants and supervisors support these programs and they have produced lower turnover, higher performance, and increased promotability.

REFERENCES

Anderson, C., ed. "Aetna Workshops in Identity." *The Career Development Bulletin*, Vol. 2, No. 2, 1981, pp. 2–3.

Anderson, C. "Corning Glass Works Career Path Review." *The Career Development Bulletin*, Vol. 2, No. 2, 1981, pp. 1–2.

Anderson, C., ed. "Self-Awareness at Honeywell, Inc." *The Career Development Bulletin*, Vol. 2, No. 3, 1981, p. 4.

Anderson, C., ed. "CitiCorp's 39 Steps." *The Career Development Bulletin*, Vol. 2, No. 3, 1981, pp. 1–2.

Bolles, R. *What Color is Your Parachute?* Berkeley: Ten Speed Press, 1981.

Cascio, W., and Awad, E. *Human Resource Management.* Reston Va.: Reston Publishing Co., 1981.

Dalton, G.; Thompson, P.; and Price, R. "The Four Stages of Professional Careers—A New Look at Performance by Professionals." *Organizational Dynamics*, 1977, pp. 19–41.

Hanson, M. "Career/Life Planning Workshops as Career Services In Organizations—Are They Working?" *Training and Development Journal*, February 1982, pp. 58–63.

Jones, R. "A Caution Signal for HRD". *Training and Development Journal,* April 1981, pp. 42–46.

Kantor, R. "Quality of Worklife and Work Behavior in Academia." *National Forum* (4), 1980, pp. 35–38.

Kaye, B. "How You Can Help Employees Formulate Career Goals." *Personnel Journal*, 1980, pp. 368–373.

Kaye, B. "The Design of Career Development Programs: A Six-Stage Model." *The Career Development Bulletin,* Vol. 2, No. 2, 1981, pp. 9–10.

Leibowitz, R., and Schlossberg, N. "Training Managers for Their Role in a Career Development System." *Training and Development Journal*, July 1981, pp. 72–79.

Otte, F. "Creating Successful Career Development Programs." *Training and Development Journal*, February 1982, pp. 30–37.

Schein, E. *Career Dynamics.* Reading, Mass.: Addison-Wesley, 1978.

Tarnowieski, D. "The Changing Success Ethic." *American Management Association Research Report*, 1973, pp. 35–42.

Zenger, J. "Career Planning: Coming In From the Cold." *Training and Development Journal*, July 1981, pp. 47–52.

12

Exit Interview

INTRODUCTION

Interviewer: Good Morning, Bob.

Bob: Good Morning, Sally.

Interviewer: Please come in and have a seat. Can I get you some coffee?

Bob: Thanks very much, Sally.

Interviewer: Bob, I'm sorry to learn that you are leaving Up-Hill Hospital at the end of the week.

Bob: Well, Sally, it's been a hard decision.

Interviewer: Bob, if you could, would you tell me why you made that decision?

Bob: Sure, Sally.

Interviewer: So, why are you leaving, Bob?

Bob: It's really very simple when you get right down to it. Short-

---

Sister Mary Schneider, the author of this chapter, is acting director of the Health Services Administration Program in the Division of Allied Health of the University of South Dakota. A special interest area of hers is the use of the exit interview as a source of important organizational data.

Stop is offering me 16.5 to start. The retirement program at Short-Stop isn't quite as good as at Up-Hill, but it's still not too bad.

Interviewer: So you're leaving for higher pay. Well, you know, with our budget cuts this year, we can't top the 16.5 you will be getting at Short-Stop. I sure would like to have you stay, Bob, but it would be unfair for me to try to stand in your way. Bob, are you telling me it's purely a question of economics?

Bob: That's about the size of it, Sally.

Interviewer: Well, thanks for telling me, Bob. I'll be sure and pass on your comments to the president—who knows, maybe someday when enough people leave because of low pay, management will see the error of its ways.

A common experience in any organization is saying goodbye. Why do people terminate one job and move to another or move from one company to another? Did you say you know the answer? Ask yourself, do I really know?

There is a process whereby upon termination the employer can uncover with the employee the "real" reasons for termination. The incident related above could be repeated and a different story uncovered. Let's do a rerun. The dialogue could continue with a few other questions and turn the interview around.

Interviewer: Bob, I hear you telling me that pay is the reason for your termination?

Bob: Yes, Sally, that's about the way it all stacks up.

Interviewer: Well, how did you find out about the opening over at Short-Stop?

Bob: Sally, I've been looking for some time just watching the ads and keeping in touch with friends.

Interviewer: I see, Bob, you've been looking for such a long time.

Bob: Yes, Sally, for over a year.

Interviewer: Why, Bob, have you been looking for such a long time? Are there some other things that have been on your mind during this time regarding your present position?

These questions and this approach now open the door for Bob and Sally to uncover the "real" reasons for termination. That is what is meant by the question, "Do you really know the real reasons?" The process can involve one or all three techniques: (1) a written form filled out by the employee, (2) an exit interview, or (3) a combination of both. This chapter will focus on the exit interview.

The information in this chapter can be divided into three parts: (1) an introduction that discusses the purpose of the exit interview, how this process relates to needs assessment, and the overall purpose of this book; (2) formats for the exit interview process; and (3) guidelines for doing an exit interview which will allow the maximum opportunity for the interviewer to elicit from the interviewee training and development needs.

EXIT INTERVIEW: THE PURPOSE

An exit interview is a means of identifying the principal causes for employee attrition. These "real" reasons, the unfolding of personal needs, are of value to the organization as well as to the employee. Employee values, ideas, and feelings hold information for the organization that can help it focus on

A. Management practices
- communication
- motivation
- leadership
- counseling
- management development programs

B. Employment, placement, and personnel planning
- matching the employee with the job and organization
- job specifications
- recruiting locations and techniques

C. Training and development
- training and development needs
- training and development processes

D. Compensation and benefits
- are they competitive?
- salary structure
- job descriptions
- job grading
- job evaluation
- range, placement, and salary structures

E. Health, safety, security
- awareness of programs
- environmental safety

F. Labor relations

G. Personnel research

The exit interview can hold a "gold-mine" of information for the organization when it is prepared for and approached with dignity.

FORMATS FOR EXIT INTERVIEWS

How does one go about the task of interviewing? An interview is verbal communication between the interviewee and the interviewer. The task of the interviewer is to set the climate, establish rapport, and promote communication with the interviewee. Careful preparation must precede any interview. This is called setting the stage. Stage setting or planning for the interview should include a response to the following questions:

1. Who is going to be responsible for conducting the interview? Will it be someone from personnel or from the department in which the person was employed? The more logical choice is personnel since the potential for objectivity and eliciting more information is greater. The personnel department is viewed as having confidentiality of information. Another plus for using personnel is that this department has ready access to such information as job descriptions, salary data, and other pertinent information which can be used in planning for the interview.

2. At what time will the interview be conducted? The termination notice should have been received prior to scheduling the interview.

3. What is the best climate for the person being interviewed? Careful planning will include the need to find a place where communication can be carried on in private without being interrupted. The environment should be warm and pleasant so as to assist in making the person feel comfortable. Comfort can decrease inappropriate stress and anxiety, factors that limit communication.

4. What type of format will best meet the needs of this person being interviewed? What kind of format am I as the interviewer most comfortable with? Designing the format should address the areas of establishing rapport; reviewing the purpose; developing questions that will surface attitudes toward the previous job, explore the possible reasons for leaving, compare previous job with the new one; and see if there are recommended changes.

Before looking more indepth at the format for the interview, it is useful to be aware of the fact that there are three general approaches which can be used in asking questions. The three are unstructured, super-structured, and patterned. It will be beneficial to briefly describe each approach and to give a few examples of the kinds of questions associated with each. First, the unstructured method uses broad, open-ended questions that do not give the interviewer much control over the interview. The person being interviewed is encouraged to express himself/herself in any area without any definite format. Thus, there is no structure and questions will not be uniform from one person to another. A definite problem is how to achieve comparability from one person to the next. A talkative person will give much information while the reluctant, hesitant person will be more reserved, perhaps giving no more information than that specifically requested. Thus, there is the inherent risk of being misled by one person versus another. Questions that might be asked are (1) tell me about your experiences with the hospital/nursing home, (2) how might you characterize the position you held?, and (3) describe the quality of your work environment.

The second approach is called super-structured. The technique utilizes questions that are basically answered by saying yes or no. Another way of describing super-structured is that it is a checklist approach. The risk here is that the person does not really say much other than yes or no. The result: little information is gained. The technique also suggests to the departing employee that the organization is not really interested in finding out the reasons for termination. A positive aspect of this approach is that it is quick and the same questions are used by every person. There is increased objectivity. Some possible questions might be (1) why are you leaving? Is it for more money? (2) were you satisfied with the hours you worked? (3) were the weekends one of the more stressful aspects of the job?

A third method is entitled patterned. This interview combines elements of both the super-structured and unstructured techniques. The objective is to combine their strengths and minimize their weaknesses. It is flexible, permits follow-up on leads and the opportunity to probe for further information. The benefit of this approach is being able to follow through on leads given by the person interviewed. It takes time and careful planning prior to the interview. This approach can best be utilized with trained interviewers. Some possible questions are (1) let's begin by outlining briefly some of the duties of your job, (2) of the described duties, tell me three or four that are crucial to your job performance, and (3) tell me some of the duties you like the most and what you liked about performing these duties.

GUIDELINES FOR EXIT INTERVIEW

Returning to the format for the interview, the first step in the actual interview is establishing rapport. This begins at the time the interview is scheduled and continues until completion. The interviewee is invited into the place for the interview and offered a comfortable chair and coffee. The purpose is to provide an opportunity for the person to relax and become comfortable with the surroundings. One can easily pursue topics of conversation not directly related to the interview. This might be the latest world news, hobbies of the person, sports, family, etc. An important remembrance for any interviewer is to realize that his or her own personal posture and mannerism are critical to establishing rapport. If you are nervous and uncertain, this will be visible to the interviewee. Your personal attitude toward life and the organization will come through and color comments. Posture and positioning of the physical relationship of the interviewer to the interviewee can create a relaxed atmosphere or add to the stress. An interviewer should be a good listener, have eye contact, and be able to gently but firmly move the conversation along. Approximately ten minutes of time may be necessary for the rapport to be established.

To begin the actual part of the interview, that is obtaining information, one should be clear in stating the purpose of the interview. The purpose may include a description of the general areas to be included. It is important at this step to assure the person of confidentiality of names brought up during the conversation. If you will be taking notes, be sure and ask permission to take notes. The person will understand the need for notes since one may not be able to remember all of the information at the termination of the interview. A conversation might go like this:

Interviewer: Bob, I want to take this opportunity to visit with you about our hospital's policies, practices, and your own personal feeling regarding the strengths and weaknesses of this institution during your time of service. I will be taking notes as we move along in the conversation so that I can remember some of the comments. I want to reassure you that what you identify here will remain confidential.

Interview questions will begin at this time. A good place to begin is with questions focused on attitudes regarding the old job. Once again, the person is given the opportunity to relax. Questions about general job duties, preference for duties, and challenges are familiar and in the forefront of the person's memory. The recall is quick and easy. The person is comfortable in relating to the known. This can open up the actual reasons for dissatisfaction without having to specifically ask a direct question. Questions about the job can lead into areas related to personal attitudes. A cumulation of data from both sets of questions facilitates the transition to exploring further the reasons for leaving and a comparison of the old and new job.

Prior to concluding the interview, it is useful to ask the interviewee what ideas he/she might have if he/she could make any changes. In concluding the time together, thank the person and see that he/she is shown courtesy upon leaving.

Figure 12-1 provides a summary of a flow of an exit interview.

Figure 12-1 Sample note-taking guide for the interviewer. Source: *The Evaluation Interview*, by Richard A. Fear, New York: McGraw-Hill, Inc., 1978.

1. Establish rapport	5–10 minutes
2. State the purpose	2–5 minutes
3. Attitudes regarding the old job	15–20 minutes
A) outline of job duties	
B) crucial duties (place A* by the duties in A.)	
C) likes	
D) dislikes	
E) critical incidents	
F) workload	
G) educational background, skills, and abilities	
H) quality of training	
I) promotional opportunities	
J) personal recognition	
K) performance appraisal	
L) morale	
M) salary and benefits	
4. Reasons for leaving	10–15 minutes
5. Changes	10–15 minutes
6. Conclusion	5 minutes
Total time	47–70 minutes

What kinds of questions open the door for identifying training and development needs? In the broad perspective, does the employee have specific career goals that are not being met? How are these going to be better met elsewhere? Does the person have the feeling that he or she is a person or a number? More specifically, the following questions can provide direct information on training and development.

1. Let's begin by your outlining briefly some of the duties of your job.

2. Of the duties you just outlined, tell me three or four that are crucial to the performance of the job.

3. Tell me about some of the duties you liked the most and what you liked about performing those duties.

4. Now, tell me about some of the duties you liked the least and what you did not like about performing those duties.

5. Suppose you describe the amount of variety in your job.

6. Let's talk about the extent to which you feel you were given the opportunity to use your educational background, skills, and abilities on your job.

7. How would you assess the quality of training on the job?

8. In assessing the quality of supervision and/or management in your area, how would you go about describing it?

9. What or who has contributed most to your self-development?

10. Many of us improve our ability to relate to people as we mature. In what ways would you say that you have improved the most over the past two to three years?

11. I hear you speaking of significant achievements made on the job. Could you describe for me what enabled you to make those achievements?

12. As an individual employee, could you capsulize the attitude that you feel the company shows toward its employees? Do you feel like you are a contributing member of a team?

13. I would appreciate hearing your description of the philosophy that permeates this organization.

Some of these questions may not appear on first glance to be able to provide you with information on training and development needs. Questions that are directed more at communication, motivation, and leadership can, however, assist in a key area of training, namely management development programs. My point is that training and development should not be limited to only enhancement of professional skills, e.g., in nursing or physical therapy or accounting. Rather, training and development is meant to encompass the totality of needs wrapped up in the human person. These include personal career needs as well as skills and facilities for competent supervisors, team leaders, and managers.

The exit interview process is synergistic and directly related to the organization's interest in the person, as well as in the organization's own growth and development. The interviewer who is convinced that the individual is the key to the organization's productivity can identify in concert with the interviewee a rainbow of ideas, challenges, and opportunities.

NEEDS ASSESSMENT FROM EXIT INTERVIEWS

As indicated in this chapter, there are a number of places within the exit interview that have relevance for the trainer. The trainer needs to explore several questions:

1. Is there an exit interview within the organization? Obviously, if the response is "no," the questions cease.

2. Does the trainer have access to the exit interview information? If not, is there a way to get access? Again, if the answer to both these questions is "no," the process ceases. If the answer is "yes," the next question comes into play.

3. Will the information contained in the exit interview be useful for me? If the response is "no," again, the process ends. If the response is "yes," the trainer proceeds to get the information.

Out of the exit interview, a variety of needs may surface. The following is a partial listing of specific areas that an individual might enunciate as training/development needs:

- Labor Relations
  - do's and don'ts during a union campaign
- Risk Management
  - energy control
  - control of chemical substances
  - safety, e.g., maintaining access to critical areas of the organization, keeping floors in a condition that prevents accidents
- Quality Assurance
  - what is it?
  - what is my role?
  - how do I assure quality?
- Educational Programs
  - how do I do one?
  - where are the resources?
  - what is best for an inservice, how can I conduct one?
- Benefits
  - what does the organization offer?

  - what do they mean to me, can I explain them?
- Staffing
  - how do I go about staffing?
  - what competencies do I need in my work area?
  - how many people do I need?
- Budgeting
  - what is expected of me?
  - I don't know how to go about budgeting.
  - all these numbers just make me nervous.
  - how many supplies am I going to use this next year?
  - how many people will be in my unit?
- Team Development
- Leadership
  - what constitutes positive leadership?
  - what is my style?
  - what are my strengths and weaknesses?
  - how can I change?
  - how can I be accepted after I change?
- Meetings and Inservices
  - these are difficult for me so I rarely have them.
  - how to become comfortable with meetings and inservice?
  - how to involve people in planning and conducting them?
- Managerial Skills

• difficulty in communicating both written and/or verbal procedures, messages, policies, etc.

• inability or difficulty in managing or resolving conflict.

• organizing responsibilities so that they are done in a timely and efficient manner (I can't seem to get things done on time. I have too much to do. Procrastination is a real struggle for me).

• feedback and listening skills (I never seem to be able to understand what she wants of me. It's hard for me to focus on the topic. My mind is constantly off on trips).

- Personal Needs

• I am unable to concentrate because my family keeps coming to my mind.

• I am so moody and can't concentrate, I just can't remember things (could be a clue to chemical dependency problems).

- I really need some help in overcoming my fears of this job.
- this place is a constant source of pressure to me—needs indicating stress reduction or environmental stress reduction.
- Managing Job and Environmental Stresses
  - work area—what is its condition, tenor, spirit, etc.?
  - organization of work so each person has time for breaks and rest.

SUMMARY

To summarize, the organization must place a high priority on the interview in order for it to be successful. The interviewer must be familiar with the process and plan for each interview. Each is unique and commands the single attention of the one interviewing. A successful interview will suggest potential opportunities for the person and organization. When well planned, this experience can be the bridge for the departing employee to look back with pride, and acknowledge that this organization does care.

EXAMPLE: ABC COMPANY EMPLOYEE EXIT INTERVIEW REPORT

Date ________

Supervisor: ____

Interviewer: ____

If the interviewer is not the employee's supervisor, explain relationship:

____

Employee's name: ____

How long with company: ____

Briefly summarize positions held while at ABC: ____________________

____

____

____

____

Current position: ____

If in a supervisory position, list names of peers in group: ____________

____

____

Results of last three performance appraisals: ______________________________

____

____

____

Has the employee found a new position? Yes ______ No ______

If yes, with what company, and in what capacity: ___________________________

____

What makes the new position more attractive than the present one? _________

____

If the employee has not found a new position, what are his/her plans? ________

____

If the employee could change any one thing at ABC Company that would cause him/her to stay on, what would it be? ______ ________________________

____

____

____

What are some other possible reasons for the employee leaving? ___________

____

____

____

REFERENCES

Pretchett, Price. "Employee Attitude Surveys: A Natural Starting Point for Organizational Development." *Personnel Journal*, April 1975.

Embrey, Wanda R.; Monday, R. Wayne; and Poe, Robert M. "Exit Interviews: A Tool for Personnel Development." *The Personnel Administrator*, May 1979.

Wehnenberg, Stephen B. "The Exit Interview: Why Bother?" *Supervisory Management*, May 1980.

Burack, Elmer H., and Smith, Robert D., *Personnel Management: A Human Resource Systems Approach*. West Publishing Co., 1977.

Miner, John B., and Miner, May Green. *Personnel and Industrial Relations*. New York: MacMillan, 1977.

Weisman, Carol S., Alexander, Cheryl S.; and Chase, Gary A. "Evaluating Reasons for Nursing Turnover: Comparison of Exit Interview and Panel Data." *Evaluation and the Health Professions*, June 1981.

Beach, Dale. *Personnel.* New York: MacMillan, 1980.

Part III

The Assessment Support System

Part III has two major chapters. Chapter 13 is concerned with the considerations involved in the construction of the assessment plan. Assessments need to be planned thoroughly to be effective. Preliminary planning saves time throughout the assessment process. There is no substitute for front-end analysis.

Chapter 13 also looks at questionnaire/interview construction. Most every assessment involves some type of questioning process. This chapter provides ideas and suggestions about that process.

Finally, Chapter 14 discusses evaluation—how do we know that the assessment accomplished what it was designed to accomplish? A series of evaluation questions are presented that provide a framework for evaluating the assessment.

13

Planning Considerations In Designing the Assessment

INTRODUCTION

This chapter is concerned with planning considerations in the design of an assessment. First, we will discuss a general generic model of planning. Parts of the model have been discussed in previous chapters. The intent of the generic model is to pull these pieces together and provide a framework to fit them in.

Second, we will discuss the questioning process as a design consideration in planning. As part of the planning time, we are concerned with questions like "What are the ways I might ask this question?" "What are the ramifications for asking questions in various ways?" "Are there special considerations when I am interviewing?" etc. The intent of this section is to address the questioning process as a critical part of the plan.

Third, the chapter will briefly discuss the planning for the analysis of the information coming out of the assessment. Obviously, an important part of the planning time is thinking about how the analysis will take place.

Fourth, time will be spent with the concept of survey feedback. At some point, it is useful to feed back to the organization the results of the survey. The organization (or some part of it) then has an opportunity to respond to the information.

THE PLAN

Developing the Plan

"Nothing is as practical as a good plan."

The above paraphrase from Kurt Lewin ("Nothing is so practical as a good theory" in Marrow's *The Practical Theorist*) is a prevailing theme in this book. An assessment plan is vital to the successful implementation of the assessment process. Without a plan, an assessment can readily become sidetracked, important information may not be properly handled, and the laxness of the assessment may make it difficult to sell the results to decision-makers. Lack of a plan will probably result in inefficiency and ineffectiveness.

A well-thought-out plan rivets the energy and resources of the persons involved toward a target. It channels people, resources, and activities in such a way as to provide a meaningful outcome. And, a plan provides a benchmark from which measurements can be made.

Thus far, the exercise sections of this book have been aimed at providing the essential ingredients of a plan. Let us take a moment and review some of those ingredients.

First, the position of training assessment was evaluated informally. A variety of exercises looked at the context in which an assessment could occur, and the place training held within the organization.

Second, a statement of purpose was written: What is the general purpose of the assessment being conducted? What is the desired outcome?

Third, the purpose was broken down into assessment objectives. A minimum of three objectives were identified, written about, and revised.

Fourth, each objective was broken down further into conditions "A" and conditions "B." Condition "A" is a specific condition pertaining to the present, and condition "B" is a specific condition desired in the future. So, the progression has been from a purpose statement, to objectives, to specific conditions currently existing and desired in the future.

Fifth, criteria critical to the needs assessment methodology before it can be adapted to specific organizations have been identified. While the criteria might change and shift at a minute's notice (e.g., we have a new CEO who wants things done her way), the tentative list has been assembled.

Sixth, and last, criteria have been matched to the methodologies. The progression has been from a multitude of methodologies to a select few.

Essentially, much of the planning work has been done. Now it is a simple matter of structuring the plan. At this point, a model becomes useful. A model for planning provides a framework for organization. A model provides a checklist of questions that need to be answered. A number of planning models for training and development might be used, e.g., Sauer and Holland (*Planning In-House Training*), Park (*Management Braining*), and Craig (*Hip Pocket Guide to Planning and Evaluation*). The framework suggested here is a combination of what has been discussed thus far in this chapter and Craig's model for planning and evaluation. Since the next chapter deals directly with evaluation, steps 5 and 6 of Craig's model will not be discussed now.

Craig's model for planning and evaluation includes the following points:

1. Defining the problem
2. Setting the objective
3. Choosing among alternative strategies
4. Preparing for implementation
5. Designing the evaluation
6. Using evaluation information

The planning model that we will discuss in detail in this section includes steps 1 to 5 of Craig's model and one additional step. The additional step is developing a purpose statement. Every plan needs to have a statement of purpose—what is it this plan is intended to do? Prior to defining the problem, this step will be included.

Plan Design

- Step 1: Develop a Statement of Purpose

A plan needs to have a statement of purpose. What is the intent of the plan? For example, a university was performing a needs assessment for a community. Its statement of purpose was

> Consistent with our goal of meeting the needs of the community we serve, we will survey community members about the activities they would like to see us offer. The result of such a survey will be targeted programs and activities to address community needs.

While this purpose statement is somewhat wordy, it illustrates some important points. First, it provides an idea of what the results will be. It will identify needs and then develop programming to meet those needs. Second, it merges this activity with a larger organizational purpose. The purpose statement demonstrates how the assessment is integral to the organizational mission statement. The purpose statement proposes the expected results and ties those results to the organizational purpose. Nadler (*Designing Training Programs*, p. 8) illustrates clearly how the change in focus (purpose) will change the model the trainer will select. Purpose is a significant variable.

- Step 2: Identify Problem

What is the problem this assessment will address? Perhaps it will address a problem of turnover. Maybe there is a problem of quality control. Whatever it may be, an important part of the discipline of assembling a plan is to cite a problem target.

A significant part of this is identifying the present condition. Documenting what is currently going on is necessary to an accurate description of the problem. What has happened to cause this problem to be identified? Or, what has not happened that has caused this problem to be identified?

Another aspect of this is identifying the one who has decided that there is a problem to be addressed. This was discussed earlier in Chapter 1. A recent example from a university provides an example. A problem was defined to be low student classroom attendance prior to the holidays. A plan was implemented to correct the condition. However, it became clear that the missing question was "For whom is this a problem?" The decision-maker made a decision presuming, "for whom it was a problem," and the result was unproductive.

Craig (p. 16) suggests that another question be asked by the planner at this time: "What is my interest in working on this problem?" The trainer needs to be aware of his/her own interests in doing the assessment. By identifying personal interests, the trainer can be aware of possible trouble areas, i.e., areas where his/her own agenda may get in the way of the assessment process. The ideal start for the plan is the identification of a specific problem to be resolved.

Warwick and Lininger (*The Sample Survey: Theory and Practice*, p. 24) suggest several important questions that can be aptly raised at this time. The major ones are "Is this survey necessary? Will it provide the information needed? Is a survey the best way of getting the information?" and, "Can the survey be merged with some other method?" Essentially, these questions question the assessment itself.

- Step 3: Selecting the Objectives

A statement of purpose has been given; a problem has been identified. Now comes the time to set specific objectives. Assume the problem identified is not having supervisory input into the supervisory training program.

One sample objective for the plan may be

> By January 1, have a specific assessment method that will be used on 60 percent of the supervisors.

Objectives provide specific benchmarks for exploration.

• Step 4: Choosing Among Alternative Methods

The plan here is one of assessment. There are many ways to conduct assessments and the purpose of this step is to identify some of those ways. By identifying the criteria that must be conformed to and finding the methods that accommodate that criteria, this step may proceed rather quickly. Chapter 4 provided specific criteria for making this selection.

In looking at each alternative another question needs to be raised: "Do we have the resources needed to carry out this alternative?" If we have been diligent in looking at the criteria, most likely the answer to this question will be yes. However, it is useful to list which resources will be needed for each method.

It is also useful to realize the quality of the alternative and the level of acceptance it needs. Maier ("Improving Decisions in an Organization") discusses these two dimensions as they relate to decisions. Quality refers to the objective or impersonal quality needed; acceptance refers to the way the people who must carry out the decision feel about it. Three types of decisions arise:

1. High quality—low acceptance. Here the focus is on "quality." Once quality is taken care of, then acceptance is discussed. A trainer involved in a purchase of new equipment may choose this alternative. In an assessment, this type of decision may be made with regard to questionnaire design.

2. High acceptance—low quality. The key here is that the process goes nowhere if it is not accepted. If the decision is not acceptable to those carrying it out, it will end at that point. Trainers are part of many decisions where high acceptance is key.

3. High acceptance—high quality. The best of both worlds. The decision about alternatives must involve both of these with equal vigor.

These decisions are summarized below:

	Low Acceptance	High Acceptance
Low Quality	XXXXX	
High Quality		

If the implementation involves a high degree of cooperation from others, it will be necessary to involve those individuals in the selection process. If, on the other hand, the strategy selected will not require significant cooperation, a high quality/low commitment decision may be made. Again recalling the discussion in Chapter 2, the "who" of this decision may be responsible for a go/no-go decision.

• Step 5: Preparing for Implementation

The strategy has been selected. It has adapted itself to criteria and practicality tests. Now comes an even closer analysis. People, resources, time, and activities need to be assessed.

One way to organize the plan is by developing a Gantt Chart. A Gantt Chart coordinates the activities that need to be done within a time frame. The steps for developing a Gantt Chart are

1. List all the activities that need to be done to carry out the plan.

2. Identify the completion date by which all the activities will need to be done.

3. Along the Y axis, list the activities.

4. The X axis will now become the time line. The end point of the X axis will be the established completion date. The line is then divided into appropriate units, e.g. days, weeks, months, etc.

5. The amount of time it takes to perform each activity is plotted on the X, Y axis.

For example, assume our project is to develop an assessment plan. The following steps have been identified: (1) develop sample questionnaire, (2) pretest questionnaire, (3) send out questionnaires, and (4) analyze and develop plan for training.

And, the steps are to be completed in 15 days. Our Gantt Chart would look like this:

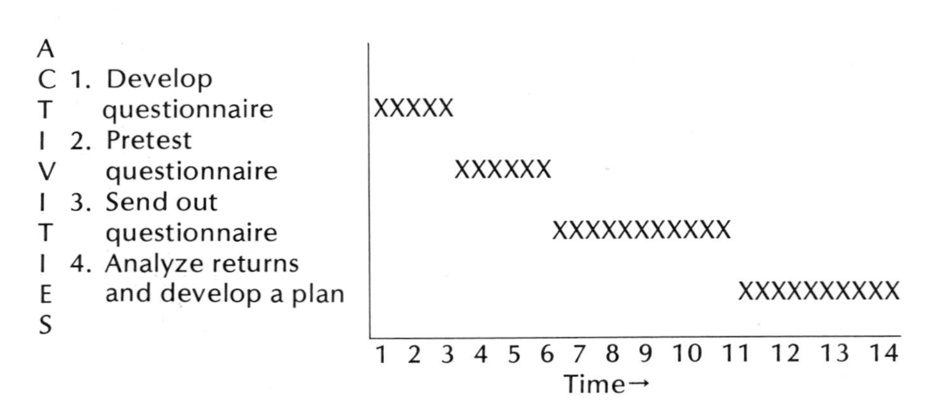

A useful spinoff from doing a Gantt Chart is the listing of activities. By identifying the major activities that need to occur and approximately when they need to be occurring, we are able to readily assign resources to the project. The following chart provides an example:

Activity	Persons Involved	Resources Involved

The plan provides a focused way of approaching the task. The needs assessment plan is designed to obtain information useful to decision-making processes.

The next two steps of Craig's model—designing the evaluation and using evaluation information—will be discussed in the next chapter on evaluation.

THE QUESTIONING PROCESS

Questioning Guides and Interviews

The plan for the assessment has been developed. Some part of that plan will deal with how information is to be collected. There are two major ways in which this can happen. The first is through observation of the work being done. The second is through asking questions.

This section deals with the art of raising questions both in questionnaires and in interviews. A note of caution regarding this section: Zemke and Kramlinger (*Figuring Things Out*, p. 158) point out that effective surveys begin with leg work, not pencil work. Getting to the point where one is ready to write questions demands doing homework. It means talking to people, making observations, reading, researching, etc. This section only makes sense after significant planning and exploring of the purpose and objectives have already taken place.

Questioning Guides

Any questioning process has at least two parts. The first is concerned with the intent and purpose of the questions being asked. This is an obvious part. The reason questions are asked is to get information. The second part, and equally important, is motivating the respondent. If the respondent is not motivated to respond, the desired information will not be obtained. This section focuses explicitly on the guides to creating questions. Later in the interview discussion, the issue of motivating the respondent will be addressed.

The design of a good questionnaire involves planning. Questionnaires just do not happen—they are created.

Breen (*Do-It-Yourself Marketing Research*) offers several guides for putting together questionnaires. First, ask only questions that relate to the purpose of the questioning process. Outline exactly what material or information is needed and proceed from that point. As you put down a question, continually ask yourself "How will this question provide me with useful information? Does it relate to the objective I have?" If your response is no, drop the question. In some cases you may be tempted to use a "hitchhiker," i.e., a question that is not directly related to your purposes. Perhaps the intention is to do some fishing, i.e., to cast about and see if a particular question can be slipped into the information you are collecting. Or it may be that the "boss" says, "Since you are circulating this questionnaire anyway, include a question about how they like the new compensation policy." The guideline is, if the question is not relevant, throw it out (and be aware of exceptions to the guide).

Second, make the questioning process as interesting as possible. This becomes a motivational matter if you are using a questionnaire—make the format as appealing as possible. A useful fantasy is to imagine yourself as the respondent holding the questionnaire and making a decision about what to do with it. What would it take to intrigue you sufficiently so that you would take the time to fill it out? Or, which question in an interview would be interesting for you to answer? Essentially, this guide focuses on how to captivate the respondent to such a degree that she is motivated to respond. Once questions are decided on, a key consideration is "How do I make these questions interesting?"

One part of the response to how to make the questions interesting depends on the words that are selected. Can I change the words in a way that sustains the original intent *and* creates more excitement? Another part is the sequence in which the questions are posed. Would a certain sequence of questions create more motivation? A third part is the design of the questionnaire itself—does it contribute to a person filling it out or not? While questionnaires are not intrinsically exciting, we need to explore how to make them sufficiently interesting for a person to read and respond to.

Third, don't ask the respondents to do work. A question that requires supervisors to go through the records of the supervisees and pull out various training records may be too demanding. Again, think about your own responses. If you are expected to do a fair amount of digging, there is a good chance that you will probably set the interview/questionnaire aside for as long as possible or file it in the circular file. The questionnaire should be designed to produce minimum effort on the part of the respondent.

Fourth, be aware of the difference between designing an interesting questioning process and being "cute," i.e., using lots of witticisms with no real significance. The pitfalls lie in either being too businesslike (dull) or being too interesting (cute). There is a middle ground. One way of finding it is to ask how you would respond to the questionnaire. Another is to ask friends how they respond to the questions. Or better yet, ask a sample of people you will be surveying for their responses.

Fifth, a major part of the battle is won if the respondent sees a relationship between the questions being asked and his personal interests. Most assessments have a clear relationship—the more accurate the information, the higher the probability that the needs will be met. The respondent should have a clear understanding about that relationship.

This relationship may be made clear to the respondent in the introduction to the questionnaire. Either verbally or in written form, the intent and use of the questionnaire must be made clear to the respondent. If the respondent sees or hears that the outcome of this questionnaire will affect her directly, and she is convinced of its impact, she will be motivated to respond.

Sixth, clarity is a crucial factor. And, clarity is in the "eyes of the beholder." You may find the questionnaire perfectly clear but does the respondent? If the respondent does not know what you are asking him, there is a good chance that the information gathered will not be good data. For example, a question like "What training would you like?" might elicit a variety of interpretations, e.g., what would I like with regard to my job, what I need for my job, anything that interests me, etc. The question is ambiguous and unclear. Perhaps the best way to avoid ambiguity is to have others look over the questions (pretest). Not only should you have the person respond with "yes, it is clear" or "no, it is not clear" but you should also have the person disclose what he is thinking as he reads the questions. Get him to think out loud in your presence, and as he does so, listen for assumptions he is making about the question. Since you have been working on the questionnaire for some time, it is probably very evident to you what the questions mean. Another person—especially one from the target group—may readily show you the areas where there is confusion. For the reader's sake, it is critical that the questions be clear.

Seventh, and pertinent to the sixth, if you have time, plan for several revisions of the questioning process. Your original draft may be reviewed by several persons or groups. After you have reworked it, you may send it out again to a few others for their critique. The result is that after a few trials the questioning process should have smoothed out the major kinks. A key method is to have your target group review the drafts. A fellow manager may understand your meaning clearly, but a first-line supervisor may not. If your target is that first-line supervisor, make sure you pretest it with her.

Eighth, use the pretest on a sample of the persons you will be surveying. This was discussed earlier and is restated here for emphasis. Plan to build from trial runs.

Ninth, and last, pay attention to appearances. This relates to the second point. Be aware of how the interview setting can facilitate or block responses. Be alert to problems of appearance within the questionnaire; there may be such things as typos, poorly mimeographed material, hard to read print, etc. Poor copy may mean poor return on the questionnaire. Pay attention to the total appearance of the questions and questionnaire.

To summarize:

1. Only ask questions that are relevant to the purpose of the assessment.

2. Make the questions as interesting as possible—remember, you are responsible for motivating the respondent.

3. Don't ask respondents to work.

4. Avoid questions that are "cute."

5. Show the respondent how the questionnaire is useful to him or her. Make that relationship clear.

6. State questions clearly.

7. Plan for several revisions of the questioning process.

8. Pretest the questioning process on a sample of people you may be surveying.

9. Pay attention to the physical appearance of the questionnaire or to the interview setting.

The above says one thing: Put yourself in the respondent's place—would you take the time to fill out this questionnaire? Why?

Kornhauser and Sheatsley ("Questionnaire Construction and the Interview Process") suggest several useful questions for you to consider as you look through the questionnaire. Some of the questions are

- Is this question necessary? How will the answer be useful for me?
- Are several questions needed in place of just one? Do I need to subdivide it?
- Is this question adequate?
- Will the respondents have this information?
- Does the question invite the interpretation I want?
- Does the question need to be more specific?
- Is the question loaded, i.e., does it invite a biased response?
- Will the respondents be willing to answer this question?

- Is the wording objectionable?
- Is there a natural progression in the questioning sequence?

The process of designing a questioning process is an art as well as an science. The guides presented thus far are intended to provide a sense of the possibilities one has when designing a questioning process. Now we will shift to the types of questions that may be asked and their uses.

Questioning Techniques

Asking a question is simple. However, asking a question that gets the information you want in a usable form may not be so simple. This may be the right context for the comical expression: "I know you believe you understood what you think I said . . . But, I'm not sure you realize that what you heard is not what I meant. . . ." There are a variety of ways to ask questions. This section will present standard types of questions that may be asked along with some of the problems associated with these types of questions.*

Direct close-ended question. The following is a direct close-ended question:

> Do you have a need for training in grievance handling?
> Yes ______ No ______.

The respondent must make an immediate choice. She either responds "yes" or "no." The value of this type of question is that it may lead one toward more detailed questions. A specific answer is given that can quickly and easily be tabulated. It is straightforward and not very demanding. The question may also be used as a screen for other questioning.

The problem with this type of question is that the respondent is forced to make a choice even though she may not have a definite answer. The question allows only a "yes" or "no" when the true answer might be "some." The respondent is forced into a polarized response.

Multiple choice. Probably there is no one who is not familiar with a multiple choice-type of question. Just in case you are not, here is an example:

---

*Much of the material on types of questions was gathered through discussion and lectures at the American Management Association Consumer Market Research Course held in Chicago, Ill., August 24–26, 1978. It has been adapted to fit needs assessment.

Which of the following training needs is most important to you at your present job?

A. Delegation
B. Conflict management
C. Stress management
D. Decision-making

There are several advantages to this type of question. First, there are more choices than "yes or no." The choice is less likely to be arbitrary. Second, with proper development, the lists may get at most of the related alternatives. Third, they are easy to tabulate and analyze. Fourth, they are not very demanding and the costs are low.

Some disadvantages: First, the crucial alternative answers may not be known. Perhaps a vital alternative is "problem-solving." However, the choice is not given. Also, the answer may have a good deal of overlap and not be differentiated in the respondent's mind. Lastly, the ordering of the responses may lead to biased reactions.

Rating scales. Rating scales ask the respondent to choose a point along some scale that best approximates his response. The following is an example:

	1	2	3	4	5
The ability to set priorities is ______ for my job.	Not Important				Very Important

The obvious advantage of a rating scale is that it provides more of a scope for a particular response—a certain intensity of feeling can be recorded. A "5" response says more to me than a "3" response. Questions are fairly easy to assemble and they lend themselves nicely to analysis.

The major disadvantages are (1) the intervals on the scale may not be clear in the respondent's mind. For example, what does 3 to 4 mean on the above scale? (2) The respondent may not have a knowledge of the different levels. (3) The terms simply may not be clear, e.g., what does "good" mean? and (4) the question may not be meaningful.

Preference questions. Preference questions get at likes and dislikes. A sample of one is

Where do you prefer training to take place?

A. In-house
B. Outside of the office at a neutral location

A preference question provides quick responses to likes and dislikes. A preference question may also involve a scale that will disclose the intensity and magnitude of the preference.

The major problem with the preference question is that it provides very little information about the preference, e.g., I have to select between two or more givens but my preference is something quite different. And they may have little relevance to what happens in a real setting. While I have a particular preference, my actual behavior is quite different from it.

Ranking questions. Ranking questions ask for an ordering of items. The following is an example:

> Rank the following four training needs from 1 to 4 with 1 being most important for you and 4 being least important.
>
> ______ ability to motivate others
> ______ ability to delegate to others
> ______ ability to manage time
> ______ ability to make decisions

Rankings provide information quickly. They can be quickly used to identify the priority need, and they provide information about what the respondents think (within the range of choices) is most important. And, they are easy to tabulate for analysis.

However, a ranking does not indicate the degree of preference between the items. We know one item was ranked 3 and another 4. But we do not know if the gap between 3 and 4 was tremendous or insignificant. And after 4 or 5 items, the job of ranking can become overwhelming. The respondent may no longer be able to discriminate clearly.

Open-ended questions. Thus far, the type of questions that we have been discussing are close-ended, i.e., a set of responses have been determined for the respondent. Open-ended questions do not have preselected responses. Two examples are

> What is your number 1 training need?
> Why did you select that need?

The first question is a kick-off question. It gets the questioning process started. The second question is a probe for more information. Many of the questions in the workbook section have followed this type of format: The first question is general and the second one is more specific.

The advantages to this type of question are obvious. The major one is that the respondent supplies the answer. The respondent selects his or her preference from numerous alternatives and writes it down. The major disadvantage is that this type of question is not easy to tabulate or even interpret. How do I know what the respondent really meant when she selected a specific item? If the respondent writes down "stress management," what is she thinking about?

The above, then, represent some of the questions that might be used. To summarize, the types of questions surveyed so far are

1. Direct close-ended
2. Multiple choice
3. Rating scales
4. Preference
5. Rank order
6. Open-ended

Obviously, there are other types of question formats that might be used, e.g., fill-in-the-blank, different rating scales, etc. The questions presented thus far are simply building blocks. They represent launching points for the questionnaire.

Also, be aware that some of the weaknesses associated with certain questions may be corrected by combining the question formats, e.g., using a rating scale but leaving room for a comment. Most of the questionnaires at the end of this chapter provide examples of combination questions.

Thus far the focus has been on discussing the interview and the questionnaire process jointly under the title of the "questioning process." However, interviewing does have some distinct characteristics that are important to recognize. The next section provides a quick look at interviewing.

The Interview

In a monogram by Webb and Slancik ("The Only Wheel in Town—The Interview"), the authors talk about the four major sources of information reporters have:

A. Observation
B. Secondhand data
C. Third-person reportage
D. The interview

The authors emphasize that of these four, the interview is the most perilous and unreliable method. Why? The interview combines all the risks of the previous methods, i.e., poor perception of what is happening, biased accounts, and is also a joint collaboration between the interviewer/interviewee. Many of these were discussed previously. Yet the interview is still one of the mainstays for gathering information. When I want to know a person's thoughts, feelings, or attitudes, the most efficient way of finding out is to ask.

The interview is a major source of information. And the interview has the same two objectives any questioning process has: (1) motivating the interviewee to share the desired information and (2) getting the desired information.

While the focus of this discussion is on the interview process, it needs to be understood that the interview is a process of interaction and influence. Kahn and Cannell (*The Dynamics of Interviewing*, p. 20) describe the interview in this way:

> If we are able to understand the process of interaction between interviewer and respondent, we cannot concern ourselves only with the mechanics of the interviewing process. . . . We must also be concerned instead with the goals, attitudes, beliefs and motives of the principals in the interview.

Interviewing needs to be seen as more than technique. It is a communication process in which both parties are involved.

Interviews may be seen as consisting of three phases: the pre-interview, the interview, and the post-interview.

Pre-interview involves the plan for the interview. What is the goal? What questions need to be asked to get the desired information? How do I order the questions in an appropriate pattern? (Note: We are talking about having a plan.) Zemke and Kramlinger (p. 101) provide several suggestions for pre-interview reflection. Some of these are (1) learn the local language. Be aware of important jargon which may be part of the interview. (2) Hold an introductory meeting with persons who will be interviewed to clarify the interview purpose. (3) Develop an actual flow chart for the meeting. (4) Don't structure the interview around yes and no responses—it is more important to let the interviewee ramble than to stick rigidly with the outline. (5) Screen your questions through a neutral person before the interview. (6) Cluster your questions topically—the interview should convey a sense of flow. (7) Conclude with an open-ended question—"Is there anything else I should have asked?" (8) Schedule the meeting at the interviewee's convenience.

Again, the preparation is necessary for the interview to be effective and efficient.

Next comes the *interview proper*. An immediate goal should be to build rapport with the person in the first few minutes of the interview. Unless some kind of trust develops, the interview stagnates. Everything, from the ambiance of the room to the kind of greeting the person receives upon entering the room, contributes to establishing rapport with the person. Without some kind of rapport, the interview may go nowhere. (This in itself will provide the interviewer with information, but probably not useful information.)

Nadler (*Feedback and Organizational Development*, p. 110) identifies the following questions that need to be resolved between the interviewer and the interviewee:

1. Who am I?
2. Why am I here and what am I doing?
3. Who do I work for?
4. What do I want from you and why?
5. How will I protect the confidentiality of your responses?
6. Who will have access to the data?
7. What's in it for you?
8. Can I be trusted?

It is important to address these questions during the early part of the interview. They form the basis for the contract between the interviewee and the interviewer.

Zemke and Kramlinger (p. 105) discuss types of tension that will be part of the interview: task tension and interpersonal tension. Interviewees will be asking three types of questions about the interviewer: (1) Why is this person interviewing me? (2) Is this person qualified to talk with me? (3) Does this person really understand my outlook?

The early stages of the interview are a time of building rapport/trust and making sure the interviewee is clear about the intent and purpose of the interview.

The following is an example of the importance of establishing rapport with an interviewee. I arrived at the interviewee's office late and in my haste to get "on with the interview," I simply jumped into the content—"the purpose of this interview is. . . ." Nothing happened. Responses from the interviewee were short and quick. Finally, I simply decided to "write this one off." The interview ended. The interviewee and I began to chat about family and weather. In a few minutes, the interviewee responded with, "You know, I have been thinking about that question you asked a while ago. . . ." Now the real interview began.

The time has come to approach the task portion of the interview. There are certain kinds of behavior that facilitate the interview. An interviewer may invite the interviewee to respond by

1. Listening reflectively—"sounds like . . ."
2. Echoing remarks—"I am . . ."

3. Redirecting the discussion back to the interview when one gets sidetracked.

4. Avoiding arguments with the interviewee.

5. Being time-conscious—don't let an hour's interview become an hour and a half without a conscious decision to extend it.

6. Maintaining a general attitude that the person you are talking with is important and has useful information for you.

8. Reinforcing transactions nonverbally—nodding your head, etc.

Genua (*The Employee's Guide to Interviewing*, pp. 59ff.) identifies a number of questioning techniques. Among these are elaboration (tell me more about that), clarification (I didn't follow that—tell me how it fits), repetition (repeating what has been said), looping back (returning to something that was previously stated), requesting specific examples (give me an example of that), exploring feelings (how do you feel when . . .), and silence (simply allowing a comfortable silence to develop). Many techniques can be used to facilitate the collecting of information.

A final note on the interview. One question that I am frequently asked is "Is it best to take notes or to record?" The question that is being raised here is how to gather the data from the interview in such a way that I do not forget it and do not interfere with the flow.

There are three major ways of recording information:

1. Remembering. The interviewer relies on his memory to remember the highlights of the interview. After the interview, notes or recordings may be made.

2. Note-taking. The interviewer takes notes during the interview. This may be a set of complex notes or it may be a shorthand method of keeping notes.

3. Audio or video recordings. This is obviously the most extensive method for keeping track of the interview. Recording frees the interviewer to give her full attention to the interviewee. And the interviewer does not waste energy "trying to remember" what has been said.

Remembering is efficient. It requires nothing other than the interviewee and the interviewer. The big drawback is the difficulty of remembering sufficient information and nonverbal clues. While persons may be trained to increase their memory capacity, the number of transactions that take place during the interview provide a great deal of complexity. Much will not be remembered.

Note-taking is next. Note-taking can be done in unobtrusive

ways that do not interfere with the flow of the interview. Zemke and Kramlinger (p. 109) provide examples of note-taking procedures. Note-taking increases the probability that key thoughts and transactions will be remembered. The problem, again, is incompleteness. Notes are taken via the interviewer's filters (something strikes me as significant and I write it down). Also, note-taking may become a stimulus-response process encouraging the interviewee to respond in certain ways (I notice that you write down things when I talk about my relationship with a co-worker but not when I talk about a subordinate). Nadler (p. 72) provides an anecdote about note-taking. Early in his career, his wife would take notes during interviews. However, they found that her note-taking became a controlling factor—she had the control because she was the one who wrote things down. The interviewees watched her every move.

Audio or video recordings provide the most extensive form of recording the interview. A major benefit is that when the interviewer goes back to the recording, she will frequently hear things that she missed during the interview. Suddenly, something said in passing takes on a new significance. New connections are made. The major drawback is intrusion into the interview. If the interviewee is uncomfortable with recordings, they may impede the process. Also, if video is used, cost may become a factor. Finally, this method may be an overkill of information. Hours of tape may be disproportionate to the purpose.

The methods one selects depend upon the nature of the assessment and the familiarity and comfort of the interviewer with the interviewee. In conformance with the theme of this book, instead of one method, one may readily combine many, e.g., not taking notes during the interview but immediately after it.

So far rapport has been built, content has been gathered, and now is the time for closure. The interview has established a relationship. The closing of it should not be abrupt. Time needs to be built into closure. There may be questions about what will happen next and in some settings, the interviewee will leave the interview with a specific action in mind. Closure is a time for confirming rapport once again.

The third phase is the post-interview. For the interviewer this is a time for analyzing and tabulating the information gathered during the actual interview. Some methods for doing that will be discussed later in another section. This is a time for summarizing the data from the interview. If the interviews are part of a survey feedback method, then one of the post-interview actions will be to send the results of the interview back to the interviewees. Interview notes may have to be typed out or recordings may need to be transcribed. This attention to detail will clarify the analysis and identify common themes.

For the interviewee, the post-interview is a time of waiting, and perhaps, anticipating the next steps. The questions asked may have intentionally or unintentionally raised expectations on the part of the interviewee. It is this author's strong belief that a crucial development during this period is providing some type of feedback to the interviewee about the results of the interview. Perhaps this might be access to a written summary of the survey, or perhaps attendance at a meeting where the summary will be discussed. The interviewee has provided input; it is appropriate that he/she receive feedback.

This is also a time of following through on post-interview actions. If the interview has identified a specific training need, it may be appropriate for the interviewer to check back and note if the interviewee has pursued the necessary training.

The major strength of the interview is face-to-face contact. Nonverbal signals become important information. The major strength is also a weakness—interviewers and interviewees influence each other by a face-to-face relationship. This may result in potentially biased information.

Both the interview and the questionnaire process culminate in the same product: a body of collected data to be analyzed and turned into useful information. That is the next section of the chapter: reflections on data analysis.

THE ANALYSIS AND FEEDBACK OF DATA

The Data Analysis

The assessment is complete. Or at least, the data has been collected. Now the question is, how do we make sense of the data? How can we take large sums of data and make sufficient sense out of it so that we can base decisions on it? Essentially, we begin to raise statistical questions.

As with most topics in this book, statistics become a tremendous study in and of themselves. The intent of this section is not to provide the reader with statistical techniques but, rather, to provide a series of suggestions for expediting the analysis. One major resource for the reader who would like to explore further is Fitz-Gibbon and Morris (*How to Calculate Statistics*). Fitz-Gibbon and Morris provide an excellent overview of statistics in a very understandable and readable way. And, if the particular assessment is even more complex than the techniques under discussion, then the next step is to find someone who has the necessary expertise. However, according to my experience, the tests suggested by Fitz-Gibbon and Morris should be sufficient for most needs assessments.

Why use statistics? Fitz-Gibbon and Morris suggest three major reasons. First, statistics provide a means of summarizing data. A median, for example, can condense a capsule of information from several hundred responses. The result is that many numbers become represented by one or just a few.

Second, statistics provide a means of measuring just how seriously we need to regard differences between results. We can begin to get a sense of how likely it is that a certain result is the product of a chance occurrence or of some form of intervention.

Third, statistics allow us to identify relationships between various sets of data. Perhaps we would like to compare a group of persons who want a certain type of training with a group that does not want that type of training. Again, we have some techniques that allow comparisons.

Regardless of the type of analysis that will be used, an important step is identifying the frequency of responses. The examples in the appendix provide samples of frequencies used with both qualitative data and quantitative data. For many needs assessments, frequency of responses will be a major tool. By developing a frequency table, one can quickly determine where the responses lie. The tables will indicate visually if the responses are skewed in one direction or another. And the frequency table will indicate if there are outlying responses. Essentially, the frequency table will provide a visual picture of the data.

For example, suppose we have a question relating to the preferred time for training. We have three options: morning, afternoon, and evening. The responses are: 15 for morning, 1 for afternoon, and 30 for evening. The responses are weighted for evening, but we may want to check the outlying responses for morning.

Beyond the frequency table, we have a number of other options readily at hand. One option is the average or the mean, which is simply the sum of the responses divided by the number of the respondents. It is useful when a whole series of numbers needs to be summarized. However, when a mean is given, it is important to include standard deviation. The reason the standard deviation is important with a mean is illustrated in the following chart. When the average is looked at alone, the results may be misleading.

Item 1:	1 3 responses	2	3 Average	4	5 3 responses
Item 2:	1	2	3 3 responses	4	5

In both Item 1 and Item 2, the average is 3. Yet there is quite a significant difference in meaning. When standard deviation is also given along with the mean, the score becomes especially useful because it shows how far a particular score is from the mean. It indicates the clustering of frequencies.

When an average is not needed for other statistical tests, but a quick estimate of the scores is needed, a median is useful. A median is the mid-score in a set of responses. It will provide a quick look at points of emphasis within a set of scores.

Many more statistical tests could be touched upon. However, the above is a quick illustration of some of the potential uses. A wholly different area deals with a comparison of responses to data sets. Again, the references touch on those.

One important note. Remember that numbers need to be demystified. It can be a trap to assume that subjective responses that have been turned into numbers can now be readily quantified. Do not read into the numbers more than what is there. The numbers simply represent the perception of a particular respondent to a particular question.

Survey Feedback

The plan for the assessment (or study) has been discussed. The typical flow for a survey will be

1. Developing the survey plan.

2. Using those methods that have been decided upon; collecting the data.

3. Analyzing the data.

4. Making decisions based on data.

Nadler provides the following model for survey feedback*:

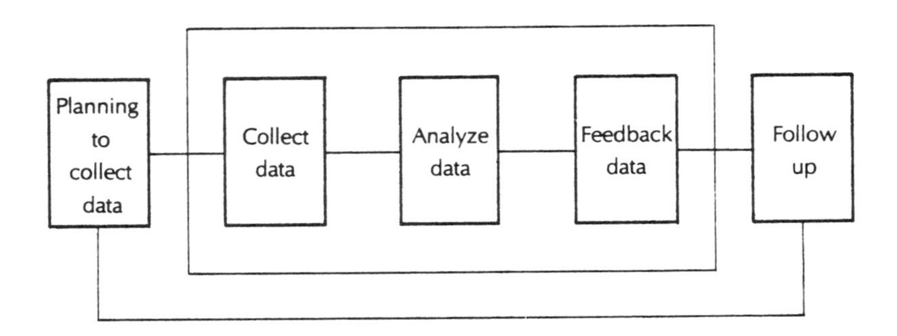

*Nadler, *Feedback and Organizational Development.* 1977, Addison-Wesley, Reading, Mass., p. 43. Reprinted with permission.

Note an important additional step in the Nadler model—the data is fed back to the client system. Instead of the assessor being the sole interpreter of the data, making assumptions about it and the training needed, the data is fed back to the participants, encouraging their interpretations as well. The appendices contain a number of cases illustrating this method.

The basic process of survey feedback might proceed as follows. First the data is collected. Next the data is analyzed and conclusions are drawn about appropriate actions. Finally, the analysis and conclusions are fed back to the client group for criticism and comments. There are several advantages to this approach. The first one is that the feedback provides an important check on the interpretations that are being made about the data; the feedback group may offer significant new insights about some of the data.

The second advantage, related to the first, is that the feedback group may develop an implementation plan of action for correcting the problems identified.

Third, the feedback method provides the feedback group with a sense of ownership—they have direct input to the interpretation of the survey and to the actions suggested. The result will be a commitment to the final plan of assessment. Instead of letting something be done to them, they have a voice in the process.

It is my belief that the feedback step is a critical part of any survey.

SUMMARY

This chapter has looked at many aspects of developing the assessment plan. A general planning process has been developed along with specific hints about questioning design, interviews, etc. The objective has not been to develop a thorough discussion of these aspects but to identify them.

Spitzer (1979) provides a nice summary of do's and don'ts about surveys. The following lists identify some of those Do's and Don'ts.*

Do

1. Begin with easy, nonthreatening items.
2. Use simple and direct language.
3. Make items as brief as possible.

---

*Reprinted with permission from the May 1979 issue of TRAINING, the Magazine of Human Resources Development, Lakewood Publications, Minneapolis, MN.

4. Emphasize crucial words in each item.
5. Leave adequate space for respondents to make comments.
6. Group items into coherent categories.
7. Have concise instructions.
8. Provide some variety in items.
9. Provide clear instructions on what to do with completed questionnaires.
10. Use professional production methods.
11. Provide incentives for a promptly returned questionnaire.
12. Plan how you will analyze data.
13. Consult experts and others.
14. Test your questionnaire.
15. Be prepared to handle missing data.
16. Provide a well-written cover letter.
17. Number and provide identifying data on each page.

Don't

1. Use ambiguous bureaucratic, technical or jargon words.
2. Use negatively worded questions.
3. Use double-barrelled items.
4. Bias responses by hinting.
5. Ask questions you already know answers to.
6. Include extraneous or unnecessary items.
7. Put important items at end.
8. Allow respondents to fall into set response.

WORKBOOK: THE PLAN

1. As you begin doing a needs assessment, think about the purpose. (You may simply think of the goals from Chapter 2.) Write a purpose statement in the space below.

2. What problem is the survey designed to address? Write it below.

3. Identify specific objectives that need to be met in addressing the problem.

4. Along with each objective, identify the major resources and constraints.

Objective	Resources	Constraints

5. What is the completion date? When does the assessment need to be done?

6. Break down the assessment process into activities. List the activities that need to be completed below.

7. Now develop the Gantt chart. List all the major activities from question 4 and plot them against the time line. Note: The finish of the time line should be your completion date.

Activities

1.
2.
3.
4.
5.
6.
7.
8.
9.
10.

Starting Time — Time→ — Completion Time

8. Finally, for each activity, assign a person responsible for completing that activity. (This is good practice even if you are the one who will be doing all the work.)

Activities	To Be Completed By	Person Responsible For

REFERENCES

Breen, G. *Do-It-Yourself Marketing Research.* New York: McGraw-Hill, 1977.

Craig, D. *Hip Pocket Guide to Planning and Evaluation.* San Diego, Calif.: University Associates, 1978.

Fitz-Gibbon, C., and Morris, L. *How to Calculate Statistics.* Beverly Hills: Sage Publications, 1978.

Genua, R. *The Employee's Guide to Interviewing.* Englewood Cliffs, N.J.: Prentice-Hall, 1979.

Kahn, R., and Connell, C. *The Dynamics of Interviewing.* New York: Wiley and Sons, 1957.

Kornhauser, A., and Sheatsley, D. "Questionnaire Construction and the Interview Process," in M. Jahoda, M. Deutsch, and S. Cook, *Research Methods in Social Relations*, Dryden Press, 1951.

Maier, N. "Improving Decisions in an Organization," in S. Tubbs, *A Systems Approach to Small Group Interaction.* Reading, Mass.: Addison-Wesley, 1977.

Marrow, A. *The Practical Theorist.* New York: Basic Books, 1969.

Nadler, P. *Feedback and Organization Development*. Reading, Mass.: Addison-Wesley, 1978.

Nadler, L. *Designing Training Programs*. Reading, Mass.: Addison-Wesley, 1982.

Park, C. *Management Braining*. Basking Ridge, N.J.: Walliker Pub., 1977.

Sauer, S., and Holland, R. *Planning In-House Training*. Austin, Tex.: Learning Concepts, 1981.

Warwick, D., and Lininger, C. *The Sample Survey: Theory and Practice*. New York: McGraw-Hill, 1975.

Webb, E., and Slancik, J. "The Only Wheel in Town—The Interview." Westley (ed). *Journalism Management*, November 1966, pp. 1ff.

Zemke, R., and Kramlinger, R. *Figuring Things Out*. Reading, Mass.: Addison-Wesley, 1982.

14

Evaluation: Feedback Through The Assessment

INTRODUCTION

How do you know that the assessment did what it was supposed to do? This is the essential evaluation question.

Perhaps an analogy is useful at this time. A group of persons come together for supervisory training. For a period of four days they live and work together. During the class sessions they experience a variety of activities, lectures, role plays, case studies, etc., which cause them to think about supervision. During breaks they talk to one another over coffee and donuts about their reactions to what is going on and about some of their problems as supervisors. At night they spend some time at the bar rehashing the day's events and their agreements and disagreements. At the end of the training period, the immediate feedback from the participants is excellent. As they go back to the job, subordinates report that useful changes have taken place. Even the hard statistics associated with turnover and absenteeism reflect positive impact. What caused the change from time 1 (before training) to time 2 (after training)?

For the trainer, the question may be obvious: his skills in design and delivery were key ingredients in the final outcome. The training design was superb. Do we stop here? Probably we do unless we continue to have curiosity about what really happened. If we begin to explore further we may find that while the trainer and the design had a significant impact on outcome, there was another factor of critical importance: the informal networking of people.

People together, talking about things important to themselves, building support systems, are referred to by the term "networking." Both the formal and informal periods allow persons to interact. Participants begin to share problems and resolutions to those problems with one another. They build relationships which allow them to return home revitalized. And when problems arise, they can call or write one another for support and advice. The result is that significant learning has taken place. Suddenly, the trainer and design take on a new purpose—to stay out of the way of networking, or at least not to inhibit networking from taking place.

The example raises questions. "Did we get the results we were after?" "What parts of what we did were responsible for the results?" In the example, the results were obtained but there is some question as to what was responsible for getting them done. Was it the training design? Facilitators' skills? "Networking?"

The same two questions are important when considering an evaluation of a needs assessment. First, did the assessment get the intended results? If the purpose of the assessment was to obtain inputs from 80 percent of the organization and to have a ranking of the top 10 training needs, did that happen? And, if it did happen, what was responsible for causing it to happen? Was it the questionnaire design? Or, was it the fact that a Vice-President told her people, "Here is something you will do!"

As trainers, it is important to be evaluators. Why? So that we do not fool ourselves about what is really happening in the training process.

Thompson and Rath ("The Administrative Experiment: Human Factors") introduce the concept of the "administrative experiment." The intent is to combine the interests of the administrator (or practitioner) with the interest of the experimenter. The administrator/practitioner's interest is getting results. We are interested in finding out if the bottom line of training is useful for the total organization. The process is oriented toward results. The experimenter's viewpoint looks toward what caused the results to come about. The experimenter is interested not only in the fact that the program had "good results" but also in what caused the results. She is interested in identifying which parts of the program seemed to be linked with the most significant output.

My suggestion is that the trainer needs to be involved in "administrative experiments." She needs to see herself as wearing the two hats of administrator and experimenter. The result: more effective training because of the constant search for causalities (for "why?").

Administrative Interest	Experimenter's Interest
Did we get results from the training?	What were the factors that caused the results of the training?

This chapter will discuss types of evaluations and present a specific evaluation model. The two key questions are: (1) Did the assessment achieve its purpose? (2) What part(s) of the assessment process were primarily responsible for achieving those results?

TYPES OF EVALUATIONS

Two uses of evaluation will be discussed simultaneously in this chapter. The first is an evaluation of the need assessment outcome and the second is an evaluation of the training outcome. Since the general principles of evaluation apply to both, they will be discussed together. The reader who is interested in reading evaluation literature in depth is referred to Suchman (*Evaluation Research*), Weiss (*Evaluation Research*) and Isaac and Michael (*Handbook in Research and Evaluation*).

There are three major types of evaluations. If an assessment is laid out along a time line, it would appear as follows:

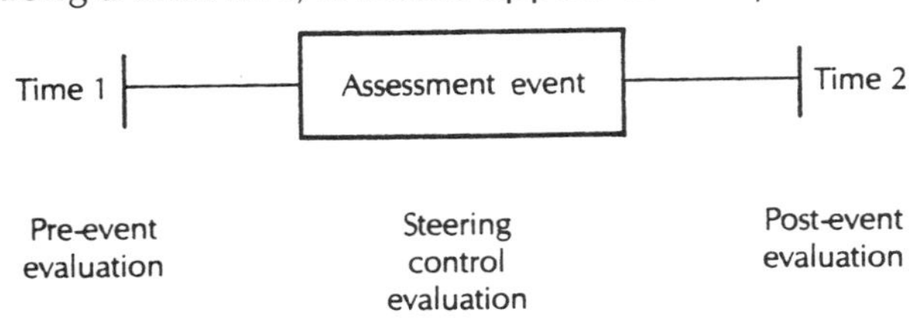

Pre-event evaluation attempts to spot and correct problems before the assessment ever takes place. For example, as the trainer begins to think about the assessment, he may suddenly realize that a particular method does not fit the objective. Perhaps one of the assessment objectives is to build rapport with the trainees culminating in greater commitment to the training. The method selected is a questionnaire. As the trainer reviews and contemplates the questionnaire, it becomes clear that this particular method does not further the objective. A remedy might be to add a survey feedback component and the objective probably will be met. Before the assessment actually takes place, the evaluation occurs, and an adjustment is made.

One exercise useful to the pre-event evaluation is making use of an ability that we all have—imagination. Imagine that the event (assessment) is over and the persons are leaving. Carry on an imagined dialogue with them about the assessment and what you hoped to get out of it. Speak as if the person were standing in front of you. Then, reflect on the imagined dialogue—what did you learn that you had not been aware of previously? Do the activities of the assessment still seem congruent with the goals? Do you need to make changes?

This exercise can be useful in identifying not only design problems but intuitive feelings about the event as well. If in your fantasy people leave angry and frustrated, this may be a clue to some unresolved feelings of your own about the assessment that may need to be reckoned with prior to the event.

Prevention is the best cure. Time spent on pre-event evaluation can be extremely valuable in clearing up problems before they develop.

The second type of evaluation is mid-course correction or "steering control" evaluation. This is precisely what the name implies. During the assessment process itself, corrective measures are taken to keep the training event on track. The following is an example.

Recently, I was involved in a training event that involved a group of administrators from an institution with which I was not familiar. The contract for the day required me to work with them on training assessments. One of the first activities I had planned for them was a 20-minute needs assessment, i.e., what did they want from a day spent talking about needs assessments? During the course of the discussion, it became clear to me (and to them) that the agenda I had planned and the one I had been asked to work with did not fit their immediate needs. Few of them had any training responsibilities. My focus was on designing needs assessments for organizations; their focus was on assessing individual needs within the organization. As this became readily apparent to me, a mid-course correction was made. I concentrated on how my examples and material might be used with an individual instead of an organization. This is an example of a "mid-course" correction.

"Mid-course" correction occurs when it becomes clear that the assessment is not doing what it was designed to do. Perhaps the questionnaire being used contains some questions that the participants are having difficulty with. Perhaps the group interview that was designed for 30 minutes has been running on for an hour. With almost *any* assessment, there arises some problem area that will need to be addressed. Steering controls or mid-course correction allows us to make changes when they are deemed important.

A word of caution about the use of steering controls: Be aware of over-correction. Be sensitive to overreacting to a person who says "these questions make no sense." If there is an isolated individual who develops a problem with what you are doing, treat that as an issue different from one with which a number of persons have difficulty.

The steering controls work only when the trainer receives feedback. In the example above, the assessment provided feedback. There are other sources of feedback, e.g., discussions over breaks, puzzled or frustrated looks among the participants, a large percentage of the audience "cat napping," etc. These are clues that tell the trainer that something is not going according to plan.

Lastly, "post-event" evaluation. The key characteristic of this type of evaluation is that it occurs after the fact. The event is now history. The assessment is finished and I can now ponder what worked and what did not work.

Post-evaluation is familiar to all of us. Typically, at the end of the training event a questionnaire of some type is handed out. Participants fill it out and return it. In an assessment process the post-evaluation questions may be, "Were the questions clear to you?" "Were there too many questions or too few?" "Were the right questions asked?" "What questions were not asked that should have been asked?"

The classroom assessment represents another type of final evaluation. Either participants pass or they do not. The finality of the evaluation may not leave room for corrective behavior. When evaluations are used with this kind of finality, problems of morale may quickly arise. If my assessment is "final" and without recourse to revision, negative feelings are likely to develop.

Another model of final evaluation is built around a concept of growth. While an evaluation may be negative, the constant question is "What has been learned from this that can be transferred to the next event?" or "What have we learned from this assessment that we can transfer to the next assessment?" This is where the "wisdom" of Sauer and Holland's (*Planning In-House Training*) "last time" discussion comes in once again. There is always a last time, and we can learn from it.

These, then, are the types of evaluations—or the points in time in which evaluations take place. All three will be involved in any assessment. An important lesson for the trainer is to think about evaluation early in the planning period. Thinking about how to evaluate during planning leads to better assessment designs. In fact, an interesting way to begin a training event or assessment process is with the question "How will we evaluate this?"

It is time to move from a general discussion of evaluation to a specific model for conducting the evaluation.

EVALUATION MODEL

Rath and Stoyanoff ("Fundamentals of Evaluation") have used a systems paradigm for evaluation. The model is as follows:

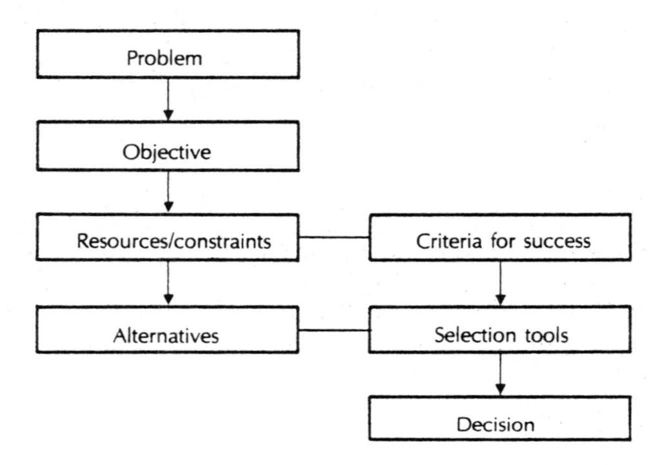

Each part of the model will be discussed in light of a needs assessment. Then, specific applications to evaluation will be looked at. Note: the model is one you will recognize since we have been using it continuously in this book.

Problem

Referring back to the needs assessment model presented earlier in this book, we know that the implicit assumption reinforcing the assessment is problem-solving. The reason for a needs assessment is a problem or to identify current problems or potential problems. A problem may give rise to a needs assessment and/or a needs assessment may isolate and identify problem areas.

Take the case of a nursing home. The home has a significantly high rate of turnover—significantly higher than is the norm for the industry. In response to the problem, the administrators decide to send out a questionnaire that assesses needs at the organizational level. The goal: to identify some of the factors involved in the problem. By identifying and addressing specific needs, the problem may be corrected. For example, it may be discovered that the orientation does not sufficiently cover the psychological impact of working in a nursing home. The remedy may be to restructure the orientation program in order to correct the deficiency.

One part of the evaluation process is identifying the problem to be corrected in the needs assessment or training process. By stating the problem clearly, the next evaluation steps are easier to accomplish.

Objectives

The next step in the process is the establishment of objectives. The objectives have a relationship to the problem under consideration. An earlier chapter discussed some of the characteristics of a "good objective," i.e., as that which answers who, what, and when questions.

With the problem identified in the nursing home, the objective may be

- "To reduce the turnover rate from 23 percent to 18 percent in the course of one year."

The objective is specific and reasonable.

In evaluating the outcome of a needs assessment program, the goal may be to identify useful training needs (as perceived by the trainees). The objectives may be to

- "Develop training programs that three out of four participants view as useful to their job."
- "Identify a minimum of four training needs."

Again, the objectives are specific.

Clearly stated objectives are a key component of the evaluation process. Without them, it becomes difficult to determine the success of a program. With them, the outcome of an assessment is much more readily identified. With each specific objective it is possible to fill in the following form:

Objective	Criteria for Success	Results	Left to Do
To identify four training needs in the next week.	To have four training needs within seven days	Accomplished goal	Nothing

The various parts of this table will be discussed later. The important thing is to see the relationship between the specificity of the objective and the ease of assessing it.

Objectives may be of many types. They may relate to knowledge, feelings, skills, behavioral changes, awareness. The following relate to the needs assessment evaluation:

- "Three of four participants report no confusion about the questions."
- "To develop a needs assessment instrument that is comprehensive in determining training needs."

- "To stay within established criteria, etc."

Rath and Stoyanoff state that, "No evaluation can be carried out without a specific statement of goals and objectives." Questions that they suggest asking include

- Do written objectives exist? If so, collect documents where they may be found.
- If written objectives do not exist, look over records, minutes of meetings, interview people, etc., to develop a set of objectives.
- Are the objectives written in measurable terms? Not all aspects need to be measurable but at least one should be.
- Agreement with institutional goals. The goals of the particular project (or assessment) need to be congruent with organizational goals.

Goals and objectives are crucial to the final evaluation. They set up markers against which we can measure our progress (or lack of it).

Resources/Constraints

What is a resource? This refers to having sufficient quantities of an item. What is a constraint? This refers to having insufficient quantities of an item.

Resources and constraints relate to the assessment itself. They may represent dollars—"to keep the cost under $1000," or persons—"to have the internal staff develop and administer the project," or time—"to have the assessment completed in three weeks."

You can readily see that each constraint or resource may be stated as an objective. When the final tabulations are in, the job of deciding whether the objectives were met or not also includes viewing the completeness of the resources and constraints. A significant cost overrun may figure dramatically into the final evaluation.

Resources and constraints impinge on the criteria for success. Criteria for success may contain implicit and explicit resources and constraints. When you look back at the chapter on criteria, notice the resources and constraints that appear.

Criteria for Success

Closely aligned with the resources and constraints are the criteria for success. Again they may be stated in terms of objectives.

One criterion may be that the work must be completed by in-house staff within a specified time period. Another might be that certain kinds of information be gathered. Still another may relate to the amount of time involvement the particular method demands.

Criteria add a note of realism to the whole process. By conforming to specific criteria, the objectives may be readily measured.

Alternatives

Alternatives refer to the method that is selected. Again, Rath and Stoyanoff suggest some questions that might be asked here (I have translated them into our words which fit our purposes):

- Is the method consistent with the goals and objectives of the assessment?
- Is the method effective? Is it meeting its goals and objectives?
- Is the method efficient? Are the resources involved being used well or is there significant waste?
- Are there side effects or spillovers from the assessment that are significantly affecting the organization?

These questions are useful in considering the various methods.

Part of this time may also be used to evaluate other alternatives. For example, if the method selected was an interview format, there may be retrospection over "what if" a questionnaire had been used. And there may even be discussion about "what if" nothing had been done at all.

Selection Tool—Model

The alternatives have been discussed. Now comes the time to weigh each one—what type of selection process will you choose? There are many.

The actual selection of the assessment method may be discussed. What actually happened with the selection? Was a formal process involved? Or was the selection made on a "hit-or-miss" basis?

The selection process may be as simple as flipping a coin or as complex as a sophisticated decision tree analysis. Whatever the selection process, it becomes part of the evaluation consideration. For example, if the selection of a method was highly influenced by a manager's favorite tool, that would need to be noted. On the other hand, if the selection process involved a detailed set of criteria, the method needed to meet those would also have to be noted.

The important question is, how did selection affect outcome?

Decision-maker

Lastly, enter the decision-maker. The information generated remains uncertain and inert until a decision-maker enters the arena and acts. What effect did the various decision-makers have on the assessment process?

Who was the decision-maker involved? Were there political interests involved that significantly influenced the decision? If more than one person was involved, how did he work with others?

The systems model, then, provides a road map for evaluation. By tracking through the process, we can begin to put together an evaluation of the assessment. Why do we put such energy into it? There may be a number of reasons. Again, the "experimenter" side of us may want to be rigorous toward what we do. Or we may want to build a case with management about the importance of needs assessment. Whatever our reasons may be, the tool provides a process from which to work.

One last reference to Rath and Stoyanoff. They make an important point when referring to an evaluation of the evaluation. They suggest that at least two questions be asked of the evaluation:

- Is the evaluation a significant factor in achieving goals and objectives? If so, it may need to be built into the ongoing assessment.
- Is the evaluation itself effective and efficient? If not, that needs to be considered.

Why an evaluation of the evaluation? Because we are interested in doing "good work."

SUMMARY

The objective of this chapter has been to discuss evaluation of the assessment process. The appendix to this chapter provides some tools to consider for evaluation.

The order in which you follow the steps in the systems model does not matter; what does matter is that each step is touched upon. If you have been following the workbook exercises thus far, you will find that you have already completed most of the steps. Now it is just a matter of reflecting on them and adding any missing parts.

The important questions to ask at each step of the evaluation are as follows:

1. Problem analysis—what is the problem we are trying to address or preclude? What is the explicit or implicit problem in the needs assessment?

2. Objectives—what are the objectives of the needs assessment? Are the objectives clearly stated or are they implied? Are they measurable? Are they consistent with the organizational objectives?

3. Criteria for success—what are the criteria? Were they spelled out? Are they comprehensive?

4. Resources/constraints—what resources/constraints were identified? Were significant ones missed?

5. Alternatives—what alternatives were explored? Which ones were developed? To what extent were they explored? Are they consistent with the assessment goal? Are they effective? Efficient?

6. Selection tool—what was the selection process? How detailed was it? Was it sufficient? Are there important "holes" in it?

7. Decision-maker—who was the decision-maker(s) involved? Do the decision-makers have important characteristics that should be noted?

WORKBOOK: EVALUATION

1. Fill in the following form. It is an evaluation matrix that should help you in the evaluation process. First list the goal(s) of the assessment. For each goal, identify the criteria, measurement tools, expected outcomes, and actual outcomes (Ulschak, 1975).

Goals	Criteria for Success	Measurement Tools	Expected Outcome	Actual Outcome

A WORKBOOK FOR EVALUATION METHODS*

The following questions are a guide for the program evaluator in gathering the necessary information to do an evaluation. Take some time to respond to each question. When you have completed the questions, you will have the skeleton for writing the final evaluation of the project.

1. Where is there a written statement(s) of goals/objectives for the program to be evaluated?

2A. List the written goals and objectives.

2B. List the goals that exist for the program, but have not been written.

3. Are goals 2A and 2B presented in operational/measurable terms? If not, rewrite in operational terms.

*Material taken from Rath, G., Stoyanoff, K., and Shawchuck, N., "Fundamentals of Evaluation," and reprinted here with permission of Organizational Resources, Downers Grove, Ill.

4. Is there a time frame (deadline) for each goal? If not, rewrite it with time limits.

5. How are the goals relevant to the mission and needs of the organization, its constituents, and all other persons who are affected?

6. Name the program(s) or activity (ies) that supports meeting each stated goal?

7. In what manner is the program(s) coherent with the stated goal?

8. What evidence is there of the effectiveness of the program? To what extent is the goal being achieved?

9. How efficient is the program? How is efficiency being measured? How does it compare to other programs? What is the relative efficiency? What is the absolute cost?

10. What are the positive and/or negative effects of the program in society, the organization, its constituents, and those who work there?

Positive:

Negative:

11. What program changes, or new programs, may be needed to achieve the goals?

12. Is the evaluation helping or hindering the achievement of the goals? How?

13. Is the evaluation producing the needed data? Is the data worth the time, money, and effort needed to gather it? How might evaluation effectiveness and efficiency be improved?

REFERENCES

Isaac, S. *Handbook in Research and Evaluation*. San Diego: Knapp, 1974.

Rath, G., and Stoyanoff, K. "Fundamentals of Evaluation." An unpublished paper, Evanston, Ill., January 1978.

Rath, G.; Stoyanoff, K.; and Shawchuck, N. "Fundamentals of Evaluation." Downers Grove, Ill.: Organizational Resources Press, 1979.

Sauer, S., and Holland, R. *Planning In-House Training*. Austin, Tex.: Learning Concepts, 1981.

Suchman, E. *Evaluation Research*. New York: Sage Pub., 1967.

Thompson, C., and Rath, G. "The Administrative Experiment." *Human Factors*, Vol. 16, No. 3, June 1974.

Ulschak, F. "An Organizational Intervention: A Case Study." Unpublished dissertation, Northwestern University, Evanston, Ill., 1975.

Weiss, C. *Evaluation Research.* Englewood Cliffs, N.J.: Prentice-Hall, 1972.

Appendix A

Case One: Needs Assessment For a Training Event

Sometimes needs assessment is seen as limited to long-range planning. This case illustrates its use in planning a specific training event. It illustrates the use of open-ended questions and individual interviews to gather information.

INTRODUCTION

The focus of this case is on needs assessment in the design of a three-day training workshop. The company has set aside three days to discuss a decision that they need to make. The decision is an emotional one involving intense feelings on the part of a variety of company employees. It was decided that a good beginning point would be a needs assessment of those involved combined with an informal opinion survey.

THE PROCESS

The process began well before the "retreat" was held. Since there were to be 25 to 30 department heads at the retreat, it was decided that the assessment process would involve individual interviews. The size was small enough to facilitate the individual interviews. The CEO set up the interviews which ran 45–60 minutes. Interviews were held in the office of the interviewee. The objective of the interview was to identify attitudes and feelings participants had concerning the upcoming retreat.

The interviewer prepared an interviewing schedule which contained open-ended questions. The following questions made up the interview schedule:

1. As you think of the management retreat coming up, what are your expectations?

2. What is an outcome of the retreat that you would like to have for yourself?

3. What is an outcome of the retreat you would like for the management team as a whole?

4. Presently, if you were to change one thing about the management team, what would you change?

5. What is the worst thing that you sense could happen as a result of the retreat?

6. What is the best thing that you sense could happen as a result of the retreat?

7. I will be the facilitator at the retreat. What questions do you have for me?

Each of the questions, along with some of the themes that came out, will be discussed.

Question 1: Expectations are of critical importance. If they are not acknowledged, they can readily become self-fulfilling prophecies. The initial question and the probing that followed began to indicate the dynamics that were likely to occur during the retreat.

Some of the actual responses were:

- "I didn't expect much of anything. Generally we just end up taking snips at one another."
- "I expect we will learn something about meeting issues head on."
- "We will end up working more effectively together. . ."
- "We are going to end up working even better together. . ."

Expectations provide insights into what may actually come to pass. Clearly, some expectations here point to team development. And, there are some cautions about past experience in the retreat setting.

Question 2: The second question focuses on what the individual wants out of the retreat. Some typical responses are:

• "Learn how to deal with my differences with others effectively."

• "'Learning to be open with my thoughts and also to know when not to share them."

• "Resolve the conflicts we have—then I can put my energy back to the real work at hand."

• "We need to air some differences and resolve them."

As can be seen from the sampling, the theme that kept recurring was managing differences with others and, in general, managing conflicts. This provides useful suggestions for the design of the retreat.

Question 3: The response to Question 3, what do you want for the management team from this retreat, was answered in much the same way as Question 2. Most indicated that they wanted skill building in how to handle conflicts. They had a particular issue that divided them and that was seen as the issue with which to work.

Responses here indicated team development and conflict management skills.

Question 4: By Question 4, the response became fairly predictable. If you could change one thing about the management team, what would it be? The responses—being able to confront a conflict, hassle it through, and leave with a sense of resolution.

The two themes of team development and conflict management were clear. Typical responses were

• "I would change it so we felt we were pulling together rather than competing as separate managers."

• "We need to feel a confidence that we can approach an issue, talk it through, and leave with a sense of 'finished business.' "

Question 5: A question that is especially useful as a follow-up to expectations is, "What is the worst thing that could happen at the retreat?" It is a question reserved for later in the interview to allow time to build rapport with the interviewee.

Probing "the worst" begins to provide a sense of the degree or depth of the problem. By playing with "the worst" it is possible to find out whether the perception of the problem is that of a minor irritation or a major blowup.

For most people in this setting, the "worst" ended up being, "We will continue on like we are and I will find myself feeling overloaded with more unresolved conflicts." For one or two, the "worst" meant that they would pick this as a time to start circulating their resumes.

The major theme was simply, "We will leave with a sense of failure and frustration."

Question 6: Following up "the worst" is a question about "the best." Again, part of the purpose is to get a sense of what options are available.

Typical of the "best" responses are the following:

- "We will leave with a feeling of satisfaction that we have resolved a specific issue and we will have confidence in our ability to do it again in the future."
- "I will have cleared the air with Mr. ____ and will be re-energized."

Question 7: Question 7 of the interview is important not only in itself—"What questions do you have for me?"—but as a process of legitimizing the facilitator. In this setting the interviewer/trainer is an outsider known to only a couple of the managers who are responsible for the retreat. One intent of the interview is to give the participants an opportunity to "check him out." This question is one that invited covert agendas into the open.

Typical questions that were asked of me included

- "What are your credentials?"
- "Who have you worked with in the past?"
- "Do you see yourself as being able to deal with us?"

The questions were responded to in a nondefensive manner providing the information requested.

THE ANALYSIS

The interviews had two major end results: (1) a good deal of information about the participants and their expectations was identified, and (2) the interpersonal process between trainer and each participant had begun—the trainer had begun to build relationships with the participants. The next phase was to analyze the data collected.

The process used to analyze the data was a form of content analysis. The responses to each question were put on a separate sheet of paper. Next, a comprehensive set of themes was developed for the responses to each question. For example, in Question 1 these themes included

- "Expect nothing will happen from this."
- "Expect that we will learn how to work together."
- "Expect that the budget issue will be resolved."

The final phase of this process involved noting the number of times a particular theme came up in the interviews. The final page, then, looked similar to this:

Question 1 Themes	Number of Responses
"Expect nothing will come out of the retreat."	4
"Expect to learn to work together effectively."	15
"Expect budget issues will be resolved."	20

The end result was a summary of themes for each question along with a frequency count. An assumption made was that valid information had been given during the interviews and it had been interpreted correctly. To check this assumption summary statements were circulated to the participants with the request that they respond to their validity—do they think that the statements adequately reflect their situation? This provided them an opportunity to make corrections the trainer may have missed. Along with it was a suggested agenda for the time based on the needs being reflected in the themes.

Generally, the responses to the summary statements indicated some minor changes. However, the overall consensus was that the information looked accurate and the interpretations fit. The design for the time was approved. The agenda was set and the training proceeded.

The training focus was on team development and skill building in conflict management. The two fit together nicely with the needs that arose during the interview and a three-day workshop was designed. During the session, a current "live" issue was also worked with.

A final checkout with the participants occurred Day 1 of the workshop. In the beginning of the training event, the summary material that came out of the interviews and the interpretations made about them were discussed. The major themes were then discussed in light of the flow of the workshop. In this way, a clear link between what came out of the interviews and the agenda was established. Participants learned an important fact—what they had said was listened to and acted upon.

The desired end result of this training was met. They did resolve the budget issue and they did leave with specific conflict management skills.

REFLECTIONS

This example of an assessment illustrates the use of open-ended questions. And the questions skirted direct confrontations about needs. Rather, they were indirect. Part of the rationale was the emotional climate that was present at the time. Feelings were running high and one objective of the assessment was to provide an outlet for the participants. It also allowed them to begin building a relationship with the trainer.

An important part of this assessment design was the survey feedback time. This was done twice—once right after the interviews and again at the beginning of the workshop. The rationale was to provide participants with reaction time. If they entered the workshop with a common agreement, the work together would proceed more easily. The survey feedback format provided two major checks: (1) Is the analysis and interpretation valid? By raising these issues with the participants, the correct analysis or interpretations could be identified. (2) By allowing the participants to respond to the data, there is a building of commitment to the outcome.

The overall flow for the time is shown in the following diagram:

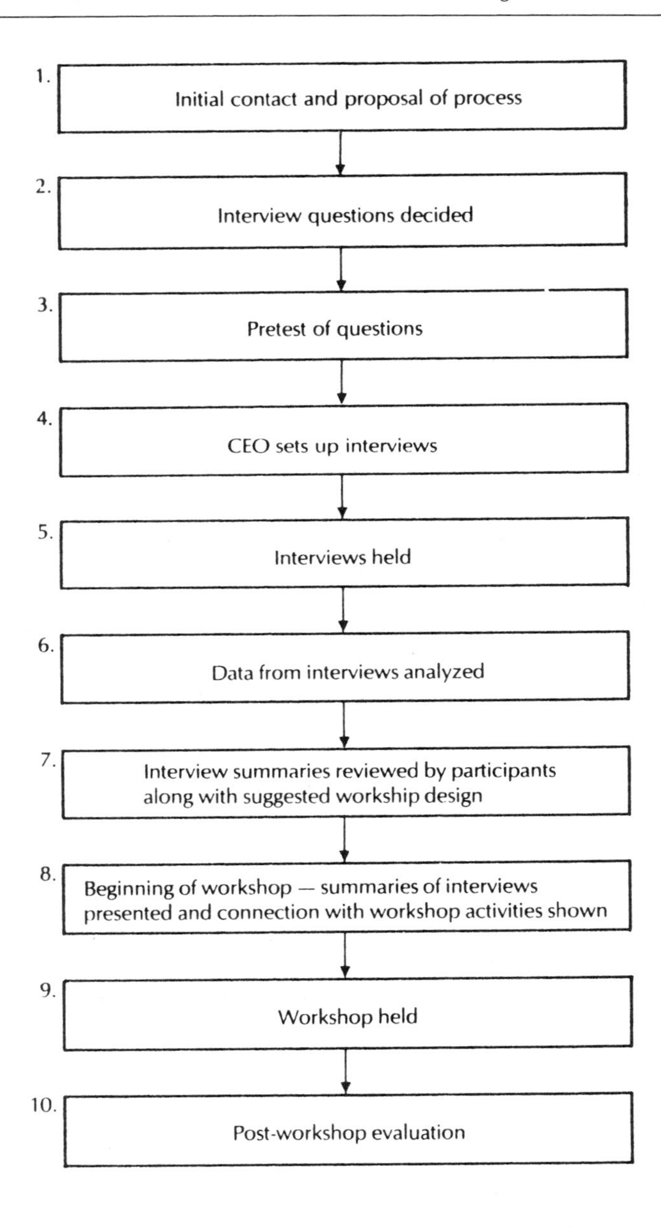
1.
Initial contact and proposal of process
2.
Interview questions decided
3.
Pretest of questions
4.
CEO sets up interviews
5.
Interviews held
6.
Data from interviews analyzed
7.
Interview summaries reviewed by participants along with suggested workship design
8.
Beginning of workshop — summaries of interviews presented and connection with workshop activities shown
9.
Workshop held
10.
Post-workshop evaluation

Appendix B

Case Two: The CEO is the Problem

What starts out as a training assessment takes an interesting twist. The initial objective is to do an organizational problem assessment. The dilemma is, what to do when the CEO is the major problem identified?

INTRODUCTION

This particular case raises a special issue—what happens when the end result of the assessment indicates that organizational relationships, not training needs, are the critical element? The initial contract with the client was to identify training needs via organizational assessment. However, the outcome indicated that the number one problem to be looked at in the organization was the style of the CEO.

BACKGROUND

A personnel director of a medium-sized hospital contracted with a consultant to do an organizational needs assessment. There were problems within the hospital that needed to be identified as it was assumed (be aware of that word) that training would be the appropriate way to address the problem.

The consultant began by developing a proposal indicating what it was he would do. The proposal to the hospital contained objectives of the assessment, the methodology involved, who would be involved in the process, a projected time line for the project, costs, and outcomes that could be expected by the hospital.

During the course of the discussion regarding training needs, it became clear that training needs were an assumed solution to problems that the organization was experiencing. As is frequently the case, a solution (training) was being suggested before the problem was defined. This led to a renegotiation of the training assessment. The suggested beginning was an organizational assessment.

The objectives became

1. Gather data on perceived problems from administrators, department heads, and employees.
2. Validate the perceived problems.
3. Develop specific action plans for addressing the problems.

The methodology was modeled on survey feedback. Step 1 involved gathering information via questionnaire and interview. Administrators were interviewed individually and the remaining interviews were held in groups of four to six participants. The objective was to have all employees provide input, and with minor exceptions, that objective was met.

The objective of the methodology was to obtain information concerning the participants' perceptions of current problems, causes of the problems, and priorities for addressing the problems.

Step 2 involved an analysis of the material developed in Step 1. Material was summarized according to themes developed and frequency counts were then made. (The method is very similar to that described in Case 1.) Step 2 was done by the consultant using the questionnaires and interview notes.

In Step 3, the feedback began. The tentative problems, priorities, etc., were presented to the participants. Again, this was done in small groups. The participants had an opportunity to respond to analysis and interpretations. The consultant presented the findings for about 15 minutes and then had the participants respond. Questions such as "Does this sound accurate?" and "Is this a fair interpretation of what this problem means?" were asked. After the discussion of the findings, the participants were asked to identify what they saw as important next steps. Two important outcomes emerged from this step: (1) validating the interpretations and findings from the assessment and (2) developing the next steps.

DISCUSSION

The above methodology seemed to work very well. The questionnaire/interview format provided a variety of opportunities for data collection.

The questionnaire consisted of two parts. Part I was a series of open-ended questions such as:

1. As you think of this organization, what do you like about working here?

2. As you think about this organization, what do you dislike about working here?

3. What changes would you like to see made in the organization?

4. What might be some things that could be done to bring about changes you would like to see in the organization?

An "additional comment" section was provided. Open-ended questions were used for a very specific reason—to have the participants identify problems in their own words. The "additional comment" question provided further opportunities for input.

Part II of the questionnaire was built on Francis and Woodcock's (*People at Work*) model of common organizational problems. Participants were asked to rate the significance of various organizational problems for their organization. Some examples include

1. Inadequate orientation of new persons to the organization. Persons coming into the organization are not given adequate orientation to their jobs.

1______2______3______4______5______6______7

No Problem Here at All — A Major Problem Here

2. Organizational structure is confused. The formal and informal way individuals are organized is unclear and inefficient.

1______2______3______4______5______6______7

No Problem Here at All — A Major Problem Here

3. Low motivation. Persons in the organization are not excited about their work or the organization.

1______2______3______4______5______6______7

No Problem Here at All — A Major Problem Here

4. Poor teamwork. Departments do not work together efficiently as a team. There is a good deal of unhealthy competition and conflict.

1________2________3________4________5________6________7
No Problem Here at All — A Major Problem Here

Once the data was gathered, the next step was analysis. Part I of the questionnaire was tabulated according to a content analysis of themes. Some examples of the analysis are shown in the following tables:

Major Likes Cited

	Frequency	Percent
Like people, good working relations	51	38
Job never gets boring—variety of experiences	27	20
Good salary—benefits	18	13
Etc.		

Major Dislikes

	Frequency	Percent
Problems with administration Administration does not back up employees; not responsive to problems; will listen but no action	62	42
Problems with supervisors Supervisors set rules but do not follow	30	22
Etc.		

Changes Like to See

	Frequency	Percent
New administrative attitude	44	35
Like to see more space available	11	24
Like to see staff meetings on regular basis	16	18
Etc.		

Some samples of the analysis of the responses to common organization problems in Part II include the following:

1. Inadequate orientation of new persons to the organization.

Persons coming into the organization are not given adequate orientation to their jobs.

					60	
1(18)	2(12)	3(18)	4(12)	5(6)	6(14)	7(30)
No Problem						Major Problem

Mean 4.4
Averages 4.4
Responses 120

2. Organizational structure is confused. The formal and informal way individuals are organized is unclear and inefficient.

					45	
1(27)	2(18)	3(21)	4(6)	5(25)	6(9)	7(12)
No Problem						Major Problem

Mean 3
Average 3.5
Responses 120

Etc.

With the results from the assessment analyzed, the next step was to take the material back to the hospital and have the participants react to it. Remember that part of the initial contract with the hospital was a stipulation of survey feedback. However, a major obstacle had developed.

From the results of the assessment, the administration was clearly identified as the major problem and, specifically, the CEO. The question became, how to feed the information back to the participants with the CEO's endorsement?

The problem was resolved in an up-front manner. The CEO was contacted and agreed to meet with the consultant in a series of off-site meetings during which time the material from the assessment was discussed.

The consultant reviewed and discussed with the CEO the material and the next steps in the process. They talked about a variety of actions that might be taken. Initially, the CEO was reluctant to have the process go forward—understandably, there was some threat involved, i.e., supervisors from throughout the hospital would be reacting to the material. However, as various consequences were discussed, he decided that the most effective strategy was to continue with the feedback session with his sanction of the survey results.

The next steps moved very smoothly. Sessions were held where the results were put on large sheets of paper. The consultant talked through the listings of the material and invited responses from the participants as to the validity of the results—does the material fit with their view of the organization? What about the interpretations? Did they fit? With minor exceptions, the results were agreed to be accurate.

The next step was the selection of a course of action, i.e., moving from assessment to action. The specific course chosen here was the establishment of a committee to be a "quality of work life" committee, i.e., they were to monitor the human environment and develop specific action plans to address problems. One immediate step they took was to set up a regular inservice training program to focus on attitudes and problem resolution. The first program selected was on "positive reinforcement."

At the same time, a coaching relationship between the consultant and the CEO was developed. This was to be one of the significant outcomes of the assessment process.

REFLECTIONS

An important part of this case was the "coaching" done with the CEO, which eventually had an impact on the CEO's managing style. It became the beginning point for significant administrative change.

Also, carrying through with the feedback had important results. Obviously, if the process had stopped prior to feedback or if the results were changed to minimize the administrative problem, the participants would have been the first to spot it. Their immediate response would have been to not trust the process further, and their belief about problems not being solvable would have been reinforced. However, in this case, the outcome was the opposite—very specific problems were addressed and resolved.

This case shows how open-ended questions may be used in a useful combination with rating questions. The end result is a mutual reinforcement of the themes coming out. If there should be a significant difference between the two sources of information, the survey feedback time is ideal for raising that observation and asking participants to explain the differences.

The flow chart of the case is as follows:

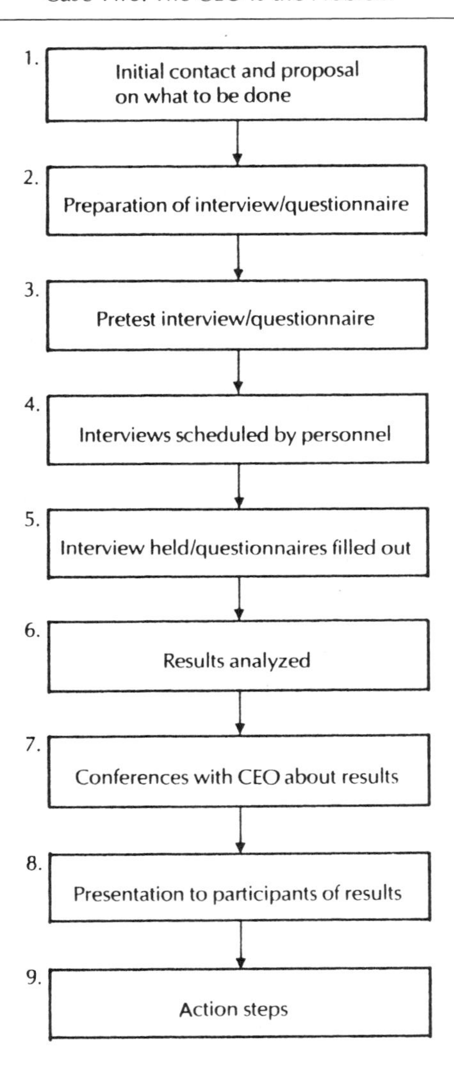

REFERENCES

Francis, D. and Woodcock, M. *People at Work.* La Jolla, Calif.: University Associates, 1975.

Appendix C

Case Three: A Hospital Reorganized

This case illustrates a questionnaire combined with the group interview method. Also involved is an example of a "hitchhiker," i.e., when the assessment has another function attached to it.

INTRODUCTION

A metropolitan hospital of about 400 beds had recently gone through a major organizational restructuring. Top management was very interested in instituting a needs analysis for the supervisors and department heads. The objective: to develop an ongoing training program. In addition to the assessment, the management wanted feedback on how the supervisors and department heads perceived the recent organizational changes. This is an example of a case where the needs assessment has a "hitchhiker."

PROCESS

The first step was to present to the management a proposal of what would be involved in the needs assessment. The proposal outlined such things as cost, objectives, methodology, time, and potential outcomes.

The objectives noted in the proposal were

1. To obtain information from the department heads, supervisors, and administrators regarding training needs for the general hospital and specific departments.

2. To obtain information from the department heads, supervisors, and administrators regarding their perceptions of the recent organizational changes.

3. To increase the commitment of the department heads, supervisors, and administrators to the hospital and the training plan by having them actively involved in participatory management processes.

Note that objective 1 included two parts. The first was identification of general hospital needs and the second was identification of specific department needs. The process needed to provide information relevant to both areas.

The outcome of identifying needs was to be a training plan. Phase Two of the project was the implementation of that training plan.

The process used to collect the actual data consisted of departmental meetings of six to eight persons lasting for about an hour. During that hour, participants were asked to respond to a questionnaire as well as to be involved in a group interview. The idea of using both methods was to provide a cross check to provide a comparison between the interview and the questionnaire. It was also a time where participants could react to the questionnaire itself.

The questionnaire had two parts. Part One consisted of two open-ended questions and two scale questions. They were

- "The best thing that has happened from the revision in the organizational structure is . . ."
- "The worst thing that has happened from the organizational structure is . . ."
- "For me, the reorganization was . . ."

(Place an X on the appropriate place on the scale.)

1	2	3	4	5
A disaster		Neutral		The best thing that could have happened

- "For the hospital, the reorganization of the structure was . . ."
(Put an X on the appropriate place on the scale.)

1	2	3	4	5
A disaster		Neutral		The best thing that could have happened

The intent of the last two questions was to get a general feeling with regard to the reorganization.

Page two of the questionnaire involved the participants in identifying training needs. It read as follows:

> Listed below are a number of training possibilities. First, go through the items in each of the major categories and check the boxes in front of the items that you sense to be important training needs for your department. If there are training needs not listed that you see as important, write them in the blank spaces provided in each major category. Second, rank order the three major categories of training from 1 to 3 with 1 being the category of greatest need and 3 being the category of least need.

____ Organizational Training Needs
- ____ Management by Objectives
- ____ Time Management
- ____ Managerial Grid
- ____ Organizational Communication
- ____ Interdepartment Conflict Management
- ____ ______________________________
- ____ ______________________________

____ Technical Training Needs
- ____ Decision-making
- ____ Goal-setting
- ____ Contracting
- ____ Systems Analysis
- ____ Problem-solving
- ____ Long-range Planning
- ____ Defining Measurable Objectives
- ____ ______________________________
- ____ ______________________________

____ Inter/Intrapersonal Training Needs
- ____ Supervisory Skills
- ____ Team-building
- ____ Interpersonal Conflict Management
- ____ Coping with Organizational Stress
- ____ Assertiveness Training

____ Transactional Analysis
____ Leadership Styles
____ Motivation
____ ________________________________
____ ________________________________

Other comments on training needs . . .

After the questionnaire was filled out, the remaining time was spent discussing the participants' responses to the items. Emphasis was on the responses to the organizational changes and the needs they were now experiencing.

It took approximately a week to gather the necessary data, i.e., to do the group interviews. The next step was to analyze the data. For the open-ended questions in Part One, a simple content analysis was used. First, all the major themes that were reported on the questionnaires were identified. After developing a master list of themes, the

Table C–1 Responses to question 1.

	General services N = 18	Personnel N = 1	Finance N = 9	Nursing N = 19	Professional services N = 15	Administrators N = 6	Total
Better communications and working between departments	3 (17)		3 (3)	9 (47)	4 (27)	3 (50)	22 (29)
Knowing who to report to; better lines of authority	4 (22)			5 (26)	4 (27)	6 (83)	18 (27)
Move information flowing through hospital about what is happening	3 (17)	1	1 (11)		8 (53)		13 (17)
Active involvement in management — more input	3 (17)		1 (11)	3 (16)		1 (17)	9 (12)
Nothing — blank	4 (22)		11 (22)	1 (5)	1 (7)		8 (10)
Better utilization of Staff				6 (31)			6 (8)

questionnaires went through a second time and the frequency of themes in the categories was noted. A final listing included the number of persons who mentioned a particular theme and the frequency of the theme. Table C-1 is an example of the responses to Question 1—"The best thing . . ."

The table was followed by a discussion of each item. Next were the questions regarding the perceived value of the change in the hospital. The responses are tabulated in Table C-2.

Table C–2 A summary of perceived value changes for self and hospital.

	Positive for hospital	**Negative for hospital**	**Neutral for hospital**
Positive for me	76% 8-A 1-B 6-C 18-D 47 8-E 6-F	3% 1-A 1-E 2	3% 1-A 1-C 2
Negative for me	5% 1-C 2-E 3	8% 4-A 1-E 5	
Neutral for me	3% 1-D 1-E 2		2% 1-C 1

Total Responses = 62

A = General Services
B = Personnel
C = Finance
D = Nursing
E = Professional Services
F = Administrators

Again, the table was followed with a discussion of the items. Next came the needs assessment material. A simple percentage and number of respondents was given for each item. The final summary table is shown in Table C-3.

With the material summarized, a final report was submitted containing the summary material. However, before a final training plan was laid out for the next year, the material as summarized was

Table C–3 Summary of training needs

	Total participants N - 68	Professional services N - 15	Nursing N - 19	Finance N - 9	Personnel N - 1	General services N - 18	Administrators N - 6
Organizational training needs							
Management by objectives	37 / 54	8 / 53	16 / 84	3 / 33	1	4 / 22	5 / 83
Time management	33 / 48	8 / 53	11 / 58	4 / 44		4 / 22	6 / 100
Managerial grid	9 / 13	2 / 13	3 / 16		1	2 / 11	1 / 17
Organizational communications	47 / 69	9 / 60	9 / 47	8 / 89	1	14 / 78	6 / 100
Independent conflict management	40 / 59	7 / 47	12 / 63	7 / 78	1	9 / 50	4 / 67
Technical training needs							
Decision making	39 / 57	6 / 40	14 / 74	6 / 67		8 / 44	5 / 83
Goal setting	31 / 46	5 / 33	13 / 68	1 / 11		6 / 33	6 / 100
Contracting	8 / 12	2 / 13	3 / 16		1	1 / 05	1 / 17
Systems analysis	26 / 38	6 / 40	10 / 53	4 / 44		2 / 11	4 / 67
Problem solving	45 / 66	8 / 53	15 / 79	6 / 67	1	10 / 56	5 / 83
Long range planning	35 / 51	10 / 67	13 / 68	4 / 44		6 / 33	2 / 34
Defining measureable objectives	32 / 47	4 / 27	13 / 68	2 / 22		7 / 39	6 / 100
Intra/interpersonal training needs							
Supervisory skills	43 / 63	8 / 53	14 / 74	6 / 67	1	9 / 50	5 / 83
Team building	30 / 44	3 / 20	7 / 37	4 / 44	1	10 / 56	5 / 83
Interpersonal conflict management	35 / 51	7 / 47	14 / 74	6 / 67	1	3 / 17	4 / 67
Interpersonal communications	38 / 56	6 / 40	12 / 63	4 / 44	1	11 / 61	4 / 67
Coping with organizational stress	40 / 59	10 / 67	10 / 53	4 / 44	1	9 / 50	6 / 100
Assertiveness training	28 / 41	5 / 33	13 / 68	1 / 11	1	4 / 22	4 / 67
Transactional analysis	23 / 33	3 / 20	11 / 58	1 / 11	1	3 / 17	4 / 67
Leadership styles	33 / 48	5 / 33	12 / 63	5 / 56	1	5 / 28	5 / 83
Motivation	33 / 48	6 / 40	12 / 63	5 / 56	1	5 / 28	4 / 67

presented to the original participants. The reason: to verify the data and interpretations.

A major two-hour meeting was held during which time the results of the survey were presented. Participants had a variety of opportunities to raise questions, make comments, etc. The end result of the process was agreement that the data as presented was accurate.

Now came the time for the training plan. The plan that developed through the assessment involved three parts. The first was an immediate training program involving communications for the supervisors and department heads. The emphasis on immediacy grew out of a feeling that the survey should be followed as quickly as possible by action. The message this would communicate was that survey responses would be acted upon. That way participants would have a sense that there were positive steps coming from the survey. These initial sessions were held away from the hospital and run by an outside consultant. Part of the purpose of holding sessions away from the hospital was to provide a sense of "specialness" to those who attended.

The second part of the training plan was the design of an ongoing monthly training event that involved a two-hour session at the hospital. Again, the starting point was the needs assessment. These monthly sessions were conducted using content that grew out of the needs assessment. At each session, a few minutes were used to gather thoughts on useful future training. Needs assessment thus became an ongoing process.

Third, since different departments had different needs, a system was devised that allowed individual departments to submit training needs that were unique to them. They were then acted on by personnel.

The end result was an ongoing training program that addressed total hospital needs as well as individual department needs and had a built-in assessment process.

REFLECTIONS

First, the "hitchhiker" provided management with useful information. Things were going much better than they had been thinking. The result for them was a feeling of movement in the desired direction. While the "hitchhiker" was not of direct relevance to the training assessment, it provided useful information to the client.

Second, a major outcome was the hiring of a training director to oversee the training development. This was a very important move. It provided for ongoing training and assessment.

Third, an important addition to this design would have been the pretesting of the questionnaire on the actual participants involved.

The questionnaire was given to management for their approval. However, the gap between management and participant was significant. For example, management knew what "MBO—Management By Objectives" was—some participants did not.

Lastly, the assessment questionnaire was weak. It was too general. Results were readily tabulated for responses to the questionnaire, but there was insufficient evidence as to what the result meant. The highest score was for organizational communications. What does that mean? The saving factor in the process was the interview that went along with the questionnaire and the survey feedback. They provided time for clarification.

The process involved

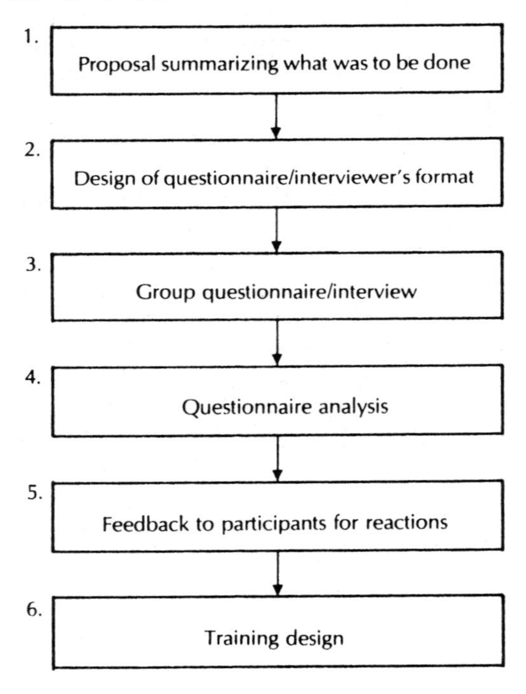

Index